LONG WALK
TO THE
SUN

Jock Miles WW2 Adventure Series
Book 1

A Novel By
William Peter Grasso

Cover design by Alyson Aversa
Cover photo courtesy of US Army Signal Corps
Map created at planiglobe.com

Novels by William Peter Grasso:

East Wind Returns
Unpunished
Long Walk to the Sun
Book 1 in the Jock Miles WW2 adventure series
Operation Long Jump
Book 2 in the Jock Miles WW2 adventure series
Operation Easy Street
Book 3 in the Jock Miles WW2 adventure series
Operation Blind Spot
Book 4 in the Jock Miles WW2 adventure series
Operation Fishwrapper
Book 5 in the Jock Miles WW2 adventure series

DEDICATION

To my grandsons Eli and Charlie—May they never
know war

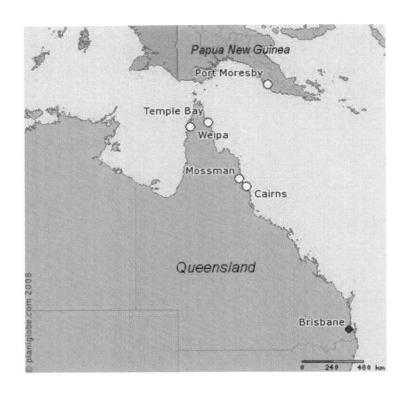

Northeastern Australia

"We had about 4.5 million barrels of oil out there and all of it was vulnerable to .50 caliber bullets. Had the Japanese destroyed the oil, it would have prolonged the war another two years..."
Admiral Chester Nimitz, Commander-in-Chief, U.S. Navy Pacific Fleet

Chapter One

December 1941

He was dead asleep when the first explosion shook his bed. More explosions rattled the open windows and jarred him fully awake.

This room looked so unfamiliar; for a few moments, Maynard "Jock" Miles was hung over and couldn't remember where he was. He checked his wristwatch—it read 7:42. *I suppose that means 7:42 in the morning*, he thought. Draped sloppily over a chair in the corner was the dress white uniform of a US Army captain. The branch insignia on the blouse's lapel was an eagle perched on a shield adorned with stars. One look at those stars and all the details of his professional life came flooding back to Captain Jock Miles—he was the aide to General Short, commander of the US Army in Hawaii. Staggering to his feet, he realized he hadn't spent the night in his quarters at Fort Shafter but at the Pearl Harbor Naval Station guest house.

The sound of airplane engines droned like a swarm of angry insects. A series of explosions, split seconds apart, rattled the entire building and sent Jock Miles diving to the floor, thinking, *What the hell does the*

Navy think they're doing? It's early in the morning...Sunday morning! This is no time for fly-bys and cannon salutes. He crawled to the window. Still on his knees, he stared in disbelief at the scene outside.

Thick black smoke billowed from the battleships moored at Ford Island. Countless single-engine airplanes buzzed low over the harbor, each in turn dropping a long, black, cylindrical object—a torpedo—aimed straight at the sitting ducks of Battleship Row. The planes all had those big red meatballs—the rising sun of Japan insignia—on their wings and fuselages. There was not an American plane to be seen opposing them. There didn't even seem to be any anti-aircraft fire directed against them.

Surely, this is just a bad dream...

On the street below his window, a group of young sailors running toward the harbor —*maybe a dozen*, Jock thought—were cut down in a hail of machine gun fire. A few were dead before what was left of their riddled bodies hit the ground. Others writhed in agony, some screaming for God to save them. The rest screamed for their mothers. A second later, the airplane that strafed them streaked low overhead, barely above the tops of the tall trees lining the street. For a brief moment, the plane's shadow—a perfect aircraft silhouette—blotted out the morning sun like a deadly eclipse.

This is a little too realistic to be a drill! And those damned planes just keep on coming!

Jock struggled into his dress whites. He balled up the necktie, stuffing it into his trouser pocket, and didn't bother to button the blouse over his half-open shirt. Such requirements of military decorum seemed ridiculously unnecessary right now. He sprinted down the hallway, trying to remember the way out of the old and stately guest house.

Where the hell did I park the car? I've got to get back to Fort Shafter! The general's probably screaming for me already!

His recollections of how he came to spend the night at Pearl, rather than his own room a few miles away at Fort Shafter, were raggedly taking shape. There had been a reception last night at Pearl, hosted by Admiral Kimmel, the US Pacific Fleet commander. General Short and his staff had attended. So had Trudy Judd, the captivating daughter of a rear admiral. Jock Miles had reserved the room at the guest house on the chance that Trudy, who he had been seeing for the past few months, might finally be inclined to slip away and spend the night with him. A neutral location would be necessary, as Trudy lived with her parents, and female guests at Shafter's bachelor officers' quarters were strictly against regulations.

And girls like Trudy Judd don't do it in cars.

But after a pleasant, arm-in-arm stroll to her family's house on Admiral's Row, they plopped into a settee on the moonlit lanai, where the evening degenerated into another frustrating episode of heavy petting and too much alcohol. By the time she sent him on his way, he was much too drunk to drive, much less find his car. How he managed to get to the base guest house was anybody's guess.

I must have been quite a sight...a drunk with a hard-on in army whites, wandering across a naval base.

He was sure he was quite a sight right now, too, in

his carelessly-donned uniform. *Dressing like this would have cost me a year of walking the area back at West Point.* But the wounded sailors he was carrying from the street to the shelter of the guest house didn't seem to care how Jock Miles looked. They clung to him like a savior sent from heaven. The dress whites were now ruined, spattered with the sailors' blood.

He had to get back to Shafter; his place—his duty—was with the general. Japs could be landing all over Oahu—all over the islands of Hawaii, for that matter. Leaving the wounded sailors in the care of a very rattled petty officer manning the guest house's reception desk, he stepped back into the street and got his bearings. His car was still at the officers' club, a few blocks away, closer to the harbor. He set out for it on the dead run. Each time he heard a plane streak low overhead, Jock dove for safety behind a tree trunk, but he wasn't strafed. The pilots had grander targets in their sights.

He was nearing the officers' club now. After a quick look for strafing planes, he abandoned the uncertain safety of trees and took a short cut, sprinting across an open field. The explosions from the harbor had become more frequent. The torpedo planes were gone; it was now the turn of the dive bombers to wreak havoc. Jock watched in horror as they released their bombs and then pulled out of nearly vertical dives to skim low across the anchorage. The bombs looked like tiny black pellets as they flew downward, some striking the water harmlessly but most exploding with terrible effect on ships and docks. There was still not a hint of opposition from American planes or anti-aircraft guns that Jock could see.

Could we have really gotten caught with our pants down this badly?

The thick, black smoke of burning vessels and aircraft was filling the air above Pearl Harbor. Jock reached the palm trees at the edge of the officers' club parking lot. His Plymouth sedan sat at the far side, the only car in the lot. He could hear an airplane very close—and then there she was, right behind him, heading straight over the parking lot toward the harbor. He hugged the nearest palm tree for cover just as the plane's machine guns announced her arrival with a bone-chilling *rat-a-tat*. The bullets plowed a trough across the parking lot, reached the other side, and turned Jock's Plymouth into a junk pile of twisted metal.

I won't be getting back to Shafter anytime soon now, that's for damned sure...not in all this chaos.

He wasn't sure what compelled him to keep running full tilt toward the harbor. Perhaps it was simply the West Point motto that kept repeating in his head: *Duty, Honor, Country*. His country was under attack. It was his duty to defend her. His honor depended on doing just that. How all that would come to pass on this Sunday morning, on the base of a rival service, he hadn't figured out yet. But he kept on going, wondering why he was the only one running toward the harbor. The few sailors he encountered were running the other way, and from their terror-stricken eyes, Jock Miles could tell they had no interest in discussing the matter.

At a dockside warehouse, he encountered a large group of sailors who were not running anywhere. They milled about outside an open doorway marked ARMS

ROOM, their frustration boiling over into rage as they tried, and failed, to get inside. A grizzled old CPO was barring their entry. From his garrison belt hung a holster containing a .45 automatic pistol.

"I told you…ain't nobody drawing no weapons until the duty officer says so," the CPO said.

The sailors beseeched the CPO as one voice, gesturing frantically at the mayhem unraveling before them. He was not moved. His jaw set sternly, the CPO responded, "Those are my orders. Fuck off if you don't like it."

Ahh, Jock thought, *the Navy has mindless pencil-pushers, too…just like the Army.*

Jock stepped to the front of the sailors. "Chief," he said, "in case you haven't noticed, we're under attack. This isn't the time to be worried about paperwork. Step aside."

The CPO did not know what to make of this bloodied man standing before him. He was not even sure what branch of service the man represented; he had never seen an army white dress uniform in his long Navy career. All he could see was the double silver bars on the epaulets, and that made him some kind of officer. And this officer was trying to pull rank on him in front of all these swabbies.

His face screwed into a sneer, the CPO said, "Look, sir, I don't know who you are or where you come from—"

Jock cut him off. "I'm Captain Maynard Miles, US Army Headquarters, Hawaii. Is that good enough for you, Chief? Now stand aside. I take full responsibility."

There was a tense moment as the CPO refused to yield. Jock began to wonder if the chief's next move would involve the drawing of his pistol. Just then, the whistling of bombs falling close by sent them all diving to the deck. The nearest impact was on the pier barely 100 yards from where they all stood, but it injured nothing more than a cargo dolly. While the old CPO struggled to get back on his feet, sailors streamed past him into the arms room, grabbing all the weapons and ammunition they could carry. As Jock offered the chief a helping hand, he noticed the pistol on his hip was not even loaded. The rectangular slot for the magazine at the base of the grip was empty.

"Better get some rounds in that weapon, Chief," Jock said. "Looks like we've got ourselves a shooting war."

The old CPO sighed and snapped Jock a crisp salute. "I hate like hell to say it, but I'm afraid you're right, Captain. Best of luck to you, sir."

A few docks away, several ships had not been so lucky. They had been hit by bombs and were belching smoke from fires below deck. Jock started to run toward them. "Good luck to you, too, Chief," he called over his shoulder. "We're going to need it."

He was halfway to the docks when he realized the anti-aircraft guns on a few of the ships in the harbor had finally begun to fire. Hearing the *THUD-THUD-THUD* of the American guns gave him some small measure of comfort:

At least we're finally fighting back.

The comfort was short-lived, for the strangest sound Jock Miles ever heard stopped him dead in his tracks. Rising above the angry chorus of Japanese engines, the roar of one aircraft had turned into a high-pitched scream that rose higher with each passing second. It was coming from the sky across the Southeast Loch, above the submarine base—and the fuel storage farm. A dive bomber—out of control, smoke streaming from its shrieking, overspeeding engine—dove straight down at incredible velocity and crashed into the top of one of the massive fuel storage tanks. The shrieking stopped abruptly; the sound of the impact that echoed across the loch was like one beat of a huge bass drum. Jock watched in disbelief as the sides of the tank buckled and split apart, leaking its millions of gallons of maritime fuel oil in thick, black torrents that quickly formed a pool within the tank's surrounding berm.

Son of a bitch! There's no fire!

Jock remembered the demonstration in a West Point chemistry lab of just how nonflammable heavy fuel oil was in a liquid state. The instructor putting on the show had stood next to an open barrel full of oil—wearing no protective gear whatsoever—and calmly tossed in one lit match after another. Rather than igniting the oil, the matches were extinguished in it. But the instructor had gone on to warn if that same oil was atomized into tiny droplets and you added enough heat for ignition, watch out! You would set off a raging inferno.

From his distant vantage point, Jock could not tell how the fire started—just whiffs of black smoke at first, then a few flames near the pipeline that ran from tank to tank along the top of the berm. Perhaps oil was spraying through a breach in the pipeline or a parted valve flange. Perhaps the crashed airplane had provided the spark or the red-hot projectiles flying everywhere had done the trick. Whatever the reason, a raging inferno had begun, spewing towering flames and thick, black smoke into the air. Inch by inch, the surface temperature of the spreading oil, licked by pools of fire at its edges, was reaching its flash point of 150 degrees Fahrenheit and igniting.

Holy shit! It's rolling like lava from a volcano!

Like moths to a flame, three Japanese aircraft in line abreast formation flew low across the eastern shore of the loch, heading straight for the fuel farm. In what seemed to Jock a choreographed aerial display, they held their formation through a gentle turn, all the while raking the length and breadth of the 24 tanks with machine gun fire.

The tanks began to resemble fountains, with black oil gushing out through scores of bullet holes in their sides. Within a few minutes, it seemed the entire fuel farm was engulfed in liquid fire; the newly spilled oil had somehow found its own source of ignition. In the ever-widening sea of flames, tank after tank buckled in the intense heat, adding many millions of gallons to the inferno. As Jock stood transfixed by this apocalyptic blaze, he didn't realize all the Japanese planes were now gone.

Fifty minutes later, while Jock Miles was rallying dockside sailors with machine guns into ad hoc anti-aircraft teams, a second wave of Japanese aircraft appeared overhead. The pilots and crewmen of those planes were surprised and delighted to see the inferno already raging below them. Despite the thick smoke that hindered visibility from above, they continued the attack on the already battered ships and airfields of the US Pacific forces according to plan.

Chapter Two

It was early afternoon before Jock Miles got back to Fort Shafter. The Japanese cabbie he'd been lucky enough to flag down outside Pearl's main gate shook his head violently when told the destination.

"I'm not going near any military base," the cabbie said, obviously terrified at the prospect. "I'm a US citizen, dammit, but you white people think I'm some kind of spy. I've had all kinds of crap thrown at me and my cab today, especially on those shot-up streets where all that anti-aircraft fire came back down. I'd probably get my ass riddled on sight if I got near Shafter."

"Then why'd you stop for me?" Jock asked, already in the cab's back seat.

The cabbie gave him an incredulous once-over. "Because it didn't look like you were wearing a military uniform at first. I thought you were a waiter or something…and you looked like you needed help."

Jock had to agree with him. In his filthy and blood-spattered dress whites, his cap long gone, he didn't look like much of a soldier anymore. He checked the cash in his wallet.

"Well, I sure do need some help. Tell you what…you can double your fare. Just drop me off near the gate, okay?"

"You're not wounded, are you? You aren't going to bleed all over my cab?"

Nodding in the direction of Pearl Harbor, Jock said, "No, this isn't my blood."

Hesitantly, the cabbie agreed. He nervously ground the gears as they drove off toward the empty streets of

Honolulu, a city usually vibrant and bright but now cowering in a colorless limbo as the smoke from Pearl darkened the afternoon sun and cast the city in gray-filtered light.

Jock thought it prudent to change from the ruined dress whites to regular duty khakis before reporting to General Short. A shave was in order, as well. The grooming mattered little, though; the general was livid when Jock entered the chaos of the cavernous room that was the command post. Keyed-up staff officers were either shouting into telephones or shuttling reports on the double to their frazzled general. Turning from the giant map of Oahu pinned to a wall, Short fixed his gaze on his tardy aide.

"Sorry, sir," Jock said. "I've been stuck at Pearl, helping out the Navy—"

General Short cut him off. "I consider you AWOL, Captain. The world is falling apart, and my aide is shacked up somewhere when he should have been right here."

"Negative, sir! My car was destroyed in the attack. I tried to call, but the phones..."

The general wasn't buying it. "I'm far too busy right now to care about your piddling little problems, Captain." Shifting to an almost fatherly tone, Short continued, "I had great hopes for you, Maynard. You would have had a fine career, but you've let me down. You've let the Army down." The fatherly tone disappeared, replaced by the stern voice of a displeased superior. "You'll be reassigned out of my command before the day is over."

Short turned his back to Jock as a major timidly approached and handed the general a sheaf of reports. They did not contain good news. Short grew more agitated as he flipped through the pages, seemingly unaware Jock Miles was still braced at parade rest behind him. The words of a naval captain still rang in Jock's ears, spoken as he left Pearl just an hour ago:

Damn fine job you did here today, Captain Miles. Those gunners you whipped together shot down at least two Japs, probably more! You should be damned proud...I'll be putting you in for the Distinguished Service Cross.

Proud wasn't the word that described what Jock felt; *relieved* came much closer. His country was suddenly at war and, much to his relief, he had finally done what he was supposed to do—what he was trained to do—without hesitation: led men in combat. He had done it brilliantly, too. It mattered not at all those he had led were Navy men. He now joined the ranks of those who had been under fire and drawn enemy blood. His boss would probably never know about it, though, consumed as he was with humiliation for being caught with his pants down by this Japanese attack. Rather than reveling in his newfound status as a decorated combat veteran, Jock Miles was trying to come to grips with being fired. He could forget about that Distinguished Service Cross.

The general seemed oblivious to Jock's continued presence. "Sir," Jock said, "am I—"

Without looking up from the reports, the general cut him off again. "Dismissed, Captain? Yes, you most certainly are. Get out of my sight."

Chapter Three

Admiral Nagumo watched anxiously from the bridge of the carrier *Akagi* as the last of his planes touched down and jerked to a halt on the deck. The first wave of Pearl Harbor attackers had finally returned, with very few aircraft missing. The deck immediately became a beehive of activity as refueling and rearming of the squadrons commenced. Speed was essential: within an hour, the planes of the second wave would return, and until Nagumo's planes could fly and fight again, the entire attack force he commanded—six carriers and their escort ships—was vulnerable to American aircraft from Hawaii.

Nagumo already knew the first wave's attack had been a success; radio reports sent when the planes were still over Oahu made that clear. The returning pilots, however, were excitedly reported a success Nagumo had not expected to hear: in addition to the battleships sunk at Pearl and row after row of parked aircraft devastated all across the island, the US Navy's fuel storage facility had been inadvertently destroyed.

"The fuel facility...how could that have happened?" Nagumo asked a flight leader.

"One of our planes...probably a dive bomber...crashed into the tanks and started a blaze," the flight leader replied. "A flight of fighters that had just strafed Hickam Field reported they were taking the initiative to strafe the tanks as well. It was quite an inferno by the time we left the area. A target of opportunity, Admiral!"

Target of opportunity, indeed, Nagumo thought. In his attack plan, the fuel storage facility was a designated target of the *third wave,* which would be launched—at his option—only after the first two waves had returned to their carriers and the situation assessed. The entire premise of a third wave had troubled Nagumo from the very beginning. The first two waves would have already crippled the American fleet by neutralizing its battleships. American defenders who had initially been caught with their guard down would be on high alert. Japanese aircrews that had already flown the 500-mile round trip and braved enemy fire once that day would have to do it all over again. Fatigue would become an issue, and fatigue caused accidents. By the time the third wave returned to the carriers, it would be dark. The now-exhausted pilots were not well trained in night landings. A day of jubilant victory could easily turn into a debacle of needlessly lost airplanes and drowned aviators.

There is no point considering it further, Nagumo thought. *We have been successful enough today. There will be no third wave.*

Once the second-wave planes were back on board ship, Nagumo's attack fleet would set a course for home.

Chapter Four

Despite its cheerful Christmas decorations, the White House was anything but a joyous place. The events of December 7, 1941, had seen to that, casting a pall over that proud edifice that promised to stretch into 1942 and beyond. Nothing being said in the Oval Office at the moment was improving Franklin Delano Roosevelt's mood, either. A cigarette in its elegant holder dangled from his lips, completing the president's pessimistic aura.

Admiral Ernest King, the Chief of Naval Operations—CNO in naval and Washington parlance—had just finished his briefing. It had summarized the devastation brought to the US Pacific fleet by the Japanese attack on Pearl Harbor. Neither General George Marshall, the Army Chief of Staff, nor Henry Stimson, the Secretary of War, had uttered a word since taking their seats. The president remained silent, his steady gaze boring uncomfortably into King, as if the bleak assessment the admiral had just delivered could be improved by sheer force of will.

Stimson began to fidget nervously in his chair. "Relax, Henry," the President said without averting his gaze from King. "I need a minute to think. I've never gotten a lump of coal in my Christmas stocking before." The room fell silent once again; no one dared speak until requested to by the president. After several long drags on the cigarette, Roosevelt perked up and propelled his wheelchair out from behind his desk. He was ready to cross-examine his military leaders. Even his cigarette holder suddenly seemed upbeat, now pointing skyward at a jaunty angle.

"So, Admiral King," the president began as he rolled to a stop before the CNO's armchair, "it's all about the oil, you say. Other than the battleships, the fleet's intact…but we can't fuel it? That is what you're saying, is it not?"

King took a long drink of water before answering. His throat was dry; he had been talking a long time. Masking his impatience behind a toothy grin, the president said, "Take your time, Admiral. I'm sure the Japanese aren't expecting us anytime soon."

Ernest King was annoyed by the president's crack, and he wasn't a man who masked his annoyance easily. This wasn't the time or the place, however, to show his notorious temper. The Navy—*his* Navy—had been caught dead asleep by the Japanese; so had Marshall's Army. The Navy, though, had paid the dearest price.

And those incompetent fools Kimmel and Short had been warned! It's all their fault, King reassured himself as he drained the water glass. *If anyone put coal in the president's stocking, it was them, not me.*

"I'm sorry, Mr. President," King said, his tone perfunctory rather than truly apologetic. "We've lost over one hundred million gallons of fuel oil. That's about a year's supply of fuel for the Pacific fleet. But we've managed to salvage some—"

The president interrupted, asking, "How much?"

"Enough to keep one carrier with a minimal screening force at sea."

"Only one, Admiral?" Roosevelt asked. "And what do you plan to do with the other two carriers?"

"Pull them back to the West Coast, Mr. President. We can't leave them as sitting ducks at Pearl. Thank God all of the carriers were at sea during the attack."

The president bristled. "I don't think God deserves our thanks right now, Admiral King. For all practical purposes, the Japanese sunk our entire Pacific fleet just by hitting that damned oil. How long will it take you to replenish our oil reserves at Pearl? And where the hell do you plan to store it now?"

King knew better than to put forth a too-optimistic estimate. The president had a special fondness for the Navy, having served as its Assistant Secretary during the First World War, and understood the workings of that service down to brass tacks; he would sniff out hogwash immediately. The admiral swallowed hard before answering, "With our current tankering capability, twelve to eighteen months, Mr. President."

Roosevelt didn't look at all surprised by the estimate. He waited impatiently for the rest of the answer.

"Regarding storage, as we can clearly see, Admiral Nimitz was correct. Our above-ground tanks at Pearl were extremely vulnerable, even to bullets."

Roosevelt *harrumphed* at the word *vulnerable*, then asked, "Nimitz…the chap you're replacing Kimmel with?"

"Yes, Mr. President. Chester Nimitz. A most capable flag officer, and he's the man responsible for the Red Hill project…the underground storage tanks that are under construction in the hills above Pearl."

"And when will this underground storage be ready?" the president asked.

"We've accelerated construction as much as humanly possible, Mr. President. It should have partial storage capability in six to eight months and full capacity by early nineteen forty-three."

Roosevelt seemed neither pleased nor displeased by the answer. He asked, "What can the Navy do in the Pacific until then?"

"We can defend Hawaii and the West Coast by the skin of our teeth, Mr. President. And that's all."

Now the President was decidedly displeased. "What about offensive operations?" he asked. "Do you expect me to tell the American people we can't strike back against the Japs for a year or more?"

"Unfortunately, yes, Mr. President," King replied. "The Pacific will be a naval war, and we won't be a serious player in that realm for a while. The British, Australians, and Dutch, weak as they are, are completely on their own for the time being."

Scowling, Roosevelt turned to his Secretary of War, Henry Stimson, asking, "What do you think about that assessment, Henry?"

"I think we should consider transferring some of our Atlantic tankers to the Pacific immediately, Mr. President," Stimson replied.

Without a word being said, it was clear Admiral King thought little of the secretary's suggestion. The president was not impressed, either. Shaking his head, he said, "No, Henry, that won't do. We've pledged our support to the Brits…to *Europe first.* You know as well as I they're in worse shape than we are at the moment. We can't cut back on them."

King added another reason. "We could send every tanker we own to Pearl tomorrow, but they'd have to tie up there as temporary gas stations for weeks or months on end. That would slow our replenishment rate to a trickle. Nobody would get enough oil…not the Atlantic, not the Pacific. And you don't build a new tanker overnight, either."

Roosevelt pivoted his wheelchair to face George Marshall. "General Marshall, how does the Army see all this?"

Marshall had waited to speak with his usual calm and reserve. At last, the floor was his. He began to state his case with purpose and precision.

"Naturally, Mr. President," Marshall said, "the Navy's diminished capabilities to transport, provide fire support, and resupply the Army will have a tremendous impact. For the moment, however, we must continue to garrison and defend Hawaii. As to the Philippines, MacArthur's grasp is tenuous, at best, and there is precious little we can do to help him now."

"So you're saying we'll lose the Philippines?" Roosevelt asked.

"I'm afraid so, Mr. President. It's only a matter of time. But we can't allow ourselves to be seen as going into a shell."

The president's enthusiasm returned as he said, "General, I agree with that sentiment completely."

"What I'm going to propose," Marshall continued, "is this: we must position all the ground and air assets we can transport to Australia as soon as possible. The Brits and the Dutch have already drained Australia of its fighting manpower to help defend the Middle East, the Far East, and the East Indies, efforts all destined to fail, and fail quickly, without the material and manpower support we are currently unable to provide. Australia is practically defenseless now...if the Japanese just walked in and established an occupation force there, they would not only control the rich natural resources of the southwest Pacific, but we would be deprived indefinitely of the only base in the theater from which we could strike back…once we were fully ready to strike back, that is."

Roosevelt looked to King and asked, "How big a force could we transport with our current limitations, Admiral?"

The CNO did a quick mental calculation and then grumbled his answer. "No more than one division every four months, Mr. President."

With eyebrows raised, Roosevelt gestured for his Army chief to respond. "That's no problem," Marshall offered. "We've only just begun to raise fresh divisions, and many of them are destined for Europe. One division every four months to Australia is about all we can handle for the foreseeable future."

"What about the Marine Corps?" the president asked Admiral King. "Are they ready to be deployed?"

King was ready to throw cold water on that suggestion, too. "As small as the Corps is, Mr. President, it's better to keep them as a mobile defense force for the time being. If we tied them up in Australia, they'd be swallowed up in a land that vast."

The president understood the subtext of King's answer: positioning marines in Australia as part of Marshall's plan would put them under Army control, and the Navy had no intention surrendering their marines to the Army.

Stimson beckoned for Roosevelt's attention. "If I may, Mr. President?"

"Go ahead, Henry."

"That might prove to be a very risky proposition," Stimson said. "The Australians feel betrayed by Britain and her Far East policies. They're expected to provide manpower to defend the rest of the Commonwealth but constantly get the short end of the stick in trade policy and military hardware. If the Japanese landed on their shores, they just might be willing to cut a deal and capitulate, quite like Vichy France. Any troops we managed to send would simply be wasted...and probably end up as POWs."

"So you're saying we do nothing, Henry?" the President asked.

"For the moment...yes, Mr. President."

"Absolutely unacceptable," Roosevelt said, his voice adamant as he wheeled about to return to his desk. "Enough of our friends have had to capitulate already. Admiral King, hold on to your marines as you suggest. General Marshall, you are to prepare your Pacific forces to assist in the defense of Australia. That's the least we can do."

"Yes, Mr. President," Marshall replied, and then added a sober assessment: "But I'm afraid it's the *most* we can do."

Roosevelt looked to the CNO once more. "And you, Admiral King, are to provide whatever ships the Army needs." Knowing King's propensity for inter-service subterfuge, the President added in a stern voice, "And I'll expect those ships to be allocated all the fuel they need to get to Australia."

Chapter Five

March 1942

A very glum thought crossed Jock Miles's mind: *We've been on this damned boat for two weeks but we're still nowhere near Australia.*

He leaned against the upper deck rail and watched as the ship's crew—sailors of the US Navy—engaged in what seemed a circus-like, but sadistic, ceremony on the main deck. This troopship, part of an armed convoy of eight ships, was crossing the Equator, and those sailors who had crossed it before—*shellbacks,* they called themselves—were hazing those sailors making their first crossing, called *wogs,* short for *pollywogs.* It was all part of nautical tradition, the 2000 Army troops on board had been told. The shellbacks wore costumes representing noble creatures of the sea. Presiding over the spectacle was a fat, bearded shellback wearing a long, flowing wig: King Neptune himself. Atop his wig sat a crown; in his hand he carried a trident. Both looked like they had been made for some grammar school pageant. Sitting primly next to King Neptune was a sailor in drag, portraying his queen. As the shellbacks were busy stripping the wogs to their skivvies, flogging them brutally with sections of hose and binding them together with hawsers, Jock reflected on his turn of fortune since December 7th.

Considering General Short got the ax less than two weeks after the disaster on Oahu, he sure didn't waste any time sticking me with a rotten report. You'd think he would've had bigger things to worry about. He really put the screws to me when he wrote, "tends to favor personal pursuits over duty." What a crock of shit...and all because I was too busy helping the Navy fight Japs to wipe some general's ass. With the war on, all the guys from my class are getting bumped up to major or light colonel and getting battalions to command...but I'm still stuck as a captain, and back as a little ol' company commander, a job I've already done twice, back in nineteen thirty-six and thirty-seven...to glowing reports. No more fast track to my first star now...more like a slow boat to nowhere. Hell, I'd get out of this damned Army if I could...but with a war on, even someone on the bottom of the promotion list isn't going anywhere.

To add insult to injury, Trudy Judd had dumped him, too. He had come to a decision as he wasted time in Honolulu, waiting for orders: he would ask Trudy to marry him. It seemed like a good idea at the time. Here he was, still a bachelor at 28 years of age, on the Army's shit list, and facing untold years at war. Maybe knowing you had a wife to come home to when it was all over would make the whole ordeal easier to bear. Armed with a far-too-expensive engagement ring, he popped the question in the sitting room of her father's house. She replied with an indifferent, *Oh, Jock...I need time to think.*

In other words, *No, thank you, soldier.*

On the deck below, the shellbacks were pouring buckets of a greasy, green fluid over the heads of the wogs. Their faces contorted in revulsion as the thick concoction dripped downward, coating their bodies. Jock thought there was a good chance the wogs would be puking their guts out any second.

Well, at least they're learning a valuable lesson:

shit runs downhill.

He didn't know many of the names and faces of the men under his command; he was handed the job only a week before marching them onto this ship in San Francisco. He thought he recognized a few of his troopers among the hundreds watching the antics on the main deck, but there was no glimmer of recognition from the men when they glanced his way.

If they're even mine, they probably don't recognize me, either. It's going to be a long, hard road making something out of this unit. By the time we get off this overcrowded tub, you'll need a microscope to measure their morale.

A man elbowed his way to the rail beside Miles. In a gruff drawl of the American South, the man said, "You know, Captain, they're all queer fellas in the Navy. Probably be corn-holing each other any minute now."

Jock smiled; the voice was one of the few on this ship he would recognize in an instant. It belonged to his company first sergeant, Melvin Patchett. "How're our boys doing, Top?" Miles asked.

"Usual stuff, Captain. Russo got hisself thrown in the brig again."

"What'd he do now?"

"Fighting over some card game. Your Lieutenant Brewster's fixing to make a federal case out of it, though."

Your Lieutenant Brewster, meaning the company executive officer, First Lieutenant John Joseph Pershing Brewster, West Point class of '39. Latest in a distinguished line of military officers dating back over a century. A regimental commander in the Corp of

Cadets. This young officer firmly believed he was on the fast track to general, just like his father and grandfather before him. Jock smiled again as he thought, *Old school NCOs like Melvin Patchett don't think much of us West Pointers, especially ones like Brewster, who think stars will fall on their shoulders just for showing up.* But Jock knew full well that Melvin Patchett was a good man to have around: he was a gruff, tough-as-nails combat veteran—a doughboy of World War One—and Army through and through. He had never bothered to take a wife, citing the old maxim, *If the Army wanted you to have a wife, it would have issued you one.* Even though Patchett was an "old man" of 42, his 24 years of service had made him most wise in the ways of the Army. Unlike Lieutenant John Joseph Pershing "Scooter" Brewster.

Before Jock Miles could ask his first sergeant to elaborate, Scooter Brewster himself came bustling down the upper deck, a sheaf of papers in his hand.

"Captain Miles," Brewster said, "I've prepared summary court martial charges against PFC Russo—"

Miles interrupted, asking, "What are the charges, Lieutenant?"

"Drunk and disorderly, sir."

"Did you confiscate the liquor?"

"Yes, sir. I found quite a stash."

Jock took the papers from Scooter Brewster's hand and gave them a cursory glance. Then he folded the papers and stuffed them into his shirt pocket.

Brewster looked perplexed. "Aren't you going to sign them, sir?"

"No, I don't think so, Lieutenant. If we locked up every dogface who got a little rowdy, half of them would be in the brig by the time this tub docks. That might put quite a crimp in our unit readiness. Tell you what…give Russo a night in the can to sober up, then release him. That sound okay to you, First Sergeant?"

Melvin Patchett nodded in agreement, trying hard not to snicker at the flustered Lieutenant Brewster.

"Was there anything else, Lieutenant?" Miles asked.

Crestfallen, Scooter Brewster replied, "No, sir."

"Then carry on, Lieutenant."

After a crisp exchange of salutes, Brewster scurried away. Jock settled back against the rail to watch the festivities on the main deck with Melvin Patchett. The hazing seemed to be winding down—if you could call being knocked down and propelled across the deck by a powerful, "cleansing" spray from a fire hose *winding down.* Soon, the wogs would rise to the status of shellback—provided the process did not kill them first.

"The way this thing is looking, the Japs are going to beat our asses to Australia," the first sergeant said. "I've just heard they bombed Darwin again and pretty much kicked the Aussie Army out of New Guinea. Those who ain't already POWs are trying to escape back home across the Torres Strait on anything that'll float. It's like a *Dunkirk down under*, they're saying. The Japs have taken the Solomon Islands, too…wherever the hell they are. They sure ain't wasting much time."

Melvin Patchett turned and gazed at the three huge crates lashed to the afterdeck, each containing a disassembled American fighter plane. "And how the hell are we supposed to stop them yellow bastards? With a trickle of route-step dogfaces and three li'l ol' fighter planes?"

"There'll be other convoys, Top," Miles said, "with more men, more equipment—"

Patchett's burst of laughter stopped Jock cold. "Meaning no disrespect, sir," the first sergeant said, "but at this rate, we'll all be dead and gone of old age before The US of A starts kicking any Japanese ass. Seems to me we're part of a show of force that ain't no force at all."

A loud, repetitive *gong* began to sound from the ship's public address system. The Navy men ceased their ceremony and sprinted to their battle stations, the old shellbacks still in costume, the new ones still soaking wet in skivvies, even before a booming voice from the speakers commanded them to do so. A destroyer off the troopship's starboard side let loose several *whoops* of its horn and, pouring thick, gray smoke from her stacks, turned hard to starboard, making maximum speed toward some submerged menace thought to be stalking the convoy.

"Probably just s'more fucking whales," Patchett said, pulling bright orange life jackets from a bulkhead rack.

"Maybe," Jock replied as he took the life jacket his first sergeant offered. "Let's just hope we don't get torpedoed and meet the real King Neptune."

Chapter Six

April 1942

It was late afternoon and the day's downpour had made its exit, but, as always, the heat and humidity remained. A strong wind pushed the storm clouds, still flashing their lightning bolts, away from the west coast of Cape York Peninsula and out over the Gulf of Carpentaria. Jillian Forbes walked briskly down the Weipa Mission dock, her riding boots making their familiar *clomp clomp* on the wet wooden planks. The wind-whipped hem of her old cotton dress flapped about her knees like a faded, flowered flag; her long, dark, untamed hair swirled crazily about her head. She was growing worried. All her fishing boats were back but one: her biggest, *Mangrove Queen*. The other five boats had already unloaded their day's catch. The boats' Aborigine crews—black men in the tattered work clothes of white men—had already gone up the road to their families in the Mission settlement. But there was something on the water, well offshore, growing larger quickly. *That's probably the Queen*, she thought, more a prayer than a certainty.

She heard the sound of another pair of boots on the dock. Constable Mick Murray was striding toward her, a very serious look on his weathered face. He looked exhausted, like he had been riding all day. The constable started speaking when he was still 20 feet away.

"Jilly, I'm going to tell you one more time…all whites are to evacuate south. That means you, too, young lady."

Jillian's eyes remained glued to the approaching speck on the water. "And I'll tell you one more time, Mick...go to hell."

Mick was now right next to Jillian, but she still wouldn't turn to look at him.

"The Japs are coming, Jilly. The *wet* is almost over...a perfect time to invade." *The wet:* the summer months of frequent, torrential rain in tropical North Queensland.

"This isn't a child's game we're playing," the constable added.

"And I'm not a child, Mick. *Aussies* don't even want anything to do with the Cape...why in bloody hell would the Japs want to come here? Besides, I've got Dad's business to look after. I won't leave."

"The Cape could turn into a battlefield before you know it, Jilly."

"I doubt that," she replied. "The only diggers I've seen around here were headed south as fast as they could go."

Frustrated, Mick pulled off his slouch hat and mopped the sweat from his balding head. Jillian Forbes had been obstinate since the day she was born. Clearly, he needed a stronger argument to convince this headstrong young woman. He tried a more ominous tack: "You know what the Japs will do to a white woman, Jilly."

She laughed and finally turned to look at him. "Mick, you may scare the Mission ladies with that talk, but I grew up here in the wild. I don't need the King of England or his lackeys in Canberra to decide what's good for me."

The constable shrugged, reached into his pocket,

and produced a document. Jillian took it from his hand, read it, and tore it up.

Mick Murray sighed and said, "Ripping it up doesn't change a thing, Jilly. The government has commandeered your vessels for the national defense. Have them ready to sail first thing in the morning. I'll be using them to evacuate the Mission folks. Why don't you plan to be onboard, too?"

Jillian's attention had turned elsewhere. She looked back over the water; *Mangrove Queen*—all 55 feet of her—was coming into clear view. She noticed something out of the ordinary right away—there were three more souls on board than when she had departed. Army green uniforms differentiated those three from the five Aborigine crewmen, even at this distance. As the *Queen* drew closer, it was clear the soldiers—the *diggers*—had seen rough times. Their uniforms were torn and soiled; their gaunt bodies had been abused by wind and sea. Once the boat was secured to the dock, the soldiers were so wobbly her crewmen had to help them disembark. Only one still had his boots. None had a weapon. They all had the same glassy stare, fixed well into the distance, as if watching a calamity from afar only they could see.

"We found them in a little boat, Miss Jilly, way out in the Gulf," Old Robert, the *Queen's* captain, called from the helm. "They rowed from Papua. It's a miracle the current in the strait didn't get them."

Mick Murray asked, "How long were you adrift, lads?"

His voice a parched croak, the one still with his boots answered, "Six days."

With the dismissive air of a know-it-all, Murray

said, "From Papua, you say…you should have just gone over to Horn Island. The Navy's been shuttling diggers like you from there down to Cairns for weeks."

Anger flared in the haggard faces of the three soldiers, but they seemed incapable of mounting a reply. Old Robert offered a rebuttal on their behalf: "Oh, no, Constable Mick…the Japs are on Horn Island now. We watch their planes come and go from the airfield there."

The soldier with the boots began to mumble, his words slow and halting: "Everything…all fell apart…the Japs…they had everything…even whores…we had nothing." His focus snapped back from that distant horizon; a look of indignation crossed his face. "The Yanks," he said, "they never came…never came."

Old Robert had more to say. "We see Jap planes flying very low all the time now over the Gulf. We can see their faces. They smile and wave at us."

Mick Murray scowled, pointed his finger at Old Robert, and said, "Let's see how friendly you think they are on dry land, when you're stuck on the end of their bayonet. Now, you blacks take these diggers up to the Mission—"

Jillian interrupted the constable. "Hang on, Mick. Don't be giving orders to my crew. They've got a catch to unload. Why don't you take these lads up to the Mission yourself? You're not doing anything useful here. Go ahead and use one of my wagons."

Murray threw up his arms in resignation. There was no point arguing with Jillian Forbes while these poor lads needed attention. After tomorrow he would be gone from here, and she would be out of his hair one way or the other. He led the three soldiers away.

Jillian's icehouse was the coolest place in the Weipa Mission, if you could stand the odor of fish that permeated its corrugated iron confines and the racket of the petrol-fueled generator that powered the place. Jillian tied her horse to the railing of the building's veranda and then looked to her six boats nestled against the nearby dock.

I'll be damned if I'm giving those boats away, not to anyone, she thought as she settled into a wicker chair on the veranda. *Dad worked too hard for them.* But she had known the government would try to take them; the Navy had been appropriating vessels all over the northern Australian coastline. She stretched her legs out and propped the heels of her riding boots on the railing. As she did, the hem of her dress slid halfway up her thighs. Unperturbed, she bunched the hiked skirt between her legs and relaxed into the chair.

The only whites left in this settlement were the Presbyterian missionaries, who were very keen on leaving, and Jillian Forbes. Less than a dozen of the missionaries remained; 50 or more had already fled on the trading schooners that worked the Gulf before they, too, had been commandeered. Six half-caste orphans remained at the Mission; they would be evacuated as well. The Presbyterians told terrible stories of what happened to missionaries in China at the hands of the Japanese. Jillian was skeptical of those stories: *Sure, they probably have a kernel of truth in them...but I'll wager they've been blown up into hysterical old wives' tales.*

Mick Murray was right, though; it didn't matter if she ripped up the government order commandeering her boats. As the sole remaining arm of government left in this area, he would just take them anyway. The only way she could stop him was to shoot him. As appealing as that idea sounded, she knew that killing Mick Murray would eventually result in a trip to Brisbane Women's Prison, probably for life.

Old Robert emerged from *The Mangrove Queen's* cabin, jumped to the dock and walked toward the veranda where Jillian sat. "All done?" she asked.

"Yes, Miss Jilly." He looked cautiously around, then asked, "Is Constable Mick really leaving with the big boats?"

"That's what he thinks."

"So we all go bush...or we starve?"

"Nobody's going to starve, Robert. Trust me."

"But the constable *is* leaving?"

Jillian nodded. Old Robert smiled, staring wistfully into the icehouse.

"Help yourself," Jillian said, motioning toward the door. "Bring me one, too."

Old Robert walked into the icehouse, patting the nose of Jillian's tethered horse on the way. When he emerged a few minutes later, his skipper's hat was cocked jauntily on his head, and he held two bottles of cold beer in his hands. He gave one to Jillian. As he took a sip from his bottle, he came face to face with Constable Mick Murray.

"Put that beer down," the constable said. "You know the law. You *boongs* can't be drinking alcohol. I can lock you up and throw away the bloody key."

Mick turned to Jillian. "You shouldn't be letting your blacks at the beer—"

"They're not *my* blacks, Mick," she interrupted. "Old Robert works for me, just like he worked for my father. Dad didn't own him, and neither do I."

Robert took another sip of the beer. Mick, his hand resting on the revolver at his hip, took a menacing step forward and said, "Don't be pushing me, *boong.*"

Like a child in a schoolroom, Old Robert raised his hand to ask a question. "Constable Mick," he said, very politely, "who's going to lock me up if you're not here?" An angelic smile remained on his face as he awaited an answer.

For a moment, Jillian thought Mick Murray's head might actually explode. Surely, Old Robert had pushed the constable too far. Mick's eyes bulged; his face was beet red. So upset was he by this insubordinate yet completely logical question that his entire body seemed to vibrate with rage.

An amused voice in Jillian's head spoke: *He looks positively ropeable.*

But Mick's tremors subsided; a calm resignation settled over him. *The abo's right,* he thought. *Once I'm gone, it'll be the law of the bleedin' jungle around here. Bloody hell...let the Japs figure it all out. And this balmy sheila wants to stay!*

"Just have those boats ready to sail in the morning, Jilly," Mick said, before striding off.

The sun had been up two hours already when the Royal Australian Navy patrol boat approached the

Weipa Mission dock. Jillian had been waiting for it, seated serenely on the veranda of the icehouse. Her rifle stood on its butt end against the wall behind her. Her boats' Aborigine crewmen lined the veranda rail, trying to hide their smiles.

As the patrol boat got close enough to the dock to read faces, the Aborigines broke into giggles; they found the astonished looks of the Navy men very funny. So did Jillian, but she remained poker-faced. All six of Jillian's boats were there at the dock, but only *Mangrove Queen* was still afloat. The other five were awash to their gunwales, their keels resting on the bottom.

While his crew manned their mounted machine guns and nervously scanned the sky, the lieutenant in charge jumped to the dock and approached the icehouse. "Who's the owner of these boats?" the lieutenant asked, while stealing his own anxious glance at the sky.

"I am," Jillian replied, without rising from her seat.

The lieutenant produced some papers from his pocket and sifted through them. "It says here I am to procure six vessels," he said. "You are Miss Forbes?"

"Yes, I'm Jillian Forbes. But you're a day late, I'm afraid. We must have had quite a blow last night. Five of the little buggers went down."

The Aborigines were snickering loudly now. The lieutenant's face reddened; he knew he was being had. But he could not stop looking up at the sky nervously.

"Expecting rain?" Jillian asked, eyeing the puffy clouds in the fair sky.

"No, ma'am. I'm expecting Japs. There's been a lot of enemy air activity reported in this sector."

"I'd be more worried about a storm coming," Jillian said. "This is still *the wet*...and I've yet to see any Jap planes around here."

As the confused lieutenant was trying to figure out what his next move would be, a parade of Mission people came down the path to the dock, led by Mick Murray. Mick's two "special constables" were supervising the Aborigine men pulling a wagon loaded with suitcases and steamer trunks.

Let's see, Jillian thought. *Ten Mission folk, six half-black children, the three diggers, Mick and those two whackers of his, and all their kit...Seems just about a right load for the Queen. Figured that real good, didn't I?*

Mick Murray's face was redder than Jillian had ever seen before. She rose to greet him with a smile as he stomped to the veranda.

"Just what do you think you're trying to pull, Jilly?" Mick said. "You've interfered with government business." He turned to the lieutenant. "This is your show, mate. Are you going to arrest her?"

Shaking his head vigorously, the lieutenant said, "I don't have time for this nonsense out here in the middle of nowhere, Constable. We really need to be leaving." He surveyed the crowd of eager voyagers. "Is this all that's going?"

Mick threw up his hands in exasperation as he replied, "Yeah...that's it."

"Good," the lieutenant said. "Everybody will fit on the one boat that's left. They'll only be on board two days, anyway." Then, he hurried back to the dock, barking orders to his men. Two of his sailors jumped on *Mangrove Queen* and fired up her engine.

As Mick and the other passengers clambered on board the *Queen*, one of the "special constables," known around the Mission as Jacko, lagged behind. He swaggered toward Jillian as she stood, hands on hips, feet apart, at the top of the veranda steps. His demented smile displayed the few, discolored teeth he had left. *Special constables, my sweet arse,* Jillian thought. *The only "special" duties these bloody thugs ever had was harassing the blacks.*

Jacko stopped at the foot of the steps. He lowered his rifle so the muzzle rested on the veranda's deck between her feet. His eyes followed the muzzle as he slid it slowly up between her boots, stopping for a moment at her knees, and then continued upward, lifting the hem of her dress to mid thigh and beyond. "Maybe next time around, Miss Jilly," he said as he lifted his grinning face to look up at hers.

What greeted Jacko's smile was Jillian's fist landing squarely and forcefully on his nose. His rifle clattered to the veranda steps, and he found himself seated on the ground with blood flowing down his face as the Aborigine crewmen roared with laughter. When Jacko looked up again, he was seeing stars and staring into the muzzle of Jillian's rifle, an inch from his face. She cycled the rifle's bolt to emphasize it was ready to fire. Her finger nestled against the trigger, she said, "Get on the boat, you bloody imbecile."

"All right, all right...don't be getting all twitchy," Jacko said as he wobbled to his feet. "I'll just be picking up my rifle..."

Jillian shook her head. "Not a good idea," she said, her rifle still inches from his face.

He tried to protest, but Jillian cut him off with the

words: "On the boat...NOW!"

Jacko stumbled toward the dock, holding a bandana to his bleeding nose. When he reached the boat, Jillian turned to Old Robert and said, "Bring him his bloody rifle. He'll need it, stupid as he is."

The lieutenant's crewmen were growing more nervous by the minute, though their machine guns tracked nothing but a sky full of fair weather clouds. As both boats prepared to cast off, Mick Murray ran to within shouting distance of the veranda and said, "You haven't heard the last of this, Jilly," before hurrying back and jumping onboard the *Queen.*

Jillian just smiled and waved goodbye. Her Aborigine crewmen did the same.

Oh, yes, I have heard the last of this, she thought. *Look at them...they're all too scared to come back up this way.*

As the patrol boat led *Mangrove Queen* out of the harbor and into Albatross Bay, Jillian turned to Old Robert and said, "Give them about an hour to get into the Gulf and out of sight...then we'll start raising the other boats."

Chapter Seven

May 1942

A scratchy recording of Wagner's *Tannhäuser* spun on the turntable, the music soothing Jock Miles's ragged nerves. *At least this old record player hasn't given up yet,* he thought, taking a moment from his mountain of paperwork to reflect on the latest dismal news. The Philippines had fallen: General Wainwright had surrendered to the Japanese. MacArthur had fled his last-ditch bastion at Corregidor, making his escape, presumably, by submarine to Australia. Suddenly, the frustrating ordeal of equipping and training his infantry company, now on Australian soil, seemed like a very small worry in a sea of Allied despair.

Periodically, First Sergeant Melvin Patchett, busy with his own administrative duties in the adjacent dayroom, would pass the open door of Jock's office, look in, and scowl. Unlike his commanding officer, Melvin Patchett was not a fan of opera. Especially not some *Kraut* opera.

The old stone building that housed Jock's office, as well as the offices for the battalion's other rifle companies, used to be a Brisbane jail. A sprawling tent city had sprung up in the adjacent field to billet the troops. While the other company commanders had elected to quarter themselves in a nearby hotel. Jock Miles preferred to sleep in his command tent, erected amidst his men's squad tents.

First Sergeant Patchett stuck his head in the door and said, "Captain, if them heinies could stop hollering at each other for a minute, we need to talk."

Jock smiled and silenced the record player. "Sure. What is it, Top? The Philippines?"

"Not much we can do about that, sir," Patchett replied. "But here on the home front, we still ain't got enough forty-five caliber ammo for the training you want with the Thompsons."

"Same story? Still sitting on a ship somewhere, waiting for the Aussies to off-load it?"

"That's what battalion says, Captain. These Aussies ain't taking this war too serious, that's for damn sure."

"Shit, Top...that really screws up the training schedule for this week."

"Begging your pardon, sir, but what do they need live-fire training with a submachine gun for, anyway? It ain't nothing but a fire hose that spits bullets. You don't aim the damn thing. You just point it...and if you hit anything farther than fifty feet away, it's just luck. Hell, if them guinea gangsters can use 'em, anyone can."

"A Thompson is the best weapon we've got for a jungle fight, Top. Fifty feet is about all you'll need...and about all you'll get. I want the men to have actually fired the thing full-auto a few times before we get shipped out."

Patchett shrugged. "As you wish, sir. Now, can I heap on a little more bad news?"

"Might as well."

"Russo's at it again," Patchett said. "He wants to press charges against Guess."

Jock sighed, steeled himself, and asked, "What for this time?"

"Attempted murder. Says Guess tried to poison him."

"Oh, for fuck sake, Top…Is there any proof?"

"Not really…just a canteen with a little Brasso in it. Lot of ways it could have got in there."

Fuming, Jock examining the ceiling of the musty office as he thought, *Son of a goddamn fucking son of a bitch! Isn't it bad enough a company commander has to ask his men to fight and die? But no…he's got to be their nursemaid, their priest…and their judge and jury, too.*

"All right, First Sergeant. Let's get this over with."

To hear PFC Nicholas Russo tell it, the whole world had it in for him, especially the fed-up judge in Brooklyn, New York, who, in 1940, gave the alleged shoplifter—previously arraigned in his court for a variety of petty crimes—a choice of jail or the Army. Once in uniform, Nicky Russo began to have serious doubts on the wisdom of his choice; he really didn't see much difference from being in prison. Now there was a war on, and he was stuck as a soldier for the duration, having to do the bidding of crackers like First Sergeant Melvin Patchett. Worse, he had to do it alongside other crackers, like that cretin J.T. Guess, who almost never spoke. When he did, it was never more than a word or two, at most.

And now, Nicky Russo was sure J.T. Guess was trying to poison him. He stood, braced at parade rest, before Captain Miles.

"No, sir, I didn't actually see him do nothing," Russo said, "but it had to be him, sir. That sneaky son of a bitch's got it in for me." With a sidelong glance at the stone-faced First Sergeant Patchett, he added, "All them rednecks do."

Jock turned to Lieutenant Brewster, his XO. "Lieutenant, did your investigation turn up any witnesses?"

Scooter Brewster snapped to attention as he replied, "Negative, sir. No one has come forward as a witness."

"At ease, Lieutenant. At ease. But you confirmed the presence of the brass polish in Private Russo's canteen?"

"Yes, sir," Brewster replied, still rigidly bracing his body at parade rest. "I did so personally."

"And how much would you say was in there, Lieutenant?"

"Hard to say, sir."

"Try, Lieutenant."

"A significant amount, sir."

"A significant amount," Jock repeated, and then said to Russo, "and nobody can tell me how this *significant amount* got there. How did you discover it was in your canteen, Private?"

"I was going to fill it. I saw some dried stuff under the cap, so I looked inside. Every swinging dick knows what Brasso looks and smells like…and that it's poison. Says so right on the can." Like an afterthought, he added, "Sir."

PFC Jeremiah Theophilus Guess stood impassively at parade rest, too, right beside Nicky Russo. Guess had not said a word; he had not yet been asked any questions. It was now his turn.

"Private Guess," Jock said, "are you in any way responsible for the brass polish in Private Russo's canteen?"

In a polite, monotone drawl, in which every word seemed to be carefully considered before being spoken, Guess replied, "If I was, Captain, I would have for damn sure done a better job of it."

Jock Miles tried not to smile; so did Melvin Patchett. Scooter Brewster seemed somehow offended by the honesty in Guess's answer.

The room was silent for a moment, until Russo blurted, "SEE? THE SON OF A BITCH KNOWS ALL ABOUT IT!"

First Sergeant Patchett was in Russo's face in an instant. "AT EASE, PRIVATE! You'll speak only when spoken to."

Jock had had enough. He rose from his chair and said, "This inquiry is closed. First Sergeant, reassign Private Russo to Weapons Platoon immediately."

Russo did not like that solution one bit. "HEY, WAIT A GODDAMN MINUTE! HOW COME I'M THE ONE GETTING FUCKED OVER HERE?"

Jock held up his hand, which stopped Melvin Patchett from the verbal assault he was about to unleash on the insubordinate private. Then, his face inches from Russo's, Miles said, "You're not getting *fucked over,* Private Russo. In fact, I'm doing you a favor by giving you a fresh start. Just try not to piss anybody off so badly in your new platoon that they want to kill you." Jock turned to Patchett and said, "First Sergeant, return these men to their duties."

Melvin Patchett snapped the two privates to attention and marched them out of Jock's office. Alone with his commanding officer, Scooter Brewster asked, "Can I have a minute, sir?"

"Yeah. What's on your mind, Scooter?"

"It's the men's morale, sir," Brewster said. "Obviously, it needs some serious improvement. I suggest we institute close order drill periods before breakfast and after supper."

"In other words, Lieutenant, the floggings will continue until morale improves?"

"Isn't that how it worked at the Point, sir?"

Jock decided it was time to play big brother. "Sit down, Scooter," he said. Once Brewster took a seat, Jock rose from behind his desk, moved next to his XO's chair and squatted beside it, so his head came only to Brewster's shoulder. A wise old sergeant had once told him, *When you want to pull someone's head out of their ass gently, don't try to do it from above.*

"Scooter," Jock began, "this isn't West Point, and the men we lead are not cadets. They were already in this Army before the war, but aside from the first sergeant, there's not an enlisted man out there whose dream was to become a career soldier. They wouldn't have joined if they could've found a job in civilian life...but the Depression, you know? It's going to get even more interesting when our ranks start to fill up with draftees."

"But they have to be made to accept that they're soldiers, sir," Brewster said.

"Right. But the way we're going to do that is by giving them the training and confidence they sorely need, not more punishment. Nobody knows better than me that everything is all screwed up right now...we can't even get our hands on the right bullets, for crying out loud...but we're going to figure this out and get it right."

Brewster shifted uncomfortably in his seat. He did not look convinced, but he offered nothing in protest.

"I need to know that I can count on your complete support, Scooter."

"Yes, sir…of course you can," Brewster replied with a hint of surprise that his captain might doubt his commitment.

"Good," Jock said as he rose to his feet. "Anything else you want to talk about?"

"Well, sir, there is. Any word on where we're getting shipped to? I hear some scuttlebutt we're planning a major offensive in the Solomons."

Jock found that amusing, but he kept his laugh to himself. In his closing minutes as a member of General Short's staff, he discerned quite clearly just how punchless the US military had been rendered. Offensives across vast seas were out of the question and would be for a while. As he walked back to his desk chair, he said, "I don't think we have to worry about shipping out, Scooter. I think this war is going to come to us."

Chapter Eight

Colonel Masaharu Najima hated being onboard ships of the Japanese Imperial Navy. Despite his rank, which sometimes exceeded that of the ship's captain, he believed army men like him never received the proper level of respect when they intruded in the nautical world. He could see it in the eyes of even common sailors: those who fought on land were inferior to those who fought on sea.

Things were better in China, Colonel Najima thought, *where the land-based campaigns made the Navy largely irrelevant.* The Japanese Army's lightning-fast victories in Malaya, the Dutch East Indies, and the Solomons that crushed the British, Australian, and Dutch forces standing feebly in their way had all been made possible by the brilliant tactics of the Navy. The devastating strike at Pearl Harbor, rendering the Americans powerless to reverse Japan's conquests, had been the Navy's doing entirely. *But the Navy is basking in far more than its share of the glory,* Najima felt sure.

The conversation in the wardroom of the heavy cruiser *Myoko* did little to comfort Colonel Najima. His dinner companion, Mister Saburo Sato, was a great fan of the Navy and had insisted they dine on board; *a ludicrous demand,* Najima thought, as the ship was at anchor in Port Moresby harbor. Excellent and far more convenient mess facilities were available on dry land. Tomorrow, *Myoko* and her supporting warships would depart that harbor, escorting barges loaded with troops of Najima's regiment to the northern coast of Australia under the protective umbrella of Japanese Imperial

Navy air power flying out of airfields on Papua and islands in the Torres Strait.

"Admiral Yamamoto expects little, if any, resistance to my plan," Mister Sato said.

Colonel Najima was surprised Yamamoto still had any say in the matter of Australia—his first two invasion plans had been unceremoniously rejected by Prime Minister Tojo. *At least Tojo…an army man, a general…is ultimately in charge of our destiny,* Najima reassured himself. The mission on which they embarked tomorrow—dreamed up by this insufferable civilian sitting across from him—left him little room for cheer, however. It mattered little to Colonel Najima how vigorously this insolent little man—who spoke English fluently and boasted of being called *Bob* among westerners—tried to defend it. *He is barely 30 years old,* the colonel said to himself. *What wisdom could he possibly offer the War Council?*

"I still would have preferred a landing near Brisbane," Najima said. "That would be the most expeditious way to neutralize American reinforcements."

"Ahh, but there was no practical contingency plan," Sato replied. "It was simply too far to support by sea and would have required far more troops than we have available. But by building airbases all along Cape York—"

Najima interrupted, saying, "Cape York is nothing but a vast wilderness. Another jungle."

"My good colonel, all of Australia is a vast wilderness! But Cape York is a *nearby* vast wilderness. Less than a day's sail! Should our enterprise fail to meet its objectives, we can easily recover back here to

Papua."

Colonel Najima bristled. "Our *enterprise,* as you call it, will not fail, Mister Sato."

"Excellent," Sato replied. "We make a fine team, Colonel. You find and secure the suitable airfield locations, and I'll procure the indigenous labor to construct them. Trust me...the Aborigines will prove quite supportive of our efforts. After centuries of being considered subhuman by the whites, they will greatly appreciate the opportunities the Empire has to offer them."

Najima's face expressed nothing but skepticism. "Cape York...we might as well be going to the moon. I would have even preferred a landing at Darwin."

Sato shook his head vigorously. "Colonel, you can't be serious. We'd be further away from the eastern coast of Australia at Darwin than we now are in Papua! All that talk of a Darwin invasion...that was a figment of the Australian imagination. We are far more clever than that."

Najima responded with a snort of sarcastic laughter. "You're sure we're more clever, Mister Sato?"

"Absolutely," Sato replied. "Very soon, all of the cities on Australia's eastern coast...Townsville, Cairns, Brisbane, even Sydney...will be in easy reach of our land-based aircraft. Our planes can then join the submarines sinking the ships that try to bring the Americans while they're still at sea."

Najima was still not convinced. "I doubt this undertaking will be quite as easy as you suggest in that wild and inhospitable land. Besides, the Germans tried the strategy of submission by aerial bombardment against the English...and they failed miserably."

Sato replied, "Ahh, Australians are nothing but displaced British lowlife, lacking the fortitude of their mother country...however hopeless that fortitude will prove...and lacking the defensive shield of the Royal Air Force. Toppling Cape York will be easier than Singapore, Colonel. Your troops easily raced through a jungle wilderness on bicycles to accomplish that."

"True, it was a jungle," the colonel said, "but at least there was an actual road through it. Unlike the Cape York Peninsula."

Sato's bravado would not be deterred as he said, "This is a golden opportunity for the Empire. Our victories have been so great, so rapid, and so widespread, we can no longer occupy all the territory available for conquest. We have simply been too successful, Colonel! But the Australians are easy pickings...See how they flee their northern territories like frightened rabbits! Their enthusiasm for this war evaporated quickly, just as I told the War Council it would. They resent being bled dry by Britain, with their manpower drawn off to defend European interests on the other side of the world. They actively subvert the feeble American efforts against us. Their dockworkers would rather go on strike than unload American supply ships! Mark my words, Colonel...in the next few months, once we have a firm footing, however small, on its soil and dominate its skies, Australia will surrender without the need for a massive invasion...an invasion we lack the resources to mount, anyway. Then the Americans will never be able to oppose us. Your regiment will lead the way to another glorious conquest for the Emperor."

Colonel Najima stroked his chin pensively as he asked, "So the War Council thinks we can bring Australia to its knees on the cheap, before the next rainy season turns the airfields we build into quagmires, to boot?"

Sato raised his glass of saké as if making a toast. With supreme confidence, he replied, "Would such a victory be diminished because your opponent never fired a shot?"

Chapter Nine

The little Aborigine girl raced up the path to Jillian Forbes's Victorian house, a tiny bearer of ominous news. Seeing Jillian tending to her horse in its stall, the girl darted toward her while yelling, "MISS JILLY! MISS JILLY! THE BOATS...THEY COME BACK!"

Jillian couldn't hear the words; the girl's approach had startled the horse and he was making a fuss. Trying to soothe the beast, she said, "Sorry, Nellie. What did you say?"

Now standing next to Jillian and gasping for breath, little Nellie said, "They come back, Miss Jilly. The fishing boats come back. We see them in the bay."

Something's wrong, Jillian knew. *It's not even nine a.m. My boats have only been out a few hours. They wouldn't come back yet, unless...*

She had no idea what that *unless* might be. *Oh, God...please don't let any of my men be injured.* Dreadful accidents on fishing boats were not uncommon, although her crewmen had never suffered more than the usual cuts and sprains. *Or maybe they tangled with sea-going bandits.* That would be rare in these waters but not unheard of: *That's why we carry rifles onboard...bandits and crocs. And please, please, please...don't tell me somebody got lost overboard.* Whatever it was, something well out of the ordinary was happening, and she needed to get to the Mission docks right now.

After swinging into the saddle of her horse, she reached down to haul up the little girl. "Come on, Nellie," she said. "Let's get you back to your mum." They were barely out of the paddock when a flight of four single-engined airplanes passed noisily overhead, low enough to see the goggled faces of the pilots, low enough to see the large red circles painted on their wings and fuselages.

Nellie asked, "Is that the Yanks, Miss Jilly?"

Jillian felt the knot in her stomach tighten a little more. "No, little one," she replied, "they're Japanese."

By the time Jillian rode onto the dock, her five boats were within hailing distance. There were many airplanes droning high and low in the morning sky, some lazily circling the bay, others making their way quickly inland. She could not see their markings, but whoever they were, they owned the sky.

The lead boat reached the dock. Old Robert called to Jillian from the helm. "Many ships on the horizon, coming down from the north, Miss Jilly. Some warships and many barges. A Japanese airplane fired across our bow, so we turn back. They don't chase us."

Low, gray shapes on the water were materializing far out in Albatross Bay. *Those must be the barges,* Jilly thought. She hitched her horse to the icehouse rail and ran back to the dock as the other four boats tied up. The Aborigine crewmen milled about on the dock, unsure what to do next.

"Go to your families," Jilly told them. "If they do land here, keep everyone calm, like nothing's wrong. And whatever you do, don't show any weapons."

Old Robert looked at Jillian with great concern and asked, "But what about you, Miss Jilly? What are you going to do?" The unspoken subtext—*what are you going to do when they rape you?*—was subtle as a locomotive.

She watched as the low, gray shapes on the sparkling blue water loomed larger. They were indeed barges, and over the rails of each were clearly visible the heads of many men, each wearing a soldier's helmet. Some of the vessels were heading straight for the Weipa Mission. Others fanned toward the thin beaches of Albatross Bay or the mouths of the mangrove-lined rivers that bracketed the settlement. Glints of sunlight reflected from objects on board, objects otherwise invisible at this distance: *bayonets,* Jillian surmised.

Suddenly feeling very mortal but strangely not afraid, she turned to Old Robert and answered his question. "I'm going to stay right here...and hope for the bloody best."

"The war is here now, Miss Jilly," Old Robert replied. "Nothing will turn out for the best."

Chapter Ten

The barges unloaded their human cargo with startling speed and cruised sedately back into Albatross Bay, toward the horizon beyond. *Looks like several thousand men,* Jillian estimated, *minus the poor buggers who'll fall victim to crocs as they slog through the mangroves.* A contingent of about 50 soldiers quickly passed through the Mission, poked tensely around the buildings but found nothing more threatening than the Mission's short-wave transmitter. They heaved the radio from the building and smashed it with rifle butts; the twin poles at each end of the long wire antenna high above the ground were quickly toppled. Then, responding to the shrill whistles of their unit leaders, all but a few vanished inland into the scrubland. Those remaining behind in the Mission strolled about, seemingly relaxed and unconcerned as they chattered among themselves. Rifles slung over shoulders, they reveled in their victory, unopposed on sea, land, or in the sky. Their only adversaries were the army of flies they continually swatted away. Not a shot had been fired.

For Jillian Forbes, the events of the morning had taken a most bizarre turn. Here she was, sitting on the veranda of her icehouse, making polite conversation with this Japanese man seated next to her—*this Japanese civilian*—under the watchful eyes of two soldiers, one on each end of the veranda. The civilian cordially introduced himself: "The name is Sato, but please call me *Bob.*" He spoke English fluently, sounding just like the Yanks in the movies. A conventional wisdom on Japanese language skills was promptly shattered; when she told him her name, he repeated it, pronouncing the "L" sound in Jillian without a hint of difficulty. He even handed her a calling card, printed in English; it announced *The Honorable Saburo "Bob" Sato, Civil Administrator, Australian Occupied Territories.* No matter how relaxed and informal their discourse seemed, though, the word *occupied* seemed to jump off the calling card. Jillian could not help but feel the yoke of a prisoner was slipping around her neck.

"And you are the only white person remaining in this area?" *Bob* Sato asked.

"As far as I know," Jillian replied.

"How many Aborigines reside near this mission, Miss Forbes?"

"A few hundred within a hour's ride of here, most of them working the stations the missionaries set up. Many more the farther you go."

"Stations?" Sato asked.

"Ranching plots, mostly, raising livestock," she explained.

Sato checked a page in the notebook on his lap. "Yes," he said. "That would agree with my research. We will, of course, be very interested in the livestock from these stations, as you call them, once adequate port facilities have been established for their shipment." He leaned closer to Jillian and asked, "So you are in charge of these blacks?"

He was startled as she threw back her head and roared with laughter. "No," she replied when the laughing was done. "I'm not in charge of anyone but myself. Like I said, some of them work for me—"

"On your fishing boats?"

"Yes, on my boats. But nobody's *in charge* of them. Not anymore."

"How many do you employ, Miss Forbes?"

"Thirty-four, most days," she replied. "Four or five to a boat...the rest here in the icehouse. Just about every able-bodied man in the Mission."

Sato considered her words for a few moments as he patted the nose of Jillian's tall, chestnut brown horse. Finally, he broke the silence and said, "This is a fine animal, Miss Forbes. What breed is he?"

"Hard to say. He's a brumby."

Sato was confused by her answer. "Brumby? Isn't that a feral horse?"

"Not after the breaker got done with him."

"I see," Sato said. "What is his name?"

"Franz," she replied.

His eyebrow raised in curiosity, he said, "That sounds very Germanic, my dear."

"I named him after Franz Liszt. He was Hungarian, you know. Not German."

"So you're a lover of fine music?"

"Bloody right I am."

"Then we must discuss the great composers some time," Sato said. "But for now, back to business. I would like you, Miss Forbes, since you are so thoroughly knowledgeable of the area, to introduce me to the local Aborigine leaders. I have a business proposition for them."

"What kind of business, Mister Sato?"

"Please...call me *Bob!* I wish to employ them in a construction venture. The armed forces of the Empire need roads, airfields, port facilities—"

Jillian raised a finger to interrupt. "*Employ,* you

say. How do you intend to pay them, *Bob*?"

Sato reached into a satchel and removed a handful of paper money, displaying it proudly before handing it to Jillian. "They will be paid in the Imperial Japanese Pound of the Occupied Territories."

Jillian inspected the bills with great skepticism. The printing on them was concise. It stated the denomination as *one pound.* The issuing agency was *The Japanese Government.* "And what exactly can they buy with these?" she asked.

Proudly, Sato threw open his arms and replied, "They can buy all the goods the Empire of Japan has to offer. Welcome to the Greater East Asia Co-Prosperity Sphere!"

Still unimpressed, Jillian had another question. "Most of the land around here belongs to the blacks. Do you intend to pay them for its use, too?"

Sato laughed and shook his head. "Does anyone really own the land, Miss Forbes? Don't we all merely borrow it from nature?"

"That's bullshit, Bob. Let's step back into reality for a minute. You haven't mentioned what's in it for me yet."

"I'd very much like to do business with you, too, Miss Forbes. I'm sure the soldiers would love having their rations spiced with some fresh fish. Nothing but rice can get so...*tedious.* "

"And you're going to pay for my fish with this Imperial shit paper?"

"Very soon, my dear, this *shit paper,* as you call it, will be the legal tender all across Australia."

"A lot of good that'll do me," Jillian replied. "Now that you're here, the supply boat won't be coming anymore. I'll be out of petrol for my boats and my generator in a week."

Sato smiled reassuringly. "No need to worry," he said. "The Imperial Japanese Navy will supply you with all the petrol you need, Miss Forbes. At no cost."

She stared quizzically at Sato, not quite believing what she had just heard. At that moment, a Japanese plane buzzed low overhead, startling her horse. Sato began to soothingly stroke Franz's head.

"I was wondering," he said, as if talking to the horse. "You wear a frock. Do you ride side-saddle?"

A chill shot down Jillian's spine. She had usually worn dresses around the missionaries; they grumbled she was *not a normal young woman* when she wore trousers. She had never seen any point in alienating them: *I needed their money and those bible thumpers were crackers enough to go hungry rather than do business with someone they considered a deviant. Hell, even as a kid, those bloody idiots said I was more a savage than the blacks.* It had all worked out; in the stifling heat of tropical North Queensland, a woman grew to appreciate the comfort a simple dress afforded. Riding in a dress or skirt had always posed a problem, though: even when side-saddle, you stood a good chance of showing off your knickers. *Funny...I never worried about showing off my knickers before...but now, there are all these little Japanese buggers walking around...*

Jillian decided to wear trousers from that moment on.

Sato took his leave, explaining he must consult with the Japanese commander. The two soldiers who had stood guard departed with him, leaving Jillian alone on the icehouse veranda. She breathed a sigh of relief; the feeling of being a prisoner in her own world had dissolved. Life would go on just as it had before, maybe better than before. The Japanese seemed to care far more about Cape York than the government of Australia ever did—at least for the time being.

Her train of thought was broken by the faint sound of distant aircraft engines far out over Albatross Bay. These did not sound like the planes that had been passing overhead all morning. There was an urgency in these sounds she had never heard before—more shrill wails than drones, like machinery being pushed beyond its limits.

Jillian could see them now, a group of airplanes— ten, maybe twelve—climbing and diving in crazy corkscrews. She thought of monkeys frolicking in a palm tree, twirling round and round the trunk as they chased each other's tails. But it quickly became clear these planes were not at play. This was a dogfight—to the death. Some of those planes were not Japanese; whether they were Australian or American, she could not tell. She could hear no gunfire, but one plane seemed to suddenly disintegrate in a bright flash to dozens of little pieces, each piece fluttering slowly down to the water. Then another plane began to trail thick black smoke, painting a gentle downward arc that soon became vertical and ended in a geyser of white water on impact. She had no idea the nationalities of the combatants who had just met their deaths.

Just as quickly as it began, it was finished. The wail of overstressed engines settled back to the more familiar drone. The planes retreated—some north, some south—until the silent dots they had become vanished from sight. The impersonal yet deadly drama of the dogfight caused a new fear to grow in Jillian's heart: there might be an armed force—Australian, American, or both—that was determined to contest the Japanese on Cape York.

Don't do us any favors, she silently begged those anonymous warriors. *We don't need your bleedin' war here. You never pretended to care about the Cape before. Please don't start caring now...and get us all bloody killed in the process.*

Chapter Eleven

June 1942

Standing ramrod straight, not even breathing hard from the 10-mile run in the sweltering midday sun, First Sergeant Melvin Patchett pulled off his steel helmet and wiped the sweat from his brow. *And they call this winter down here,* he thought. On the dusty track before him, the weary men of his company jogged past in a column of twos, their bodies bending but no longer breaking under the weight of packs and weapons. *Slowly but surely,* Melvin Patchett felt certain, *these doggies are getting whipped into shape. They're running ten miles like it's nothing now.*

He thought of what an old drill sergeant had told him many years ago: *If you can run ten miles, you can walk a hundred.*

The first sergeant bellowed, "COMPANY...HALT!" One hundred marching men stopped on a dime simultaneously. "FALL OUT," Patchett commanded, and then added, "Take five, ladies...and there's no smoking out here on the range. We don't need no more fucking brush fires." He ignored the widespread grumbling that followed.

A jeep crammed full with the company's officers approached and came to a stop. With a smirk, Patchett said, "Grenade gets you all, gentlemen."

Jock Miles smiled as he hopped from the jeep. "Very funny, First Sergeant," he said. "How'd the live fire exercises go?"

"Another circle jerk, sir. Shot up a lot of ammo, but they still maneuver like a goddamn Chinese fire drill.

I'm telling you, sir…no matter how many posters the Army puts it on, that old saw *kill or be killed* won't sink into their thick heads until they have to cart away some of their buddies in mattress covers. But I'll bet watching them fuck up was more inspiring than y'all's dog and pony show up at Division. Did you find out anything good?"

"Same old bullshit, Top. The Aussies keep promising to pick up the pace unloading our supply ships, the Air Force swears it's going to get its shit together any day now and start hitting New Guinea and the Solomons…but they still can't stop the Japs from knocking out the airfields we're trying to build up in northern Queensland."

Patchett nodded knowingly. "Any news from back home, sir?"

Jock's face became grim. "Ever hear of Midway Island?" he asked.

Patchett shook his head.

"Well, it's a little spit of an island way out west of Hawaii," Jock continued. "If I hadn't spent all that time in Hawaii, I might not have heard of it either. Anyway, we abandoned it to the Japs last week. Wasn't worth fighting over, I guess. Hawaii's like a powder keg now, just waiting for the Japs to come and light the fuse. And they're still all panicky on the West Coast…blackouts every night…rumor has it a TWA plane got shot down by accident near Sacramento."

"Anything about the Aleutians, sir? I think I've got me a kid brother up there."

"Well, Top, Washington thinks that's just a feint, to draw the Navy away from Hawaii. Apparently, the Japs dumped a couple of thousand troops on a few of the islands and left them there, sitting on their hands, freezing their balls off."

That brought a smile to Melvin Patchett's weathered face as he scanned the desolate Australian countryside before him. "Sounds kinda like our situation, don't it, sir? At least we ain't cold. Hell of a war, ain't it?"

Miles nodded in agreement. "Did the men eat, Top?" he asked.

"Yes, sir. The cooks trucked out a good, hot meal. None of that Vegemite shit the Aussies think is so goddamned wonderful."

"Outstanding," Jock replied. "But listen...I've been ordered to meet with Colonel Snow up at Regiment at fourteen hundred hours. Lord only knows why. With all the traffic jams in Brisbane these days, I'd better be heading back pretty soon. Lieutenant Brewster and the platoon leaders will stay with the company for the rest of the exercise."

"Very good, sir," Patchett replied. "I believe we can handle it."

Colonel Snow had the annoying habit of knocking his West Point class ring on the desk as he spoke. So many grads from the Academy had that same habit; those in the Army not blessed with its diploma derisively called them *ring knockers*. The *tap-tap-tap* was meant as a subtle reminder the wearer of the ring was a vested member of the military profession's premier fraternity, and as such, no harm could come to him from those without the ring.

What's with that damned tapping? Jock Miles brooded. *I'm the only other son of a bitch in this office, and I know he's got a ring. I've got one, too...not that it's done me a whole lot of good lately.*

"I've got to be frank, Captain," the colonel began, "I'm a bit disappointed with you at the moment. On paper, you're my most experienced company commander and my most senior captain from the Point...yet your company's performance in training has been merely average, no better than any of the others. It seems to me like you're just coasting...not pushing yourself or your men. We're at a crucial juncture in history, and no man from West Point can be seen as losing his fire in times like these. What do you have to say for yourself?"

What Jock wanted to say was, *Cut the crap, sir. You didn't call me here for a career pep talk. Get to the point.* But he knew better. *Just shut up and roll with the punches,* he told himself. *He's not interested in what you have to say, anyway. They never are. Just play it by the book.*

"No excuse, sir," Jock said. "I take full responsibility for my company's performance."

"Damned right you do," Snow said. He rose from behind the desk and began to pace the small room.

A cynical voice in Jock's head began to speculate on the colonel's motivation: *But what the hell's going on here? If he wanted to relieve you, he'd just get your battalion commander to do that over the phone. He wants something from you...maybe this is the setup for some shit detail? You know how it works...he gives you the Dutch uncle act, gets you all shaky, then offers you a chance to be his number one boy again. If he starts pretending to be your buddy now and calls you by your first name, you're screwed.*

Colonel Snow stopped at a window and looked out. Like some serene visionary beholding some new reality only he could imagine, he fixed his gaze far in the distance and said, "Jock, I'm going to give you a chance to redeem yourself. Despite all your fiddly-fucking lately, I believe you're just the man for this job."

The cynical voice in Jock's head spoke again: *There it is, pal...the first name bullshit. Bend over and prepare to take it up the ass.*

Turning to a faded map of eastern Australia on the far wall, the colonel said, "Almost two weeks ago, a small force of Japanese infantry...we reckon no more than a battalion's worth...landed near here." He pointed to a spot on the map in the northwest corner of the Cape York Peninsula. "A little place called Weipa. It's spelled like *wee-pa* but the locals say it *way-pa*. There was a Presbyterian mission there, but all the whites have been evacuated so there's nothing left up there but some abos running around bare-assed naked. The Aussies didn't have any troops up that way, so the landing was unopposed. It's very rough terrain, with no roads to speak of. The usual way in and out is by boat. The Aussies talk about it like it's part of some other world. MacArthur's put a news blackout on the Jap landing but, of course, anyone with a short-wave receiver tuned to Radio Tokyo will figure it out eventually, no matter how MacArthur tries to deny it."

"Just a battalion, sir?" Jock asked.

"Yep. A couple of hundred men, give or take," Snow replied. "We figure they're some kind of reconnaissance in force. There's not enough of them to do anything else. But they're not likely to find much up there except a whole lot of nothing. Like I said, that peninsula is one big wilderness."

Jock listened in silence. He had no idea yet where all this was going.

"Now we've got ourselves a couple of problems. The Aussies are afraid the Japs are trying to recruit the Aborigines…maybe trying to turn them into a partisan force to fight against us. It's no secret the abos have no love for the white man. And Washington's got its tit in a wringer because the Japs just strolled right on in." The colonel paused for dramatic effect. "That makes our mission here look ineffective…like some paper tiger."

Jock might have seemed serious and attentive on the outside, but inwardly he was laughing at the terms *ineffective* and *paper tiger.* That seemed to describe the Americans' presence in Australia quite well—at least, so far.

"Neither Washington nor Canberra wants those Japs getting too comfortable up there," Colonel Snow continued, "and we can't tolerate any more of them coming ashore. Now here's the thing…we sent a few photo recon planes up there right away, and none of them came back. So…a couple of days after those Japs landed, the Aussies sent in a small force of scouts on horseback…*Nackeroos*, they call them. Pretty stupid name, eh?" He pointed to a spot on the map. "Anyway, they dropped them off by boat here, at Archer Bay, about sixty miles south of Weipa. Their mission was to find the Jap command post and direct a bombing raid against it. Trouble is, they were never heard from again."

Jock asked, "Why'd they land so far away, sir?"

"Remember what I said about those recon planes not coming back? Jap air and sea power from Papua and the Torres Strait are mighty strong up that way, Jock. Those *Nackeroos* had to sneak in at night."

"Begging your pardon, sir...but with the Jap airpower that strong, how does anyone plan to mount an effective bombing raid?"

"Don't you worry your head about that, Captain Miles. Give those flyboys the map coordinates of the target and they'll do it at night. The Japs can't do shit against them in the dark. We'll cut the head off the snake and the rest of it will just wither and die. But they've got to have exact coordinates to bomb a target that small."

Jock searched the map for landmarks. Aside from a river or two—thin blue lines etched in the faded green denoting vast, flat woodlands—and the settlement at Weipa, there didn't seem to be any geographic point of reference for over 100 miles in any direction. He noticed the date on the map legend was 1910. He couldn't help but wonder how accurate its features were after 32 years.

"Maybe the Aussies just had radio trouble?" Jock asked.

"Afraid not," Snow replied, "Radio or not, the boat was supposed to pick them up at Archer Bay on the eighth day. The boat was there. They weren't."

Jock got a sinking feeling in his stomach. He was beginning to understand why he was sitting in Colonel Snow's office. Getting right to the point, he said, "Now, I suppose, it's our turn to find the Japs, sir?"

Colonel Snow was beaming from ear to ear as he patted Jock on the back. "You catch on real fast, Jock my boy. I knew you were the man for this job! Since it's an American mission now, with our planes doing the bombing, the big brass want it to be our boys on the ground calling the shots. And Jock, you're going to have the honor of leading those boys."

Honor...there was that word again. The centerpiece of that holy triplet *Duty, Honor, Country* that had shaped Jock Miles's life and somehow managed to derail his army career at Pearl Harbor. The words that had seemed so straightforward and worshipped with easy conviction on the parade fields at West Point now, in the face of actual combat, took on a variety of murky meanings. The way Colonel Snow said *honor* had the distinct tone of something to be bestowed posthumously.

Yet, as if seized by some involuntary reflex, Jock snapped to attention and said, "Yessir!" with great enthusiasm. He was not sure from what depth of his being this sudden enthusiasm had emerged. Perhaps some small part of him desperately wanted to believe the colonel was offering a chance at redemption, even though that chance came with the odds stacked squarely against success and survival. Perhaps it was the chance to do the job for which he had so diligently trained—a job he, and he alone, believed he had done splendidly at Pearl Harbor—but this time in an arena sanctioned by the starry gods in green. Or perhaps the inviolable motto of the parade ground was more deeply ingrained in Jock's soul than even he realized. Whatever the reason, Jock Miles found himself nearly giddy with eagerness.

The burst of enthusiasm drained quickly as practical considerations began to flood Jock's mind. He studied the old map closely, using spread fingers like dividers to measure distance: from Brisbane to Weipa was 1200 miles as the crow flies. For a soldier on foot, it was a hell of a lot farther.

"When are we planning on doing this, sir?" Jock asked.

Still beaming that smile, the Colonel replied, "You move out in three days, Captain." Undaunted by the stunned, disbelieving look on Jock's face his answer had caused, Snow continued, "Don't worry, three days is *plenty* of time. Let me give you a brief overview of how you're going to do this thing..."

Chapter Twelve

The dusty streets of Brisbane were so thick with military vehicles, he might as well have been driving in convoy. Jock Miles was paying the slow-moving traffic no mind, though. His thoughts were elsewhere as he drove the jeep back to his company area. There were so many unanswered questions about the mission he had just been handed—questions that were now up to him to solve.

First, how the hell do I pull off this fool's dream of a recon mission without getting every last one of us killed?

We can't go in with vehicles...there's no way to refuel out there and hardly any roads. I've got to keep this small...maybe take only a dozen or so of my best men. I don't need the whole damned company tromping around in the middle of nowhere, and we've got to stay concealed. We're going to have a ton of walking to do, no matter where the Aussies drop us off.

How am I going to figure out our exact location out there? There are no landmarks. We'll need to navigate by radio somehow. My celestial nav skills are way too rusty, dead reckoning's certainly not going to cut it...but the smallest radio direction finder that's accurate enough for the job needs to be hauled around in a jeep trailer, so that's out.

And speaking of radios, the company's communication radios will be useless for this mission. Their range is just a couple of miles. But the Colonel says I'm getting a team assigned to me...three men...with the newest, whiz-bang portable field radio. Without it, there's no mission.

The Colonel said we're supposed to get a crash course from the Aussies on living off the land in the bush. But they won't send a guide with us. Supposedly, they're ticked off the job got taken out of their hands after they screwed it up.

Lost in his thoughts, Jock didn't notice at first the US Army truck in front of him had come to a halt at an intersection. As he stood on the brake pedal, his jeep skidded noisily to a stop, bucking like a bronco the last few feet. It stopped within a hair's breadth of the truck's towing hitch. Another inch and the hitch would have been rammed through the jeep's radiator. Several wide-eyed American soldiers riding in the truck's bed peered down over the tailgate at the flustered captain behind the jeep's wheel.

An American MP corporal, who had been directing the dense traffic at the intersection, was now walking quickly toward the jeep. "Hey, pal!" the MP called to the jeep's still-anonymous driver. "What the fuck's the matter with you? Get your head out of your—"

The gleam of captain's bars, now clearly visible on the jeep driver's collar, cut the corporal's tirade short. "Sorry, sir," the flustered MP said, snapping a salute. "I didn't realize—"

"That's okay, Corporal," Jock interrupted. "My fault entirely. Consider my head *pulled out.*"

Much relieved, the corporal said, "Very good, sir." He turned and headed back to his duties at the intersection. "Have a good day, sir…and take it easy."

Take it easy…that's easier said than done, Jock told himself.

When he walked into the company dayroom, Jock found his first sergeant and executive officer squared off in confrontation, standing nose to nose. The first words Jock heard were spoken by an exasperated Melvin Patchett: "Negative, Lieutenant! Negative. You told those men 'you don't want to get caught lying down in grazing fire.' Those were your exact words. I'm living proof, sir, there ain't nothing you *can* do except lay down in grazing fire! Would you rather they stand up and get chopped off at the knees?"

Brewster, arms folded defiantly across his chest, was adamant. "As I told you before, First Sergeant, you do not contradict an officer in front of the men. Is that clear?"

His face beet-red, Patchett replied, "With all due respect, Lieutenant, what's clear to me is that dumbshit instructions like that will get a lot of men killed for nothing."

Brewster dropped his hands to his hips like a scolding school teacher. "That's it, First Sergeant," he said. "I've had enough. I'm bringing you up on charges for insubordination!" Without looking, he spun around to storm out of the dayroom, but with his first stride collided with Jock Miles.

Jock steadied his agitated XO with a hand on his shoulder. "Easy, Lieutenant," Jock said, his voice irritated. "Now, Brewster, would you like to explain to me just what the hell is going on here?"

"The First Sergeant was disrespectful to me in front of the men, sir," Scooter Brewster replied.

Jock rubbed his chin as if deep in thought. After a moment, he said, "Let's you and me go into my office, Lieutenant." He turned to Patchett. "First Sergeant, I want a meeting of all company officers and NCOs at eighteen hundred hours, right after supper. I've got something real big I need to discuss."

The look of irritation on Patchett's face had cooled to its usual indignant scowl. "Very good, sir," he replied, and went about his business.

As he took the few steps to Jock Miles's office, Scooter Brewster fantasized that *the real big thing* the company commander needed to discuss was the replacement of Melvin Patchett as company first sergeant. *That insubordinate old cracker needs to be put out to pasture, anyway. Now we can court martial him...let him rot with a few less stripes in some pencil-pushing job with all the other fossils while the new breed goes out and wins this war.* His chest puffed proudly when the words *new breed* passed through his head.

As soon as they were inside the office, Jock said, "Shut the fucking door, Brewster." Like a punctured balloon, the air escaped from Scooter's chest—and from his fantasy—as soon as Jock's irritated words were spoken.

"Sir," Scooter pleaded, "you're not going to tell me it's okay for an NCO to chew out an officer like that?"

Jock settled into his chair and held the officer before him in a stern gaze. "Did First Sergeant Patchett call you a disrespectful name or use disrespectful language or tone of voice in front of the men?"

"No, sir, not really, but—"

"I didn't ask for any explanation, Brewster. Just yes or no answers will do. Now, from the little I've heard here, the First Sergeant corrected some point of tactical instruction you were giving the men. Do I have that right?"

Brewster hesitated before answering, "Yes, sir." He wanted to say so much more, to plead his case, one West Point officer to another. But something told him he'd better not.

"Do you have any reason to suspect, Lieutenant Brewster, that your rather limited...no, make that *nonexistent* combat experience might have more validity than that of a man who, when you and I were still having our asses wiped by our mothers, actually had to lie down and crawl across no man's land under grazing fire?"

There were a few moments of awkward silence before Scooter Brewster replied, in a voice barely above an embarrassed whisper, "I suppose not, sir."

Jock rose from his chair. "So," he said, "let me get this straight. You want me to court martial the most experienced and valued man in my company because your pride was hurt?"

There was another moment of silence before Scooter said, "I guess not, sir."

"We should all be thanking our lucky stars Melvin Patchett had the good sense to lie down on that battlefield in France," Jock said. "Now I'd like you to suck it up like a man and apologize to the first sergeant."

Bristling, Scooter Brewster asked, "Apologize for what, sir?"

"How about mistaking pride for wisdom, Lieutenant?"

It took Scooter Brewster several seconds to shake off the waves of revulsion that passed through his body.

His face contorted into a grimace as if he smelled some terrible odor. This was not the way things were supposed to go in his promising military career. *I'm a Brewster, goddamn it! We don't "suck it up" for anyone, especially not subordinates. What's this Army coming to when another West Point man will shit all over you like that?*

Scooter would put in for a transfer to another unit first thing in the morning, and he would get it; the general commanding the division was an old friend of the family. Before he did that, though, he would wait and see what this company meeting—with its promise of a *real big thing*—was all about.

Brewster snapped to attention, but before he could say anything, Jock added, "By the way, Scooter, when the phrase *with all due respect* is aimed at you, it means you've already made a complete jackass out of yourself."

Chapter Thirteen

Jillian watched them march in step up the path to the icehouse veranda: a tiny Japanese Army officer carrying a satchel, with two equally tiny soldiers two paces behind. The officer was so short the tip of the sword hitched to his belt nearly dragged across the ground; the bantam soldiers seemed strangely unencumbered by the absurdly large rifles they carried at shoulder arms. As they made their way forward with serious faces, rigid postures, and synchronized limbs, they looked more like children playing warrior than conquering heroes of the Empire.

She did not bother to rise from her armchair as the officer bowed, deposited the contents of the satchel at her feet, snapped to attention, and fell back in step with his escorts as they marched away as if in some comic opera. Jillian bent over and scooped up the money at her feet—the week's accounting of Imperial Japanese Pounds of the Occupied Territories, payment for the fresh seafood her boats had supplied. She began to count it, then thought better of it: *They're not interested in short-changing me...at least not yet.* She carried the money into the icehouse, spun the dial on the safe she had never bothered to lock before, and placed the Japanese money inside. It nestled on top of the many bundles of Australian pounds no one had any use for at the moment. *And if this Japanese money turns out to be worthless...well, I guess we can always use it to wipe ourselves.*

Jillian settled back into her chair on the veranda and waited for her boats to return with the day's catch. They would be flying those oversized white flags on which the Japanese had insisted. *Don't think of it as a symbol of surrender,* Bob Sato had told her. *It's for the safety of your boats and their crews in these transitional times. We must assume vessels such as yours, flying the Australian flag, have hostile intent, just as the Allies will assume the same for anything flying the Japanese flag.* Grudgingly, she had conceded his point. The waters of Albatross Bay had never been so busy, with the daily landings of Japanese barges on the shores in and around Weipa. They brought construction vehicles, fuel tankers, artillery pieces, and supplies under the protection of warships and the usual flock of aircraft. It would only take one trigger-happy soldier or sailor to cause a tragedy of mistaken identity. *And when all this is over,* she thought, *I wonder what the flag of the Occupied Australian Territories will look like. A kangaroo on a white background?* The thought depressed her: *I need a bloody drink.*

Jillian fetched a beer, allowing herself a bottle of Australian from the chiller. She had taken to rationing the last of the Australian beer, for once it was gone there would be nothing to drink but Japanese beer. She had tasted a bottle of the stuff soon after they had landed last month; Bob Sato had brought a case as a goodwill offering. Aussies always referred to their beer as *piss*—but Sato's gift had brought a new, quite literal meaning to the term.

She had barely sat back down when a small utility vehicle with Japanese Army markings drove up. Vehicles seemed to be multiplying like rodents as more and more roads were cut through the eucalyptus forest into the bush beyond. Bob Sato popped from the passenger's seat as the driver shut off the engine. "May

I join you, Jillian?" Sato asked.

"If you like," she answered.

He eyed her bottle of Australian beer. "Would you fancy one?" she asked.

He nodded eagerly, and she disappeared into the icehouse. When she returned a few moments later, she handed him a bottle of Japanese beer. He took the proffered bottle, his face registering abject disappointment. Jillian managed—just barely—to mask the smirk trying to spread across her face.

"You've been bridging the river, I see. So how many of your soldiers did you lose to the crocs today?" she asked.

The question—and the reality it reflected—made Sato uncomfortable. He squirmed in his seat as he answered, "Oh, I suppose the usual number...one or two, perhaps."

Jillian relaxed into her chair. "Did you ever notice," she asked, "how your black laborers rarely get eaten by crocs? It's usually the crocs getting eaten by the blacks."

"Yes," Sato replied, "It's been duly noted." After a long pull on the beer bottle, he said, "There is something I must discuss with you, Miss Forbes."

She turned in her chair to face him and instinctively began to cross her legs. Then she realized there was no need for modesty: she was wearing trousers. She propped the heels of her riding boots high against the veranda's railing instead.

"I've taken great pains to establish a stable currency here, just as I have done in the other occupied territories," Sato said. "But I fear you've been undermining my efforts...unintentionally, of course."

"I'm doing *what*?"

"Undermining the stability of the occupation pound."

"And how the bloody hell am I doing that, Mister Sato?"

"Please do not misunderstand, Miss Forbes! I appreciate that you don't realize the results of your actions..."

Jillian was becoming hot under the collar. "Are you calling me stupid?"

"No, no! It's just that...you...you don't appreciate the economic impact of your actions."

"WHAT BLOODY ACTIONS, MISTER SATO?"

Sato sighed. He had meant this conversation to be enlightening, not adversarial. "The wages you pay your crewmen, Miss Forbes...they're much too high. I hear many complaints from my black laborers, who are paid much less."

"What business is it of yours...or theirs...what I pay my crewmen, Mister Sato?"

"Please...call me Bob!"

"I don't bloody think so."

"Please, Miss Forbes...can we be businesslike?"

"Not when you're sticking your arse into my bleedin' business, we can't."

"That's just my point...our businesses are very connected now. The Weipa Mission is a microcosm of Australia's future economy."

Jillian glared at him and took another pull on her beer, prompting Sato to ask, "You do understand what I mean by *microcosm,* Miss Forbes?"

She nearly spit the beer in his face. "Of course I know what *microcosm* means. Insulting my intelligence is a bloody awful way to talk business, Mister Sato. Get to the fucking point, already."

"Very well, Miss Forbes. The exorbitant wages you pay your crewmen are putting inflationary pressure on the occupation pound."

"Excuse me?"

"Inflation, Miss Forbes. You're paying them more than their labor is worth, which drives down the currency's value."

A light went on in Jillian's eyes. She was ready for battle. "In other words," she said, "you think that my pay rates are putting upward pressure on the pay of the blacks you employ as laborers."

Sato clapped his hands with delight. "Yes, Miss Forbes! That's exactly it!"

"Well, Mister Sato, there's just one problem with that. We're fishing in different ponds. I already employ all the men I need. I'm not looking for any additional help. Since I have no interest in hiring men away from you, I have no impact on what you pay the laborers you employ. And since there is a more than ample supply of blacks for you to employ on Cape York, you have no need of the men who work for me. Like I said…different ponds."

Sato was flustered. He began to sputter, "But that's academically incorrect! That's not how the value of money works!"

Jillian smiled, settled back into her chair, and said, "It's how it works around here." She paused before adding, "Unless you want to catch your own bloody fish." She drained what was left in her bottle as Sato shifted nervously in his chair, struggling to compose a rebuttal.

"Besides," Jillian said, "outside our little world, in the *macrocosm,* we still don't know if this funny-money of yours is really worth anything. We may all be paying our men absolutely nothing."

"Perhaps, in time, Miss Forbes, you'll better understand the economic workings of the Empire. But now, there is another issue we must discuss."

An amused smirk on her face, she said, "Oh, wonderful! There's more?"

"Yes, Miss Forbes, there is. Tomorrow, a ship will arrive bearing a contingent of what the Army calls *comfort women.* "

Jillian thought back to the bedraggled diggers her crew had rescued at sea, only days before the Japanese landed. She remembered clearly something one of them had said about the Japanese in Papua: *They had everything...even whores.*

"These *comfort women*," Jillian said, "they're whores, right?"

"We prefer to think these women provide a service which is very beneficial to the morale of our troops, Miss Forbes. Colonel Najima has kept a very tight rein on his men. There has been none of the unfortunate *abuse* the other occupied territories experienced. The troops have earned some...shall we say, recreation." He paused, looked straight into Jillian's eyes, and said, "Surely, you wouldn't want them turned loose on the local females."

As those words came off his lips, Jillian saw the change in Sato's demeanor. For the first time in the weeks she had known him, the tone of his voice made no attempt to be friendly and conciliatory. She heard in that voice a transparent threat, something he had always been so careful to conceal behind a veneer of partnership and fairness until that moment. Those were the words of a man who knew he held all the cards and could do whatever he pleased.

But those words were met with nothing but Jillian's impassive glare. *Stupid little man,* she thought. *As if it was some big secret that they could rape and kill every one of us in this bloody place if they wanted to.*

After a few more moments of expectant silence, Bob Sato smiled; the spirit of cooperation and friendship had made its return. "Since it's no longer in use, we plan to billet the ladies in the main Mission House," he said. "Do you think the community would find that acceptable?"

Jillian found that riotously funny. "Acceptable?" she said, trying to catch her breath between howls of laughter. "Whores in a church house? That would be the most acceptable thing anyone around here has seen in quite a while."

"Excellent!" Sato said, joining in the laughter. "Now, the ladies will require substantial quantities of ice from your facilities to cool themselves during their labors. Let's negotiate a price per pound."

"I'll tell you what, *Bob,*" Jillian replied. "I'll give them the bloody ice for free. It's the least I can do to help keep your lads happy…" She finished the sentence in her head: *…and out from between the legs of every female around here.*

Chapter Fourteen

Jock Miles reckoned he had never been so busy in his life—or had so much on his mind. He'd hardly slept last night and hadn't even found time for breakfast yet. The plans for the mission Colonel Snow had given him yesterday had been drawn. He had followed the KISS doctrine to the letter: *KISS—Keep it simple, stupid.* But even simple plans can have a thousand details that do not solve themselves.

Let's see who we've got, Jock thought, as he reviewed the roster of those selected for the mission, now known as Task Force Miles. *Besides me and the first sergeant, there are two five-man scout teams with a decent sergeant in charge of each one. Everyone's in great physical shape...we should be able to handle a week or two of walking our asses off in the middle of nowhere, eating nothing but these new-fangled K rations and D bars. All we need now is that three-man radio section that's coming from Division and a medic.*

Melvin Patchett had given him some bad news right before last night's cadre meeting: the company medic had gone to sick call with *a drip.*

My medic, of all people, caught the clap! You'd think he'd know better, at least. Shit...we've got to find somebody to replace him, fast! I'm not taking my men into the bush without a doc.

Jock lingered over two names near the bottom of the mission roster: Russo and Guess. *I looked kind of cross-eyed at the first sergeant when he picked them...but they haven't been at each other's throats lately, and Top is right: they're the best men for the job. Guess is the finest sharpshooter in the company, maybe the division. And Russo, since his assignment to Weapons Platoon, has all of a sudden become the proudest, most proficient machine gunner I've got. He's a wizard with the air-cooled thirty caliber...and we'll sure as hell need a good machine gunner if we have to fight our way out of a jam or fend off some airplanes, just like we had to do at Pearl. As good a weapon as those Thompsons are for a close-in fight, they'll be next to worthless for hitting anything more than fifty feet away. The air-cooled thirty is a lot heavier than a BAR, but its better sustained rate of fire is worth it.*

And on top of everything else this morning, the company needs a new XO. Brewster stormed off like a little girl last night when I wouldn't pick him for the mission. Went straight to his buddy the general at Division, looking for an immediate transfer. He'll get it, too, but so be it. I just don't think he's ready to lead men in combat yet...and a team this small doesn't need more than one officer. The little asshole never did apologize to Top like I told him to, either. Good riddance to you, Scooter.

But I still can't get out of my head that thing Patchett said to me after the meeting:

"Anybody who gets handed a mission like this has already been designated expendable. What do you say we don't give them sons of bitches the satisfaction and actually pull this damn thing off?"

The cocky Australian Army captain giving the briefing was fast getting on Jock's nerves. The rest of Task Force Miles found the Aussie just as irritating.

Melvin Patchett's whispered comment to Jock was especially telling: "The little prick acts like he's doing us a goddamn favor letting us clean up their shit."

If the Aussie sensed their annoyance, he wasn't showing it. He digressed from his tactical presentation for a moment to boast of his credentials. "I am a graduate of the Royal Military Academy, Sandhurst," he said, his nose in the air. "It's like your captain's West Point, only quite a bit better."

At the back of the room, PFC Nicky Russo mumbled, "You'da been better off going to the Jap military academy, numbnuts." The men within earshot began to snicker.

The Aussie captain did not hear Russo's comment or at least pretended not to. As he continued the briefing without missing a beat, Melvin Patchett slipped behind Russo and whispered icily in his ear, "One more peep, son, and you and me gonna lock asses." The sound of the first sergeant's voice, even at a whisper, caused the snickering to cease as if a switch had been thrown.

"The Catalinas will drop you off here, at Temple Bay," the Aussie continued, pointing to a spot on the map far to the north on Cape York Peninsula's east coast. "You'll land at first light—"

Jock jumped from his seat and interrupted the Aussie. "That's no good. We'll be on those damned planes all night. We'll be exhausted before we even get started."

"There is no other choice, Captain," the Aussie replied. "Japanese air power is too strong to risk the flight in broad daylight. Once the Catalinas drop off you and your men, they'll depart with great haste, I assure you."

Jock scowled and sat back down. There was no point debating operational plans with a mere briefing officer. "Go ahead," he said to the Aussie. "Let's see what other gems you've got up your sleeve...so I can get them all changed at once."

The Aussie shrugged arrogantly and returned to the map. "It's about eighty miles due west across the peninsula from Temple Bay to Weipa. A detail of Nackeroos"—Jock's men snickered again at the mention of that name—"will meet you with vehicles and transport you to here." He pointed to a dot on the map about halfway across the peninsula, a place called *Moreton,* where a thin black line—a road, maybe just a trail—met a thin blue line: a river. "Moreton—that's as far as the trucks can go cross-country and still get back on their petrol load." With a cocksure grin, he added, "There are no petrol stations in the bush, Yanks." He paused, waiting for the laughter he felt sure would come. It never did. The Aussie broke the awkward silence with, "You'll be on foot from there."

Jock wasn't happy with the plan at all. "About forty miles on foot," he said, "a good two days' forced march...totally on our own, in the middle of fucking nowhere." It came out as more of a lament than a statement of the obvious.

"You may not need to walk that far to find the Japanese, Captain," the Aussie replied. "But it will be a nasty walk, regardless...just you, the abos, and the crocs."

"Speaking of Aborigines," Jock said, "why can't you provide us one as a guide?"

It was the Aussie's turn to snicker. "Oh, you don't

want that. Didn't you get the word? We expect the abos to collaborate with the Japanese. Any guide familiar with Cape York will have tribal ties there and cannot be trusted. The same goes for any abos you encounter along the way."

In a stage whisper, one of Jock's men wisecracked, "Why don't they just shoot us all now?" Another faceless voice added: "Yeah. Save the Japs the trouble."

"All right, men...at ease," Jock said, and the room fell quiet. Turning back to the Aussie, he asked, "What's the plan for getting us back out?"

"It's expected that your removal will be the reverse of your insertion, Captain Miles. But of course, high command prefers to remain fluid, based on your circumstances."

Jock could not hide his disgust as he said, "In other words, you have no plan." Turning to Patchett, he said, "First Sergeant, move the men out. We're done here."

The Aussie was suddenly flustered. "But I'm not finished," he said.

"Yeah, you are," Jock replied. Not bothering to shake the Aussie's hand, he added, "I realize you're just the messenger boy here...but thanks for nothing, *mate*."

As the men of Task Force Miles—exchanging wisecracks once again—filed from the room, Patchett said to Jock, "Maybe we oughta take ourselves a chaplain, too, sir? You know...for the last rites?" He followed his gallows humor with a wink and a wry smile.

Waiting outside the briefing room was another Australian Army officer, this one a major. As First Sergeant Patchett formed the men for the march back to the company area, the Aussie major approached Jock

Miles. His uniform was ill-fitting, as if he had carelessly donned someone else's. He had none of the arrogance of the captain who had given the briefing. His manner was casual and confident, as if accustomed to receiving respect without having to demand it.

"Captain Miles," the Aussie major said, offering his hand rather than returning Jock's salute. "I believe you're in a need of a medic? I'm Dunbar Green. Perhaps I can help. May I call you Jock?"

Jock thought that perhaps he should pinch himself, in case he was dreaming. In the midst of a day that had offered nothing but dismal news so far, he had just been cut a terrific break. Major Dunbar Green, Royal Australian Army Medical Corps, was far more than the medic Task Force Miles so sorely needed. He was a full-fledged doctor—and he was volunteering to go with them into the Cape York wilderness.

Even better, he was familiar with the terrain, wildlife, and people of the Cape. "I've spent a few months working at the missions up that way," Doc Green explained. "Even been to Weipa once," he added, "though it was quite a while ago."

"But how did you find out about this task force?" Jock asked. "Don't tell me the whole damned world knows about us? It's supposed to be a secret."

"No, I don't think the whole world knows, Captain. I was only told because I'm assigned to give you lads your briefing on the Cape York environment tomorrow...you know, natural hazards, diseases, hygiene—"

"But Major—"

"Please...call me Doc."

"Okay, Doc it is. But aren't you assigned to duty here in Brisbane? How can you just pick up and go to the field with us?"

Doc Green found that funny. "They'd be more than glad to get rid of me for a while. My CO at the surgical hospital and I know each other from our mufti days. We worked at the same hospital in Sydney. Let's just say we're not exactly chums."

Jock didn't want to look a gift horse in the mouth, but something was still troubling him. Hesitantly, he said, "Begging your pardon, Doc, but I'm a little...I don't know...*uneasy* that you outrank me. It could lead to confusion for my men...maybe bring up questions of who's really in command."

Green began to laugh again as he pointed to the insignia of rank on his epaulets. "Jock, I only wear these crowns because that's what they pinned on me when I was inducted. I'm no more a soldier than the bloke in the moon. You'd be the boss, always...I'm just the doc."

"Okay, fine," Jock said. "But why do you want to go with us at all?"

"I'm not doing much good around here, Jock, and I'd love one more chance to help stick it to the bloody Nips. I was in Papua, you know...bloody shame, it was. And I heard some of the bullshit that wanker of a captain was shoveling at you. To be honest, Jock, there're good reasons almost nobody lives on the Cape. The Japs may prove to be the least of your problems. You're going to need all the help you can get just to survive."

"I guess I can't argue with any of that. Welcome aboard, Doc."

They shook hands with great enthusiasm. "Outstanding!" Doc Green said. "When do we ship out?"

"In two more days."

"I'd better get packing, then. May I billet with you and your men right away? Like right now?"

"By all means, Doc. By the way, you said 'surgical hospital.' You're a surgeon?"

"No, Jock...I'm a gyno."

The next words that came from Jock's mouth sounded like those of a man who fully understood what he had just been told but refused to believe it. "A *what?*" he asked, his voice climbing half an octave on the *what.*

"A gynecologist," Green replied.

The stunned look on Jock's face prompted Doc Green to expand on his answer a bit. "But don't worry," he added. "I know all the man parts pretty well, too."

Chapter Fifteen

The three-man radio team had just arrived from Division. They snapped to attention at Melvin Patchett's command as Jock Miles entered the dayroom. There were other new arrivals, too: sitting in the middle of the floor were three large, olive drab backpacks. Each pack was box-shaped and looked like it weighed a ton. One of the new men, wearing the newly-introduced rank of T/4—a buck sergeant with a capital T under the chevrons, designating technical expertise—said, "Sergeant Botkin, reporting as ordered, sir."

"At ease," Jock replied. "Introduce me to your men, Sergeant Botkin."

Pointing to a tall, strapping red-haired young man, Botkin said, "This is PFC McGuire. And to his right, we have PFC Savastano."

"Where do you men call home?" Jock asked.

"I'm from Springfield, Illinois, sir," Botkin replied.

Then it was McGuire's turn: "Boston, sir." It came out *Baasten,* with that broad, flat *a*.

Jock smiled and said, "Beantown...who wouldn't have guessed that? How about you, Savastano?'

"The Bronx, sir."

Melvin Patchett grumbled from behind his desk. "Great...s'more damn Yankees."

"Don't mind Top," Jock said. "He can't help it he's from Alabama. I'm a Massachusetts man myself, McGuire. I'm from Pittsfield."

McGuire's eyes brightened as he joked, "So you're from way out west, eh, sir?"

"Yep, about as far west as you can go and still be a

bay stater," Jock said as his attention shifted to the three backpacks on the floor. "Are those the radio sets? How many did you bring?"

"Only one, sir," Botkin replied. "It breaks down into these three packs."

"And if anything happens to any one of these packs?"

"We're out of commission, sir."

Swell...and the whole mission goes to shit.

Botkin was eager to press on. "Can I give you the two dollar tour, sir?"

"By all means, Sergeant."

Botkin and his men went to work. In a few minutes, they had assembled the bulky receiver-transmitter unit onto its short-legged folding table, attached its vertical antenna, and wired it to a hand crank generator. With Botkin crouched before the console, he began his presentation. "This is the latest in field radios, sir...the SCR-284. It transmits high-frequency signals on either AM voice or CW...that's continuous wave transmission using Morse code...with a CW output of twenty-four watts." He ignored the brief frowns of the company commander and first sergeant; apparently, they knew damned well what CW meant. "It's the only radio in our inventory with the range required for this mission. With the right atmospheric conditions, they should be able to copy our CW signal halfway around the world."

Jock had a question. "The right conditions, you say, Sergeant...Will we be able to communicate with Brisbane reliably from way up north in Cape York? Won't the mountains on the east coast disrupt radio signals?"

With easy confidence, Botkin answered, "Normally, they might, sir. But we've established fixed radio stations on a number of peaks in the Gregory Range to snoop on the Japs. Those stations are only three to four hundred miles from where we'll be, and they all have very sensitive antenna arrays. We've just set up a station at Iron Range, too, where we've been trying to build that airfield. That's only about a hundred miles away. None of those stations will have any trouble working us and relaying our messages. And they all have excellent direction-finding capability, which we'll need to pinpoint our location. We can use the azimuth vectors from two or more DF stations to figure out exactly where we are. That's how we've been getting fixes on the Jap ground transmitter up there ever since they landed—"

"Wait a damned minute," Jock interrupted, suddenly agitated by what Botkin had just said. "You mean to tell me we know where the Jap transmitter is?" From the corner of his eye, he could see Melvin Patchett's face growing red, too. He knew what the First Sergeant was thinking: *Ain't that just like the goddamn Army to send you looking for something when they already know where it is? And we've got to find this out from a lowly little buck sergeant, to boot?* Jock was thinking exactly the same thing.

"Well...yes and no, sir," Botkin replied. "Their transmitter keeps moving."

"Moving? Where?"

"So far, sir, it's been within a two hundred square mile area north, south, and east of Weipa. It may even be more than one transmitter moving around. Even though it transmits at the exact same time every night, at twenty-two fifteen hours, the signal never comes from the same place twice."

Jock thought that over for a moment before saying, "So the Air Force can't bomb something we can't pinpoint."

"Exactly, sir," Botkin said. "We haven't been able to crack their code yet, either, so we have no idea what they're saying. We're pretty sure they're giving status updates to their base at Rabaul, though."

Jock felt himself calming down. Perhaps he had been a little too quick to judgment. *Who can blame me for being jumpy? After all, just about everything else about this mission has been a circle jerk from the word go.* He could see the normal color returning to Patchett's face, too.

It was time to get back to technical matters. "How does this setup work, exactly?" Jock asked.

"Well, sir, one man does the sending and receiving," Botkin said, tapping a few dots and dashes on the Morse code key attached to the unit's table. "The other two take turns cranking the hand generator. The one not cranking stands guard. All three of us are qualified radio telegraph operators, and I've been to the tech school on this unit. I can repair it in the field, if necessary."

"That sounds fine, Sergeant," Jock said. "But I have one more question. How good at weightlifting are you three?"

"I beg your pardon, sir?"

"The three packs the set breaks down to…how much does each one weigh?"

"About fifty pounds a piece, sir."

"They did explain to you up at Division that this

mission is a long-distance foot recon patrol that could last a week...maybe more by the time we walk back out?"

The look on Botkin's face could not have been more earnest. "Yes, sir. We understand that. Fully."

"So tell me, Sergeant...how do you expect to do a forced march of twenty or more miles a day with all that weight on your back...in tropical weather...for a week or more?"

A look of relief came over Botkin's face. Almost apologetically, he said, "Oh, no, sir...we don't plan to carry them on our backs. We used some Yankee ingenuity and built little carts for them."

Miles and Patchett spoke the same word almost at once: "Carts?"

"Yes, sir," Botkin replied. "You remember *Radio Flyers?* Those little red wagons kids play with? Lightweight, man-carryable, sturdy as hell...just about indestructible? Well, we modified three of them...put on fatter wheels so they wouldn't sink into soft ground and drilled some holes in the bed so they didn't fill up with water. Of course, we painted them army green, too. One pack fits in one wagon perfectly, with room to spare. We could drag them around at normal walking speed for months." He paused, savoring the astonished expressions on the faces of the captain and first sergeant. "*Radio Flyer*...that's a pretty appropriate name, don't you think, sir?"

Chapter Sixteen

Franklin Delano Roosevelt was in a buoyant mood. Maybe it was caused by the lovely June morning outside the Oval Office windows. Perhaps it was just the afterglow of his latest therapeutic trip to the Little White House in Warm Springs, Georgia. Whatever the reason, he felt triumphant. *Surprising,* he thought, *considering how little my military chiefs have given me to feel triumphant about lately.* But as he gazed upon those military chiefs now sitting before him, he somehow had the feeling *this* morning might be different. He was ready for some good news for a change.

Admiral King, Chief of Naval Operations, would have the first chance to disappoint the president, although he believed he was doing just the opposite. "There's good news from Hawaii, Mister President," the CNO said. "Nimitz reports excellent progress on the Red Hill Project. We're well ahead of schedule and now have nearly fifty percent storage capacity available."

FDR was grinning from ear to ear. "That's wonderful! How soon can we fill that capacity with fuel oil for the fleet?"

"We're already thirty percent full, Mister President. We've been working the tanker fleet to exhaustion, but so far they've handled the challenges magnificently. At our current replenishment rate, we can hit fifty percent by the end of July."

The president restrained the urge to feel giddy. Treading carefully so as not to be let down too hard, he asked, "And what does that fifty percent get us in terms of naval capability?"

"Well...it expands the range of our one operational carrier group defending Hawaii, Mister President."

"That belabors the obvious, Admiral," FDR said, his impatience flaring. "What I want to know is what *new* capabilities it gives us."

King knew what the president wanted to hear. What the president might want, though, and what the CNO thought was a good idea were not necessarily the same thing. Steeling himself, he replied, "Theoretically, it gives us the capability to make another carrier group operational in the Pacific—"

"I'll take it," FDR said, his fist gleefully pounding the desk, a gesture that mimed *rubber-stamping* his approval.

"I said *theoretically,* Mister President."

"You can either fuel your ships or you can't, Admiral King. What's *theoretical* about that?"

"There are many thorny issues yet to be resolved, Mister President. Having the fuel in storage tanks on land is not the same as having it in a warship's bunker."

"Again, Admiral, you belabor the obvious. You already said you've worked wonders with the logistical issues. I expect you to keep doing so."

King realized he had made a mistake and was now on dangerous ground. You could not be vague with Franklin Delano Roosevelt about nautical matters; he simply had too much experience in the Department of the Navy. The CNO had no choice but to come clean about his reluctance to deploy a second carrier group in the Pacific. The president, though, beat him to the punch.

"I understand your unwillingness, Admiral King,"

FDR said. "You don't want to commit to the fight at anything less than full strength. There's a great deal of merit in caution...but right now, caution is a luxury we don't have. Whatever naval capability we can reacquire, we must find a way to put it to offensive use against the Japanese immediately. The American people demand it, and we must deliver. Do I make myself clear?"

"Crystal clear, Mister President."

"So when can a second carrier group return to operations in the Pacific?" the president asked.

King pretended to do a quick mental calculation, much to FDR's silent amusement. The president knew full well his admiral had the answer to that question long before setting foot in the Oval Office, but he allowed his fellow Navy man a moment to play-act.

His bogus deliberations done, King replied, "By the end of September, sir. Mid-October, the latest."

FDR said, "Excellent, Admiral, excellent!" Then the president upped the ante. "In one week's time," he continued, "I'll expect a detailed briefing on the offensive operation in which the Navy intends to use that carrier group."

The president turned to his Army Chief of Staff. "Now, General Marshall...what good news do we have from Australia? Have we bombed any Japanese airfields on New Guinea? The Torres Strait islands? The Solomons?"

In his usual, measured tones, Marshall said, "No, Mister President...we have not been successful in doing so. Not yet...but the strength of our air force continues to grow on Australia, slowly but—"

FDR cut him off coldly, asking, "Grow? In what

way? Have our pilots downed any Japanese planes?"

"We have several unconfirmed kills reported, sir."

"Nothing confirmed?" Roosevelt asked.

"No, sir. Not to my knowledge."

"Are you telling me your squadrons...few in number as they are...are still short fuel? Hasn't the Navy's resupply rate for aviation gasoline improved yet?"

"Negative, Mister President. We continue to receive only the minimum allotment."

Admiral King came to the defense of his navy. "It's like blood from a stone, Mister President. We burn fuel just to transport fuel. It's a delicate balance...the Navy's doing all it can."

Roosevelt cast a scowl in Admiral King's direction and then let out a sigh of exasperation. Turning his wheelchair so he could gaze out the window, he said, "Fuel...it's always about the damned fuel, isn't it?"

Grasping for anything that could be considered positive news, FDR looked to his Army chief and asked, "The Japanese interlopers on Cape York...are your boys dealing with them yet?"

"Yes, sir, they are. The mission to locate and target the Japanese landing party will kick off within the next two days. We've selected a crack recon unit to do the job."

The president raised an eyebrow skeptically. "A crack unit, you say? Didn't you tell me last week the readiness level of our ground units was still marginal?"

"Yes, sir, I did. But in the weeks since MacArthur has assumed command of the Allied effort in the Southwest Pacific, signs of great progress are beginning to emerge."

FDR believed he had found a ray of hope after all. "Very good," he said. "I look forward to hearing of our first victory over Japanese forces very soon, General Marshall. Just do me a favor and make sure the Australians don't feel like they're playing second fiddle in their own country."

Confidently, Marshall replied, "I understand, Mister President. If anyone can bring about understanding and cooperation between our forces and the Australians, it's Douglas MacArthur."

On the other side of the world, some of that *understanding and cooperation* with the Australians was being inflicted on Jock Miles. In a meeting meant to iron out the details of moving his task force by air the 1400 miles from Brisbane to Temple Bay, the Royal Australian Air Force pilot leading the briefing had just thrown a big monkey wrench into Jock's schedule. Rather than the 24-hour movement—with one stop— Jock had envisioned, the RAAF flight lieutenant had just announced the flight would take four days, with three overnight stopovers.

"That's just piss-poor execution," Jock said, not caring if his snide tone offended the collection of pilots in the room. "My men need to be on the ground and moving across Cape York a whole lot faster than that. Every day they rot while sitting in an airplane takes away another big chunk of their combat effectiveness."

The indignant RAAF pilots seemed to puff out their chests, as if presenting the pilot wings residing there was all the justification needed. Jock ignored their studied arrogance and pressed his case.

"Look, my time in Hawaii made me pretty familiar with the capabilities of the Catalina flying boat. You fly the same ones the US Navy does, and they can keep them in the air for over twenty hours at a stretch—"

"As can the Royal Australian Air Force," the flight lieutenant interrupted. "But our hands are tied here, Captain Miles."

With an incredulous laugh, Jock asked, "Yeah? By who?"

"Your General MacArthur, *our* Supreme Allied Commander," the lieutenant replied, emphasizing the *our* with a tone that implied MacArthur's authority over the Aussies was most unwelcome. "He has ordered that no long-range combat missions be flown by any of the allied forces until further notice. Too much precious fuel wasted, he says, with little in the way of results. We're only to fly close-range, defensive missions until the fuel situation improves. Unfortunately, the flight leg you suggest…Brisbane to Cairns…violates your general's order by a sizeable percentage."

Jock thought he had heard it all in his army career, but this took the cake. "That's bullshit," he said. "I might as well take the fucking train to Cairns."

Looking smug, the flight lieutenant said, "Feel free to do so, Captain."

Jock knew the attitude well; the US military had been putting up with it ever since it landed in Australia: *Typical bloody Yanks…they want everything, and they want it yesterday.* And now, his own commanding general was giving the Aussies another excuse to drag their feet. But he tried to reason with this collection of intransigent pilots one more time. "Look, I'm pretty sure you're misreading the order. The only *combat* part of this mission looks to be the last leg…the flight from Cairns to Temple Bay. That's only four hundred miles. The thousand miles before that is just a straight transport flight, something I'll bet you guys do every day."

His assertion must have been close enough to correct, because the RAAF pilots shifted uncomfortably in their seats. But Jock could tell from their faces none of them were willing to make the distinction he had just suggested. "Well, then," Jock said, "I'm wasting my time here. I'm taking this matter up the chain." As he shuffled his mission papers back into their folder and prepared to take his leave, an authoritative voice spoke from the doorway.

"No need for that, Captain Miles," the voice said in a mild but unmistakable Australian accent. "The *chain,* as you call it, has come to you…and I'm inclined to agree with you."

Jock turned to see the speaker, a smiling Royal Australian Air Force wing commander whose embroidered pilot's wings seemed to glisten like spun silver against the khaki of his shirt. The other pilots in the room shot from their chairs and snapped to attention.

"I'm Wing Commander Tim Wells," he said as he extended his hand to Jock. Wells did not bother to tell his braced pilots they could relax and take their seats until the handshake was done and they had both settled into chairs at the briefing table.

Tim Wells's manner was relaxed and confident. Turning to a junior pilot officer, he said, "Do we have a kettle on? I could use a cup. Bring one for our guest, too."

Turning back to Jock, the wing commander said, "Sorry to have not joined you sooner, but contrary to the impression these lads might have given you, some of us do actually fly from time to time. I heard the tail end of your discussion. I'm afraid my lads may be more intent on having a naughty or two with girlfriends along the route than getting you to your destination in a timely fashion. Perhaps we can arrive at a more equitable solution."

"That would be great, sir," Jock said, fumbling over the *sir*. He was not quite sure how to address Tim Wells. To an American, *wing commander* sounded almost silly, like something out of a Buck Rogers comic book. If Wells had been a US officer, he would simply be called *colonel*. Since the wing commander did not correct him, Jock assumed *sir* would be just fine. As laid back as Wells seemed to be, though, Jock half-expected him to say, *Call me Tim.*

Wells's pilots, so haughty and unyielding just a few moments ago, sunk glumly into their seats like schoolboys caught cheating by their headmaster. They could only watch silently as their wing commander took center stage.

Studying the aviation chart sprawled across the table, Tim Wells said, "My lads seem to have overlooked one thing. If your General MacArthur is really so keen on conserving fuel...and he really wants us to fly you and your men to Temple Bay...making all those unnecessary stops along the way would actually cost us *more* fuel. Nothing burns petrol like taking off and climbing to altitude. Why do it four times when we only need to do it twice? And why would I want to tie up two of my Catalinas for four bloody days...not even counting the trip back?"

Jock nodded in eager agreement as he thought, *Finally...a brass hat with some common sense!*

With his finger, the wing commander traced a line on the chart up the east coast of Australia, from Brisbane to Cairns. "That's a leisurely day's flying. About a thousand miles...we'd be airborne a little over nine hours. Is that more what you had in mind for the first leg, Captain Miles?"

"Yes, sir, it is."

"Good," Wells said. "And the chance of running into Japanese aircraft between here and there is pretty slim. North of Cairns, though...not so slim, I'm afraid."

"I understand, sir," Jock said. "And I understand you need daylight for the water landing at Temple Bay."

"Absolutely, Captain...landing at first light will be best, after we've flown that last four hundred miles in darkness. Much safer that way. If there are any Japs about, they'll have a much harder time finding us." Wells jotted a quick calculation on the edge of the chart. "Let's say we depart Cairns at oh two thirty? I don't fancy water takeoffs in the dark, but the weather looks good and we should have decent moonlight. It's a risk we'll have to take to keep you on schedule."

Jock could feel a wave of relief sweeping over him. It would be a piece of cake working with Tim Wells.

"Yes sir, that would work fine," Jock said, and then added, "Unfortunately, you'll still have to fly out of Temple Bay in broad daylight after you drop us off."

Tim Wells just smiled and said, "Can't have everything we want now, can we, Yank?"

The hot tea Wells had requested was placed in brimming cups before them. After a sip, Jock held his mug high and said, "Well, sir, here's to a great plan."

As they clinked mugs to toast their venture, Tim Wells replied, "A great plan, indeed. I like it so much, in fact, I think I'll fly the lead ship myself."

Chapter Seventeen

As she rode through the Mission, Jillian could not decide which was the more humorous sight: the line of several dozen Japanese soldiers at the door of the Mission House, impatiently waiting to avail themselves of the comfort women's talents, or Nathan Gooreng pacing the veranda of the icehouse like some crazed wind-up toy, gesturing wildly as Old Robert sat and listened, looking for all the world like he would rather be someplace else.

The image of Nathan that seemed so comical from a distance, though, grew more serious the closer she came. When Nathan noticed her approaching, his pacing stopped suddenly, as if this large, imposing man was embarrassed she had seen him so upset. His arms, which a moment ago had been flailing to make some point, were now held open in a gesture of welcome to her.

"Got your knickers in a twist, Nathan?" Jillian asked as she dismounted and hitched Franz to the veranda rail.

She had never before seen Nathan Gooreng upset. Even though he did not work for her on the boats, she knew him well. Everyone in Weipa did. He was the finest carpenter in the Mission and a natural leader. It came as no surprise when Sato made him foreman of the Aborigine laborers. But now, after unburdening his troubled soul to Old Robert, Jillian was sure Nathan was fighting back tears.

His deep voice trembling, Nathan said, "Mister Sato does not keep his word, Miss Jilly."

She felt a knot tighten in her stomach as she

thought: *Is this the moment when it all falls apart? Is this when our coexisting with the Japanese starts to unravel...and we start to become their slaves?*

She tried her best to hide her anxiety, but her voice trembled just like Nathan's as she asked, "What happened?"

"The airfield...it is nearly done," Nathan began. "They say airplanes can come tomorrow. We set many fires...burned away many trees."

"Yeah, we know. We've been gagging on the smoke for days," Jillian said. "But you weren't supposed to be done for another week. How many workers did you have?"

"About one hundred...from Weipa and Aurukun. We thought the Japanese would be very happy..."

Old Robert had been gently stroking Franz's neck, letting Nathan do the talking. He had always been a hard man to read, but Jillian could tell her captain was deeply agitated, as well. Still gazing into the eye of the contented horse, Old Robert said, "Tell Miss Jilly what they did to my son."

Jillian felt the knot in her stomach take another twist: *He didn't say his son's name! Blacks never speak the names of the dead.* She wouldn't speak the young man's name, either, pleading with her eyes instead: *What happened to Old Robert's son? What happened to Jonathan?*

"They beat him, Miss Jilly," Nathan said. "Tied him to a post and beat him. Just like those soldiers who were stealing rations." He paused, and Jillian found herself unable to breathe until he mercifully added, "Then they made him go back to work."

She breathed a sigh of relief, but in a moment she

was scolding herself. The fact that Jonathan was still alive hardly signaled the end of anything. Jillian reminded herself: *This is probably just the beginning.*

Laying a comforting hand on Old Robert's shoulder, she asked Nathan, "How did all this happen?"

"Jonathan told Mister Sato we should get more money for working so fast. I told him to hold his tongue but he did not listen to me."

"The young ones never listen," Old Robert said.

His voice more steady now, Nathan continued, "Mister Sato says we don't work fast enough. He will pay us less to build the next airfield—"

"That son of a bitch," Jillian muttered.

Nathan's tale was not finished. "When Jonathan told Mister Sato, 'That's not fair,' he answered, 'Then go work for Miss Jilly if you don't like it.'"

Shit! Jillian thought. *I should have seen this coming. Business partners, my arse!*

"So what are we going to do?" Nathan asked.

"What can we do?" Old Robert replied. "They treat us better than the whites did…at least until this. I think they want to teach my foolish son a lesson."

Jillian slumped into a chair. Her mind wrestled with her anger over what had just happened at the airfield and her guilt for helping to cause it. *Sato's probably trying to teach me a lesson,* she thought.

A young Japanese soldier scurried up to the veranda, bowed, and handed Jillian an envelope. Bowing again, he ran off, back to the Mission House. Inside the envelope was a note from Bob Sato. It invited Jillian to dine that evening with him and Colonel Najima. There was no provision for an RSVP; there was no option to refuse. She knew she had just been given an order.

Chapter Eighteen

The word about Doc Green had spread like wildfire through the ranks of Task Force Miles. All the men were now aware of his *lady doctor* specialty and his easy-going, decidedly unmilitary nature. A few of them decided to test just how *easy-going* he was at the weapons range.

Jock Miles had insisted that Doc and the three radiomen get familiar with their newly-issued Thompson submachine guns before the task force set out from Brisbane. Sergeant Tom Hadley led the detail that would conduct the live-fire training. As Doc Green arrived at the firing range, Hadley commanded, "ATTEN-HUT." Rather than snapping to attention, however, his men—all except a sullen J.T. Guess— offered a very special "salute." They threw themselves onto their backs and raised their legs in the air as if in the stirrups for a gynecological exam. Nicky Russo shouted, "UP ON THE TABLE AND SPREAD 'EM, BOYS."

The dumbfounded Hadley, a straight-laced fireplug of a buck sergeant, looked ready to blow a gasket until he saw Doc Green convulsed with laughter. "Very good, fellows...Very funny," Green said after catching his breath. Waving the muzzle of his unloaded Thompson in the air, he added, "Now get up and show me how this bloody thing works."

Hadley wasn't sure why the doc even needed to make an appearance at the firing range. "Sir, are Aussie medics allowed to carry weapons?" he asked.

"Everyone's entitled to a means of self-defense, Sergeant," Doc Green replied.

Much to their surprise, the doc proved to be a natural with the submachine gun. His hands were steady and confident, not tentative and shaky like those of a novice. Calmly, he put the weapon to his shoulder and with the first burst, he ripped the heart out of the bull's-eye at 30 yards. "Not much different than shooting a Bren," he said. "Just a hell of a lot lighter."

Surprised, Sergeant Hadley asked, "You've fired a Bren Gun, sir?"

"Sure," Green replied, "In Papua. It bloody well saved my life a couple of times. And please…call me Doc."

Like wide-eyed, reverent children, Hadley's team asked in a collective voice, "You were in Papua?"

The bonding came quickly after that, the yet-to-be-blooded soldiers hanging on every word of the combat veteran. They listened in rapt attention as he told stories of the Aussies' failed attempt to hold back the Japanese advance and the terrible human cost of that failure.

"My friend…a coast watcher…he didn't make it," Doc Green said, his voice detached and emotionless, as if this rote recitation was the only way to relate a nightmare. "The Japs cornered him. We found his decapitated body while we were running for our lives."

Sergeant Hadley had a question. "Doc, those Aussies who went in before us…the Nackeroos…do you think we'll find them with their heads cut off, too?"

"Maybe," Green replied, "if we find them at all. I wouldn't expect much from the Nackeroos, though. They've never left Australian soil, and they're very lightly armed. They're nothing but coast watchers with somewhere to run." He paused, and then added, "I wasn't too thrilled to hear they'll be the ones driving us into the bush. Bloody stupid name, too, if you ask me."

The mood was getting too somber for Doc Green's taste. He shrugged, put a smile on his face and said, "I've got to be getting back. I'm supposed to give you blokes a class later. Everything you need to know about crocs and snakes and such..."

After the doc had gone, J.T. Guess confronted Nicky Russo. "That was a damn stupid thing to do, lying on the ground like a buncha women. You coulda got us all in deep shit, you Yankee moron."

Russo responded with an extended middle finger. "Fuck you and the horse you rode in on, cracker. All you rednecks should get *slow stomach cancer.*" Then he pushed J.T. Guess hard in the chest.

Guess did not yield his ground. They stood nose to nose; their old animosities had never really healed. They had only been in remission. It was a blessing all the ammunition for the Thompson submachine guns they carried had already been expended.

It was Guess who broke the tense silence: "Touch me again, Yankee, and I'll—"

Sergeant Hadley jumped between them. "KNOCK IT THE FUCK OFF, BOTH OF YOU," he yelled in a command voice of surprising power from a man so short. "SAVE THAT SHIT FOR THE JAPS, YOU KNUCKLEHEADS."

A man's size didn't matter if he had three stripes on his sleeve; ignore him at your peril. As Guess and Russo shuffled back to their respective duties in prudent silence, Tom Hadley, with his voice now barely above a whisper, added, "You're going to need it."

In the commandeered office building that served as American Forces Headquarters in downtown Brisbane, this was Scooter Brewster's third visit to the latrine in an hour. He hadn't needed to answer the call of nature on any of the visits; he just wanted to stand before the mirror and admire the new insignia that adorned his collar: the eagle-on-shield of a general's aide had replaced the crossed rifles of an infantryman. He smiled proudly, straightened his tie, and headed back to his desk outside the office of his new boss, Major General Samuel Briley, the division commander. Very soon, the general had promised, Brewster would be trading in the single silver bar of a first lieutenant for the double bars of a captain, too. *Life is good,* Scooter thought as he began to whistle Glenn Miller's *In the Mood.*

He found several packets in his "in" basket, fresh from the morning mail delivery. Most contained documents on administrative and logistical issues already acted upon by division staff officers; they merely required General Briley's signature, which he usually affixed without even bothering to read them. The packet at the bottom of the pile caught Brewster's attention. Within it was the paperwork to process a soldier for a decoration.

For an army that had not yet done much in the way of fighting, processing decorations was a rare occurrence. Especially decorations being awarded for *extraordinary heroism while engaged in an action against an enemy of the United States.* True, MacArthur's soldiers and airmen in the Philippines had fought bravely in a losing battle, and no doubt some of them deserved to be decorated, but there was little urgency in the Army to process that paperwork. Those who had not been killed in action were, for the most part, dying a slow, miserable death in POW camps.

So who the hell in this command is up for a medal? Brewster wondered as he spread the documents before him on the desk. The intended recipient's name practically jumped off the page in capital letters: MILES, MAYNARD CAPTAIN USA. Seeing that name rubbed salt in a wound that still felt very fresh to Scooter Brewster.

With disbelieving eyes, he read through the oldest document, signed by an admiral and stamped US NAVAL PACIFIC FLEET HEADQUARTERS, PEARL HARBOR, HAWAII. In the narrative block used to justify the decoration, those eyes fell on the phrase:

...showing conspicuous gallantry and leadership under fire, Captain Miles rallied an undirected group of Navy personnel into an effective ad hoc anti-aircraft unit, successfully downing at least two of the attacking Japanese aircraft...

"What a bunch of horseshit," Brewster mumbled as he scanned down the page. He came to the block listing the recommended decoration:

Distinguished Service Cross

"A DSC?" Brewster said, his tone incredulous and loud enough to make the Aussie secretaries in the office cast curious glances his way. Lowering his voice so no one would hear, he said, "Fucking swabbies blow everything way out of proportion." The secretaries went about their business with knowing smiles on their faces. Brewster had only been in their midst a day, but they had already dubbed him *Lieutenant Douchebag.*

There were two more documents, each processed by a different stateside Army command. According to the date stamps, each had languished on some staff officer's desk, or been in transit halfway around the world and back, for months at a time. Both documents rejected the recommended decoration of its predecessor and kicked the award down a notch without explanation. The current request on Scooter Brewster's desk proposed to award Jock Miles a Bronze Star. Now it was up to the division commander to approve or reject entirely; there was no lesser award for combat heroism to pin on a soldier's chest.

Looks like there's no rush on this nonsense, Brewster thought as he scooped up the documents and stuffed them into a desk drawer. *General Briley's got far more important things on his mind at the moment.*

Chapter Nineteen

Jillian was struggling with an eerie feeling of vulnerability as she tottered with uneasy steps from the icehouse to the Mission House. *Maybe it's the way I'm dressed,* she thought. She had ridden Franz down from her house, put him away at the icehouse paddock, and splashed on a dab of perfume from a bottle that had sat on her dresser, unused, for years. She then changed from her usual trousers and riding boots into a dress and what she called her *funeral shoes.* They were cloth pumps with thick, two-inch heels, the only high heels she owned. She had only worn them once prior to this evening, at the funeral of a white missionary woman who had died suddenly last year. *Maybe I should call them my "white funeral shoes,"* she thought, *since at funerals for the blacks, you don't need shoes at all.* Somehow, going to dinner with Sato and the Japanese colonel seemed very much like going to a funeral. A white funeral. *Her* white funeral, perhaps.

She towered over the two sentinels who stood like toy soldiers at the Mission House door. They snapped to attention as she approached. The waning light of sunset glinted for an instant off the cold steel of their rifles' long, thin bayonets. Her steps began to falter, not because of the unfamiliar heels she wore or the tools of violent death on display but the sounds she heard coming from within the Mission House. A performance on piano of Liszt's *Hungarian Rhapsody No. 5* played softly from some sort of record player deep within the house. The scratchy quality of the recording and the somberness of the piece's minor key added to the funereal feel in her soul. But she thought she heard another sound, far more chilling and not quite masked by the music: the muffled screams of a woman. Jillian's forward progress slowed to a stop as if wading through molasses.

Bob Sato appeared in the doorway, smiling broadly. "Come, Jillian," he urged her. "Dinner is about to be served." The woman's screams trailed off into moans and sobs, barely audible, as if she had abandoned any hope of mercy from her tormentor. Hesitantly, Jillian climbed the stairs and stepped across the threshold into the flickering lantern light of the Mission House. Bob Sato continued to pretend nothing was out of order.

In the entrance hallway, Jillian could hear more than just the woman's moans beneath the music. A man's grunt, followed a split second later by a sharp *thwack,* preceded each moan, the sickening sounds of a beating administered with some sort of stick. She had seen and heard men beat animals—and sometimes their women—with sticks before. Her steps faltered once again; it was impossible to ignore the sounds of the beating or hide the distressed look on her face.

"Listen," Bob Sato said, "I've played Liszt for you!"

A particularly emphatic *thwack* and moan escaped from the depths of the house.

"You didn't play it loud enough, I'm afraid," Jillian replied, her eyes searching but failing to find the hidden source of the distressing sounds.

"Oh, that woman? Don't concern yourself. The colonel is displeased with one of the comfort women. It's a routine matter."

The sound of the beating ceased, replaced by the

steady *clomp* of an object on wooden floors, growing nearer. Sato offered his arm to Jillian and escorted her to the candlelit dining room. As they reached its threshold, Sato removed his boots. Taking his cue, Jillian removed her *funeral shoes.*

Colonel Najima appeared, already shoeless, wearing a kimono and carrying a large bamboo stick in his hand like a walking cane. He was red in the face; perhaps administering the beating had gotten the better of him. The cane made one final *clomp* as the colonel stopped, gestured graciously for Jillian and Sato to *go inside*, and then followed them, setting the bamboo stick upright and prominent in a corner of the room. The three comfort women fluttered silently about, waiting to attend to the colonel and his guests, casting furtive, fearful glances at the stick.

Jillian had been in this room many times before, but it was arranged quite differently now. The long dining table and its chairs had been removed. In its place was a low table, its top only a foot or so off the floor, surrounded by cushions on which to sit. The music was coming from a Victrola—the old, wind-up type, with a large horn sitting on top to project the sound—that sat on a sideboard in the corner of the room. The colonel settled onto the cushion at the head of the table. He spoke something gruffly in Japanese; Jillian understood not a word. She found the sound of the language harsh and guttural, like the speaker was always clearing his throat. One of the comfort women quickly silenced the Victrola before following the other two into the kitchen.

"The colonel wishes to converse without the distraction of the music," Sato said.

Sato picked up a small pitcher and poured Jillian a cup of *saké*—Japanese rice wine—and then did the same for the colonel. The colonel, in turn, poured a cup for Sato. With a lengthy torrent of words as he held his cup high, the colonel seemed to be proposing a toast. Jillian's hapless smile made it plain she had understood not a word once again.

Sato provided the translation. "The colonel wishes to express our regrets for the unpleasantness at the airfield earlier today. He hopes we can renew our spirit of cooperation."

"Why is he telling *me* this?" Jillian asked. "He should be talking to Nathan Gooreng...and that poor lad Jonathan who took the beating."

As Sato repeated her words to Colonel Najima in Japanese, Jillian wondered how close his translation actually was. She watched the colonel intently, trying to gauge his reaction. She was relieved—and a bit surprised—he did not seem in the least upset. The colonel responded with another lengthy dissertation.

Sato smiled knowingly as he provided the translation. "He's telling *you*, my dear Jillian, because there is no one the Aborigines respect and trust more than you. They hold you on a pedestal. Whether you realize it or not, you *are* their leader."

Jillian furrowed her brow. "I told you before...I'm not anyone's leader. And if I was, do you really expect me to help you justify cutting their wages?"

"That was merely an empty threat, Jillian...ill-considered and made in haste."

"So you have no intention of cutting their wages?"

Sato took a moment to relate the dialogue to the colonel, who, after a moment's reflection, merely nodded in agreement and made a gesture with his hand, an unmistakable directive to continue.

Sato did just that. "The colonel believes cutting the wages of the Aborigine laborers would be a terribly counterproductive thing to do, don't you agree?"

Now it was Jillian's turn to nod in agreement and make the same *continue* gesture the colonel had just made.

"The colonel shares my concern, however, about inflationary pressure on the occupation pound..."

Here we go again, Jillian thought. *In about two seconds, they're going to ask me to cut the wages of my crews again.*

"It is important we keep prices well under control," Sato said. "I'm alarmed at the rise in price of many goods at the general store...goods the Empire was pleased to supply at less than wholesale. It seems the store's Aborigine management—"

"Aborigine management? That's a bit *grand,* isn't it, Bob? You're talking about one person here...Alice Tookurra, who was only the shop girl when the Mission people ran the place."

"Yes, and your Alice seems to have graduated from shop girl to profiteer very quickly."

"Alice doesn't keep the money. It all goes to their country."

Sato looked confused. "Country? Do you mean Australia?"

"No, Bob...Weipa, their Aboriginal community...*that's* what they consider their country. The concept of Australia means nothing to them."

"It makes no difference where the money goes, Jillian. It's still profiteering and will lead to inflationary pressure on the occupation pound."

Sato held up a finger, demanding her silence so he could translate the conversation for Colonel Najima. The colonel's response was terse; he looked irritated now. Before Sato could relate Najima's comments to Jillian, the comfort women reappeared with plates of food for the table. The meal looked sumptuous: a variety of seafood served on beds of rice. The centerpiece of the offering was large slabs of broiled shark steak.

It took Jillian several tries to get that first bite into her mouth as she struggled to master the art of eating with chopsticks. Sato began to speak again, this time in those chilling tones of transparent threat she had heard only once before, the last time she and Sato had discussed wages. "Quite simply, Jillian, the colonel and I feel we have been more than generous with the people of Weipa. But we feel a certain lack of...shall we say *gratitude?*...for the warm welcome we have extended into the Greater East Asia Co-Prosperity Sphere. We would appreciate a gesture from you, as the leader of this community, to show our generosity has not been wasted effort."

Jillian's appetite had vanished. The bamboo stick stood in the corner as a reminder of how life around Weipa could become something very different: a brutal prison—or a slaughterhouse. She realized she now had no choice but to assume the mantle of leadership being thrust at her. The peace of the Weipa community—and the lives of everyone in it—depended on her.

Glancing down at the shark steak on her plate, a great calm came over her. That piece of fish had inspired the answer she so desperately needed. Bursting with confidence, she said, "You know, gentlemen...I can solve your money problems very easily. And I'm not talking about lowering the wages of my men. You know as well as I the effect of that would only be a drop in the bucket...but I can do two things that will have tremendous impact. First, I'll get Alice to lower the prices at the store. Believe me, she had no intention to do any harm...and her actions haven't yet caused any real harm to the occupation pound."

She pointed with her chopstick to the shark steaks on the serving platter. "And second, I'm going to cut the price of the fish I provide to you in half." For graphic emphasis, she sliced one of the tender steaks right down the middle with the chopsticks. She let her proposition sink in for a moment before asking, "What do you think of that?"

The exchange in Japanese between Sato and Colonel Najima was brief. Smiles spread across the faces of both men. They turned to Jillian, bowed their heads, and then began to applaud her.

"Now," Sato said, "the colonel would like us to enjoy both this delicious meal and our renewed spirit of cooperation."

As great as Jillian's relief was, Sato's was greater. One of the things the colonel had told him in the conversation leading up to Jillian's concession was this: *Get this foolish girl and her lazy primitives to do my bidding without question before this entire venture falls apart...and I scatter your ashes in this wasteland along with theirs.*

When dinner was over, Sato walked Jillian back to the icehouse. Two soldiers—Sato's bodyguards—marched behind at a discreet distance. The saké had made him glib and his gait unsteady. Perhaps a bit amorous, too. He offered her his arm; she did not take it. "No, thanks, Bob. I've been standing up by myself for a long time."

Not so sure about you, though, you little sot. Can't stand a man who can't hold his grog.

"That's a very generous and noble thing you proposed, Jilly."

"Don't call me Jilly. Nobody calls me that nowadays but the blacks. It's an expression of affection…and you're not black."

Sato chuckled tipsily at the rebuff. "Okay, fine, *Jill-ee-un.* But seriously, to sacrifice profit for the general good is a generous and noble thing." He had made the comment so effusively he nearly toppled over.

"Don't get all wobbly, Bob," she said without offering a steadying hand. "It's not that big a deal. Profits are the last thing on my mind at the moment."

The saké had not affected Jillian's balance or thought processes in the least. She unhitched Franz and mounted him side-saddle, taking great care not to flash her knickers at her inebriated admirer.

"So what is on your mind?" His drunken leer turned the question into a sexual overture.

"A good night's sleep." As if she had not already made her rejection plain enough, she added, "Alone."

"Perhaps I can call on you tomorrow evening," he said. "We can listen to Liszt together…"

Jillian wanted to laugh out loud for a variety of reasons. Listening to a drunk try to pronounce *listen to Liszt*—which came out as an almost unintelligible slurry of *sh* sounds—was only the first reason. But she contained her mirth, thinking instead, *It might not be so bad to enjoy and discuss great music with someone who knew what he was talking about.*

"Fine, Bob," she said as she wheeled Franz around and began to trot away. "Just leave the saké at the whorehouse."

Chapter Twenty

Of the 16 men in Task Force Miles, only Jock and Doc Green had ever flown in an airplane before. As the 14 first-time flyers climbed down from the deuce and a half to the boat dock at Brisbane River, they looked with a mixture of awe and trepidation upon the two dark blue RAAF Catalina flying boats afloat at their moorings. One was marked with a large block letter "L" in dull white next to the RAAF roundel on the fuselage, the other with an "M."

Even to experienced flyers, the first look at a Catalina—*Cat* for short—rarely inspired confidence in its abilities as a flying machine. It looked more like a long, squat boat which someone, as an afterthought, had decided to suspend from a wide slab of wing. Then they stuck some tail feathers at the aft end. The two engines that sprouted from that wing seemed tiny and insufficient to get the awkward contraption into the air. The dark blue paint looked faded and shabby even in the gentle, forgiving light of sunrise. Machine gunner Nicky Russo summed up everyone's feelings: "We should've taken the train…or another goddamn boat."

"These things look god-awful enormous when you see 'em overhead," Melvin Patchett added as he took the airplanes' measure. "They don't look near so big when they're sittin' in the water. We're all gonna fit in just two?"

"There's enough room inside, Top," Jock said. "Let's form the men up and do a weapons check."

"Very well, sir," Patchett replied. Within moments, he had the task force's enlisted men in inspection ranks. "HEAR ME GOOD," the first sergeant bellowed. "THE

RULE FOR PASSENGERS IS *NO LOADED WEAPONS ONBOARD THE AIRCRAFT.* ANY ONE OF YOU TOUCH-HOLES EVEN THINKS ABOUT PUTTING A ROUND IN THE CHAMBER BEFORE WE GET TO TEMPLE BAY, YOU'LL WISH YOU NEVER FELL OUTTA YOUR MAMA'S TWAT."

The RAAF men on the dock were getting one hell of a kick watching Melvin Patchett lay down the law.

"AND ANOTHER THING," Patchett continued. "IF YOU PUKE, YOU CLEAN IT UP. NOW, SERGEANT HADLEY, YOUR TEAM RIDES IN THE AIRCRAFT MARKED 'L FOR LOVE' WITH THE CAPTAIN AND THE DOC. SERGEANTS ROPER AND BOTKIN, YOUR TEAMS RIDE WITH ME IN THE AIRCRAFT MARKED 'M FOR MOTHER.' ANY QUESTIONS?"

There were no questions, to no one's surprise.

"OUTSTANDING! THOSE LAUNCHES WILL TAKE US OUT TO THE PLANES...LET'S MOVE OUT!"

The launches brought them to a waist gunner's blister on the aft fuselage of each aircraft, its clear canopy rolled open. The men of Task Force Miles quickly began to hoist themselves and their equipment onboard. Once inside and struggling to cram themselves into the crew's bunk compartment, they found themselves even less confident in their mode of transportation. Directly above them sat the flight engineer, manning his control panel in the cabane strut that connected the fuselage to the wing. Jock's men felt like they were being wedged into the bottom of a flimsy tin can. And it stunk to high heavens—a pungent combination of decayed food, sea water, chemical toilet, and body odor.

Nicky Russo surveyed the cramped confines, the belts of .30 caliber machine gun ammo crisscrossing his torso making him look like some Mexican bandit. Shaking his head, he loudly expressed the collective dismay: "I don't think this piece of shit's gonna fly...and it smells like my grandfather's ass in here!" To everyone's mute surprise, he walked back to the waist gun blister and announced, "I'm getting off this son of a bitch." In another moment, he was climbing out of the plane, back into the launch.

Jock Miles, in the cockpit going over maps at the navigator's table with Wing Commander Tim Wells, was unaware of Russo's vanishing act until he heard Sergeant Hadley yell, "Hey, Russo, where the fuck do you think you're going?"

"Ahh, shit," Jock said. "What the hell is going on back there? Could we hold up for a minute, sir, while I square this away?"

Tim Wells nodded sympathetically. "By all means," he replied.

Jock climbed out of the flying boat and into the launch with Nicky Russo and the puzzled Aussie helmsman. Russo was standing aimlessly amidship, arms crossed, his grand, mutinous exit complete. Once back on shore, he expected to be dragged off by the MPs, who would lock him up in the stockade pending his court martial. He had it all figured out:

Court martial...big fucking deal. They take away my one stripe and throw me in the can for a couple of months...maybe a couple of years. Better than playing hide and seek with the Japs in the middle of nowhere. Who knows...maybe the captain won't even come back

*from that circle jerk...or that redneck prick first
sergeant, either.*

But the look on Captain Jock Miles's face was not
what Nicky Russo expected. Rather than the hard-set
jaw and pinpoint stare of a military man about to
dispense military discipline, Captain Miles studied him
with an air of easy surety. He had the look of a man
who had faced—and beaten—his demons a long time
ago. There was even a slight, but comforting, smile on
his face as he said, not in the strident voice of a hardass
company commander but a father confessor, "You've
come a long way to let yourself down like this, Nick."

The first thought that raced through Nicky Russo's
mind was, *Don't bullshit a bullshitter, Captain.* But
Miles's words had stung him; he *had* come a long way.
He had finally become best at something—the machine
gun—and with that status had come benefits: nobody
had tried to fuck him over ever since. And they would
not, unless he gave them an excuse. At the moment, he
was creating one hell of an excuse.

*The captain is looking right through me! He knows
I'm just scared out of my fucking mind. Who wouldn't
be? But am I that big a pussy that I won't get back on
that airplane?*

Nicky Russo answered his own question. As his
fingers played with the ammunition belts draped around
him, he thought, *If I'm going to dress up like Pancho
Fucking Villa, I'd better play the part.*

Jock watched Russo's defiance crack away, a little
piece at a time. It was like watching those films of
melting icebergs, where huge sheets suddenly break off
and slide away into the sea. It takes some time, but the
mammoth iceberg disappears into the warm, welcoming

water.

"I just needed a breath of fresh air, Captain."

Inwardly, Jock breathed a sigh of relief. *It would have been so easy just to throw PFC Nicholas Russo in the stockade. The mission would have carried on without him, even if he was the best machine gunner I've got. That's the way the brass hats would want it, but that wouldn't have been real leadership in my book...not the kind of leader I want to be, anyway. He's just scared. Shit, we all are...Hell, even an old bulldog like Melvin Patchett would try to relight a guy's fire one last time before snuffing it out for good.*

Another launch circled alongside. Its helmsman made an impatient *what gives?* gesture, with arms open, palms skyward. Jock put his hand on Russo's shoulder. "Come on, Nick, we're holding up the show."

Russo climbed back into the flying boat first. Once in the cabin, he turned to Jock, and with his best *bullshitter's* smile on his face said, "But it still smells like an elephant took a shit in here, Captain."

"Probably not an elephant," Doc Green said, who, in preparation for a nap was fluffing his pack to use as a pillow. "But perhaps a mob of kangaroos..."

The Cat's flight crew, at least, found that very funny. With a big smile on his face, Tim Wells addressed his passengers. "Sorry about the rank odor, lads, but that's what happens when these girls get flown 'round the clock. But trust me...the only aroma you have to worry about is the smell of petrol. If you start to get a whiff of that, we're all in big trouble."

"Why, sir?" Nicky Russo asked. "Does that mean we've got a leak...and we're going to blow up?"

Jock had watched the fear creep back into Russo's

face as he spoke. *There better be a hell of a punch line coming, Wing Commander, or I'm back to square one with Russo.*

"Blow up from a leak? Maybe," Wells replied, very nonchalantly. "But worse than that, your General MacArthur will surely beat our brains in for wasting precious fuel."

The Aussie flight crew was laughing again but stopped suddenly when two massive .50 caliber machine guns were hoisted onboard. As the gunners loaded thick belts of ammo into the fifties—with bullets that looked the size of Coke bottles—the somber realization they would soon be flying into harm's way returned to everyone onboard the Cat.

"Now we're ready to fly," Tim Wells said.

The engines coughed to life in great puffs of grayish-white smoke, and Wells addressed his passengers one more time: "I'd like all you lads to put those life vests on now. There may not be much time if we have to go for a swim."

Despite the doubts of Jock's men, the Catalinas did eventually fly. The takeoff run down the river seemed to go on forever, thumping and bumping along in the light chop—and occasionally slamming hard, like a speedboat crossing a wake—until the Cats finally broke free from the water's surface and the ride suddenly felt very smooth. They certainly were not fast, but in the 15 minutes since lifting off the river, the flying boats had climbed to 5,000 feet and were heading north, up the east coast of Australia. *L for Love*, with Tim Wells at the controls, was the lead plane. *M for Mother* flew in trail, slightly below and off the leader's right wing.

For all the wonder and grandeur of flying, an airplane passenger's existence at cruise is mostly spent fending off boredom and imagining the passage of time has come to a screeching halt. A few of Jock's men tried—like Doc Green—to sleep the flight away, but the unfamiliar sensations of being airborne in this ungainly machine kept all the first-time flyers wide awake. Fortunately, it had been a smooth flight so far, with little of the sudden ups and downs that displaced one's stomach. But the drone of the props, the rumble of the engines, and the steady whistle of the slipstream over the airframe made normal conversation difficult.

A protocol was devised—mainly with hand signals and a few shouted words—so each man could, in rotation, spend some time in the waist gun blister alongside the gunner, viewing the panorama of land, sea, and sky. Out the left blister were the rugged mountains extending far inland from Australia's east coast, a few rising as high as their aircraft. Out the right blister was the shimmering blue of the Pacific, dotted by a small handful of ships bringing more American troops and supplies to Australia. When viewed against the backdrops of an endless ocean and the vastness of Australia, those ships looked like they could provide little more than a drop in the bucket for the war effort. The gunners kept the blisters closed, with the .50 calibers inside, as they scanned their sectors for any threat. Should enemy aircraft be sighted, they would quickly roll open the blisters. The machine gun would then be swung out into firing position.

Sergeant Hadley shouted a question to one of the

gunners. "How come you just don't leave them open, with the guns at the ready?"

"Because it's bloody noisy enough in here as it is," was the reply. "It only takes a couple of seconds to get the gun ready to fire." Despite the Aussie gunner's air of experience, the American sergeant hoped with all his heart that *a couple of seconds* would be enough if they got jumped by Japanese fighters.

"You ever run into any Jap planes around here?" Hadley asked.

The gunner nodded, pointing to some small, patched punctures in the cabin's thin aluminum skin. Hadley had not noticed them before—a dozen, perhaps, each patch covering what was once a bullet hole.

After his turn in the blister, Hadley climbed over his sprawled team members, making his way to Jock Miles. "Sir," the sergeant said, "those mountains all along the coast...they look pretty rough. We won't have to climb any like those to get inland, will we?"

"No," Jock replied, "the mountain chain starts to level out north of Cairns, just like I showed you on the map. We'll be in the trucks when we go through what's left of them."

About an hour into the flight, Tim Wells left the cockpit to use the chemical toilet which sat prominently in the aft end of the cabin, affording its user no privacy. Stepping around the men of Task Force Miles and their equipment, he startled them all by dropping his trousers and skivvies to his ankles and plopping down on the bowl. Sergeant Hadley began to admonish his men, who were all gawking in astonishment at a sight they had never seen and were unlikely to see again: a wing commander—equating to a lieutenant colonel in their army—relaxing on the throne. Even the latrines they had dug during maneuvers had separate accommodations for the officers, screened off by a tarpaulin.

"GIVE THE WING COMMANDER SOME PRIVACY," Hadley barked. "AVERT YOUR EYES."

Nobody in the aircraft was laughing harder at Tom Hadley's ridiculous demand than Wing Commander Tim Wells. "That's all right, Sergeant," Wells said once he caught his breath. "There's no such thing as privacy on a bird like this. When you've got to go, you've got to go."

His business finished, Wells hitched up his trousers and beckoned Jock to join him in the cockpit. "My navigator noticed something I think you should see, Captain Miles," he said.

Jock joined Wells and the navigator, a prematurely gray flight sergeant, at the chart table. "Flight Sergeant Wilcox will explain," the pilot said.

"Something fishy with your maps, sir," Wilcox began, folding one of Jock's topographic maps so its lines of latitude and longitude at Temple Bay aligned with the aviation chart on the table. "They're very old...based on a 1910 survey."

"Yeah, I know," Jock said.

"We've come up with new charts," Wilcox continued, "based on surveys done last year. I know your Yank aviators have the latest ones, but I guess they didn't get them out to you ground troops yet." He laid a plotter on the aviation chart. "Look at the coordinates for the most westward point on Temple Bay, sir, where we'll be landing tomorrow."

Jock leaned over the table, moving his fingers

along the plotter's smooth, clear surface. "Okay, got it," he said.

"Now, let's do the same thing on your map," Wilcox said, moving the plotter over. "See the difference? That same point on Temple Bay is off by almost a minute north and east on your map. If you're trying to use it for celestial or radio DF navigation out in the middle of nowhere, you could be about a mile away from where you think you are."

Jock felt his mood darkening. "Son of a bitch," he said. "That could really screw things up, and there's not much margin for error when you've got to walk everywhere. I don't suppose you've got extra maps I can have?"

"Sorry, sir...afraid not," Wilcox replied. "I'd give you this aviation chart, but it won't do you much good as a topographic map once you're on the ground. Everything's hard to come by these days...maps, petrol, spare parts..."

"Yeah, I know, I know," Jock said. "Any chance of radioing ahead to Cairns? Maybe they can drum up a few for me."

"Certainly," Tim Wells replied. "We'll give it a try."

Jock smiled in gratitude. "Well, even if they can't come up with any," he said, "at least I'm aware of the problem."

Scooter Brewster was desperate for an excuse to enter General Briley's office. Colonel Snow was in there with the general, and he felt sure they were discussing Task Force Miles. Brewster's curiosity was killing him.

One of the Aussie secretaries gave him the excuse he needed. As she approached the office door with a pile of dispatches for the general, Brewster stopped her and took the papers from her hands. "That's okay, Miss Cobham. I'll bring them in," he said.

Annie Cobham raised a skeptical eyebrow. Ordinarily, this pompous little wanker of a lieutenant would never lower himself to do *women's work.* But here he was, volunteering.

The dickhead must want to get in there awfully bad, she thought. *Oh, well...no skin off my nose.*

She shrugged and walked away. Triumphantly, Brewster knocked on the office door.

"Ahh, Brewster," General Briley said. "What've you got there?"

"Just the afternoon dispatches, sir."

Now it was the general's turn to raise a skeptical eyebrow. "Why are you bringing them?" he asked. "Did all the young ladies break their legs?"

"No, sir...I didn't think you'd want any secretary hearing your discussion."

Scooter placed the papers on Briley's desk. Once that was done, he braced to parade rest. Colonel Snow, standing silent with pointer in hand at a large map of Australia hanging on the wall, did a slow burn.

"You're absolutely right," the general said. "A secretary should not hear what's being said in here...and neither should you. You are dismissed, Lieutenant."

Once Brewster had slunk from the office, the general cracked a grin and said to Snow, "Some gall on that young man, eh?"

Snow didn't get the joke. He nodded in enthusiastic agreement. "Yes sir! Some gall indeed, sir!"

"Oh, come on, Colonel. The boy's all right. He just needs that ambition of his properly channeled, that's all. Hell, by the time this war is over, I'll bet he'll be wearing one of those chickens on his collar...just like you, Colonel."

They returned to the discussion of Task Force Miles. "In summation, sir," the colonel said, "I'm quite afraid Supreme Command has forced upon us an objective that is a bit obscure...and an execution that is much too rushed."

General Briley said nothing for a few moments; he sat with a serene smile on his face, enjoying the familiar sight of an anxious subordinate squirming before him. Finally, he said, "Colonel, one thing you'll learn working for MacArthur. Sometimes it's more important to be seen as doing *something*. Doesn't matter what it is. Just do *something*."

Chapter Twenty-One

Onboard the Catalinas, the men of Task Force Miles watched as the coastal mountains of northeast Queensland began to cast long shadows toward the blue, shimmering sea below. It was the same body of water they had flown over all day, but it was no longer called the Pacific. It was now the Coral Sea.

The two planes began a gentle descent for landing. The flight had been relatively easy on their bodies. Only two of Jock's troopers on *L for Love* had gotten airsick. Whether it was due to motion sickness or the American revulsion to the Vegemite sandwiches the Aussies provided, no one was sure.

Suddenly, the radio operator sat bolt upright and clasped his headphones tighter to his ears. Jock could tell from the tension in the man's face the message he was receiving was no routine weather report; it was a matter of grave importance.

"Cairns is reporting a Jap air raid, sir," the radio operator yelled to Tim Wells and everyone else in the cockpit.

"Shit," Wells muttered as he scanned the sky above his aircraft. A deck of cumulus clouds had formed a few thousand feet above, looking like so many fluffy sheep grazing on a broad, invisible plain. They would provide a splendid place to try and hide from Japanese fighters. "Pilot to Flight Engineer," Wells said into the interphone. "We're going to climb back to six thousand. What does that do to our fuel reserve?"

Without waiting for the answer, Wells eased the throttles forward and pulled the plane's nose up sharply, instructing his co-pilot, "Tell the lads in the back we may be in for it." Then he turned to the radio operator and said, "Tell Mother to spread out and play hide and seek."

Headphones crackled with the flight engineer's report on fuel reserves, and the news was not good. Expressing the frustration of the entire RAAF, Tim Wells said, "Only thirty fucking minutes left! Bloody MacArthur! I'll wager his airplane gets all the fuel it needs!"

Trading speed for altitude, *L for Love* struggled to reach the cloud bank. The radio operator clamped the phones to his ears once again. "Yank fighters are trying to intercept the Japs," he said.

"That's just bloody wonderful," Wells replied, but his sarcastic tone left Jock Miles puzzled. Seeing Jock's confused look, Wilcox, the navigator, set him straight: "We're delighted you Yanks are finally trying to do something, sir, but at the moment we're just as worried about getting shot down by one of your trigger-happy flyboys as by the Japs. It's happened a couple of times already."

In the Cat's cabin, Jock's men were startled when both gunners suddenly flung open the blisters and swung their .50 calibers to battle stations. As Jock passed through the bulkhead hatch that separated cockpit from cabin, his men's voices peppered him with a flood of words that all boiled down to the same question:

What do we do, Captain?

Even Doc Green had awakened.

"Take it easy, fellows...we're still okay," Jock said, trying his best to sound calm and collected. "The place we're heading to...Cairns...they're having a Jap air raid. We're going to hide out in the clouds until it's all clear..."

Fortunately, they could not hear the words completing the sentence in Jock's head: *if we don't run out of gas first.*

"But they've got the guns out, sir!" Sergeant Hadley said. "Shouldn't we be loading our weapons?"

"Negative, Sergeant," Jock replied. "Do you see any gun ports for us to shoot from?"

Already in the gunners' compartment, Russo called through the open hatch to the bunk room, "Captain, we could shoot from the blisters."

The Aussie gunners took a dim view of that suggestion. Shaking his head adamantly, one of them said, "How about you stay out of our bloody way and let us do our bloody job?"

"That's good advice, men," Jock said. "Just sit tight. This crew knows what they're doing."

By now they had leveled off in the cloud deck, coasting along, using just enough engine power—and petrol—to maintain altitude. They vanished into a huge, white puff of cloud, then reappeared, only to quickly vanish into another. If it wasn't for the gunners scanning their sectors, fingers on triggers, it would have been idyllic. They seemed alone in a marshmallow sky.

The shadows on the cabin sidewall gently slid upward, a sign the plane was in a shallow bank. With no visual horizon to reference, they were the only indication of the maneuver to those in the cabin. After a few moments, the shadows slid back down the sidewall. They were in level flight again. The cabin darkened a bit; the clouds around them had grown thicker now. Only rarely—and for a brief moment—could they catch a glimpse of the Earth's surface through the cabin's small windows.

Trying to spread some optimism, Jock said, "Those clouds make for great concealment, don't they, men?"

The optimism lasted only a second. The left waist gunner screamed, "BLOODY HELL!" His words dissolved into the roar of his .50 caliber as he squeezed off a long burst.

Hunched low, their faces pressed against the small cabin windows, Jock and his men strained desperately to see the gunner's target. But all they saw was the same field of cottony white for one second, two seconds, three...until the fluffy whiteness suddenly turned into the mottled green and brown of a twin-engined airplane with a big red meatball on its side flying directly abeam and parallel off their left wingtip. It was a Japanese bomber the Allies called a *Betty*. She was so close they thought they could touch her.

The .50 caliber roared again, a longer burst this time. On the Betty, a turret at the aft end of the long greenhouse canopy winked flashes from its guns. A half-dozen thin horizontal shafts of pinpoint light instantly appeared in the Cat's cabin, traversing the dusty air above their heads, each shaft made of sunlight that a new bullet hole allowed inside. PFC Boudreau, one of the men in Hadley's team, began to gyrate in a frenetic dance as a glowing fragment from a tracer round ricocheted from a fuselage frame and landed squarely on his shoulder. Its velocity spent, it lacked the energy to puncture skin, but it was still hot enough to ignite the fabric of his fatigue shirt on contact. Doc Green smothered the flare-up quickly with a towel from his kit.

The Betty popped in and out of view through the milky clouds as if being viewed through a shutter. Much faster than the Cat, it moved farther ahead with each appearance. In a few more clicks of the shutter, it vanished.

"ANYONE HIT?" Jock asked, scanning the cabin for casualties. Everyone, even PFC Boudreau with the burn on his shoulder, seemed to be all right. As Jock stood, his body intersected the shafts of light left by the Japanese bullets. They made neat, bright circles on his chest. As he touched his fingertip to the little spots of light, Jock thought, *That was a real good time not to be standing up.* He hoped nobody noticed how badly his knees were shaking.

It was then he glanced aft, into the waist gunners' compartment, and saw the man who dueled with the Betty. He was without a scratch and still seemed ready for action, scanning the sky with his machine gun. But now he was trembling from head to toe and trying to wipe away tears of fear and frustration from his eyes.

L for Love skimmed the clouds for another 10 minutes. They had not seen another airplane since the close encounter with the Betty and had only caught fleeting glimpses of ground and sea. Jock Miles was summoned to the cockpit.

"Cairns has given us the *all clear*," Tim Wells said. "Trinity Inlet, where we'll be landing, isn't beaten up too badly. We can't waste any time getting down...petrol's too low...so have your men holding on tight."

The descent felt like the downhill run of a roller coaster. "Bogater" Boudreau, wearing his singed fatigue shirt like a badge of honor, said in his slow, bayou drawl, "Pretty hard to talk with your innards all up in your neck."

And then they were down, bouncing and lurching along the water's surface as the Cat slowed to taxi speed. Nicky Russo was seated on the catwalk as he packed his gear, his feet dangling into the bilge. Those feet promptly became soaking wet. "WATER!" he screamed. "WE'RE TAKING ON WATER!" His panicky words could be heard even in the cockpit.

With the *whoosh* of a fired carbon dioxide cartridge, Russo inflated his life vest. He jumped onto the highest crew bunk like a housewife standing on her kitchen table, frightened by a mouse. Then he tried to claw his way up to the flight engineer's perch in the cabane strut but was stopped by the sole of the man's shoe pressing firmly on his head.

"Relax, mates. Relax," the engineer called down to the Americans. "The bilge pump will take care of it."

Jock and his men really wanted to believe the engineer, but the water level never receded. If anything, it rose higher. Even the waist gunners seemed to be getting a bit apprehensive, their fingers toying with the inflation lanyards on their life vests. "Keep your knickers on, Yanks," one of the gunners said, trying to sound reassuring. "We're almost to the ramp."

The Cat coasted to a stop adjacent to the shore. Her engines fell silent; the beat of her windmilling props against the air diminished quickly until it, too, was gone. There were sounds of many men's voices, accompanied by loud *clunks* from outside the fuselage as ground crewmen attached the beaching gear—three sets of tandem wheels, one on each side of the forward fuselage, one below the tail. The bilge water sloshed forebodingly as the Cat was rotated until her tail was toward land. A tractor's engine revved—and she was slowly towed backwards up the launching ramp to her parking spot.

Spilling to the ground from *L for Love,* the men of Task Force Miles expected far worse than the sight that greeted them. A few of the hangars and buildings at the seaplane base had suffered damage, some of it severe. What had been a US Navy Catalina was now a smoldering heap of skeletal metal. A ground crewman reported there had been a few injuries, but no deaths reported. At least not yet.

As they unloaded their gear from *L for Love,* the other Catalina, *M for Mother,* was towed alongside. Melvin Patchett was the first man down the ladder. As he strode toward Jock Miles, it was not hard to detect the wobble in his step. As he got closer, he was obviously a little green around the gills.

"Have a good flight, Top?" Jock asked.

Putting on the brave show, Patchett replied, "Never been so bored in my life."

"So I guess you didn't run into any Japs, then?"

Patchett looked surprised. "Japs? Never saw another airplane the whole trip. Couldn't even see you most of the time." Color was coming back to the first sergeant's face. His expression became stern as he scanned the damage on the airfield. "Why, sir? Did you?"

"Damned near kissed a Jap bomber up there in the clouds." Jock pointed to the bullet holes in *L for Love's* fuselage. Steady streams flowed from a number of punctures in the lower fuselage. The water they had taken on during landing was now leaving the flying boat the same way it entered.

"Holy shit," Patchett said, squinting for a better look at the airplane's punctured skin. "Everyone okay?"

"Boudreau got burned a little...shell fragment or something. Looks like it hurt his shirt worse than him...but he just might be our first Purple Heart."

"Son of a bitchin' Japs," the first sergeant muttered. "Can't wait to shove this Thompson right up their asses. I just heard some of the Aussies talking...they say Cooktown and Mossman got bombed, too."

"Yeah, I heard that, Top." Pointing to the unblemished hangar before them, Jock added, "We'll billet in there. Let's get a hot meal in them and then try to get us all some rest."

"Takeoff still planned for oh two thirty, sir?"

"Affirmative, Top...Oh, and I found out we've got a little map problem. We'll try to get that cleared up before we leave here."

Chapter Twenty-Two

In the drawing room, the upright piano lay open, its tuning pins exposed. As one finger repeatedly tapped the high C, Jillian gave a gentle tug on the tuning hammer with her other hand. "There...that should do it," she said. There was no one to hear her except one of the Mission dogs, sprawled by the couch in the hot, darkening room, cooling himself by alternately playing with and then licking a small chunk of ice. She had been so consumed with the piano tuning she had forgotten nightfall was nearly here, and the coming darkness had once again silenced the drone of Japanese airplane engines.

It was an unseasonably hot evening for *the dry*—the winter—in Cape York. Barefoot and wearing baggy shorts, Jillian had long ago unbuttoned her shirt, exposing the sweat-dampened men's undershirt she wore beneath it. The room took on a warm glow as she lit an oil lamp, the light playing off hundreds of books that lined shelves on the rich, wood-paneled walls. There were well-worn volumes on history, economics, marine biology, music, and anthropology. Literary classics adorned their own, special shelves.

Returning to the piano, she wiped away the sweat that had dripped on the keys during her labors. Then, she played a brisk arpeggio starting at the lowest note and traveling all the way up the keyboard, her hands expertly crossing over repeatedly until the last key was struck.

Not bad, Jillian thought. *I might actually get good at tuning this thing with a little practice. But if I break any more hammer springs I'm in big trouble. I don't imagine I can get piano parts from the Japs, too.*

She reinstalled the articulating cover that also served as the piano's music stand and closed her toolbox. Settling onto the bench, she arranged the sheet music before her. When done, she took a deep breath, head hung down, eyes closed in concentration. Softly, she began to play the first notes of Liszt's *Vallée d'Obermann.*

She drew power from the music she was making. The somber feel of the piece's introduction, occasionally spiced with notes that gave hints of optimism and promise, began to liberate Jillian from the reality of her life. The music transported her to a plane of existence far more exquisite than the one she was actually living. She did not even notice when the dog, bored now that the ice had melted and every drop licked up, sauntered out the back door to seek amusement elsewhere.

Minutes ticked by as she played on, flipping the pages of sheet music with mounting anxiety as the piece approached its complex crescendo; this was where she always faltered. The swirling, staccato melody demanded the hands exchange roles at a lightening pace as it traversed octaves. Only a true virtuoso had a fair chance of the hands landing on nothing but the correct keys throughout the entire passage.

She winced as she made the first mistake but played on. The second mistake followed quickly, then another. Too frustrated to continue, she slammed her open palms against the keys in defeat, letting the discord ring in the sultry night.

Her heart lurched when a man's voice pierced the

stillness. "Why did you stop?" Bob Sato asked. "You were doing so well."

"What the bloody hell are you doing here?" she asked, startled and annoyed but not afraid. "And how long have you been standing there…inside my house?"

Still seated on the piano bench, she turned to face him. In the frail, flickering light of the lantern—her hair hanging damply across her face, little beads of perspiration clinging to the valley between her breasts, just visible above the scooped neck of the undershirt—Jillian had never looked more beautiful to Bob Sato.

"I said I would call on you tonight."

"You were pissed," she replied. "I'm surprised you remembered." She pointed to the bottle he carried in his hand. "But I told you… none of that grog of yours. You didn't bloody remember that."

Sato held out the bottle of saké to her. "Consider it a house gift."

After a moment's hesitation, she snatched the bottle from his hands. "Thanks," she said, then pointed to what his other hand carried. "What've you got there?"

"Just a few recordings I thought we might enjoy. Liszt, Chopin…even Wagner."

Jillian rose from the bench and walked to the front window. "Where are your bodyguards?" she asked, scanning what little she could see in the twilight.

"I released them for the evening. No doubt, they're at the Mission House—"

"With the whores."

"Comfort women, Jillian. We call them comfort women."

"A rose by any other name, Bob…The Victrola's

over there in the corner. Why don't you crank it up. Let's hear someone who can *really* play."

He selected a recording and set it on the turntable. Jillian recognized the tender but resolute melody immediately: Chopin. Sato took a seat at one end of the couch.

Jillian decided it would be impolite not to serve the saké Sato had brought. *He'll have to settle for sherry glasses...I don't have anything like those silly little cups they use.* She sat at the opposite end of the couch, more than an arm's length away from him. Even though she poured herself a glass, she made it a point not to drink more than a sip or two. The rest went into the vase on the table next to her when he was not looking. Frequently, he had to pop up to select a new record; that was the best time for disposal.

By his fourth glass, the saké was taking hold of Sato. He lost interest in the music and became more interested in making conversation. Like a conspirator, he asked, "You received your petrol supply today, I trust?"

"Yes, I did. My tanks are full once again. Thank you very much."

"This is a lovely house, Jillian. Classically Victorian. How long have you lived here?"

"Most of my life. It was my father's house."

"I see," Sato said, adopting a cautious tone for his next question. "And your father is...?"

"Missing, presumed dead. Went out hunting one evening and only his horse came back. We never found his body. Crocs, probably."

"Perhaps he was waylaid by thieves...or blacks?"

"Nah," she replied with a shake of her head,

"thieves don't clean up after their dirty work as well as crocs do. And blacks? Not possible. They loved my father."

"Just like they love you, Jillian?"

A coy smile was her only reply.

Sato asked, "And your mother?"

Just for a moment, her expression became one of deep pain. The tone of her answer, though, was very matter-of-fact: "Never knew her. She died giving birth to me."

That stopped the conversation dead in its tracks. Sato floundered, trying to think of a graceful way to get it rolling again. Several long, awkward moments passed before he asked, "Your father...when did that happen?"

"Nineteen thirty-seven."

"And you've been running his business ever since?"

Jillian nodded. Her glass of saké was still half-full. Whether the conversation had made her uncomfortable, or just thirsty, she was not sure. The half-glass did not go into the vase. She downed it in one swallow.

Sato made a mental calculation, no doubt slowed a bit by the saké. "But that was five years ago. You would have only been—"

"Nineteen, Bob. Nineteen years old. Plenty old enough to run a business I've known all my life."

"We are closer in age than you might realize," he said. "I'm only thirty one."

Neither spoke as she refilled their glasses. The bottle was now nearly empty. Jillian returned to the far end of the couch, tucking her bare legs beneath her as she sat, and fearlessly took another sip. The alcohol would pose no problems. She knew from last night's experience she could hold her liquor far better than her guest.

Sato broke the silence; he began to wax philosophical. "This is truly a very generous thing we Japanese are doing for Australia," he said.

"Generous? How's that, Bob?"

"We're allowing you to become part of a new era...with very little sacrifice on your part."

"Maybe you should define 'very little sacrifice,' Bob. Those airplanes that fly from your airfield...I don't suppose they're dropping candy and biscuits on the lucky people of Australia."

Sato chuckled and shook his head. "No, of course not. It will be necessary to make a show of force against a few of your cities...Cairns, Townsville, Cooktown, Mackay, Brisbane, even Sydney...to drive home how foolish it would be to resist."

Jillian leveled him a skeptical look. "Your planes can reach all those cities from here? Mackay, Brisbane, Sydney...they're all bloody far away."

"No, not yet," Sato replied. "But our enterprise here on Cape York has gone swimmingly. In a few months, before the wet season begins again, we'll have airfields far to the south, right down to the Gregory Range. Those cities will then become much closer. All for a very small investment in men and equipment. When faced with that threat, we will expect to receive Canberra's full cooperation with the Empire."

"You really think it's going to happen just like that?"

"We've never had any doubt, Jillian. Australia is simply too vast to be defended by its meager forces. The Imperial Japanese Navy's brilliant stroke at Pearl

Harbor has rendered the Americans barely able to help themselves, let alone Australia."

Jillian pondered his words for a few moments. Suddenly, her face brightened like a schoolgirl who had just solved the teacher's riddle. "Wait a bloody minute," she said. "If Australia is such a pushover, why don't you just march in right now with a whole bloody army and take whatever you want?"

"There's nothing in this place we *want,* Jillian. We already control all the vital resources in the Southwest Pacific."

"Bullshit," she replied. "That's not it at all. You're spread too thin now, aren't you? Your bloody army and navy are trying to hold down half of Asia, the Philippines, the East Indies... You don't have the men or equipment for any more conquests, do you? That's why there's only a tidy handful of you walking around on Cape York."

He tried to put that tone in his voice—the one he had used before to assert superiority and imply a threat of destruction—but the saké had thickened his tongue. His rebuttal sounded more like that of a whining ideologue, trying to refute an obvious truth. "The forces of the Empire have proved invincible so far, my dear young lady."

Jillian knew she had opened a door Sato meant to keep closed. She had nothing to lose now by plunging ahead; her debating skills were far less impaired by drink than his. The saké had done nothing but jack up her courage, and she was enjoying this feeling of having the advantage very much.

"No, Bob," she said, moving in for the kill, "there *is* something you want here. You want to make sure that nobody, like the Yanks, for instance, can get strong in Australia and use it as a base against you...because you couldn't lift a bloody finger to stop them if they did. So you're going to try to bluff Canberra into surrendering."

She leaned back against the cushion, very satisfied with herself. Sato looked so pitiful, not saying a word, like a crestfallen child who had been caught telling tall tales. But Jillian could not resist rubbing salt in his wound.

"If *I*"—she made a grand, theatrical gesture of pointing to herself—"could figure that out, Bob, don't you suppose those bloody wankers down in the capital have already done the same? Whose brilliant idea was this, anyway?"

His silence was all the answer she needed. Trying not to sound too giddy, she asked, "Oh, goodness...it was yours, wasn't it, Bob?"

Now she thought he might actually break down and cry. To her great surprise, she found herself feeling sorry for Bob Sato. She was still fully aware that Colonel Najima's troops could, at their whim, slaughter every last man, woman, and child in and around Weipa. But Jillian now knew their presence was just a ruse—a sideshow playing to a meager captive audience, removed from the far bigger stage of a world at war—that could collapse like a house of cards with the slightest puff of wind. Somehow, bullets and bayonets aside, they suddenly seemed irrelevant and ridiculous.

Just humor them a little longer, she thought, *and they'll be gone.*

The saké had dimmed Sato's mind but bolstered his courage. With a speed and deftness that belied his advanced state of inebriation, he slid across the couch to Jillian. One hand began to caress her neck, the other the smooth skin on the inside of her thigh.

"You're a very perceptive woman, Jillian," he said, his face hovering closer, his words slurred.

She was startled but not repulsed, despite her reflex to retreat. But there was nowhere to go—she was already wedged against the armrest. He was not an enemy because she did not consider herself at war, and the touch of his soft hands was gentle and comforting. Bob Sato would probably make a very suitable lover, she thought, someone with whom you could discuss music and politics when the bed play was done—if it was not for that *one thing...*

"Bob, I won't sleep with you."

My goodness, she is painfully direct! Please don't tell me she believes that nonsense that all Japanese men are poorly endowed.

"Why?" he asked, the pain of a fresh wound on his face. "Is it because I am...Japanese?"

"No, Bob, it's not that. Not at all. I won't sleep with you because...because I can't sleep with any man."

Confusion kept Sato silent for a few moments. When he finally did speak, his words were cautious and fumbling: "You're not...not a..."

Her laughter shook the room. "A virgin? No, Bob, I'm definitely not a virgin."

Seeing the hurt on Sato's face was now mixed with confusion, she added, "And no...I'm not a lesbian, either."

Again, he asked, "But why?"

"Because it will hurt. Unbearably."

His hands returned to his lap. He considered asking her to clarify, but not knowing what or how to ask, thought better of it.

"Maybe you should go join your friends at the Mission House," she said.

Sato shook his head dismissively. "Those women are for the soldiers." The way he slurred *those women* made the words sound dirty and repulsive.

Drunk or not, he knew a rejection when he heard one. This didn't seem like one you could reverse with some smooth talking, either. Assuming, of course, he was even capable of smooth talk with so much saké in his belly. He rose to collect his records.

"Thank you for a most enlightening evening, Jillian." His words sounded sincere, almost too formal.

Jillian stood and waved goodbye as he walked out the door, stumbling twice along the way. Then she sat back down on the couch and breathed a deep sigh of relief. She smiled, reveling in the verbal thrashing she had just dished out, but her joy quickly turned bittersweet as she thought, *Why does sex have to hurt so bloody bad?*

Chapter Twenty-Three

Sleep proved an elusive refuge for the men of Task Force Miles. Melvin Patchett had little trouble rousing his edgy troopers at the designated 0100 wake-up. Two US Navy cooks had been detailed to serve them a hot breakfast at 0130: eggs to order, bacon, toast and jam, and coffee. The food was delicious and therapeutic to everyone's tense nerves. The knowledge that it was the last hot meal they would enjoy for the immediate future made it taste even better. From this point on, they would be eating nothing but the newly developed K rations and D bars they carried with them. Designed to provide the combat soldier just enough calories to maintain normal physical activity, they were certainly no taste treat, especially the D bars. Although resembling a thick candy bar, D bars had a bitter taste akin to baker's chocolate. As Melvin Patchett had told his complaining troopers when they first sampled them, *They made it taste like shit so you touch-holes don't eat it like candy.* The rations were compact and light, though; each man carried 14 days' worth of sustenance in his pack, with room to spare.

Tim Wells and his crew looked refreshed and ready to go. They were used to catching sleep whenever and wherever they could, even onboard the droning Cat in flight. The weather forecast had held. The sea breezes were light, the surface of Trinity Inlet placid. A few wispy clouds proved no impediment to the moonlight illuminating the flying boats' watery runway. Even *L for Love's* wounds had been healed with more patches and rivets. She and her sister ship stood poised on their beaching gear, noses to the water, looking as eager to fly as the ungainly aircraft possibly could.

Not everything had gone so well during the stopover at Cairns. The search for up-to-date maps had proved fruitless. The only ones Jock Miles could find were at least as ancient as the ones he carried. He'd have to make do with the maps he had.

Another problem: the burn to PFC Marcel "Bogater" Boudreau's shoulder looked more serious once they were back on the ground. "It's a second-degree burn," Doc Green said as he examined the wound closely. "Small area…but still, it's blistered and sensitive. Even bandaged, there's a risk of infection. You shouldn't carry anything like a weapon or a pack strap on that shoulder. Not until it heals."

"How long will that take?" Jock asked.

"About two weeks."

Jock and First Sergeant Patchett exchanged worried glances. The last thing they needed was a man who could not carry his weight. Without the need to speak a word, they had come to a decision.

Bogater Boudreau had seen this moment coming. Ever since Doc Green had started fussing with his wound, he knew they would want to leave him behind. But he would have none of it. Before Jock Miles could say anything, Boudreau laid out his case.

"It's no problem, sir," he said. "Look…"

Bogater hoisted his horseshoe pack into position, one strap over his good shoulder. He had modified the other shoulder strap so, instead of going over the top of the shoulder, it would now loop under his armpit and across his chest before hooking to the other strap. The pack hung crookedly on his back, but it wouldn't fall off and did not impede his movement in any way. Most importantly, no weight was hanging from his burned shoulder.

Patchett was the first to change his mind. "Looks like a little Cajun ingenuity there, Bogater. I'm impressed."

"And it ain't even my shooting shoulder that's wounded," Boudreau said.

Jock was still not convinced. Even without the irritation of the pack's strap, the wound could fester in the bush. Infection would rob Boudreau of his energy and impose another burden on the team. *We might have our hands full with sick and wounded men once we're out there. Let's not start off bringing a liability with us. We can manage with one less man.*

"That looks fine," Jock said, "if we were just going on an admin march for a couple of hours. But we're going to be walking through the bush for days. With all that weight on one shoulder, you'll wear out fast."

"I can handle it, sir," Boudreau replied. "I'm damn sure tougher than that."

Jock wanted to believe him. But there were the lives of 14 other men to consider, too. He shook his head: *No.*

Bogater screwed up his face in protest, but the first sergeant cut him off with a terse, "At ease, son." Turning to Jock, Patchett asked, "If I may, sir?"

Jock nodded, yielding the floor to his top sergeant.

"Show him the leg, son," Patchett said to Boudreau.

Bogater Boudreau quickly dropped his pack to the floor, undid his right legging and pulled up his trouser leg to the knee. His shin and calf were a mass of purple scars. A few of the scars had a nasty concavity where flesh had been carved out. Once upon a time, something had taken quite a bite out of Bogater Boudreau.

He began to tell the story behind the wound. "When I was fifteen, my kid brother and me...we was fishing. Gator got a hold of my brother. I wrassled him, got my brother free, but he was bit up real bad." He pointed to his leg. "He got an itty-bitty piece of me, too...before I stuck my knife through his eye."

Boudreau ran his hands through his blond, close-cropped hair before continuing. "I carried my brother all the way to the doc in town...some twelve miles...and we both come out okay."

Melvin Patchett smiled. He could see the story was having the desired effect on Jock Miles.

"So if you think I ain't man enough to carry this little ol' pack, Captain, I gotta beg to differ with you."

Jock's resolve had softened halfway through Boudreau's story. If he insisted on dropping Boudreau, he knew what the first sergeant would say next: *If we start leaving men behind for every little scratch, in no time flat it'll be just you and me, sir*. And he'd be right, as usual.

"All right, Private Boudreau. Welcome back to the team," Jock said.

Doc Green had watched Boudreau's display in quiet amazement. He had remembered the young private as being especially unimpressed during his briefing on the hazards posed by crocodiles and other Australian wildlife. Now he knew why. He lingered to speak with Bogater Boudreau after Miles and Patchett had moved on to other business.

"So tell me, Private," Green said, "did you get that nickname *bogater* because of that incident you just described?"

"No, sir. In *Loosiana*, a blond boy is just about always called bogater. It's short for albino alligator...and both are rarer than a virgin in Brisbane."

With a delighted laugh, Doc Green said, "A man of the world, I see...but just the same, we'll have to keep a very close watch on that burn."

Boudreau still seemed unimpressed as he said, "Suit yourself, sir."

Her engines were already running as *L for Love* rolled slowly down the ramp toward the water, restrained by the tractor's towline hooked to the beaching gear beneath her tail. Once afloat in the water, the towline held her fast as the ground crew, working only by the dim light of their torches, performed the ritual of removing her beaching wheels. Tim Wells waited for them to finish, his fingers thrumming impatiently on the control column as he and his co-pilot scanned the surface of Trinity Inlet.

"It looks clear, sir," the co-pilot said.

"Yeah," Wells replied, and then turned to Jock Miles, seated on a milk crate between the pilots' seats. "A water takeoff at night is the same as one during the day, except you can't see a bloody thing, of course."

Jock hoped he was just trying to be funny. Judging by the tense faces of all the crew, though, that didn't seem to be the case.

"The real problem is debris in the water," Wells continued. "There could be a log floating along and you wouldn't know it...until it tore the bottom out of her hull."

Okay, he's definitely not joking, Jock thought. *But this was the trade-off...the shortest flight so my men aren't too fatigued, plus that flight had to be made in darkness, yet arrive at dawn...So how come it doesn't sound like such a hot idea all of a sudden?*

"I wish we had the bloody Mark Three already," Wells said, to no one in particular.

"What's a Mark Three?" Jock asked.

"A Catalina amphibian...flies off land or sea. We've only got a handful right now. Obviously not in this squadron. Your Navy seems reluctant to let go of them."

A waist gunner's voice came over the interphone, reporting the ground crew was done removing the beaching gear. They were clear to taxi. Wells advanced the throttles and *L for Love* pushed forward, into the darkened void that was Trinity Inlet. Aside from the blackout lights of vehicles on the shore—tiny pinpoints of white and red vanishing and reappearing with each twist in the road—the moon was their only source of illumination. The city of Cairns, flanking the inlet's north bank, was as dark as the seaplane base. Sometimes, the Jap bombers came at night. There was no point making themselves easier targets.

The radio operator called out, "*M for Mother* is in the water, sir. They'll hold position until we start our run."

"Very good," Wells replied. He asked his co-pilot, "I reckon we're in the middle now, don't you?"

"Yes, sir, this looks about right."

Jock wished both pilots sounded a little more certain.

With a blast of differential engine thrust, Wells pivoted *L for Love* eastward, pointing down the inlet toward the sea. Then he pulled the throttles back to idle and took one long, last look across the moonlit water. When it was done, Tim Wells, looking like a man not enthused about what would happen next, turned again to Jock and said, "I need you back with your men in the bunk house now, Captain. Tell them everything looks fine, then all of you hang on for dear life until she's in the air. And take that bloody milk crate with you. We don't need it bouncing around up here right now."

When Jock joined his men in the dimly-lit bunk compartment, he was surprised how relaxed and confident they all seemed. No one had the wide-eyed look of apprehension that punctuated their first flight. Not even Nicky Russo.

I wonder how relaxed they'd be if they just saw what I saw up in the cockpit.

"Hang on good and tight, men," Jock shouted over the roar of throttled-up engines. "It might get a little bouncy."

He knew those words were probably unnecessary; all the men were seated, their feet braced against the catwalk, their hands holding onto anything that was well nailed down. He was not ready, though, for the look they returned *en masse*. That look could only mean one thing: *Gee, Captain...No shit!*

They could see nothing but the blackness of night through the small cabin windows, but they could tell they were accelerating across the surface of the water. The Cat seemed to be evolving as a vessel as it picked up speed: first, it was a slogging launch; then an eager but encumbered motorboat, gently bouncing off the ripples. Now, she had become a sprightly speedboat, going fast enough for her hull to rise on step. What had been gentle bounces were now quick, harsh jolts that made you flinch. Jock looked across the faces of his men, each with an expression of joyful excitement unmistakable even in the dim lighting. They were trading boisterous comments he could not hear above the din, looking no different than kids enjoying an amusement park ride. All the fear of what they might shortly encounter in the bush was forgotten for the moment.

These are the shared experiences that bring a unit together, Jock thought. *Only one flight under their belts, but my guys consider themselves seasoned airmen now...*

Suddenly, it was all shattered. PFC Rex Billings and Nicky Russo were in an awkward shoving match, each trying to use the other to pull himself upright and get in position to throw a punch. A particularly wicked bounce on the water thwarted their efforts and landed them both back against the sidewall, still clutching each other by the life vests.

"I DON'T SEE NO FUCKING STRIPES ON YOUR ARM, YANKEE," Billings yelled over the roar of the engines. His high-pitched, North Carolina drawl became all the more shrill at high volume. "YOU CAN KISS MY REBEL ASS."

"KNOCK IT OFF, YOU TWO," Jock bellowed. "SIT YOUR ASSES BACK DOWN. I DON'T NEED ANYONE BANGED UP BEFORE WE EVEN GET AIRBORNE!" A different thought flashed through Jock's mind, too: *Some of these southerners are never going to give up fighting the Civil War, are they?*

It took them another moment to realize they were already airborne. The jolting had stopped; they were now floating on air instead of water. They had been too distracted to appreciate that sweet moment when earthbound mortals begin to soar with the eagles.

"All right, men...at ease," Jock said. Sliding across the catwalk to Billings and Russo, he asked, "Now what's the problem here?"

"I ain't got no problem, Captain," Russo said, still coiled like a spring. "*He's* got the problem."

"Damn straight I got a problem, sir," Billings said. "He ain't got no rank on me, so he can't be giving me no orders. Sure, I'm toting ammo for him...but that don't make him in charge of nothing."

Jock asked, "What kind of *orders* are we talking about here, Private?"

"He's telling me...no, *ordering me*...that when we land, *I'm* gonna tote the machine gun. Well, sir, I say bullshit on that. He wanted to be the hot-shit gunner, and with that honor, you get the gun...that big, heavy old gun. All thirty-two pounds of it."

There was no mistaking the looks on the faces of Hadley, Pacheco, and Boudreau: they agreed completely with Billings.

So did Jock. He took a deep breath. *Here we go again,* he thought. *It's time to play nursemaid, priest, judge, and jury all rolled into one.*

"Listen up...and listen good," Jock began. "Like I said before we ever left Brisbane, you're carrying the thirty cal as an *individual* weapon, Russo. That's why it's on the bipod and has the stock attached. We left the tripod behind because we don't need to be carrying the extra weight. Now...you got the job because you're the best at it. When we need that gun, we're all counting on it being in *your* hands. It *better* be in your hands. Do you understand?"

As expected, Russo had the look of a child who had just been spanked. He took a moment before answering, "Yes, sir." There was no rancor in his voice. Jock allowed himself to think Russo even sounded contrite.

"Shake hands, you two," Jock said. Coming from the captain, that was an order, not a request. Russo and Billings complied quickly, if not wholeheartedly.

Their little world began to tip sideways as *L for Love* banked, beginning a slow turn to the north toward Temple Bay. There was nothing more to see or do for the next four hours, until they met the sunrise at their destination. Jock and his men took a cue from Doc Green and tried to catch a nap. Some were even successful.

M for Mother followed well behind and slightly below, just close enough to keep *L for Love's* recognition lights in sight. Any closer, and the risk of a mid-air collision in the dark was just too great. Just like Tim Wells and his crew, *M for Mother's* crew had breathed a mighty sigh of relief when their ship finally lifted off the water. Their takeoff run had been a good deal rougher than *L for Love's*; they had to contend with remnants of the lead ship's wake.

The bunk compartment of the trail ship was more crowded than the one in which Jock and his men were trying to sleep. There were the extra men from the radio section plus all their radio gear, including the three *Radio Flyer* wagons. First Sergeant Patchett had dozed off several times, only to be jostled awake by the restless stirrings of Sergeant Jed Roper, leader of the second scout team, who was seated next to him.

"Didn't they learn you Texas boys to sleep when you can?" Patchett asked Roper. The question sounded gruff and fatherly at the same time.

"I tried, Top, but it ain't no use. Got something on my mind."

Patchett gave him a surprised look. "Well, there damn sure must be something on your mind, son. That's the most I ever heard you say in one breath. You wanna talk about it?"

At first, Melvin Patchett thought the usually laconic Texan would not talk at all. He looked sorry he had even brought it up, perhaps. Jed Roper would probably get up and walk away rather than say any more, the first sergeant thought, but there was nowhere to go inside this airplane.

Finally, Roper said, "There's been some talk, Top…about Captain Miles…that he's a meatball…a real fuck-up. And to make himself look good and save his own ass, he volunteered us for this mission."

Patchett's stomach clenched at Roper's words. From firsthand experience, he knew rumors like this could get out of hand quickly and destroy a combat unit, making it more of a danger to itself than the enemy. He'd have to set this nonsense straight, and right now.

"Let me tell you a little story, Jed," Patchett began. "Back in the Great War, I was just a private in a rifle company. Our company commander, a real fine man, got killed in a barrage one night, and the next morning, we had ourselves a new one...a brand new captain, a West Pointer—"

Roper snickered at the mention of West Point. "And you got no use for West Pointers, right, Top?"

"That's another false assumption you gotta get out of your head. Now don't interrupt my story again...Anyways, that night, we got told we were going over the top. There was intel that Gerry had pulled back. We were to confirm that intel and hold the new line until the rest of the battalion advanced. Of course, nobody was real eager to go over the top and out into no man's land. If Gerry was still there, we'd be lambs to the slaughter. And we were doubly pissed because we'd been on the line for two straight weeks, getting our brains beat in daily, and it was our turn to come off. So, sure as hell, by supper time, the rumor started spreading like wildfire that our brand new captain had volunteered us for the job. How the hell else could we have gotten fucked over like that? This sound familiar so far?"

Roper nodded eagerly. "Yeah, Top. Real familiar."

Patchett frowned. He did not think his young buck sergeant was listening in the proper frame of mind. At least not yet. He pressed on with his story.

"So, clever young bucks that we were, we decided if the captain wanted to get hisself a posthumous medal, we were gonna let him. When he blew the whistle to go over the top, we just all sorta stood there...just to see what would happen...and wouldn't you just know? The captain climbs up the ladder alone, stands straight up...all exposed like a sitting duck...and yells, *Come on men! Let's go make history!*"

Roper snickered again. He still didn't have a clue where this story was going.

"And you know, he stood there for what seemed like a lifetime...and not one Gerry shot at him. So we all just sorta shrugged and thought *what the hell...*and over the top we went."

Patchett paused to take a sip of bottled water. Before he began to speak again, his expression changed. It became less of an older man imparting wisdom to one younger and more of a man confessing something of which he was deeply ashamed.

"But we still figured the captain was showboating with our lives...so we advanced *reeeeeal* slow, stepping around the barbed wire and shell holes...and it being dark and all, pretty soon the captain was way out in front of us, so far we couldn't see him any more. So we stopped...just stopped, right there in the middle of no man's land...and hunkered down. It was so quiet...so unlike any other night in the trenches. We must have just sat there for four, maybe five minutes...when suddenly we hear some yelling and a couple of rifle shots...and we high-tailed it back to our lines. The rest of that night was quiet as quiet can be. No barrages, no gunfire, no flares...nothing. We kept peeking over the top of the trench to see if the captain was coming back...but he never did."

Patchett was disheartened to see the smug look on Roper's face, a look that said, *Yeah! Serves the stupid bastard right.* But there was still more story to tell.

"Next morning, some scout plane flies over and drops a message saying there were no Germans in front of us for miles. So this time, the whole damned battalion started walking across no man's land...in broad fucking daylight...and when we got to the German trenches, all we found was our captain's body. The Gerries must have left a couple of men behind at a listening post when they pulled back. He probably walked right into them...and they riddled his ass. We thought we were so fucking clever...at least for a little while, anyway."

Suddenly not so sure of the story's outcome, Roper asked, "Why, Top? What happened?"

"Well, later that day we got pulled off the line, just like we were supposed to. Back at the rest area, we ran into some old sergeant from HQ, and he told us the real story of how we got that mission. Turns out our captain hadn't volunteered us at all...*he* was the one who got volunteered because the other company commanders, who had been in the battalion for a while, knew how to bullshit the battalion commander. So they got this walk in the dark across no man's land *volunteered* to the new guy. This sergeant said our captain even tried to talk his way out of it, saying stuff like, *He didn't even know his men's names yet, let alone what they could do as a unit.* But that didn't cut no ice. He had his orders. Once the captain was outside the CP, that sergeant said he saw the man break down and cry, that's how frustrated he was."

Roper was finally starting to get the point.

"Funny thing is," Patchett said, "if we had all stayed together, one little ol' listening post wouldn't have posed no problem. They probably would have run away if they heard a whole company tramping towards them. And nobody would have died. Not that night, anyway."

Roper slumped back against the cabin sidewall, his

bravado totally deflated. "So you're saying it was Captain Miles who got *volunteered,* Top?"

"That's exactly what I'm saying, Tex. Now listen good...you ain't in some Waco gin mill no more, where a bunch of ignorant, liquored-up buttfucks think they get to make the rules in their little shithole of a world. This is the army, son...and you don't get to make no rules. Captain Miles is our commander, and we follow him, no questions asked. And one more thing...he ain't no fuck-up. Just the opposite. The way I hear it, he was a goddamn hero at Pearl Harbor but got hisself on the wrong side of some brass hat doing it. That happens to a lot of good officers...the ones who can think for themselves and don't need to be sticking their noses up their commander's asshole all the time."

Patchett let those words sink into Roper's head before adding, "And I'm making it your personal business to stifle those rumors, Sergeant. Without delay. Do I make myself clear?"

"Yes, First Sergeant," Roper replied, wishing he could disappear into his helmet like a turtle into its shell. "Perfectly clear."

Chapter Twenty-Four

Jock Miles knew it was a dream, but it confused him nonetheless. A friendly, attractive young woman sat behind a desk in an opulent office, sunlight streaming through grand windows. She possessed an effortless but unyielding air of command that he envied. Yet he felt threatened by it at the same time.

Wagner was playing from somewhere, another room, perhaps. He recognized it immediately as the finale of *Götterdämmerung*. But something was off in the performance. The soprano's voice faltered; when she soared for the high notes, they came out flat.

He was telling the young woman about the Cape York mission—how he organized it, how it unfolded, and how he had totally succeeded: the Japanese had fled like terrified children. All the way back to Tokyo. He was flush with his victory, but behind her polite smile, she was unimpressed. Throughout his narrative, she would frequently interrupt with these words:

It's time to move on, Jock.

In the dream, he pretended not to hear her words, but each time they were repeated he felt less sure of his victory, less sure of himself. Had he made some crucial mistake, not apparent at the time and only rearing its ugly head now? Had his success been only an illusion? *And what the hell does "it's time to move on" mean, anyway?*

Suddenly, the young woman was gone, vanishing to the hidden lair where subconscious creatures dwell. The walls and ceiling of the office collapsed like a house of cards into a pile of splintered lumber and shattered glass. The sunlight that had lit the office was now trapped below the rubble. Its dim glow still lit the dreamscape, leaking from within the pile in dusty rays, like so many searchlights scanning the night sky. He was still seated amidst the destruction, untouched by its chaos. But his body was shaking...

Flight Sergeant Wilcox had shaken Jock three times before his eyes opened and let in the dawn's light, now streaming through the cabin windows. His men were awake and anxious. They fussed with their equipment, their nervous hands needing to do something—anything—to ease the tension. They were almost there. Jock could not believe he had slept the flight away.

"The wing commander wants you in the cockpit, sir," Wilcox said. "We're coming up on the landing area."

"Yeah, okay," Jock said, rubbing the sleep from his eyes. "I guess it's time to move on."

Flight Sergeant Wilcox replied only with a quizzical smile. Jock knew what that smile meant: *He has no idea what I'm talking about...and neither do I.*

When Jock got to the cockpit, the view out its windows startled him. They were so low—just a few hundred feet up—and flying just inland from the shoreline of a bay that formed a shallow horseshoe, curving gently for miles. Jock felt he could count the leaves on the trees beneath them.

"That lagoon off the right nose," Tim Wells said, "that's where the Nackeroos are supposed to meet us. We'll pass over it...maybe we'll even see them...then turn inland and circle back so we can land out to sea, into the southeast wind." He took another glance to his right, looking out his co-pilot's side window. "The swells don't look bad. We shouldn't bounce around too much. Just make sure your men are snug."

Jock took in a quick lay of the land below. He was relieved to find what he saw agreed very closely with the impressions he had formed from map recon and aerial photographs. There was some high ground a bit farther inland but nothing like the mountains they had passed farther south. Through the gaps in the high ground, he could see flat, wooded terrain stretching toward the western horizon—and Weipa. The trees and foliage directly below were abundant but not dense, offering cover and concealment without impeding movement. For as far as his eye could see, there did not appear to be a structure of any sort. Or a living soul.

"Pilot to gunners," Wells said into the interphone. "Five seconds to rendezvous point, one o'clock. Any sign of them?" He listened as the reply came into his headphones and then told Jock, "Yeah, we've found the Nackeroos. The man in the right blister saw them. They waved to us."

They flew on for another minute, and then Wells began a tight left turn that traversed almost 270 degrees, first taking them farther inland and ending when they were headed toward the sea. They caught a glimpse of *M for Mother* as they came around, just beginning her turn to follow them. As Wells began the slow descent to the water, he said, "The only problem with landing out to sea like this is the long taxi back to shore. We're ten times more vulnerable as a boat than a plane."

With that comforting thought, Jock returned to his men in the cabin. As he passed through the hatch linking the compartments, their taut faces turned to greet him. Nicky Russo sat with the machine gun across his lap, its loading cover open, a belt of ammo in place, the first round ready to be chambered. All the others had a magazine of .45 caliber ammo for their Thompsons in one hand, their weapon in the other. As soon as Jock gave the word, the weapons would be ready to fire.

But it was not time yet. "Not so fast, men," Jock said. "We have to land first...we're going to bounce around a little...we don't want any accidental discharges. Once we're taxiing to the shore, *then* I'll give the word. Not before. And we keep all weapons on *safe* until we're out of the aircraft. Is that clear?"

Reluctantly, they nodded as one. Somehow, having a round in the chamber makes one feel less vulnerable.

"When are we going to be landing, Captain?" Sergeant Hadley asked.

"Any second now. Everybody hold on tight."

They counted the seconds—*five, ten, fifteen*—and then there was that first, soft *bump,* followed by a gut-wrenching feeling of floating. Another bump—and then a *thud* and the sound of water coursing against the hull. They were down, riding the sea swells like a roller coaster.

Russo yelled to the waist gunners, "Hey! We ain't gonna fill up with water again, are we?"

The response was less than reassuring: "There may be some water, mate. We are a boat, after all. Nothing like last time, though. No bullet holes down below now."

The gunners added to the collective sense of uneasiness by rolling open the blisters and deploying the .50 calibers. *L for Love* slowed to taxi speed. With a blast of differential thrust from her engines, made noisier by the open blisters, she pivoted in a wide arc toward shore. Halfway through the turn, the starboard waist gunner called out, "*M for Mother* just touched down." Both gunners broke into an off-key rendition of *Hail, Hail, the Gang's All Here.* Only Doc Green joined in.

"Okay, men...*now,*" Jock said, and with a single, loud, metallic *clack,* the loading of weapons was completed in unison.

It took fully 10 minutes to taxi back to the rendezvous point, riding the swells toward shore. A few of the crewmen were on top of the fuselage now, preparing to deploy a sea anchor from the bow. She turned in a semicircle, then coasted to a stop a hundred yards offshore. A large pram approached the port blister with three men onboard: two Aborigine oarsmen and, standing at the bow, a grinning, tanned white man. All three were shirtless, barefoot, and wearing tattered khaki shorts of the Australian Army. Other than large knives on their belts, none seemed to be carrying a firearm.

"Welcome to the bloody Cape," the white man shouted in an unmistakable Australian accent above the Cat's idling engines. "I'm Corporal Cockburn of the Nackeroos, sir. How many to come ashore?"

Standing in the open gun blister, Jock replied, "Seven on this ship, nine on the other. All with full equipment. How many boats do you have?"

The Aussie seemed amused by the question, shaking his head with that *bloody impatient American* expression Jock had gotten used to in Brisbane. "Just this one, Captain," Cockburn said. "Just this bloody one."

It would take four trips with that pram to get everyone and their equipment off the two planes. *M for Mother* was still a good five minutes' taxi away from anchoring. It could be the better part of an hour before everyone and their gear was on shore. "Another typical Army cock-up," Tim Wells said, standing next to Jock with a very disgusted look on his face. "That's too long for us to be sitting here." Turning to his gunners, Wells said, "Break out one of our rafts. Let's get everyone ashore in one shot. Signal *M for Mother* to do the same. Use the blinker light."

Jock scanned the shore. It looked empty of men and equipment. He asked, "Where are the trucks, Corporal?"

"They're tucked back in the bush, sir. Real beauties they are, too...and pretty hard to come by in these parts."

Refusing to get swept up in Corporal Cockburn's optimism, Jock said, "Let's hope so."

An inflatable raft—one of two onboard the Cat, stowed no bigger than a steamer trunk—was shoved out the starboard blister and its cartridges fired. With a loud *hiss,* the raft unfolded and grew into a capable vessel.

Well, at least the damned raft floats, Jock thought. He delegated Doc Green to skipper the raft, taking Sergeant Hadley, PFC Russo, and PFC Billings with him. In less than a minute, the raft was loaded and on its way to shore. Hadley and Billings were doing a competent job with the paddles. Russo sat at the bow of the raft, his machine gun at the ready. Jock couldn't tell if the grimace on his face was one of fear or determination.

Jock, Corporal Pacheco, and PFC Boudreau joined

Cockburn and the black oarsmen in the pram. As they began to pull away from the Cat, Jock called back to Tim Wells, still standing in the blister. "What about the raft, sir?"

"Keep it," Wells replied, as his crew began hauling in the sea anchor. "We're off, Captain Miles." He snapped a salute and added, "Glad to have been of service. Best of luck to you."

"Thank you, sir," Jock said, returning the salute. "You won't forget about picking us up when we're done, will you?"

"Say the word and we'll be here."

"They'd better be," Corporal Pacheco mumbled, just loud enough for Billings to hear.

"You got that right, George," Billings replied.

Pacheco rolled his eyes in annoyance. "Not George. *Jorge.*" He repeated his given name, dragging the syllables out: "*Horrrrr-haaay.* How many times do I have to tell you crackers? And that's *corporal* to you, Private."

The pram handily won the race to shore. No sooner had it deposited Jock and his men on the beach than it was on its way to *M for Mother*, now waiting offshore with a bright yellow raft blossoming alongside. *L for Love* was already airborne and heading south.

Corporal Cockburn, still standing at the prow like Washington crossing the Delaware, pointed back into the tree line as he yelled, "The trucks are right over there, sir, with the rest of my blokes. Be back in a jiffy....Oh! And don't be cutting no holes in the raft. We can use it."

First Sergeant Patchett had it all under control on *M for Mother*. The radio section and all their gear—including the *Radio Flyer* wagons—had been loaded into the pram and were beginning their trip to shore. Patchett, Sergeant Roper, and his men climbed into the raft donated by the Cat's crew. Roper did a quick head count: Corporal McMillen was there. So was PFC Guess and PFC Simms. But that made one man missing: PFC Mukasic.

The first sergeant noticed Teddy Mukasic missing, too. He had already started to climb back into the flying boat to retrieve him. He found him, huddled in a corner of the bunk compartment, his knees tight to his chest.

"I ain't going," Teddy Mukasic said, bracing for the blow he fully expected at the hands of the first sergeant. But Patchett just stood there, arms folded, looking down at him without a hint of violence in his gaze. If anything, the gaze was empathetic.

"Suit yourself, son," Patchett said over the steady rumble of the Cat's engines, "But I'm here to tell you...these Aussies got no use for you. They'll just throw you in the water and fly away. Wouldn't it be better to stay nice and dry in that raft?"

"I can't move, First Sergeant," Mukasic said, his lips trembling. He clenched his knees tighter to his chest. Patchett could see his hands trembling, too.

The first sergeant squatted before the terrified private and put his hands gently on the boy's shoulders. "Even if these Aussies took you back to Brisbane, they'd just be bringing you to a firing squad. And that's no shit, son. If you think you're the only one who's scared, think again. The only difference between you and me is you're afraid of what you *don't* know, and I'm afraid of what I *do* know."

Mukasic looked into Patchett's eyes. "You're really scared, Top? You?"

"Only a crazy man ain't scared, son. So you see what you're facing? Either the Aussies or the brass in Brisbane's gonna kill you if you don't get off this airplane. That's guaranteed. You're better off taking your chances with me and the Japs."

Patchett could see Mukasic's defenses starting to crack. He added one more point to his argument. "Besides, we're all depending on you, son. You're not gonna let us down now, are you?"

The tight ball of Mukasic's body relaxed. He wiped away a tear and took a deep breath. "But what're we going to tell them, Top? They'll all think I'm yellow."

Patchett eyed the chain around Teddy Mukasic's neck. "What's that hanging there, son?"

Teddy pulled the medallion out from beneath his shirt. "This? It's my Saint Christopher's medal."

"Good. We'll say you dropped it down in the bilge when you were getting your gear together. It took you a minute to find it, that's all."

Mukasic considered that for a moment. Then he stood, grabbed his gear, and headed for the open gun blister. "Sorry, Sarge," he said to Roper as he dropped into the raft. "I couldn't find my good luck charm there for a minute. But I've got it now." He held out the Saint Christopher's medal for all to see.

Roper's displeasure spread across his face like a storm cloud. "Oh, ain't that just fucking wonderful, sweetheart. I was beginning to think you—"

Melvin Patchett's reproachful glare silenced Roper like a switch being turned off.

"Pick up those fucking oars and let's get moving," the first sergeant said. "We've done enough dicking around for one morning."

The crew of *M for Mother* wasn't much for dicking around, either. They were airborne long before their passengers reached shore.

Chapter Twenty-Five

Jock Miles found two trucks parked in the tree line, just where Corporal Cockburn of the Nackeroos said they would be. He was having a difficult time, though, squaring the vehicles he was looking at with the requirements spelled out in the operations order. That order had specified *two each wheeled vehicles of not less than one-ton capacity, capable of overland operations, able to travel no less than 160 miles without refueling.*

What Jock saw before him were two battered, very small trucks, no larger than what would be called a pick-up truck back in the States. Here in Australia they'd be called *utes*—short for utility vehicle. He couldn't tell their vintage, but they closely resembled the model he had driven for his part-time job in high school, circa 1930. He knew from hard experience they could climb a steep hill at no more than walking speed if loaded with more than 500 pounds, a figure they were about to exceed by a healthy margin. They looked more like they had been abandoned there, rather than poised to take him and his men into the unknown. Doc Green made a whistling sound that could only mean *oh, brother…you've got to be kidding* when he laid eyes on the trucks.

Sergeant Hadley's men were dispersed in a loose perimeter around the vehicles. Jock was pleased Hadley had immediately deployed his team in proper tactical fashion without having to be reminded. He did not want his men wandering around like tourists with their thumbs up their asses, like they forgot they were in a combat zone.

But, hell...my men tangled with Japs before we even got to Cairns, so they'd better believe they're in a combat zone.

Slack discipline could be contagious, and what little Jock had seen of the Nackeroos so far seemed to set new standards for slackness.

Maybe Cockburn and his men have just "gone troppo," like those Aussie troops who had been in the New Guinea jungle too long. But speaking of Cockburn's men...where the hell are they?

Sergeant Hadley provided the answer in short order. "Captain," he called, "you'd better come see this."

Tom Hadley had indeed found the rest of Cockburn's Nackeroos—all three of them. They were bearded, shirtless, and in shorts, just like their corporal, but at least they had boots on their feet and each man carried a Lee-Enfield rifle. They stood in a small clearing, in the process of having group photographs taken by a bearded man in civilian clothes. Each soldier grinned broadly, proudly brandishing his weapon for the camera as if he had just won the war single-handedly. Like the Nackeroos he photographed, the civilian had the rumpled dress and suntan of one who had been in the tropics for a long time. Too long, perhaps.

"Just what the hell is going on here?" Jock asked, making no secret of his displeasure.

"Ahh, the Yanks have finally arrived," the civilian said in a thick accent that sounded decidedly German. He was older—in his forties, perhaps. The Nackeroos stopped posing and began to mill around, looking embarrassed, like kids caught playing hooky.

"It's nothing, sir," the tallest of the Aussies said. "Just some pictures for the folks back home."

Ignoring the speaker, Jock turned his attention to the civilian. "Identify yourself," he said, punctuating his question by pointing the muzzle of his Thompson at the man with the German accent.

"There's no cause for alarm, my friend," the civilian replied, his hands in the air. "I am Heinrich Van Der Hoorst. I am a Dutch citizen and a correspondent for the BBC. I'd like to ask you a few questions about the American—"

"Nobody's answering any fucking questions, *my friend,* except you. How the hell did you get here?"

"He jumped ship off a coastal trader, sir," the tall Aussie spokesman said.

"I didn't ask you, soldier," Jock snapped. "Let me hear it from Mister Whoever-The-Fuck here."

"I see there are just a handful of you Yanks," the Dutchman said, brazenly clinging to his own line of interrogation, "and I see the rank on your collar. You are a captain of the US Army, are you not?"

"Like I said, pal...you don't get to ask questions."

"But if you and your men represent the sum total of your government's response, Captain...coupled with the feeble Australian attempts at defense—"

"Hey, wait a bloody minute," a voice called from behind Jock. It was Corporal Cockburn, and he seemed mighty upset. "Who the hell do you think you are, giving us a gobful like that, after we—"

"That's enough, Corporal," Jock said. Pointing his Thompson once again at Van Der Hoorst, he asked Cockburn, "Do you know this man?"

"Not really, sir. He just showed up yesterday. He

would have drowned getting ashore if we hadn't pulled him out."

"Has it occurred to you, Corporal, that he could be a Jap spy? The *Dutch* bit could be a good act, too. He still sounds awfully German to me."

The Nackeroos' rifles were now pointing at the Dutchman, too.

"He did have that Jap *funny money*, Harry," a Nackeroo reminded Cockburn.

"I explained that," Van Der Hoorst sputtered. "I got it from some of your diggers in Singapore."

One of Cockburn's men walked over to a duffel and pulled out some green paper currency. He handed the money to Jock. It was a one pound note. The issuing agency was *The Japanese Government.*

As Jock examined the money, Sergeant Botkin and his radio section approached from the beach, each man pulling one of the olive drab *Radio Flyers.* Van Der Hoorst burst out laughing. With derisive delight, he said, "There you have the American response to Japanese aggression…in children's wagons, yet!"

Cockburn was getting embarrassed and a bit flustered. "I didn't think it would be any harm if he hung around, Captain. I—"

Jock interrupted, asking, "Did your commander authorize any civilian to be hanging around?"

"No, sir. But he's a—"

"Then what the hell were you thinking, Corporal? This guy could compromise the whole goddamn mission. And if he really was a newsman, he'd know damn well anything he tried to write about us would be censored straight into the trash can. We've got to—"

The Dutchman, beside himself with sarcastic glee,

said, "There you have it, ladies and gentlemen, a fine example of coordination between the Allies! The world has a right to know just how cocked up..."

As he spoke, Van Der Hoorst reached impulsively into the rucksack hanging from his shoulder. That was his last living act. The lone shot that rang out rattled everyone; each man checked his weapon, unsure if he was the one who fired.

A wisp of smoke from the barrel of a Lee-Enfield betrayed the shooter. It belonged to the tall Aussie—the spokesman. His eyes were wide as saucers, his mouth hung open. It looked like he just might pull the trigger again and not even realize it. Cockburn gently pried the rifle from his hands.

"It's all right, Billy," Cockburn said, his voice gentle, his arm around the young man. "It's all right."

The rest stood and stared at Van Der Hoorst as he lay dead on the ground, arms and legs askew, a bullet to his head. A river of his blood flowed across the ground. Small drops of pink matter from his brain were sprayed across the vegetation at the edge of the clearing. After the briefest examination of the Dutchman, Doc Green turned to Jock and shook his head, confirming what everyone already knew:

No use. He's gone.

Sergeant Roper's team arrived from the beach raggedly dispersed in line abreast formation. Despite Melvin Patchett's prodding, the pace of their advance was less than eager. The sound of the shot had terrified them and set their senses tingling. Patchett made a bee-line for Jock. No words were necessary between the captain and first sergeant. They both knew what had just happened was the best possible outcome for their mission. Even if it was a ghastly mistake. Secret missions weren't a secret if the whole world knew about them.

As everyone watched, Patchett carefully pulled the rucksack from the Dutchman's body and peered inside. "Go slow when you do this," he said as if giving a class. "Those Japs like to booby trap things." He pulled a pistol from the ruck—a Webley revolver, typical British Commonwealth issue, all chambers loaded. There was a notebook and some documents, still a bit soggy. The notebook was full of text in a language that looked similar to the little bit of German Patchett knew. The documents purported that Heinrich Van Der Hoorst was a foreign correspondent of the British Broadcasting Corporation. They lacked any sort of official stamp. There was no passport.

Patchett broke open the Webley, spilled its bullets onto the ground and held it up for all to see. In a deadpan voice, he said, "Would've looked a lot better if this was a Jap Nambu, though."

A queasy look came over Cockburn. He asked Jock, "What are we going to do with him, sir?"

"We leave him, Corporal. You can come back and bury him later, if you like...once you take us where we've got to go. I want these trucks on the road in five minutes...and get your men in proper uniform right fucking now. This isn't some Tarzan movie."

Chapter Twenty-Six

According to Corporal Harry Cockburn, he and his men knew this route like the backs of their hands. You couldn't really call it a road. It was just a dirt trail, carved by many horses and a few wheeled vehicles from Temple Bay westward, into the bush. The trucks were climbing the high ground just inland from the coast, not really mountains anymore but still obstacles you'd prefer not to cross on foot, especially with the loads the men of Task Force Miles were carrying.

As Jock had surmised when he first saw the two old trucks, their progress up the hills would be very slow. They chugged along in low gear, the ruts in the trail pitching their occupants roughly about. Jock had already returned his folded map to the safe place between his steel helmet and its wooden helmet liner, where no rain or perspiration could ruin it. For the meantime, the map was useless; there were no landmarks to confirm position. As long as they were heading due west, they were at least headed in the right direction. Once the truck ride was over, Jock would get a fix from the radio section to pinpoint exactly where in the middle of nowhere they were.

Little conversation had transpired in the cab of the lead truck between Jock Miles and Harry Cockburn, who was at the wheel. The shock of the Dutchman being gunned down had left them disinclined to talk, and Cockburn was consumed by the effort necessary to keep the truck on the winding trail.

It didn't take long to crest the hills, even at the snail's pace they were forced to maintain. Now Cockburn had to ride the brakes, still in low gear, to keep from plummeting out of control on the downslope to the plateau that would carry them toward Weipa. Once at the bottom, the Aussie corporal breathed a sigh of relief. He had a burning question for Jock: "Tell me, sir...why was it so bloody necessary for my men to put their shirts and hats on? We usually muck about in the bush wearing as little as possible, since it's so bloody hot."

Jock answered with dead certainty. "Because when bullets start flying, your bearded, bare-chested troopers don't look much different from Aborigines. My men are green and under enough stress as it is. If we get into trouble, I want it to be as simple as possible for them to figure out who the bad guys are. Otherwise, you and your men could end up accidentally dead. Just like the Dutchman."

Cockburn winced at the mention of Van Der Hoorst. "You know, Captain," he said, "we're not going to get attacked by blacks."

"That's funny. Your high command told me the Aborigines were not to be trusted. They'll probably side with the Japs."

"The abos aren't on anyone's side, sir. They never are. They just look out for themselves."

Jock thought about that for a moment before asking, "By the way, what happened to those blacks in the rowboat?"

"They left as soon as those Cats were unloaded," Cockburn replied. "That's all I paid them to do. They live a few miles south of where you came in. They took their boat and rowed straight home. These *utes* are borrowed, too, from some miners near Iron Range," Cockburn added, patting the steering wheel. "I've got to return them as soon as we're done with this little exercise. They're holding our horses as collateral. I'll have to borrow these sorry bastards all over again when it's time to pick you up."

"And what will you be doing while you're waiting to pick us up again?"

"Our job, sir...watching for Japs on the northeast Cape with the rest of our outfit."

They were making better speed now, almost 20 miles per hour across the flatter ground. Jock looked out the cab's rear window to see how his men were faring. Sergeant Hadley's team was nestled in the truck's bed along with PFC Savastano from the radio team, Doc Green, and Nackeroo Billy, the man who shot Van Der Hoorst. They were all alert, scanning the surrounding terrain, weapons at the ready. Russo was standing with his machine gun resting on the cab's roof, scanning the sky for aircraft, bobbing and ducking occasionally to avoid being swatted in the face by low-hanging branches. Every inch of space in the bed was crammed with men and their gear, including one *Radio Flyer*. Jock was glad to see two hand grenades hanging from each man's web gear. Not wanting them rolling around in the Catalinas, he had delayed the grenades' planned distribution until they were on the beach at Temple Bay. In the chaos with the Dutchman, though, he had forgotten to do it until Melvin Patchett gently reminded him.

The first sergeant saved my ass again. He even had them bury the packing the grenades came in, in no time flat.

Jock could see the second truck, lightly veiled by the dust the lead vehicle kicked up. It followed at proper tactical interval some 50 yards behind. Nackeroo Ben was at the wheel, with First Sergeant Patchett riding shotgun. Sergeant Roper's team and the rest of the radiomen filled the bed, with Nackeroo Roddy, now wielding a Bren Gun, posted as air guard.

"I don't like all this dust we're kicking up," Jock said. "Makes us too easy to spot from the air."

Cockburn just shrugged. "It's *the dry,* sir. We'd kick up dust just walking on this trail. Do you want me to drive slower?"

Jock shook his head vigorously. "Hell, no! Let's get there as quickly as possible. We'll take our chances."

A far different conversation was going on in the bed of the lead truck. The shock had worn off, and the enormity of what he had just done was fraying Nackeroo Billy's nerves. Desperately, he searched for affirmation that the Dutchman's death at his hands was perfectly justified.

"But he had that money," Billy said, for perhaps the tenth time. "And he's a bloody German…"

In the most conciliatory tone he could muster, Doc Green replied, "There's a good chance he was Dutch, son, not German…and what happened was an accident. An unfortunate accident. Things like that happen in war. Nobody's blaming you."

Billy desperately wanted to believe Doc's words. They did nothing, though, to ease the tightness in his chest, the bitter taste washing into his mouth, or the rhythmic convulsions of his stomach. The look on his face gave him away; Doc knew the young man was on the verge of nausea. He managed to get Billy's head over the tailgate just before the heaves began. The others looked on with a mixture of sympathy, distaste, and relief. They were all thinking exactly the same thing: *At least he didn't puke on me or my gear, the poor bastard.*

At this pace, the ride to the drop-off point would take almost three hours. They had been on the road a little over an hour and were making their way through lush stands of eucalyptus trees, which provided excellent cover from aerial observation, even with the dust they left in their wake. This would be a great place for a piss stop.

"Don't get your willies bitten off by a croc, mates," Cockburn yelled as the soldiers climbed from the trucks.

That reminder—there was more to fear in the bush than the Japanese—gave Jock's men a moment's pause. All except Bogater Boudreau.

"Ain't gonna be no crocs around here," Boudreau said. "Not enough water to suit them."

All the same, the men looked around very carefully before selecting a spot of ground to anoint. Wordlessly, they went about their business, until a shriek cut through the air—and the *bup-bup-bup* of a Thompson's short burst.

The shriek had come from PFC Simms, one of Roper's team. He had backpedaled in terror so quickly he fell flat on his butt. Feet churning, he continued to scoot backwards while still seated on the ground. At least one bullet from his Thompson had torn into the long body of the python he had disturbed, lurking beneath a fallen tree. The wounded snake was now thrashing about in plain sight.

First Sergeant Patchett was red-faced with

annoyance. "DO NOT WASTE ONE MORE ROUND ON THIS CREATURE, ANY OF YOU," he said. "Simms, you get up now, before you piss yourself. That's just an itty-bitty ol' snake. He didn't bite you, did he?"

Doc Green stepped forward for a look. "No, he's not bitten," he said. "Wouldn't be poisonous, anyway. Pythons constrict you to death." He turned to the other stunned troopers. "Remember what I told you lads about snakes?" he asked, pointing to the fallen timber. "That was a perfect spot to find one."

Jock Miles shook his head in frustration. *It's never going to end, is it? Just one fucked up thing after another.* But it was time for him to take back command.

"All right, men," he said, "let's put the cocks away and get back on the road."

As they shuffled to the trucks, Bogater Boudreau broke away and returned to the writhing snake. In the blink of an eye, he cut its head off with his bayonet. "Hey, Doc," he called out, "can we eat this son of a bitch?"

The Doc's reply was a tentative, "Yes, you can, but—"

"Well, somebody come give me a hand, then," Bogater said as he tried to coil the still squirming body of the decapitated snake. End to end, it must have been 12 feet long. "I'm tired of them K rations already."

"Kiss my ass, redneck," Russo said from the truck's bed. "I ain't riding with no fucking snake. Dead or otherwise."

"I ain't no redneck, you stupid Yankee. I'm Cajun."

"KNOCK IT OFF," Jock said. "Boudreau, leave

the fucking snake and get in the truck."

Reluctantly, Bogater Boudreau complied. "Yes, sir," he said, "but I'm betting a couple of days from now some snake's gonna look mighty tasty."

They had only been back on the trail for about 15 minutes. At first, they all thought the airplane hadn't seen them. She wasn't very high—perhaps a thousand feet, Jock estimated—and kept heading north after her shadow rippled across the terrain ahead of the trucks. She vanished as quickly as she had appeared, obscured by the trees flanking the trail.

But the dust! He's got to see the dust we're kicking up.

Her pilot did see the dust. The Jap fighter descended and, turning in a tight circle to the left, set up for a head-on attack at treetop level. She came back into view leveling out of the turn dead ahead of them. She was rapidly growing in the windshield of the lead truck, as if planning to chop them all to pieces with her propeller.

Jock began to scream a command, but at that exact instant Russo opened up with his machine gun. The pounding noise of the gun, amplified by the thin metal roof of the cab on which it rested, was all Cockburn heard as he watched the rapid movements of Jock's mouth, issuing what must have been very emphatic orders. He had no idea what the American captain had just commanded, but Jock's hand reaching over and jerking the steering wheel to the right provided the answer. The truck departed the trail and bumped to a stop just as Japanese bullets plowed the dirt where they had just been. The second truck, its Bren Gun spitting bullets at the plane, left the trail in the opposite direction. It, too, escaped being hit.

As the Jap plane flashed overhead, close enough, it seemed, to touch the big red circles on the bottom of her wings, a chorus of Thompson submachine guns firing wildly upward added their noise to that of the two machine guns. As the firing died out, the sound of the plane's snarling engine could still be heard, but the trees blocked all sight of her once again.

"KNOCK IT OFF WITH THE THOMPSONS," Jock yelled to the men in his truck. "THAT'S NOT WHAT THEY'RE FOR. SAVE YOUR AMMO...LET THE THIRTY CAL AND THE BREN DO IT." He glanced across the trail and saw Melvin Patchett berating the men in his truck, no doubt delivering the same message.

"GET MOVING," Jock yelled to Cockburn.

"WHERE, SIR?"

"BACK ON THE TRAIL. WE'RE SITTING DUCKS HERE."

"I DON'T KNOW IF THAT'S SUCH A GOOD IDEA, SIR."

"WELL, I DO, CORPORAL. NO FUCKING TIME TO EXPLAIN. GET MOVING."

Sixty seconds later, the duel began again. This time, they saw the Jap fighter from a long way off, coming at them from the rear. Both air guards on the trucks started firing their machine guns. Contrary to their leaders' instructions, though, just about every other man on board the trucks began to discharge his weapon, too. Terror overrode fire discipline once again;

they simply couldn't help themselves.

She streaked over them without firing a shot in return. The sound of her engine changed. Its smooth rumble turned to the screech of rending metal for a few moments and then, with one final groan and a wisp of black smoke, fell silent.

She veered left and vanished from their sight, once again hidden by treetops. Over the noise of the truck motors, they couldn't hear the *crack* as she met the trees or the *crump* as she bellied into the ground far ahead. They drove for several minutes more before they found her. She sat in a clearing of her own making, crumpled but intact, some 50 yards off the trail. There was no post-crash fire. Her pilot was nowhere to be found.

"He can't have gotten far," Cockburn said. "Let's track him down."

"Negative," Jock replied. "We're getting back on the road."

From their faces, Jock could tell some of his men wanted to chase the pilot, too. It was time to nip that sentiment in the bud.

"Let me remind you we're on a recon patrol, men," Jock said. "The point is to *avoid* contact with the enemy so we can collect information *in secret*." He noticed Melvin Patchett was already checking the cockpit for any information they might use.

Cockburn still wasn't convinced. "But sir, he probably radioed where we are."

"All the more reason we don't want to be hanging around here, Corporal. Now everyone...mount up. I'm thinking we've got another hour on the road until our drop-off point. This is a big country. Let's get lost in it."

As the men climbed back into the trucks, Jock asked Patchett if he had found anything in the cockpit.

"Nah," the first sergeant replied. "They're pretty disciplined little bastards. They take all their garbage with them."

"Speaking of discipline, Top...how many rounds of Thompson ammo do you figure we wasted shooting at that plane?"

"Probably not as bad as it sounded, sir. Look at the bright side...at least they fired back, instead of crawling inside their helmets, crying for their mamas. Maybe we're learning them something after all."

Chapter Twenty-Seven

They bounced along the trail for another hour. They hadn't seen another airplane or another living soul the entire time. Now, looming ahead just as Jock had predicted was the sight they were looking for. It seemed completely out of place in this wilderness: a line of telegraph poles, running across the trail north to south, as far as the eye could see in either direction. A dirt trail wide enough for heavy trucks ran beside it.

"We reached these buggers just in time, Captain," Harry Cockburn said. "This is as far as we can go. Our petrol supply will be down to fumes by the time we get back." He pulled the truck under the cover of some eucalyptus trees and stopped.

Jock touched his finger to a spot on the map, *where a thin black line— a road, maybe just a trail—met a thin blue line—a river,* the same spot he had circled during that first mission briefing. The thin black line was the Telegraph Track, carved into the bush when they laid the telegraph wire to the northern end of Cape York in the late nineteenth century. As they looked to their right, they could see the track dipping sharply where it crossed a narrow span of the Wenlock River.

"Over by the river is the Moreton relay station, Captain. Of course, it's been evacuated, like everything up this way."

"Yeah, this looks like the place," Jock said. It was barely midday; Task Force Miles could cover a lot more ground on foot before the sun set. "What's at the northern end of this telegraph line, Corporal?"

"Japs, probably, sir."

First Sergeant Patchett dispersed the two scout

teams into a defensive perimeter. When he was satisfied with their placement, he joined Jock Miles, who was bidding farewell to Harry Cockburn. "Thanks for the ride, Corporal," Jock said. "I must admit I had my doubts about the mode of transport..."

"We've all got to make do with what we can find, sir," Cockburn replied as he offered a salute and a smile.

Melvin Patchett had his own words of farewell for the Aussie. "You watch your ass going back, son. Make good use of that Bren if you need to."

"Will do, First Sergeant. Good hunting to you!"

With a final wave from the Nackeroos, the trucks set out down the same trail from which they came, headed back to Temple Bay. As the sound of their engines faded and died, Jock's men were able to hear only the raucous noise of a thousand birds crying out all at once—until raised voices from the perimeter, where Russo's machine gun covered the Telegraph Track, added their own discord. Russo and Guess were at each other's throats once again.

"You're full of shit, Yankee," Guess said. "We was all firing at that plane. No telling who brought it down."

"None of you assholes stood a chance to hit it with them pop-guns," Russo replied. "Like the captain said, 'Let the thirty cal do it'...and I fucking did."

Now they were standing nose to nose. It only took a second for the shoving match to start and a second more for punches to be thrown. By the time Sergeant Hadley got to them, they were wrestling in the dirt. Hadley pulled them apart as Jock and Patchett arrived.

"Are you trying to get us all fucking killed?" Patchett said, his voice surprisingly calm. "Do either of you two idiots understand the term *noise discipline?*"

Russo directed his appeal straight to the captain. "But sir, ain't it more likely that I shot that Jap down?"

"For crying out loud," Jock said, "who can say who knocked that plane down? Could have been any of you...or it could have been all of you. Why don't we look at it that way? We all worked together...and we didn't have to bury anyone."

"Maybe the poor bastard just picked a bad time to have engine trouble," Patchett said. "I didn't notice any bullet holes on that wreck. Did you? With the amount of lead y'all flung at that thing, it shoulda looked like Swiss cheese."

They all had to admit the first sergeant was right. They hadn't noticed any bullet holes.

"Okay," Jock said, "let's forget about handing out medals for the time being and focus on doing our jobs before we all get our asses killed. Top, assemble the team leaders right here. Let's have us a little chat before we start our *walkabout*."

"*Walkabout?* As I live and breathe, sir, I do believe you've gone troppo on us," Patchett said.

Jock would have felt better if the first sergeant had laughed when he said it. He would have felt better, too, if that murderous look on J.T. Guess's face had softened to something more benevolent.

They walked for hours, heading west, making good time across the flat terrain. Sometimes they were beneath a canopy of eucalyptus trees, other times they crossed open ranges of sparse grass or low scrub.

Flying insects were everywhere, prompting some of the men to joke about *the Australian salute*—the constant need to swat flies away from your face. It was hot beneath the mid-afternoon sun. At Doc Green's suggestion, most wore their army green towel draped across their neck and used it often to wipe the sweat from their eyes.

The men were getting more confident about picking spots to cross streams and small rivers; twice they had spotted fresh water crocs submerged just below the surface and given them a wide berth. Like Doc Green had said, the fresh water variety, smaller than their vicious salt water cousins, usually didn't attack humans unless provoked. The soldiers kept their distance, anyway.

Sergeant Roper's team led the column, with J.T. Guess as point man. It made good sense to have the boy from the backwoods of north Georgia as the first man in the entire column. He was used to moving swiftly and stealthily through the woods, stalking game while avoiding Mother Nature's deadly pitfalls. He seemed more aware of his natural surroundings than any of the others. In the Army, that was called *terrain appreciation.*

As the sun began to lower in the western sky, they found themselves navigating a field of termite mounds. There must have been over a hundred of these spires of earth crowning the insects' underground nests. Some of the mounds were taller than a man. Corporal Jorge Pacheco had tried to count them all but gave up at 50. It was too hard to keep track of which ones he had already counted. The mounds seemed other-worldly, like something that belonged on some imaginary planet in a

Buck Rogers movie, and the thought of millions of insects so close unnerved him. *Please, God...don't let the captain lay us up for the night near these things.*

To Pacheco's relief, they pushed on. Later, when they came to a briskly running stream, First Sergeant Patchett put the corporal in charge of water purification. "Pa-*cheek*-o," Patchett said, "make sure every swinging dick puts a Halazone tablet in each and every one of his canteens. Don't need nobody getting the shits."

"Yes, First Sergeant, will do...But it's Pa-*chek*-o, not Pa-*cheek*-o."

"Hmm...that sounds kind of Russian to me, Corporal. I thought you were a Mexican."

"I'm a *New* Mexican, First Sergeant...and it's still Pa-*chek*-o."

The shadows grew long across the bush as the sun approached the horizon, looking like a shimmering tangerine hanging low in the sky. In a stand of trees stretching across a broad rise, Jock figured he had found his place to spend the night.

"What do you think, Top? Shall we set up camp here?"

"Looks good to me, sir. I'll give Hadley's team first watch. I'd better get them started on weapons cleaning, too, after that little firepower demonstration before."

"Get the machine gun cleaned and back in action first, Top, before we break any other weapon down."

Immediately, Jock felt silly for saying that. Even though Patchett's reply—"Affirmative, sir!"—was full of gusto, the look on his face said, *Do you really think you needed to tell me that? How dumb do you think I am?*

Patchett had it all organized in no time flat. Hadley's five-man team manned the star-shaped perimeter, each man digging in with his entrenching tool at a point of the star. Roper's team was assigned to dig what would double as sleeping and fighting holes for everyone else. They took to the task with much grumbling.

Jed Roper asked, "You ain't really gonna make us dig in just to catch some sleep, are you, Top?"

"You bet your sweet ass I am, Sergeant," Patchett replied, fixing Roper in a stare that would bore holes in steel.

"I suppose you want a latrine, too," Roper said.

"No need...Every man'll bury his own shit for now. Once those K rations start working their magic, you'll only be crapping a little pebble about once a week, anyway."

The radio team assembled their set in the middle of the perimeter. "Get us a position fix, Sergeant Botkin," Jock said. "I'm sure we're all dying to see just where the hell we are. I know I am."

PFC Billings, digging his hole on the perimeter, found he had some company watching him from a distance. "Hey, look!" he said. "Those are the first kangaroos we've seen since Brisbane."

Doc Green strolled over for a look. "No, those aren't kangaroos," he said. "But you're close. They're wallabies. See how they're shorter than the 'roos you're used to seeing down south...and with a thicker body, too?"

"Yeah, I guess so. They are smaller," Billings replied.

"Up here in the Cape, you won't see very many

kangaroos, if at all," Doc said. "But I'll wager those won't be the last wallabies we see."

Bogater Boudreau shook his head in aggravation. "I thought Australia was fucked up enough as it is, but then we come to the Cape where we've got crocodiles that ain't really crocodiles, kangaroos that ain't really kangaroos...Maybe we'll run into Japs that ain't really Japs, too."

Everyone in earshot found that funny except Doc Green. "Bogater," he said, "if the blacks side with the Japanese and take up arms, you just may be right about that."

Boudreau asked, "You think they will, sir?"

Doc held up his arms in a *who knows?* gesture. He took a step closer to Boudreau, his gaze fixed on the young Cajun's shoulder. There appeared to be a telltale stain on the shirt's fabric; his wound might be oozing. "Let's have a look at that burn, soldier."

"It's fine, sir. No problem."

"Let's look anyway."

Reluctantly, Boudreau removed his shirt. The bandage beneath showed tinges of red and yellow stain. "Damn," Doc said. "You sure you haven't been carrying anything on that shoulder?"

"Might have laid my weapon on it a couple of times while we was walking."

Doc grimaced as he peeled off the bandage. "I don't want you doing that. If this burn gets aggravated any worse, we're going to have big problems out here. I'll get my kit...we've got to get you patched up again."

First Sergeant Patchett, doing a check of the perimeter, stopped to join them. "We got trouble here?" he asked.

"Not yet," Doc replied.

The first sergeant didn't look convinced, but he had some wisdom to dispense. "Y'all listen up," he said. "It'll be dark real soon. Don't anybody go wandering around in the dark...not even to take a shit. Before you know it, you could be outside the perimeter, and one of your trigger-happy buddies is gonna shoot your ass." Patchett didn't wait for a response. He hurried away; there was much he needed to check on in the camp before nightfall.

Jock was startled to find how loud the *whir* of the radio's hand-cranked generator sounded out here in the bush. It hadn't seemed nearly as loud when he first heard it demonstrated back in the dayroom. Now he was sure the racket PFC Savastano was making as he spun the handles could be heard half a mile away. Botkin was busy at the telegraph key, alternately transmitting, then pressing the earphones to his head to better hear the reply. He and PFC McGuire had very serious looks on their faces as they worked with the code book to decipher the message. He kept the transmissions as short as possible; the Japs might be listening, and while they probably couldn't break the code, they had direction-finding capability, too.

"I've got three lines of position, Captain," Botkin said. "Not much radial spread between two of the stations but the third one is from *waaaay* out west at Mount Isa. They all say we're pretty weak...they had a rough time locking us in. These are their best guesses." He handed Jock a message slip with the three azimuths: *Mossman station: azimuth 325 magnetic. Iron Range station: azimuth 280 magnetic. Mount Isa station: azimuth 020 magnetic.* Jock went to work plotting them on his map.

The results were less than encouraging. Instead of the three lines of position converging at a single point, they formed a triangle with an area of about 15 square miles. The center of the triangle was some 25 miles east of Weipa. Task Force Miles was somewhere in that triangle. Probably.

"Shit," Jock said. "We need to be a hell of a lot more accurate than this to call in the bombers. I wonder how much of the error is being caused by this damned map."

Botkin offered a note of optimism. "Conditions might improve after dark, sir. Maybe on a higher frequency."

"Let's hope so, Sergeant. Let's fucking hope so."

Chapter Twenty-Eight

Jillian was exhausted; she had captained one of her boats today, taking the place of the usual captain who needed to care for his sick wife. It looked like she'd need to do that for a few more days, at least. She had just sat down to supper when she heard footsteps on her veranda. The dog sleeping on the kitchen floor raised his head, offering a grumble that was more curious than threatening before laying his head back down.

She met Nathan Gooreng at the back door before he even had a chance to knock. She hadn't seen much of Nathan, the foreman of Sato's Aborigine workers, since the last labor dispute at the airfield. His showing up like this couldn't be just a social call.

"Sorry to bother you, Miss Jilly," Nathan said, "but there is a problem. Again."

She invited him in. Though he hungrily eyed the food she had set out, he refused Jillian's offer to join her at the table, preferring to squat next to the dog and pet its head. He didn't refuse the offer of a cold beer, though. After quenching his thirst with a long drink that downed half the bottle, he began to tell his story.

"Our work for Mister Sato takes us farther and farther from our country," he said. "Soon, we will finish a road from Weipa airfield to the place of the next airfield. It will be farther south and more inland, on Coen River."

"That's over fifty miles from here, and it's nothing but bush," Jillian said. "How long does it take you to get there on this new road?"

"Nearly two hours. They have been driving us from here to there in Army trucks. But they say now that it is too far to do that every day, so they want us to live at the work site."

"For how long?"

Nathan shrugged. "Forever, I suppose."

Jillian stared vacantly into the mug of tea clasped between her hands. She needed to be thrust back into the role of peace keeper at this moment like she needed a hole in the head.

"Nathan, you know they'll kill you if you refuse."

"If they kill us, Miss Jilly, they'll have no one to do the work."

Jillian shook her head. "No, Nathan...they'll kill *you* first as an example to the others."

"If they kill me, the others will not work."

"But Nathan, you'll still be dead. I can't let that happen."

Deep in troubled thought, she began to pace the kitchen. She was running out of ways to placate Bob Sato, yet it fell to her once again to keep the threat of Japanese violence from becoming a reality. "Let me try to think of something," she said. "Now go home to your family, Nathan."

Jillian had been unable to eat another bite since Nathan's visit. Her mind was full of terrible images: Japanese soldiers burning black settlements to the ground; the wailing of terrified children; men being led off for slave labor, those refusing being killed on the spot; women being gang-raped.

What if those stories from China aren't such old wives' tales after all? Did it start the same way there?

No, it couldn't have...the Chinese actually tried to resist them from the very first, army pitted against army, with the people in the middle. Would it matter that Australia did not...no, could not...resist? Probably not.

She kicked the sideboard with a violence that set the alarmed dog to barking. Slowly, as if the weight of the world was pushing her down, she slid with her back against the wall to a seated position on the floor and buried her face in her hands.

A vehicle came to a stop outside; its driver shut off its motor. There were footsteps on the veranda once more, this time stopping at the front door. Bob Sato had come to call again. Standing in the fading light of day, he seemed nervous yet hopeful, scrubbed and groomed in freshly laundered clothes a tourist might wear, holding a spray of wildflowers in one hand like a young boy on his first date.

Jillian almost didn't open the door. She now felt a revulsion toward this man—this *Japanese* man—she usually reserved for the degenerates who roamed the Cape earning their living as croc hunters and livestock thieves. Yet he seemed so harmless; how could this innocuous looking man—this academic—hold so totally the fabric of her life and the lives of everyone she knew in those soft hands?

Tucked under his arm was a stack of phonograph records. "I brought Chopin," he said.

She rolled her eyes. *Chopin! How bloody romantic! I really am the only game in town, aren't I?*

With a cheekiness born more of exhaustion than wit, she asked, "What? No saké?"

His face broke into a broad smile. "Actually, I have some in the vehicle..."

"Well, leave it there, Bob. We're going to need stronger stuff than that tonight."

Once settled in the drawing room, Jillian broke out the dark Australian rum. Sato was a quick and easy drunk. She felt sure he wouldn't stand a chance against the rum's potency. *All I've got to do is get him drunk and he'll agree to anything. Of course, I've got to come up with a plan for him to agree to first.*

He placed a record on the Victrola and turned the crank. A Chopin etude began, its notes galloping merrily across the piano keyboard, conjuring images of children happily at play. Sato took delight in the precise, *allegro* rhythm of the piece, waving his forefingers like a conductor setting tempo as he returned to the couch. He took a sip of the rum, struggling to keep his smile as the dark liquid burned its way down his throat.

"This has quite a kick," he said, contemplating the glass he held in his hand.

"Oh, you bet it does, my friend."

She bided her time, letting him finish the first glass before saying, "There's some business we need to discuss, Bob."

Sato looked surprised. "Why, yes," he said, "there's something I need to discuss with you, too."

Refilling his glass, she said, "You go first, Bob. The floor is yours."

"I'm afraid I'll need your help again with the blacks, Jillian."

She played dumb and asked, "Really? What's the problem now?"

"We have a few too many of them. Our situation has changed in a most unexpected way. Since neither the Australian nor American armies have mounted any sort of challenge whatsoever…and seem unlikely to do so in the foreseeable future…our soldiers have become bored. We need to give them something to do before morale collapses completely. Colonel Najima has decreed soldiers will replace some of the black laborers. Work will bolster their spirits."

"How many blacks do you have to sack?" she asked.

He took a big swallow of rum before answering, "About a third."

She considered what he had just said as she swirled the rum in her glass, from which she had yet to take a sip. Her body might be tired, but her mind was still razor sharp. Bob Sato, on the other hand, was already glassy-eyed. It was time for Jillian to crank up the theatrics and move in for the kill.

"You miserable son of a bitch," she said, her enraged tone a very convincing job of acting. "All this big talk about your Greater East Asia Co-Prosperity Sphere. Total bullshit! First you jack these blokes up with your big talk and a fat paycheck, and now you want to kick them out on their arses. Just how do you plan to pick the one third who are out of luck?"

Sato's hand reached clumsily for her arm. She slapped it away. "Don't fucking touch me, Sato," she said. Even the sleeping dog awoke and began to growl.

Cringing, he offered an answer to her question: "I was hoping you'd help me determine who to sack."

Just a short while ago, he felt sure this was the night he would break through her silly excuses—*Oh, it will hurt, Bob! Boo hoo!*—and make passionate love to her. At the moment, though, he was more concerned with blocking any blow her hands or feet might deliver. But she just sat there, curled into her corner of the couch, glaring hatefully at him.

Jillian's expression slowly transformed itself into a satisfied smile, for Sato had just provided the answer she had been searching for ever since Nathan's visit. She grabbed a pad and pencil and began to construct a chart resembling a calendar. "I'm going to make your life very easy, Bob Sato," she said. "Have another drink while I do a little figuring here."

Looking ready to agree to anything she might suggest, he did as he was told. In a few minutes, Jillian had constructed a formidable-looking work schedule. Holding it up for him to see, she asked, "You've got about one hundred black laborers...most from Weipa, the rest from Aurukun, right?"

"That's correct," he replied, his speech now slurred.

"Good. As you can see, I've divided the work force into six crews."

He squinted at the chart. It was obvious to Jillian he couldn't see a blessed thing.

"I've set up each crew on a four-day-on, two-day-off schedule. On any given day, two of the crews...exactly one third of your work force...will be off. Your problem is solved and nobody gets sacked."

And you won't have about thirty angry blacks looking to rip your bloody head off, you stupid Jap bastard.

Sato didn't understand the chart, with its array of columns, rows, symbols, and arrows. He was much too drunk for any sort of mathematical reasoning. Now that the threat of physical violence seemed to have passed, all he could think about was what Jillian Forbes would look like without her clothes.

"This is wonderful, Jillian," he said. "A perfect solution." He took her hand—she let him this time—and kissed it.

"Ahh, that's sweet, Bob. Now, it's your turn to solve *my* problem."

A voice in Sato's head screamed, *Yes! She wants me to make love to her! I will solve your problem, my lovely white flower!*

Instead of peeling off her clothes, she began to write again on the pad. She was composing some sort of document. His euphoria sagged back to Earth like a punctured balloon.

Jillian thrust the pad in front of him. "Sign it," she said.

To his bleary eyes, the words looked as indecipherable as the work schedule she had drawn. After trying—and failing—to make any sense of them, he said, "I cannot read this."

"It's very simple, Bob. It affirms that you will not sack any of the black workers, and they will always be transported back to their countries to enjoy their two days off."

Sato tried to protest. "But the distances...the vehicles...we can't..."

"Oh, sure you can, Bob. You run trucks from the harbor here at Weipa down to your work sites all day and night. By the way, do you plan to move your whores down south, too?"

"No...the *comfort women* will stay at the Mission—"

"Excellent. The drivers who bring the blacks back

to Weipa can spend the night getting *comforted* and then bring the new shift back the next morning. Everybody wins." She thrust the pad at him again. "Now sign."

Sato took the pad and scrawled a rough approximation of his name across the bottom of the page. He leaned forward, trying to hand the pad back to her, but his sense of balance betrayed him. He toppled from the couch, and despite flailing efforts to arrest his fall, ended up face down on the floor.

Without lifting a finger to help him, Jillian asked, "Steady on, Bob! Are you all right?" Somehow, she managed not to burst out laughing as she said it.

He tried to get up, but for Bob Sato, the room was spinning crazily. The floor on which he lay was tilting back and forth, too. It felt so much better just to remain prone, his arms and legs splayed to grip the out-of-control gyroscope on which he was riding. He wouldn't try to rise again, not for a long time. The dog was now standing over him, licking the upturned side of his face. Whether this was a show of canine compassion or simply curiosity, Sato didn't know. But he was certain this was the most intimate act he would share with another living creature that night.

Jillian bounced up from the couch, retrieved a blanket and draped it over Bob's torso and legs. Smiling down at him, victorious once again, she asked, "How do you like your eggs in the morning, Bob?"

The thought of food made his stomach lurch. He struggled to fight off the bile rising in his throat.

"If you puke, you clean it up," Jillian said as she headed to her bedroom. "G'night, Bob. Sleep tight." She locked the bedroom door behind her.

Chapter Twenty-Nine

Walking carefully, Jock picked his way through the darkness to the radio set in the center of the perimeter. The red lens in his flashlight allowed little of its brightness to reach the ground before him. Twice he nearly stumbled over members of Roper's team as they caught some sleep before their turn on watch. Without the red lens, though, his flashlight would be a bright beacon in the bush at night, advertising his unit's presence for miles in all directions.

He finally saw the boxy silhouette of the radio console. As he drew near, he could just make out Sergeant Botkin's face in the dim, green glow of its dials. One of Botkin's hands pressed a headphone to his ear; his other hand alternately flipped the pages of the codebook and wrote feverishly on a pad.

It was strangely quiet around the radio set. PFC Savastano was poised at the hand generator cranks, but he wasn't turning them now. He stood at the ready, waiting for Botkin to tell him when it was time to crank again.

Before Jock could move any closer, the shape of a man holding a weapon at the ready stepped before him. "I challenge *Duluth,*" the man said just above a whisper, but the unmistakable Boston accent of PFC McGuire, the third member of the radio team, was still obvious.

"*Delicious,* McGuire," Jock replied. "I authenticate *delicious.*" Jock had selected passwords heavy with "L" sounds for this mission, in keeping with the folklore that Japanese could not pronounce the letter L. "Good job, McGuire. That's the way to challenge."

Moving past McGuire, Jock asked Savastano, "How are the receiver batteries holding up?"

"Pretty well, sir. The little we've been using this set out here, we'll be changing batteries about every two days."

"And you've got five spares, correct?"

"Yes, sir. Good thing we've got the wagons, because those bastards weigh about six pounds apiece."

"But you can't transmit without using the generator?"

"That's correct, sir."

Botkin pulled off the headphones. "Okay, sir," he said, "the Japs broadcast at twenty-two fifteen, just like clockwork. Their signal was strong as hell...almost blew my ears off...but what they're saying is still Greek to me. But they're not very far from here, that's for sure." He tore off the top sheet of his message pad and handed the decoded information from the American stations to Jock. "Here's the azimuths the DF stations got on both the Japs and us, sir. They reported our signal as much stronger than it was this afternoon."

"That's good news," Jock said as he spread his map across the radio's case. It took him a few minutes to plot the vectors in the glow of the red flashlight. He was mildly encouraged by what he saw as the lines converged on the map.

"Well, we've gotten our location nailed a little bit better," Jock said. While the vector lines to Botkin's transmitter didn't intersect in a single point, the triangle they formed was much smaller than before, only a few square miles this time. The lines to the Jap transmitter, with its much stronger signal, were far more precise. "That puts the Jap transmitter just about thirty miles west of us. Practically in Weipa."

"At least that's where it is tonight," Botkin said.

"That's right, Sergeant."

Perhaps it was just a trick of dim light and shadow, but the look on Botkin's face had changed. Normally earnest, it now seemed skeptical. He raised his hand to ask a question, just like he probably did in a schoolroom not so long ago.

"Something on your mind, Sergeant?"

"How do we know the Jap headquarters is located anywhere near that moving transmitter, sir?"

"We don't...but it's a pretty good bet they're not too far apart. That's what we're going to figure out."

Franklin Delano Roosevelt decided to take his after-supper coffee in the Oval Office. Exhausted and feeling unsociable, he wanted a few minutes alone to compose himself and organize his thoughts before General Marshall and Admiral King arrived for the nightly briefing. He very much wanted to seem upbeat and full of confidence to his war leaders. Lord knows he didn't feel that way at the moment. This war his nation was still incapable of waging was wearing at his soul.

By the time they arrived 15 minutes later, the president had transformed himself. Grinning broadly, he launched the briefing with the gusto of a much younger, much healthier man.

"The Australians are in a tizzy, gentlemen," FDR began. "Three of their east coast cities were bombed last night...or was it actually today? I can never get these time and date differences straight."

"The reports of damage and casualties were light, Mister President," Admiral King said.

Roosevelt's smile faded quickly. "That comes as little comfort to the people being bombed, Admiral. We can't let our allies lose faith. Every day that passes without an offensive action by our military makes us look increasingly irrelevant. Did we at least shoot down some of their planes?"

"We have no confirmed reports of that, Mister President," General Marshall replied.

"We'll be on the offensive very soon, Mister President," King said. "Our Navy's counterattack in the Solomons is on schedule for the end of September."

FDR couldn't help his sarcastic outburst: "Oh, hallelujah, gentlemen! Say a prayer that the Japs decide to stop where they are. In another month, they could be in Mexico."

"Unlikely, Mister President," Marshall replied. "The Japanese simply don't have the capacity to expand their defensive zone any further. They've captured all the resources they need…now they just want to hold on to them."

Roosevelt pressed his questioning. "And those interlopers on Cape York, General? Have they been expelled yet?"

"Our commandos were successfully inserted and are moving into position, Mister President."

"Ahh, so now they're *commandos,* are they? A few days ago, they were *a crack recon unit,* and before that, they were just ordinary soldiers. Was that MacArthur's idea? Using escalating vocabulary as a substitute for concrete action?"

"Mister President," Marshall replied, "what we call them is of little importance—"

"You're damned right about that, General. What matters are results. Do we have any results yet?"

"The mission is still ongoing, Mister President. We don't know—"

The president's fist slammed angrily on his desk as he said, "That's the trouble, gentlemen...we don't *know* anything. We need a victory...*any* victory...to give to the American people. Do I have to remind you the next election is only two years away? A new president can pick his own generals and admirals, you know."

Neither Marshall nor King said a word in reply, but their expressions were telling. Marshall was imperturbable as always, absorbing the president's dissatisfaction without a hint of emotion. King was sullen and irritated, chafing behind the bit of the one man on Earth who held authority over him.

Calm once again, the president said, "So I ask you one more time, General Marshall...will they have success expelling this mere handful of Japanese from Cape York?"

Marshall replied, "We suspect they will be successful, Mister President."

"I don't need your suspicions, General. I need your assurances."

Jock found it impossible to sleep. It wasn't the demands of his job keeping him awake or the fear that a Jap patrol might stumble into them. It was the sounds of the night, an incredibly loud assortment of diverse noises, shattering the impression they were alone in this pitch black wilderness: the calls of countless birds, the wind rustling the treetops, and the intermittent cries of unseen animals all played their parts in this natural symphony.

But there was more. His men were doing their best to add their own sounds, most unnatural in this wild setting and quite capable of bringing death and destruction down on all their heads. Coughing seemed to be contagious; first one man coughed, then two more, and in a minute, everyone within the perimeter joined in. Jock could hear First Sergeant Patchett moving around the perimeter, his words softly hissed and undecipherable, but Jock knew their message: *Keep fucking quiet, you morons!*

Someone had taken the first sergeant's warning not to wander out of the perimeter to heart. Jock could hear the man urinating a few yards away, the steady stream sounding like a babbling brook as it anointed hard ground and foliage. Other man-made sounds were interspersed, too: the *clack* of bolts being driven home as men cleaned and checked their weapons; the crinkling sound of a K ration's cellophane wrapper being torn open as some bored, hungry soldier—despite the need to make his rations last—helped himself to an unscheduled, late night snack; the loud *snap* as another snacker broke off a piece of rock-hard chocolate from a D bar. The occasional exchange of the challenge *Duluth* and the password *delicious* between comrades moving about in the darkness was made loud enough to be heard across the entire perimeter. Somewhere in the middle of the position, a soldier snored loudly.

Our noise discipline is pathetic. Might as well just

put up big fucking signposts pointing to our position.

If Jock couldn't sleep, he might as well check the perimeter. It was past midnight, so Roper's team would be on watch and Hadley's men would be catching some sleep. As Jock moved from point to point of the star-shaped perimeter, he found each of the first four points manned by a nervous but alert sentry. When he got to the fifth and final point, manned by Sergeant Roper, he found him dead asleep, his Thompson lying on the ground beside him. Jock picked up the Thompson before jarring Roper awake.

Feeling around him frantically, Jed Roper said, "Is that you, Captain? Where's my fucking weapon?"

"It's right here in my hand, Roper."

"That's *Sergeant* Roper, Captain."

"You won't be after the court martial," Jock said. "You were asleep at your post. I'm relieving you as team leader, effective immediately."

His defiant words still slurred by sleep, Roper said, "You gotta be crazy, Captain. You can't relieve me...not in the middle of all this. Not now."

"I just did, Roper. I'm putting Corporal McMillen in charge of the scout team."

Roper was wide awake now, shifting nervously in the fighting hole. Jock tossed the Thompson back to him. He caught it surely in one hand. "Stay alert," Jock said. "Dying in your sleep isn't all it's cracked up to be."

First Sergeant Patchett wasn't too surprised when Jock told him about Roper. "That boy's turned into quite a disappointment," Patchett said. He had the change of scout team leadership sorted out in short order. When he reported back to Jock, he said, "Once this last watch is over, I'm putting Roper under Hadley and shifting Pacheco over to McMillen's team. That okay with you, sir?"

"Yeah...that'll be fine, Top."

Patchett's tone turned fatherly. "Maybe if Roper changes his tune and does good out here, we can go a little easy on him, sir?"

"First Sergeant, he's going to have to win the fucking Medal of Honor before I change my mind about the court martial."

They were interrupted by a breathless Corporal McMillen. "Roper's gone, sir," McMillen said. "Guess saw him beat it into the woods. Took his pack with him and everything...might have even stole some rations from the other guys."

"Now the son of a bitch deserts," Patchett said. "Looks like the case for a court martial's getting stronger by the minute."

McMillen asked, "Shouldn't we go after him, sir? Suppose the Japs capture him and he tells them—"

"Absolutely not, Corporal," Jock said, cutting him off. "Nobody else is going anywhere. Top will get you another man for the perimeter."

A few feet away, the sleeping figure of Doc Green stirred and sat upright. "I'll do it," Doc said, reaching for his Thompson. "Let the other lads catch their beauty sleep. I've had more than anyone tonight."

Once Doc settled into the fighting hole Roper had abandoned, the ambient sounds of the night returned to their usual riotous melody. It stayed that way for five minutes, ten minutes, and maybe a few more, until the shrieks of a man in mortal terror sliced through the darkness, jarring even the sleeping soldiers awake. The shrieks were coming from somewhere to the east, well outside the perimeter but not very far away. They were from the same direction in which Roper had made his escape. They didn't last but a few seconds.

Without being told, Hadley's team joined McMillen's on the perimeter. So did the radio team. Every set of eyes peered into the darkness, expecting the whole of the Japanese Army to materialize out of the void. Suddenly, it was dead quiet; even the birds had gone silent. A man's whisper could be heard for 20 yards, a footstep in the crackling brush for a quarter mile. Yet they heard nothing. Only the dawn several hours later confirmed what they refused to believe in the darkness: they were totally alone.

In the new daylight, it didn't take long to find what was left of Roper's body. It was in a thicket just a few minutes of backtracking to the east. One leg had been torn off, his torso disemboweled, his face hideously disfigured and unrecognizable. The dog tags still hanging from what was left of his neck confirmed his identity. The pack had been ripped from his back but was otherwise undisturbed. It was indeed full of rations he had pilfered before going AWOL. His Thompson lay half-buried in the sandy soil, still unfired.

"Wild boars," Doc Green said as he examined the wounds. "He probably stumbled right over them."

Nicky Russo couldn't believe what he was hearing. "Fuck me!" he said. "It ain't bad enough we've got crocs and snakes and God knows what else...but we've got fucking killer pigs, too? Get me the fuck out of here!"

J.T. Guess said, "Pigs did us a favor."

"All right, men," First Sergeant Patchett said.

"Let's get our heads out of our asses. Police up his weapon and gear." He asked Jock, "What do we do with him, sir?"

"We bury him right here," Jock replied. "We can't have the Japs finding his body. They'll be doubly on the lookout for us then."

"Make the hole good and deep," Doc Green said. "We don't want any animals digging him up. We'll be right back where we started."

McMillen's team did the digging while the others provided security. Grimly, they slid his remains onto the ground sheet from his bedroll and lowered them into the hole. The bloody soil was used first to cover him. One of Roper's dog tags was left around his neck. Jock placed the other dog tag in his own pocket. When the burial was done, you couldn't tell this had been a place of death. Patchett made some marks with his bayonet—a cross with Roper's initials—in the bark of the nearest tree as Jock marked the location of the grave on his map. The location would be duly reported if and when they returned from this mission. Maybe Graves Registration would be able to reclaim the body at some point in the future, if the data from Jock's old and suspect map proved accurate enough to locate it.

When they headed west once again, their column shortened by one, a newfound soberness had settled over the men of Task Force Miles. Yesterday, they acted more like cynical, detached spectators to an unfolding drama; today they had become determined protagonists in that drama. Melvin Patchett smiled; he knew the phenomenon well. He said to Jock, "Look at them, sir…nothing tightens up a slack unit like planting one of their own in the ground." After a few more steps, he added, "Hell of a way to beat a court martial, though."

Chapter Thirty

They marched through the day, making good progress westward across the level, forested terrain. The only man-made sounds they heard were the ones they created themselves: the scuffle of occasional clumsy footsteps; the soft *clink* of metal hardware on a man's gear coming together; the hushed rumble of the *Radio Flyers'* tires along the ground.

As the afternoon wore on, a new sound began to rise out of the west: the faint hum of airplane engines, arriving in waves that seemed to flow right through the trees. "Sounds like a bunch of planes landing," Melvin Patchett said. "We've got to be awfully close to an airfield...and it sure as hell ain't one of ours. Can't be more than a couple of miles away."

"Yeah," Jock replied. "We've got about three hours of sunlight left. Let's see if we can put eyes on it before dark."

They advanced more slowly now, with Hadley's team in the lead and Bogater Boudreau as point man. Jock stayed near the front of the column, with Doc and the radio team in the middle between the two scout teams. First Sergeant Patchett brought up the rear, making sure there were no stragglers.

The last airplane engine sputtered and died. It was quiet again—so quiet every man could hear the beating of his anxious heart. Still they saw nothing but the trees. An old cliché crossed Jock's mind: *Can't see the forest for the trees. Can't see the damned Japs for the trees, either...and I sure as hell hope they can't see us.* The late afternoon shadows were growing longer. He checked his watch; almost an hour had gone by since the sound of the airplanes stopped. *And I'm betting we've only gone a mile in that hour.*

Suddenly, Boudreau, the point man, dropped to one knee, signaling with a raised hand for the column behind him to stop. The hand signal passed rapidly from man to man until everyone in Task Force Miles had stopped and made himself invisible, either prone on the ground or behind a tree. Even the army green *Radio Flyers*, camouflaged with vegetation refreshed regularly during the day's march, seemed to become part of the forest.

Jock low-crawled forward to Boudreau's vantage point. "The clearing up ahead, sir," Boudreau whispered. He didn't have to say anything else. A hundred yards in front of them there was a saddled, chestnut brown horse hitched to a tree. Using his binoculars, Jock saw clothes hanging from a low branch: a white shirt and dark green trousers, just like a Japanese officer would wear. On the ground below the clothes could be seen the tops of a pair of tall, brown riding boots. Just like a Japanese officer would wear.

Melvin Patchett crawled up alongside Jock and took a look through the binoculars. "What do you make of this, sir?" the first sergeant said as he took in the sight before them. "Some Jap making hisself croc bait?"

"I'm going to get a closer look," Jock said. "I'll take Hadley and Boudreau with me. Top, you hold position here with the others."

"Y'all be real careful now," Patchett said. "Come at him from around the other side so you stay downwind of the horse. Don't let that four-legged fucker's nose give you away."

"No shit, Top," Jock replied, trying to hide he hadn't considered the sensory abilities of the horse at all. "I'm just hoping that horse'll lead us to what we're looking for."

There was a slight rise at the far side of the clearing. It took Jock, Hadley, and Boudreau a good 10 minutes to get there, most of it in an adrenaline-fueled low crawl. By the time they neared the edge of the rise, their knees and elbows were bruised and sore, but they were too pumped-up to care. What they saw when they peered over the crest stunned them: it wasn't a Japanese officer at all but a white woman—damp and naked—drying herself after what must have been a dip in the small pond that filled the clearing. The three men were too startled for words. The last thing they had expected to lay eyes on this day—or any other, for that matter— was a nude goddess. Especially one who seemed so comfortable in a wilderness they found so totally alien. She took her time drying her hair before slipping back into clothes. The three issued a collective, barely audible groan of disappointment as the panties slid into place and another as her breasts hid beneath the undershirt she pulled down from over her head. The blouse and trousers, which from a distance looked so much like parts of a Japanese officer's uniform, bore no such resemblance at close range; neither did the broad-brimmed hat she placed on her head. Jock recognized the melody she whistled loudly as she dressed. It was Wagner: *O Du, Mein Holder Abendstern,* the beautiful but bittersweet aria of unrequited love from the opera *Tannhäuser.*

Once the men found their voices again, they could express their surprise only in hissed whispers. Tom

Hadley, his eyes still full of wonder, said, "I thought there wasn't supposed to be any white people here."

"Yeah, that's what they told us," Jock replied, trying to shake off his lustful bewilderment and figure out what to do next. Further muddling his thought processes was a voice in his head saying, *Wagner? Maybe that babe's a Kraut?*

Whatever sexual impulse Boudreau enjoyed was gone; he had the woman zeroed in his gunsight. "Maybe she's with the Japs," he said. "A nurse or something." He snugged his cheek against the Thompson's stock and wrapped his finger tight around the trigger.

"For God's sakes, Boudreau, don't shoot her," Jock said. "We've had enough people die for nothing already...and she might not be alone."

Indecision and sexual frustration had made Hadley jumpy. "So what the hell are we supposed to do now, sir?"

"We calm the fuck down and see where she goes, Sergeant."

"She's got a rifle hanging from that saddle, sir," Boudreau said, still squinting down his gunsight.

Jock took a quick glance at the rifle through his binoculars and managed to catch a magnified view of the woman's nether region, its contours etched distinctly against the tightly stretched fabric of her trousers as she bent forward to pull on her boots. "Looks like a hunting rifle, not military," he said. "Definitely not Jap. As long as she's not shooting it at us, we're okay."

The woman unhitched the horse, swung up into the saddle, and reined her mount to the west. After a few steps, she pulled the horse up and looked back over her shoulder, directly toward the stand of trees where Melvin Patchett and the rest of Jock's men lay concealed. In just a few seconds, she and her horse were headed straight toward Patchett's position at a brisk trot.

"Oh shit," Jock said, the horse and rider now between him and Patchett's group. "What the fuck is she doing? Come on…we've got to get back to the team."

Jock, Hadley, and Boudreau moved as quickly as they could and still maintain some semblance of concealment, but the woman on horseback was into Patchett's position before they got very far. From his vantage point some 80 yards distant, all Jock could see through the trees was the horse rearing up, the woman toppling to the ground, and green-clad shapes of his men pouncing on her. None of this happened silently. The horse whinnied loudly and continuously. The woman swore a blue streak at the top of her lungs—in English, with a decidedly Australian accent—before her angry words became muffled somehow.

We're fucked, Jock thought as he stood upright and ran the rest of the way, abandoning concealment for speed. *You can hear all that noise a mile away.* When he reached the melee, two of his men were sitting on the prone but wildly struggling woman, trying—and failing—to pin her flailing hands behind her back. Melvin Patchett crouched next to her, the skin around one eye growing puffy and turning vivid shades of purple. A field dressing had been stuffed in her mouth to silence her, but she managed to spit it out just as Jock joined the chaos.

"GET OFF ME, YOU FUCKING SONS OF BITCHES," she said as she ripped one of her hands from its restraining grasp and took an ineffectual poke at Patchett. "MAYBE I'LL BLACKEN YOUR OTHER EYE, TOO, GRANDPA."

Barely able to control his rage, Patchett said, much too loudly, "She had a weapon, sir."

Despite his desperate gestures to *keep it down,* Jock's words also came out much too loud. "All right...everyone, calm down! Simms, Mukasic...get off the lady. Now, miss, you've got to be quiet."

"Oh, bloody hell...you're Yanks," Jillian Forbes said, now sitting up and shaking with exasperation. "Now everything's going to go to shit." She spun around, anxiously looking for her horse but found Franz under control with J.T. Guess's steady hand holding the reins.

She leveled an icy glare at Jock. "And you must be the head wanker."

"Wait a minute," Jock said. "What do you mean by *everything's going to go to shit?*"

"Because you're going to try to fight the Japanese...and all of us who live here are going to pay the bloody price."

"We were told all whites had been evacuated," Jock said. "Do you really live here?"

"Well, whoever told you that was bloody wrong, wasn't he? Of course I live here...right over in Weipa. Imbeciles!"

"Look, miss...I'm really sorry we got off on the wrong foot—"

"That's a bloody understatement, Yank."

"Yeah, I know," Jock replied. "But I've got to

ask…how the hell did you see us?"

She pointed to the *Radio Flyers*. "Those big boxes sitting in the middle of the bush…are those really *kiddie wagons?* They caught my attention, you bloody idiot. The scrub you used to try and hide them…that doesn't grow around here."

"Listen…miss…my name is Miles. Jock Miles. I'm a captain in the US Army."

The rumbling of airborne engines rose again, this time from the east. A flight of Japanese Betty bombers—just like the plane they had tangled with off Cairns two days ago—passed low and slow overhead, minutes from landing. As Jillian caught a glimpse of them through the trees, a look of loathing spread across her face.

"Bloody savages," she said, shaking a fist at the planes. "I wonder what poor bastards they bombed today?"

Jock's manner became more soothing. "Okay, I told you who I am. Can I ask your name, miss?"

"Forbes. My name is Jillian Forbes."

Doc Green was examining the first sergeant's black eye when he heard Jillian say her name. He promptly did a double take. "Forbes," he said. "You wouldn't be related to Bull Forbes, would you?"

"He was my father. How on earth did you know Dad?"

"I was on a medical team that visited Weipa Mission about a dozen years ago. I was just a student in medical school. My name is Dunbar Green. I'm sorry…did your dad pass on?"

"Yeah, he did," Jillian said. Then her face broke into a smile. "I guess everyone knew Dad in these parts.

You know, I think I remember you. I was just a kid back then, of course, but weren't you a lady doctor?"

"Like I said, medical student, studying to be a gyno."

"Oh, yes," Jillian said. "A lady doctor. All the black women called you *Mister Happy Fingers.*"

Jock's men thought *Mister Happy Fingers* was a pretty good nickname for the doc. A few laughed out loud.

"Shut the fuck up," Melvin Patchett hissed at the laughing soldiers. "You want to bring the whole fucking Jap Army down on us?"

"Oh, I wouldn't worry about that, Grandpa," Jillian said. "Airfield Number One is about four miles east of here, and the Japs never patrol out this far. Not anymore."

Patchett's blackened eye was swollen practically shut now, making him look like he had a permanent squint. With gruff skepticism, he asked, "They don't patrol? Why the hell not, girlie?"

"Too many of them became croc food," she replied. "Why the hell do you think I carry a rifle? And by the way...do you really think I hit like a girl?"

Jock had another concern. "You said 'Airfield Number One.' There's more?"

"Yep," Jillian replied, "Airfield Number Two is almost finished. It's about fifty miles south. And they plan to keep building them farther and farther south until they can bomb Brisbane...even Sydney." As she spoke, she mentally counted the men in Task Force Miles. "Is this the lot of you?" she asked.

When no one would offer an answer, she added, "Well, you can keep it a secret if you like, but I'm telling you...what you've got here is not nearly enough of you to take on a regiment of Japs."

"A regiment? We've been told only a few hundred of them are on Cape York," Jock said.

Jillian chuckled as she shook her head. "A few hundred? Oh, no, Captain. Try again. It's more like a few *thousand.* That's a regiment, I believe."

Ever the skeptic, Melvin Patchett was the first to voice what the others were thinking. "How the hell do you know all this, sweetheart?"

Raising two fingers in the V sign, knuckles out, she flicked Patchett off—the Commonwealth equivalent of the raised middle finger in the US—and then reached into her pocket and triumphantly held out Bob Sato's business card. "I know because this wanker told me."

Patchett snatched the card from her hand, glanced at it while shaking his head in rejection, and passed it to Doc Green. Doc examined it, remained poker-faced, and passed it to Jock, who quickly decided *maybe we should listen to what this young lady has to say.*

She proceeded to tell them the whole story of the Japanese occupation. They weren't surprised to find the Aborigines working for the Japs. She made a compelling case why the people of Cape York cared not a whit about the military misfortunes of Australia, a nation whose government alternately harassed and ignored them.

Despite Patchett's initial grumblings of *collaborator* and *profiteer,* they ultimately accepted that Jillian had little choice but to do what she had done. Her flatly stated rhetorical questions were convincing enough: "What the hell was I supposed to do? Get us all bloody killed?" She sealed her logic with an irrefutable statement: "It's not like any of you blokes were around to help out."

They chuckled when she described Sato's attempts to have it off with her. It took more than a few grains of salt for them to accept the Japs were trying a cheap bluff to take Australia out of the war. But they shook their heads in disbelief when she related there had only been one incident of violence—and a minor one at that—by the Japanese against civilians on Cape York. Doc Green found that detail especially hard to swallow.

"I've been *north of Alice*, Jillian," Doc said, "and I've been to New Guinea. I've seen the brutality the Japs are capable of."

"But they haven't done it here," she said.

Doc raised an eyebrow. "Not yet, dear lady," he replied. "Not yet."

Shaking her head wistfully, Jillian said, "Maybe so, but you're the only soldiers who've pointed a gun at me so far."

She had been so involved in telling her story, she lost track of time. Only now did Jillian realize the sun was about to set. "Shit! It's too dark to get back home," she said.

"How far do you have to go?" Jock asked.

"Too far...almost five miles. It's much too dangerous to be roaming about in the dark. That's how we lost Dad."

"Yeah, we know about the dark," Jock said. "We lost a man last night...to wild boars."

"That's awful," she replied, her words deeply sincere. "So you know what I mean."

Doc Green had a question. "What were you doing out here, anyway, Jillian?"

"I'd been out on one of my boats all day and stunk of fish. I needed a ride and a bath." She pointed toward the pond in the clearing. "That's the only fresh water pool around here the crocs don't fancy."

"Yeah, we saw it," Jock said.

"Wait a minute," she said. "You saw *it?* Or you saw *me?*"

Jock replied with just an embarrassed smile.

"You cheeky little bastard," she said, but with a smile, too. "Now that you've seen the big show, how about some tucker? My horse eats grass, but I don't...and I'm starving."

Nobody in Task Force Miles could quite believe that Jillian Forbes loved the taste of K rations. She had wolfed down every crumb of a meal package, even consuming the entire bitter D bar with great glee. "These are wonderful," she said, smearing the last of her canned cheese on a cracker. "I don't know what you Yanks are complaining about. Can I have more for later?" Happily, she stuffed the ration packages they offered into her rucksack.

Task Force Miles—and their female guest—settled into their defensive perimeter for the night. J.T. Guess turned out to be a godsend in dealing with the horse. "Don't you worry about old Franz, miss," Guess told Jillian. "I've got him calmed down just fine."

Watching as Guess and the contented animal relaxed in a patch of low grass, Melvin Patchett said, "Us good ol' boys sure know how to handle our animals." As he walked off to check the perimeter, he mumbled to himself, "But that young woman...she needs a good horse-fucking. That'd calm her down right quick."

While Botkin fired up the radio for the nightly position fix, Jock and Jillian were deep in discussion. He had decided to divulge the nature of his mission and to ask for her help in pinpointing the Japanese headquarters. In the dim shadows cast by the red flashlight, Jock could see the distress etched into her face.

"Can you stop them from bombing the cities?" she asked, her words more a plea than a question.

"If it makes it any better," Jock replied, "their bombing hasn't been very effective."

"No, Jock...that doesn't help a bit."

"If we're successful, the bombing will stop...and the Japs should be gone."

"But I need to keep the blacks safe," she said. "This isn't their war...they don't deserve to be caught in the middle. Promise you'll tell me what's going to happen so I can keep them at a safe distance?"

"You have my word, Jillian."

She considered his answer for a moment. Then she crawled into the borrowed bedroll laid out for her next to Doc's and closed her eyes. "I'll draw you some maps in the morning, when I can see what I'm bloody doing." Against Patchett's wishes, Jock let her keep her rifle at her side. But it had been the first sergeant's idea to bunk her next to Doc Green, telling Jock, "Doc can look after his little Aussie hellcat so I don't have to."

As Jock started to move away, Jillian's voice called to him in the darkness. "Jock, I'll take you at your word...but don't cross me on this. Please."

In the darkness, she couldn't see his smile as he replied, "That's funny...I was just going to ask you the same thing."

"Then we understand each other," she said.

As Jock plotted the azimuth vectors Botkin had handed him, Melvin Patchett whispered, "I still don't trust her, Captain. Don't you be thinking with your pecker, now. If we let her go, she could run straight to those Japs she's so chummy with."

"Duly noted, Top, but if she's on the level, she can save us a whole lot of trouble. And I'm pretty damned sure she's on the level. If she's not...we're really not much worse off, are we? We've still got this big ol' peninsula to hide our peckers in."

Patchett didn't look convinced, but there was no doubting his sincerity as he replied, "As you wish, sir."

Chapter Thirty-One

Jock Miles snapped awake to a variety of sounds. The first was the drone of many aircraft engines revving up in the distance. The second was the alarmed whinnying of Jillian's horse. The third was the sound of men brawling.

In the pre-dawn glow, Jock could just make out Guess and Russo going at it again. They were standing, each with a two-handed grip on the same entrenching tool, trying to wrest it from the other. If one of them succeeded, he would no doubt try to beat his opponent senseless with it. As Jock raced closer, he noticed they were smeared with some dark, gooey substance. Jillian had the reins of her frightened horse firmly in hand, leading the creature away from the fighting men.

At the sight of their commander, the two troopers stopped fighting and snapped to attention as the entrenching tool fell to the ground. From the look of their fatigues, they must have rolled through a pile of horse excrement. Without waiting to be asked, Nicky Russo stated his grievance. "This dumbass cracker made that horse take a shit right in my hole."

"Did not," Guess replied. "A horse gonna shit where he wants. If you don't like it, Yankee, here's the fucking shovel." He kicked the entrenching tool into Russo's shins.

Jock could hear the irritated words Jillian was mumbling: "And this is the army that's going to save us?" He could only assume she said it to the horse.

Russo didn't retaliate; he didn't move from attention at all, despite the painful blow to his shins. But his voice took on a menace Jock had never heard from him before when he said, "I'm going to kill this fucking redneck...maybe all you fucking rednecks...if it's the last thing I do."

Melvin Patchett's icy voice spoke softly from somewhere behind Jock: "I'd think real careful about what the next words out of your mouth are going to be, son." Patchett laid a hand on Jock's shoulder. "I'll get these two touch-holes straightened out and cleaned up, Captain. You've got more important things to do."

Jock and Jillian settled into those *more important things.* While delightedly wolfing down a K ration breakfast, she asked, "Are things always this cocked up in your army?"

Jock's smile was bittersweet; he'd asked himself that same question many times before. Trying his best to sound flippant, he replied, "Actually, this is a pretty good start to the day."

She began to draw diagrams of the Japanese facilities around Weipa in Jock's notebook. "You say you want to bomb their headquarters," she said while sketching a rough layout of Airfield One. "It's on this airfield somewhere, I'm sure, but Colonel Najima, the regimental commander, is never there at night. He spends his nights here,"—she turned back to the diagram of the Weipa Mission and pointed to a big rectangle—"at the knocking shop."

Seeing the confused look on his face, she elaborated. "Knocking shop. Brothel. Whorehouse. The Japs bring in their own prostitutes. They call them *comfort women.*"

"Hmm, that's interesting," Jock said. "Are there a lot of troops in the Weipa Mission?"

"Not really. There's a small guard detail at the

whorehouse…maybe a dozen men…plus a fair mob of eager lads having their naughty around the clock."

"It sure sounds like there's a lot of nightlife in Weipa," Jock said. "Don't the Japs black the place out at night?"

Jillian shook her head. "There's no need. Weipa's not exactly a big, bright city, Jock. There aren't many lights there in the first place. The only electricity is at my icehouse, from my own generator. Everything else is oil lanterns."

She took Jock's map and drew a line running south from Weipa. She pointed to the line's southern end. "With Airfield One up and running, the colonel spends most days here, supervising the construction of Airfield Two. Once that's done, I'm sure he'll move south again to wherever they decide to build Airfield Three, probably halfway to Mitchell River. Now this line represents the road they've built to link the airfields. We call it Yellow Vermin Road."

"Very appropriate name. How many men are at Airfield One?" Jock asked.

"Not sure…a few hundred, maybe?"

Melvin Patchett approached and took a seat on the ground with them. There was enough light now to see his eye was still a vivid purple. "Good morning, Grandpa," Jillian said, her eyes twinkling mischievously. "How's the shiner?"

"I've had much worse, young lady."

"Ooo, now it's *young lady*," she said with delight. "Yesterday, it was just *girlie.*"

Jock almost burst out laughing but caught himself just in time. Quickly changing the subject, he asked, "Have you seen their radio station? You know…their wireless? I'm not talking small tactical sets—"

"Like the ones on your kiddie wagons?" she asked.

"Right. Not like those. I mean a big, high-powered wireless."

"Of course I've seen it," she replied. "Everyone has. It's on a truck. Some nights they park it right in the middle of the Mission and string up that big wire aerial of theirs."

"How do you know there's just one truck?" Patchett asked.

"The vehicle numbers are painted on, *First Sergeant,* and they're always the same." Despite her sarcastic tone, she nodded respectfully as she spoke his rank.

"Hmm. I guess that makes sense," Patchett said. "The headquarters stays put. Only the transmitter moves. Good way to confuse our Air Force."

"It's worked for them so far," Jock said.

Jillian went back to work marking the map. "Let me give you some landmarks so we can meet and exchange information. I don't expect you'll want to be strolling into Weipa to talk with me." After putting a name on every river and creek, she said, "Be careful around water from here to the shore. The crocs you'll run into are deadly. Shoot them in the head if they're coming for you. That's your only chance."

Jock asked, "You mean salt water crocs?"

"Exactly. The worst kind. I've had to shoot a few in my time. We suspect they're what got my dad. Don't play around with the snakes, either. They'll kill you, too. It just takes a little longer."

"Yeah," Jock said, "Doc briefed us on the wonders of nature around here."

"But look at the bright side...the fishing's wonderful! Maybe we can figure out a way to get you blokes a seafood dinner?"

Jock looked into the K ration package he was eating with little enthusiasm and said, "That would be really great."

The hum of aircraft engines at Airfield One turned into a rasping growl as Jap planes took off for the day's sorties. Jillian scowled and flicked a V sign in the direction of the airfield. "Bloody bastards," she mumbled, and then went back to marking the map. "These are the red cliffs, a few miles east of the Mission," she said. "If you ever need high ground, that's all there is around here. And these are the middens..."

"What are they?"

"Mounds of shellfish remains. The ancient blacks piled up what was left of the shellfish they ate for centuries. Now, over here is an abandoned black settlement...or what the termites left of it. Meet me there tonight, before dark. About seventeen hundred hours, okay? It'll be a safe place for your blokes to camp out."

"Okay," Jock said. "By the way, do you have any topographic maps of this area?"

"No...but I've got nautical charts from here to the Solomons. A cabinet full."

Trying to rein in his rising hopes, he asked, "How far inland do they cover?"

"A couple of miles."

"So Airfield One and Two's locations would be on the charts?"

"Sure."

Jock delivered the big question: "How up to date are these charts?"

"As up to date as they can be," she replied. "I just got new ones a few months ago."

"Good. Bring them tonight."

Dawn had broken. Jillian took the notebook again, opened it to the Weipa Mission diagram, and pointed to a spot on its edge. "This is my house, the only Victorian for a hundred miles...but promise me you won't mark the location..."

"In case this notebook happens to fall into Jap hands?" Jock asked.

She nodded, grateful that he understood her concern so instinctively.

"Look, Jock...I've got to get home. I'm already late. I've got to captain one of my boats again today."

"Hey, before you go...can I ask you one more thing, Jillian?"

"Sure."

"The Wagner piece you were humming yesterday..."

"Oh, bloody hell...you mean when I was naked?"

"Yeah. That one. Wagner's my favorite composer. Are you a fan, too?"

"When he suits my mood," she replied. "But I'm always partial to Liszt."

"Ahh, so you're a romantic, Jillian?"

"Yeah, that's me. Romantic as all bloody hell."

From where Melvin Patchett sat, it certainly looked like they were flirting.

Chapter Thirty-Two

Her horse seemed genuinely delighted to finally be out of the bush and back home in its paddock. Jillian was no less thrilled as she walked through the back door of her house. Setting the rifle in a corner of the kitchen, she flung the rucksack onto the table and pulled off her boots. It would feel so wonderful to have a quick sponge bath and put on clean clothes, at least for a short while. In no time, she'd be back on the boat and mucked up all over again.

Her blouse was already in a crumpled ball on the kitchen floor as she passed into the drawing room, momentarily sightless as she pulled the undershirt over her head. The sound of an unsteady yet belligerent voice stopped her cold in her tracks: "Where the hell have those tits been all night, *Miss Jilly?*" She didn't need her eyes to know it was Bob Sato's voice. She quickly pulled the undershirt down over her torso.

He was seated on the couch, quite drunk. An open saké bottle lay on its side on the floor before him, quite empty. He had gotten into her liquor cabinet, too. Open bottles of whiskey and dark rum sat on the table beside the couch. With the amount of liquor he had apparently consumed, Jillian was amazed this easily inebriated little man was still conscious. He rose from the couch and began to stagger toward her.

Bloody hell! He can stand up, too.

"I asked you a question, *Miss Jilly.*"

"You can shove your bloody question right up your arse. Get the hell out of my house."

He kept coming. "Finding comfort in another man's bed? A black man's bed?"

"GET THE FUCK OUT OF HERE, BOB!"

She turned to hurry back to the kitchen—and her rifle—but he was on her with surprising speed. He grabbed her hips and tried to pull her back to him in a clumsy caress, but she spun and cracked him firmly across the jaw with a flying elbow. He staggered, released his grip on her, but didn't go down. She ran to the kitchen, her socks sliding across the hardwood floor until she crashed headlong into the corner where the rifle stood. But the relief of having the weapon in her hands faded in an instant.

If I shoot him, they'll know I did it. I might as well shoot myself, too.

She needed to get out of the house. The back door was closest; Sato was somewhere between her and the front door. She tried to move, but what she saw on the table froze her in her tracks: spilled from her rucksack, in plain view, was a K ration box.

When she looked up again, Sato was standing in the archway of the kitchen entrance, leaning against its structure to steady himself. His eyes fell on the thin cardboard box, too, its black lettering bold enough to be read even by a drunken man 10 feet away: US ARMY FIELD RATION K. It took no time at all for the meaning of the little box's presence to sink into his drunken head. Once it did, the jealous anger he felt was stoked to murderous rage. He pulled out the Nambu pistol concealed beneath his jacket and stepped forward, blocking her path to either door.

With his free hand, he picked up the K ration box, waving it unsteadily before him like some scolding pendulum. At first he said nothing; the fierce look on his face was already speaking every hateful, corrosive word one human being could hurl at another. But after a few moments, his feelings of lust, betrayal, and rage finally coalesced and spat forth their acidic brew:

"So the Americans feed you as well as fuck you?"

He took an unsteady step into the kitchen, then another. He tried pointing the Nambu in her direction, but his movements were so shaky and uncoordinated the pistol was just as much a danger to himself as to her.

Her dilemma—*I can't shoot him! They'll know it was me!*—was solved in a rush of revelation: a hunting rifle can have more than one dangerous end. The stock, too, can be a powerful weapon when the rifle is swung by the barrel like a club. That stock met Sato's bewildered face with terrifying force before he could take another step.

He backpedaled out of the kitchen into the drawing room, the motion of his legs more like those of a crazed marionette than a man. His balance became more precarious with each faltering step. Jillian watched in what seemed like slow motion as his heels finally lost their purchase and he toppled over. Halfway down, the back of his head struck the edge of the piano's keyboard cheek with the sound of a melon being cleaved by an ax. His lifeless body crumpled and hit the floor with a dull *thud,* like a sack of potatoes being dropped.

At first, she had no recollection of rolling his body onto a blanket and dragging it out the back door, down the steps, and into the fodder bin. When her cognition returned, she was on her knees, wiping the last of Bob Sato's blood from the floor beneath the piano. She froze in horror as the whole sordid scene replayed in her head, right up to the mighty swing of the rifle. She remembered nothing after that. But by the look of the crimson-tinged rags and water in the bucket, someone had surely been mortally wounded in this house.

But where the bloody hell is that little bastard?

Then it all began to come back, little pieces at a time, in no specific order. As if by intuition, she retraced her steps to the fodder bin. Using the pitchfork, she gingerly lifted the pile of feed—and saw the face of Bob Sato. That same look of bewilderment that greeted the rifle stock's blow was still there, but his eyes had taken on the lifeless quality of a fish too long out of water. She lifted the pile a bit more and found his Nambu pistol resting on his chest. Right where she must have put it. There was no point poking the body with the pitchfork. Bob Sato was dead. She had killed him.

And I've got to get this body out of here before his little mates come looking for him.

Back inside the house, as she gathered the K ration packages, the rags, and the bucket, the grandfather clock chimed 7:30. *Shit! We should have been out on the water by now.* The clothes she wore, still grimy from yesterday's adventures, now displayed the same incriminating blood stains as the cleaning rags. She'd need to burn them all before showing her face at the Mission.

Chapter Thirty-Three

The never-ending clash between Nicky Russo and J.T. Guess wasn't the only personnel problem facing Jock Miles that morning. Doc Green had some bad news: Bogater Boudreau had awoken weak and listless. The wound on his shoulder had festered. Doc Green administered a knockout dose of antibiotics, but Boudreau was unfit for duty. His strength was sapped.

"This is what can happen to wounds in the tropics," Doc said. "He'll need to take it easy for at least a couple of days and stay on antibiotics."

Jock barely managed to keep the frustration those words triggered at bay. "Easy?" he said with a sarcastic snicker. "Nothing's going to be easy from here on in."

A new concern popped into Jock's mind. "Are you treating him with penicillin instead of sulfa powder?" he asked Doc Green.

"Yeah, I've got no choice now," Doc replied.

"As little penicillin as we've got, I thought we were saving that for really serious wounds."

"How serious would you like his wound to get, Jock? The sulfanilamide didn't do the job against the infection. Another day without penicillin and we'll have to carry him everywhere..." Doc's voice dropped to a whisper only Jock could hear to add, "...until maybe he dies. We knew we took a risk bringing him out here. We gambled...and lost."

For once, Bogater Boudreau didn't argue and insist he could do the job. He sat sullenly against his pack, his face sallow, picking at the food in a K ration package. They hadn't even met the enemy on the ground yet, but already nature had conspired to decrease their number by two.

"This kind of screws up our plan for the day, sir," Melvin Patchett said. "If you're gonna take Hadley's team with you, you'd better pick up another man from McMillen, too."

"Yeah...I'll take Guess."

The look on Patchett's face made it clear he didn't think much of that idea. "Are you sure about that, sir?" he asked. "That'll put him with Russo. Just a little while ago, they were ready to beat each other's brains in."

"Yeah, I'm sure, Top. After what that Forbes woman said, I've been thinking about the Jap colonel's nightly habits. We might need ourselves a sharpshooter...and we have no one better than Guess. I want him to see the target area in daylight first."

Nothing Jock said erased the disapproving look from Melvin Patchett's face. If anything, the disapproval grew stronger. But all the first sergeant said was, "As you wish, sir."

The plan for today's recon was simple: Patchett would set up camp at the abandoned Aborigine settlement Jillian had identified. He would keep the radio team and Doc Green with him and use McMillen's team for perimeter security. Even Boudreau could help out by manning a perimeter fighting hole. Someone else would have to dig it, though.

The camp would be a little over a mile east of Airfield One. Jock would take Hadley's team—now with Guess replacing Boudreau—and advance farther, all the way to the edge of Airfield One. That would involve crossing Yellow Vermin Road—a potentially risky proposition in daylight—but what about this mission wasn't risky? Once at the airfield, they'd get a map fix on the Japanese headquarters for the bombers, who would attack—hopefully—the next night.

Something else had been on Jock's mind ever since this morning's discussion with Jillian. *We're supposed to pinpoint their headquarters...but what is a headquarters, anyway? Is it just the tent or building the commander works in? Or is it the commander himself? The bombers will come at night...but according to Jillian, the colonel will probably be shacked up with some government-issue whore in the middle of Weipa Mission, a couple of miles away. We can't very well call in the bombers on the Mission...too many innocent black people will get killed. But when the bombs start to fall, that should draw the colonel out...and we get him, too, right there, with a sniper's bullet.*

Then...we run like hell. Mission accomplished. In total. Ding-dong the colonel's dead. Isn't that what they really meant when they told me to "cut the head off?"

Jillian was surprised to see all her boats still at the dock at nearly 8:30 in the morning. Old Robert offered the explanation: "We were worried about you, Miss Jilly. Theo went by your house at sunrise and saw Mister Sato on the veranda. He looked very drunk...and there was no sign of you."

"Well, he's not drunk anymore," Jillian said, looking around to make sure no Japanese were in earshot. "He's dead. I killed him...and now I need your help."

No words were necessary from her black crewmen.

It was obvious from their demeanor: as always, they were ready to do anything for Miss Jilly.

"Listen," she said, "When we're done here, I'll take out *Mapoon Maiden.* The rest of you, cast off now, just like nothing's wrong."

As the other four boats cranked their engines, Jillian told the four-man crew of *Mapoon Maiden,* "Fill a wagon with some fish and ice. We'll take it up to my place and swap the fish for the body, then we'll bring it back here and hide it in the icehouse for the day. Tonight, after it's dark, we'll feed it to the crocs."

Yellow Vermin Road was more than just a dirt trail carved through the eucalyptus forest. It was a major thoroughfare, two lanes wide and heavy with traffic. Jock and the men of Hadley's team heard the noise of the road's traffic well before they saw it. Just beyond that thoroughfare lay Airfield One.

"I wasn't expecting the traffic to be quite this thick, sir," Sergeant Hadley whispered to Jock as they crouched in thick undergrowth 50 yards from the road's edge. Trucks of every type passed in both directions, kicking up clouds of thick dust in their wake. Some were heaped high with supplies and construction equipment; others towed artillery pieces or carried troops and Aborigine workers. Tanker trucks shuttled gasoline from lighters at Albatross Bay to the airfield.

"I wasn't expecting it, either," Jock replied, swatting away a swarm of mosquitoes from his camouflage-darkened face with a similarly darkened hand.

"These fucking flies," Hadley said, doing some swatting of his own. "This insect repellant they gave us isn't worth a shit, sir. We're all going to get malaria."

"Ever the optimist, eh, Sergeant? Now let's stay focused...We still can't see the airfield from here. We've got to get closer. Got to find a way across this road."

Tom Hadley had an idea. "Maybe if we head south along the road, past the airfield, the traffic will thin out and we can slip across."

Jock liked that idea; he had been thinking exactly the same thing. "Sounds good, Sergeant. Let's try it." Hadley issued a flurry of hand signals, and the dark green shapes of Privates Russo, Guess, and Billings, their faces and hands blackened with camouflage, seemed to materialize out of nowhere and began to move south without making a sound.

Hadley was right. After nearly an hour of creeping through the forest, they had moved past the airfield, and the traffic volume had dropped significantly. Those vehicles continuing south to the construction site for Airfield Two were fewer and farther between. Sometimes, there was no traffic at all for several minutes.

Hadley, very eager to be on the other side of the road, asked, "Should we cross all at once, sir?"

"Negative," Jock replied. "We go one at a time." His reasoning was simple: *if there's a shit storm waiting for us on the other side, we don't die all at once.*

The last in a line of trucks passed. Guess crossed first, quickly vanishing into the thick trees. A minute later, he popped back into view and signaled *all clear.*

Hadley went next, followed at intervals of several seconds by Russo, Billings, and Jock. They huddled to formulate the next part of the plan.

Russo seemed perplexed by their good fortune so far. He asked, "How come these Japs ain't patrolling, Captain?"

"Good question," Jock replied, "but they must have *some* kind of security. We just haven't run into it yet. Listen up...we'll push north now, towards the airfield. Judging by how quiet it is, most of the planes are probably gone. We may not see much through these trees until we're right on top of it. Everyone stay alert."

As they started moving again, Jock scolded himself. *Stay alert? For crying out loud, Miles...do you really think you needed to say that? Their eyes have been wide as pie plates all morning. They couldn't be more fucking alert. Try not to sound like some jackass shave-tail. They deserve better than that.*

They had only moved a few hundred yards when Hadley, who was now walking point, signaled the team to halt. As Jock moved forward to Hadley's position, the reason for the halt became obvious: there were 50 yards more of thick, shady forest before them, and after that, the world was suddenly much brighter. They were coming to a clearing—a very big clearing. Big enough to be a runway.

"I think we're at the south end of the airfield, sir," Hadley said.

Jock took a look through his binoculars, then handed them to Hadley. "Look two fingers to the right of the split tree," Jock said.

"Holy shit," Hadley said, looking at the nose of an airplane concealed among trees some 300 yards distant.

"Looks like a Betty. I can see guys working on her." He handed the binoculars back to Jock.

Scanning the rest of the airfield, Jock said, "There's a bunch of single-engined fighters parked on the other side...probably Zeroes. Some anti-aircraft guns, too. And there's a tent city at the northeast corner. You getting all this?"

Hadley nodded as he sketched the airfield layout into his pocket notebook.

Jock focused the binoculars on the tent city. He shook his head in disbelief as he said, "Everything is all bunched together! Lots of personnel running around like ants. Their headquarters is probably in that second tent from the right. The sides are all rolled up so I can see inside. There are lots of Nips with swords and white shirt collars sticking out of their tunics...only officers dress like that. A lot of guys without tunics bowing to them, too. Only a headquarters has that many officers running around. You'd think they would have learned something about dispersal by now."

"Maybe they're getting sloppy," Hadley said. "They're getting used to not being shot at."

"Well, that's good for us...and too bad for them," Jock said. "Now we've got to figure some good map coordinates on this place."

Hadley looked puzzled. "Can't we just dead reckon them, sir?" he asked. "It's not like there are any landmarks around...and we can't bring the radio set here..."

But Jock had already dropped his pack and his Thompson and was shimmying up the stoutest tree in the stand. "I'll bet I can see the rooftops of Weipa Mission from up there, flat as this place is," he said.

"Maybe even those red cliffs Jillian was talking about."

Jock was right: once in the tree's crown, he could see the rooftops clearly. Their tin roofs glistened in the late morning sun, even through the filter of dust being kicked up by the trucks on Yellow Vermin Road. The high ground of the red cliffs was impossible to discern; the terrain relief presented itself only as a continuous green carpet of forest canopy. One hand firmly gripping a branch that swayed beneath his weight, Jock pulled his notebook from his shirt pocket with the other hand and flipped to the diagram Jillian had drawn.

That highest roof...that's got to be the whorehouse. The long, low roof a little to the west...that's got to be the icehouse. I make them both at about four thousand yards.

Slipping the notebook back into his pocket, he shot the azimuths to both structures with his compass. Looking west-northwest, he realized he could discern where the waters of Weipa harbor met Albatross Bay. He shot the azimuth to that point, too, before sliding down the tree. Once back on the ground, he immediately recorded the azimuths before the numbers jumbled in his memory.

Hadley asked, "What did the airfield look like from up there, sir?"

"It looks pretty damn well concealed," Jock replied, donning his pack once again. Even if we were running photo recon flights up this way, I'll bet they'd have to catch a plane sitting smack out in the open to tell this was an airfield."

It was time to make their escape. But no sooner had the team formed up behind Hadley, he signaled for them to *hit the deck.* As they dove for concealment in the knee-high grass, they heard what Tom Hadley had already seen: the loud, high-revving sound of a vehicle's engine to their left front. In a few moments, they could all see it, even with their heads only inches off the turf in the tall grass: a Japanese armored car, complete with machine gunner perched in its turret, moving very slowly in low gear. Well behind it walked a squad of soldiers—a dozen or more in column— scanning the forest around them, rifles at the ready. The slender bayonets at the muzzle of each man's rifle flashed glints of reflected light, even in the forest's shade, as if the devil was winking. The bayonets looked long enough to impale several men at once.

A shot of panic coursed through Jock's veins. *They didn't see me up in that fucking tree, did they? We're way outnumbered...and they could drive that armored car right up our asses! And the only retreat is onto the airfield...*

But the Japanese soldiers didn't seem to be looking for anything in particular. If anything, they were engaged in a dull routine. Several of them showed outright disinterest, staring at their feet as they shuffled along when they thought their leader, a chubby sergeant toward the front of the column, wasn't looking. As long as Jock and his men didn't move a muscle, the Japs would pass about 30 yards to their front and be gone. It wouldn't take more than a few minutes.

The only sound to be heard was the raucous throb of the armored car's engine—until screams rose from the grass where Nicky Russo lay: "OH GOD OH GOD OH JESUS GOD! I'M BIT! A FUCKING SNAKE! OH GOD I'M BIT!"

Jock and his men could hear Russo's constant

screams—and while the armored car crew would never hear them over their vehicle's noise—the Japanese foot soldiers, once they were close enough, would hear the screams, too, no matter how much noise the armored car far to their front made.

"OH JESUS GOD OH MAMA PLEASE I DON'T WANNA DIE!"

Jock felt like he was crawling through a field of molasses, making no progress. He couldn't see Russo but tried to home in on the sound of his hysteria. But that wasn't working—the screams wrapped themselves in the noise of the armored car's engine and seemed to be coming from everywhere at once.

I'm going in circles...Why can't I find him?

Hadley and Billings looked over their shoulders at Jock as he crawled past. Suddenly they looked so much younger—so much more innocent—than they had just a few minutes ago. Their eyes seemed to say what their lips couldn't: *It's okay, Captain. We don't blame you.* They held their Thompsons in one hand and a grenade in the other, ready to play the final act of their lives.

But where is Russo? And where is Guess?

Jock crawled a few more feet before those questions were answered. The sole of a G.I. boot protruded from a patch of tall grass, toe pointed up, twitching crazily. Russo's screaming stopped abruptly. The sound of the armored car's engine peaked, then began to fade as it crossed before them and moved on through the woods. Jock parted the grass with the muzzle of his Thompson. He wasn't quite prepared for what he saw.

Russo lay flat on his back, with Guess on top of him, face to face. Guess held a bayonet in his hand, its blade dripping fresh blood. Russo was still making some noises, but they were soft gurgles, inaudible more than a few feet away, as the last essence of life drained from him. There was a gaping incision across the front of his throat, still spilling a steady red flow that turned the brown soil black. The headless body of a brown snake lay beside them, its long, thick body in weakening convulsions, signaling its own death throes were nearly complete, too. "It's one of them brown snakes, like Doc showed us," Guess said, pointing to the two puncture marks on Russo's cheek. "He must've fell right on it. Real deadly...ol' Russo didn't stand a chance."

The look on Guess's face struck Jock as the most peaceful, compassionate look he had ever seen on another human being. "Somebody had to do it," Guess said as he wiped the bayonet clean on Russo's sleeve. "It's *kill or be killed,* right, sir?"

The sound of the armored car had faded to a distant murmur. It had gotten so quiet, Jock could hear the shuffling of the Japanese soldier's feet as they walked past, oblivious to anything but their own boredom.

They couldn't leave Nicky Russo's body to be found by the Japs. J.T. Guess had fabricated a stretcher from his and Russo's fatigue shirts, using the sniper rifle and a fallen tree limb for poles. During the long walk back to the camp, Guess wouldn't relinquish the spot of lead stretcher bearer and never seemed to tire. The other three alternated often as trail stretcher bearer; about 10 minutes was all any of them could manage before exhaustion set in. No words were spoken; none were necessary. They moved as if of one mind. A glance or gesture conveyed as much as a torrent of words.

No one had protested when Guess threw the dead snake—body and severed head—onto the stretcher with Russo. "I need to show it to Doc," he said.

As they lay concealed in the woods beside Yellow Vermin Road, waiting for a long line of trucks to pass before they could cross, Sergeant Hadley couldn't keep the question bottled up inside him any longer. "Sir," he whispered to Jock, "you're going to court martial him, aren't you? I mean...*for murder? At least manslaughter, right?*"

Jock was truly surprised his young sergeant still seemed concerned about the military justice system when, for at least this moment, the cold realities of combat and nature had mangled the letter of civilized law so thoroughly. "Yeah, I'm afraid so, Tom," Jock said, the slip to first name seeming not at all out of place. "But I'm not sure I wouldn't have done the same thing myself if I'd gotten there first." He paused, then added the question that left Hadley silent and squirming in its uncomfortable truth: "Wouldn't you?"

Chapter Thirty-Four

She wasn't sure how much more pain she could take or how much longer her shoulders would stay in their sockets. The rope binding her wrists behind her back had turned her hands numb as they hung from the block and tackle's hook. With each question, a military policeman—a *kempei*—pulled the rope to the pulleys a bit more, raising Jillian's bound hands slightly higher, bending her further forward, stretching her body even more and straining her shoulders to their limits. Now, only the toes of her fisherman's boots had a firm purchase on the icehouse floor. It wouldn't take too many more pulls on the rope before she would be off the floor completely, her entire body weight hanging from those arms pulled painfully high behind her back.

But she still hadn't told them a thing.

She had been detained by six men of the Japanese military police—the *Kempeitai*—just as she was about to cast off on *Mapoon Maiden*. They brought her to the icehouse, the same place she and her crewmen had stashed Sato's body 10 minutes before, invisible in a large steel bin beneath a load of ice and fish. The *kempei* had been instructed by Colonel Najima to question her about the mysterious disappearance of Mister Sato. According to the *Kempeitai* doctrine of *kikosaku*, nothing produced information better and faster than the prolonged infliction of physical pain.

A young, mustachioed sergeant was the leader of the *kempei,* pacing the icehouse with a decidedly, stiff-legged limp as he conducted the interrogation. He spoke English almost as flawlessly as Bob Sato. When first apprehended, she asked how he had become so

fluent. The four letters he gave in terse response—
UCLA—meant nothing to her. She stopped asking
questions when two *kempei* grabbed her arms and the
coarse rope began to bite into her wrists. Her crewmen
could only stand on board and watch helplessly as a
kempei brandished his pistol, holding them at bay. They
had little doubt the policeman would use it if necessary.

They had been at it for almost two hours, and the
limping sergeant was growing bored with the whole
business. He had already questioned the two soldiers
who served as Sato's escort. They said they had seen no
sign of Jillian Forbes when they dropped Sato off at her
house last night. They had been instructed to wait at the
Mission House—with the *comfort women*—where Sato
would rejoin them at sunrise. When he had not shown
up, they went back to the Forbes woman's house to
look for him. They found neither her nor Mister Sato.
The sergeant had never encountered a civilian who
could take as much pain as this woman and not tell him
whatever he wanted to hear, whether the words the pain
inspired were true or not. Maybe she really didn't know
anything, after all.

*The colonel always said Sato was a fool...and a
disgracefully bad drinker. Maybe he did just wander off
drunk and become some wild creature's dinner. It's
better we're rid of him. Now the colonel will have to
depend on my skills in dealing with the primitives.*

Two of the *kempei* relaxed against the bin
concealing Sato's body, enjoying the perverse thrill of
watching the woman being tortured. They were
oblivious that the answer to their questions was just a
few feet away, packed in ice and fish. Through the
searing pain, Jillian was thankful for their cluelessness.

"Let me ask you again, Miss Forbes," the sergeant said. "Where were you last night?"

"I told you...I spent the night in the bush. Alone." Her voice quavered and cracked under the strain of the ropes.

The sergeant struggled to sound skeptical through his indifference. "Help me to understand, Miss Forbes, why anyone would do that."

"We all need to go walkabout sometimes. You'd never understand...you're not from here."

"And I'm very grateful for that, Miss Forbes. Living here obviously makes one crazy." He made a chopping motion with his hand to the *kempei* manning the rope: *cut her down.* The rope slackened abruptly, and Jillian toppled to the floor. She lay still as her wrists were cut free and didn't try to move as sweet relief began its battle to overcome the throbbing pain still coursing through her body.

"We're done with you...for now," the sergeant said as he led his men out the door to their vehicle. A small but resentful crowd of blacks had formed outside the icehouse, and they parted sullenly to let the Japanese through. As soon as the *kempei* drove away, Jillian's crewmen raced inside.

"They are not our friends, Miss Jilly," Theo, the first mate, said as the crewmen helped her to her feet, relieved and grateful to find her still alive. "Say the word and they're dead men."

"No, Theo," Jillian said, trying to rub the feeling back into her hands. "Those bastards have never been our friends....but I won't have you trying to fight them." Jillian cast a long glance at the tub that concealed Sato's body. "This isn't over yet," she said, "not by a bloody long shot."

Chapter Thirty-Five

One look at Jock Miles's face told Melvin Patchett something had gone terribly wrong. Then the rest of the patrol—complete with stretcher—came into view through the trees. Patchett did a quick mental roll call and one man didn't answer: Russo.

"We didn't hear no gunfire, sir," Patchett said to Jock. "You didn't have to go hand-to-hand, did you?"

Jock shook his head. Try as he may, he had no words to say yet. This was not going to be an easy story to tell.

"So you didn't get spotted?" Patchett asked, making his way to the stretcher.

"No," Jock replied, his mouth finally in sync with his brain once again. "Thank God for that, anyway...and we did find the headquarters. It's right on the airfield. We've got an excellent position fix for the bombers."

Guess and Hadley laid the stretcher down. The first sergeant began to kneel next to it, then recoiled when he saw the dead snake tucked next to Russo's body. He recovered quickly and lifted the towel covering Russo's face. It took a few moments to make sense of what he saw.

Doc Green hurried over with his medical kit but stopped cold in his tracks still 10 feet away. He could see all he needed from there: the fang marks on Russo's face, like black quotations marks in the skin, set in a field of mottled purple and yellow; the gaping, mortal wound across the throat. "Bloody hell," Doc murmured.

"Somebody want to tell me what the fuck's going on here?" Patchett said.

Jock took a deep breath. He began to plod through the tale of what happened at Airfield One as Guess displayed the snake proudly. As it dangled from his outstretched arm, a few inches of the snake's tail still managed to coil on the ground. With its head attached, it would have been nearly six feet long. As the story neared its end, Patchett was fixated on Guess's grinning face, trying to decide if this young man didn't understand the enormity of what he had done or if the stress of coming face to face with the enemy had driven him out of his mind. Melvin Patchett had seen more than a few cases of mental breakdown from combat, though, and they had never looked quite like this.

When Jock had finished speaking, it was deathly quiet for a few moments. Guess broke the silence: "This *is* a killer snake, right, Doc?"

"Yes, son, it can be," Doc Green said. "Being bitten in the face like that…that would be difficult to treat, for sure. But it's never certain if someone is going to die from snakebite. You never know how much venom was injected or how great a man's resistance to it is. If death did come, though, it would take some time…hours, maybe days." He measured his words as if preparing testimony for Guess's court martial. "One thing I'd have to say, though," Doc added. "Even without hearing Captain Miles's retelling, it's fairly obvious the throat wound would have killed that man long before any snake bite."

Guess's smile faded. "But he was making so much noise," he said. "We would've all been dead."

Patchett put a hand meant to be comforting on Guess's shoulder. "You could be in some real deep shit here, boy," the first sergeant said, his tone of voice showing a surprising hint of compassion. That compassion promptly vanished as he added, "Now let's get this man buried. Get rid of that fucking snake, too."

This eventful day was still only half over. Jock Miles tried to bolster his flagging strength with a D bar as he and Melvin Patchett went over plans for the afternoon's patrol to Weipa Mission.

"You sure you're up for this, sir?" Patchett asked. "I mean, this little trip could be a big waste of time. There's no guarantee that Jap colonel's going to be dipping his wick."

Jock was adamant. "I want to cover all the bases, Top."

"And how are you even gonna know if you've got the right guy or not?"

"I'm still working on that one, Top."

"As I live and breathe, Captain...why on earth are you trying to freelance this mission now? We're supposed to be just recon. Nobody said nothing about setting up no ambush. Ain't that the kind of thinking that got you in trouble back at Pearl?"

"At ease, First Sergeant," Jock replied, his command voice bristling with annoyance.

"Sorry, sir...but permission to speak freely?"

Jock had a sudden change of heart. Maybe this wasn't the time to be getting on his high horse with a top-notch NCO like Melvin Patchett. He softened his tone. "All right, Top. Go ahead."

"With all due respect, sir, do you think that's gonna get you back in the Army's good graces? After the way they screwed you? Shit, you shoulda been a light colonel by now, at least. Look, you found the fucking headquarters, just like you were ordered to. Now let's call in the bombers and get the hell out of here. Mission accomplished."

Patchett stopped himself from adding, *Or are you wanting to stick around just to get into that crazy Aussie woman's drawers?*

But the first sergeant could tell right away he had wasted those words. His captain obviously had no intention of backing down. "Negative, First Sergeant," Jock said. "That's not the way we're going to do it."

There was no point arguing anymore. Melvin Patchett decided to try and make the best of what he considered a very bad situation. "Okay, sir, as you wish. But if we're gonna pull off an ambush, we're going to need a sniper...and Guess is the only one we've got."

"I fully intend to use Private Guess, Top."

"I think that's a pretty piss-poor idea, sir," Patchett said, scratching his head in bewilderment. "Don't you think that boy's gone a little off his rocker? Technically, he's under arrest for murder, ain't he?"

"Sure he is, Top...but how exactly do you hold someone under arrest out here? It's not like there's a stockade...or spare men to guard him. Best thing to do right now is just keep him doing his job—"

Patchett interrupted, throwing up his hands in a cautioning gesture. "How well do you think the others are going to work with him now, Captain? They're already calling him *Killer*...although I doubt any of them are gonna miss Russo much."

"They'll all do their jobs, Top. They've got to...or

the Japs will kill them...and they know that for a fact."

Melvin Patchett sat silently for a few moments, deep in thought. Finally, he asked, "Do you mind if I have a little talk with him first, sir?"

"Talk? About what, Top?"

"I just want to make sure that li'l ol' country boy just got hisself scared out there and he ain't gone crazier than a shithouse rat. Because if he even begins to look like he's thinking about doing another one of us in, I'll cancel his ticket myself. And that wouldn't be no bullshit *mercy killing,* neither, sir...that'd be self-defense."

It didn't take much talking to convince Melvin Patchett that J.T. Guess wasn't crazy. A bit fatalistic, perhaps, but he still came across to the first sergeant as the best soldier in the unit.

Hell, Top, Guess had said, *if we ever get out of here alive, maybe then I'll worry about some firing squad.*

When the first sergeant cautioned him to put any thoughts he might have about going AWOL out of his mind, Guess replied, *I saw what happened to Sergeant Roper, Top. I ain't running nowhere.*

Now, as his exhausted comrades from this morning's patrol to the airfield rested at the abandoned settlement, PFC J.T. Guess, once again clutching the Springfield sniper rifle, was enthusiastically beating his way through the bush with Captain Miles, Corporal Mike McMillen, and PFC Teddy Mukasic.

They moved north, staying in the forest well east of

Yellow Vermin Road and getting closer to Weipa Mission. What they didn't realize was there were other, smaller roads—just narrow trails, really, barely wide enough for a vehicle, hidden by the forest until you stepped onto them—branching east from the main road to where some Japanese units were bivouacked. It was a heart-stopping moment when an army truck suddenly rumbled by, just 10 yards in front of them, through woods so dense it seemed a bicycle couldn't find a path. The truck's occupants were as oblivious to the Americans' presence as the Americans had been to the trail.

Jock and his men crept to within 50 yards of a bivouac, hidden in the shadows among the thick stand of trees. It was just a small clearing with a smattering of weather-beaten tents, accommodating no more than a platoon. About a dozen men idled without weapons within the bivouac area, talking loudly, engaging in horseplay, or bathing in metal drums filled with water warmed over open fires. None of the soldiers appeared the least bit concerned about security. They might as well have been on a camping vacation.

"We could take 'em all out in a second," Corporal McMillen whispered to Jock as they crouched in high grass.

Jock whispered in reply, "Don't get too carried away. Let's not blow the mission now, when we're so damned close to pulling it off."

"Oh, I know, sir. But the urge to empty a couple of magazines into them....especially when they've got their heads so far up their asses..."

Jock patted his eager corporal on the helmet. "Just keep it in your pants a little bit longer, Mike. Now let's get moving."

By mid-afternoon, they had gotten as close to their objective as they could in broad daylight. The forest ended abruptly some 150 yards from the Mission buildings; there was little natural coverage from that point to the water's edge at Albatross Bay, another 400 yards distant. Industrious land clearing, first by the missionaries, now by the Japanese, had seen to that, and gave the Americans an unsettling view of a Japanese warship loitering offshore. Moving laterally a few yards, they found a clear field of fire through the trees to the Mission House.

As J.T. Guess sighted his Springfield rifle from a prone firing position, the telescopic sight centered on the Mission House's front door, he announced, with all the confidence in the world, "This is plenty close, sir." He adjusted his aim slightly to take in the lanterns hung by the door. "Just so there's a little bit of light, it'll be like shooting fish in a barrel."

Mike McMillen wasn't convinced. "In daylight, maybe. I hope you can tell officers from enlisted men in the fucking moonlight," he said.

"As long as they still got them swords on, it won't be no problem," Guess replied.

"Even pissant sergeants can be wearing a sword, Guess," McMillen replied. "That don't mean shit."

They all took a good look at the Japanese soldiers milling around the settlement. McMillen had a point. None of the Americans could tell the rank of any of the Japanese from this distance.

"How are we supposed to identify this colonel, sir?" McMillen asked. "In the dark, yet?"

As Jock pondered the question to which he didn't

yet have an answer, J.T. Guess said, "It don't matter...I'll just shoot 'em all."

Heading back to their staging area at the abandoned settlement, Jock took his patrol well to the east. He was hoping to avoid any more surprises, like the hidden roads and Japanese bivouac earlier. That proved to be wishful thinking.

They had only walked about 10 minutes when, in the distance ahead, a house appeared through the trees. It was small, but a stately Victorian nonetheless. Jock checked the sketch Jillian had drawn; he remembered her pointing to the corner of the sketch, where she had purposely not made a mark: *This is my house,* she had said, *but promise me you won't mark the location.* They advanced a bit closer; the paddock and small horse barn behind the house came into view.

But there was more to see, as well: two Japanese staff cars were parked, one in front of the house, one in back. A few moments later, two men—they appeared to be Japanese soldiers—left the house and began walking between the house and barn. Their eyes were cast down, their bamboo swords flicking at the ground. They were searching for something. Whatever it was, they didn't seem to be finding it.

Jillian appeared on the veranda; Jock and his men recognized her instantly. She was followed by a man who appeared to be a Japanese sergeant. His uniform was different—more formal, less practical for the tropics—than those they had seen on the soldiers at the airfield and at the Weipa Mission. Looking through his binoculars, Jock could tell the man had a mustache and was sweating like a pig. When he walked, he limped, favoring his stiff left leg. He and Jillian were in what appeared to be a business-like conversation, although they could not hear a word that was being said.

"I don't know, sir," Mike McMillen said. "She looks awful chummy with them to me."

"We don't know what they're saying, Corporal," Jock replied. "Don't rush to judgment, okay?"

Out of the corner of his eye, Jock noticed J.T. Guess crouching into a shooter's stance, his rifle pointed toward the veranda where Jillian and the Japanese man stood. "Stand down, Guess," Jock whispered. "We're not shooting any Japs yet."

"Who said I'm aiming at the Jap, sir?" Guess replied, his eye pressed to the telescopic sight.

"Goddamn it, Guess, put the weapon down," Jock said.

Through the telescopic sight, Guess had a bird's-eye view of the slap the Japanese sergeant had just delivered to Jillian's face. Lowering the weapon, he pointed toward the house and said, "You better take a look-see at what's going on up there, sir."

Like watching a silent movie, Jock stared through his binoculars as two more soldiers appeared from the house and restrained the struggling Jillian by the arms. The sergeant repeatedly slapped her face while saying something—Jock couldn't read lips, but it appeared he was saying the same thing over and over again—as if the blows would eventually coax the demanded response. But she was saying nothing, just struggling and kicking to no effect. One of the men restraining her produced a bamboo sword and smacked Jillian across the head. She collapsed to the deck of the veranda, lying motionless on her side. The sergeant signaled to his men, and they headed for their cars. Before leaving, though, he tried to clumsily kick Jillian with his game leg, aiming for her stomach but striking the shins she had curled defensively before her. Frustrated, he kicked her shins several times, almost toppling himself in the unsteady attempt before giving up and striding away.

While the kicks were still flying, Jock took the sniper rifle from the startled Guess. Try as he might, Jock couldn't center the Japanese sergeant in the crosshairs—his hands trembled too badly. He could feel his heartbeat pounding in his temples, his ears, his fingertips. He had fired at men before without difficulty—at Pearl, they were just abstractions, generic Japanese enemy in airplanes. But this was the first time he had wanted to kill a *specific* man, for a very specific reason: what he was doing to Jillian Forbes. He took a deep breath and held it. His hands obliged and steadied for a moment. His finger tightened around the trigger—until McMillen's disillusioned voice broke the target fixation:

"So we're not recon anymore, sir? Now you want to shoot 'em?"

Jock lowered the rifle and got a hold of himself. *Holy shit...what the hell am I doing? The mission, man...the mission comes first. Always. We're recon...we can't expose ourselves.*

He handed the Springfield back to Guess and then patted McMillen on the shoulder. "Good call, Corporal," Jock said. "Thanks."

The Japanese staff cars wound their way down the trail toward Weipa Mission and were soon out of sight.

Cautiously, Jock led his men closer to Jillian's house. They were still concealed among the trees when Jillian pulled herself to her feet. The distance, the green of their clothing, and the blackening of their faces made no difference: she saw them right away, like strange animals that didn't belong in her part of the world. She didn't seem glad to see them.

Jock recognized the meaning of her furtive hand gestures immediately: *Stay away! Don't come here!* Her head swiveled nervously while her hands spoke, as if expecting the Japanese to return at any moment. She pulled out a pocket watch, pointed to it quickly, and flashed five fingers. Jock got the message:

Five. Seventeen hundred hours. She'll meet us then, just like we agreed.

Reluctantly, he retreated with his men into the woods. They made their way back to the abandoned settlement to rejoin First Sergeant Patchett and the rest of the team. The only Japanese they encountered on this leg of the journey were four soldiers frolicking naked in the river where it narrowed southeast of Weipa Mission, either unconcerned or totally ignorant of the threat posed by crocodiles. Their uniforms hung from branches well away from the river bank.

"Let's take their clothes, sir," Mike McMillen said, fully expecting his captain to slap down the idea as being far too risky.

But much to his surprise, Jock replied, "Yeah...why not? Go ahead...they'll think some of their own guys pranked them."

Not wasting a second, Corporal McMillen organized the raid. "Killer, Mook...you snatch the duds. Me and the captain will cover you. Don't fuck up, now…The guys back with Top will be so ticked off we got souvenirs and they don't."

It took Guess and Mukasic only seconds to grab the clothes and return. "Those Nips never saw a thing," Teddy Mukasic said, gloating over the bounty. "Too busy playing grab-ass, like a bunch of queer-boys."

Laying the shirts out on the ground in front of Jock, Guess asked, "Can you read these ranks, Captain?"

"Looks like we've got three senior privates…and a lance corporal," Jock said.

"Three *naked* senior privates and a *naked* lance corporal," McMillen said, his eyes gleaming with mischief. "How come you didn't take their shoes, too, Mook?"

"They look like they got the jungle rot worse than ours do," Mukasic replied. "Who needs 'em?"

"Okay," Jock said, "enough fucking around. Let's get the hell out of here."

Chapter Thirty-Six

Jock and his men had been back at the camp in the abandoned settlement for about an hour. They had spent the time since their return trying to clean themselves up. The first sergeant had scrounged a bucket or two from the termite-riddled remnants of shacks around the settlement and filled them with fresh water from a nearby stream.

"Don't go drinking that water now," Patchett said. "It ain't treated. Good for washing up, though…give yourselves a helmet bath. And make sure you change your socks and use plenty of powder on them doggies. We don't need no trench foot out here. Doc would have my ass."

After three days in the bush, they were all sorely in need of some washing up. PFC Billings, the North Carolinian of the group, had summed up the collective state of their grooming this way: "We all smell kinda like a road-kill skunk. No wonder them flies love us so much." Billings might have a point: the mosquitoes had been brutal since the move to this new position. The Americans were constantly swatting them away from their faces.

Seventeen hundred hours came and went without Jillian's arrival. "Maybe she's spooked now, with them Japs beating her up and all," Patchett said, shading his eyes as he scanned the woods for any sign of visitors. "Kinda curious, though, as to why, all of a sudden, they ain't being so friendly as she claimed."

"Give her time, Top," Jock replied. "She'll be here…" His voice trailed off, exposing the certainty he tried to express as merely wishful thinking. After what he saw happening to her a few hours ago, he knew that if she didn't come, it was because something terrible was happening to her all over again—and he wished against all reason he had pulled the trigger when the limping Jap was in his sights.

It was nearly 1730 when Corporal Pacheco, manning the north position in the perimeter, suddenly forgot all about the mosquitoes bedeviling him and was jarred into a blood-pumping state of awareness. Something was coming through the woods straight for him—*it looks like a horse...it's someone riding a horse.* His finger tightened around the Thompson's trigger—and then he saw it was *a woman on a horse:* Jillian Forbes.

"Aren't you going to challenge me before you shoot me?" she asked, as her horse walked right up to Pacheco. Then she added, "You mean I remembered that bloody password all day for nothing?"

Embarrassed, Pacheco lowered his weapon and waved her into the perimeter.

Melvin Patchett got to her first and helped her down from the horse. He studied the bruises on her face. "They hurt bad, miss?" he asked, his concern sincere.

"The slapping was the easy part. I got a lot worse this morning. I'm still sore all over from that."

Jock was now at her side. He had been so relieved to see her—and then he heard those words *a lot worse this morning.* "What do you mean? What happened this morning?" he asked, bracing himself for what the answer might be.

"First things first," she said. "Now that I see it's safe, I've got a surprise for you blokes. Please...tell your men not to shoot." She put her fingers to her lips and let out a shrill whistle of several alternating notes, which seemed more like the call of some exotic bird than any sound a human might make.

Two black men came out of the woods, leading a donkey hitched to a cart. On the cart were several barrels. One was full of fresh drinking water. The others were filled with the seafood feast she had proposed last night.

"Now, if only I could have brought some music, too," Jillian said.

Jock whispered in her ear, his words tense and irritated. "I thought you wanted to keep the blacks out of this...so you bring two of them right into my camp?"

Jillian found his annoyance wonderfully naïve and funny. So did the two black men, who, without hearing his words, had understood what he asked by the look on his face. "Oh, Jock," she replied, "they've all known you were here for the past two days. Bloody hell...they could smell you a mile away. And all the bloody noise you make? Believe me, you can trust them...and you've been trusting them, whether you know it or not, ever since you set foot in their country."

She directed Jock's attention back to the barrels, which his men were eagerly emptying. "We smoked you some fish and steamed you some crabs," she said, "since you probably don't want to be making any fires. I'm sure we've brought more than enough...there's fifteen of you, right?"

"More like fourteen now," Jock said.

"Oh, dear God...what happened?" she asked.

"Let's get them eating first, then I'll tell you all about it."

The two black men departed with the donkey and cart as quietly as they had arrived. "Where are they going?" Jock asked.

"They've got something to do for me," Jillian replied.

As he watched the blacks depart, Jock noticed something odd. They never had to swat any flies away. In fact, the flies didn't seem to come near them. Or Jillian, either, for that matter.

"Why do the flies leave you and the blacks alone?" he asked.

"The blacks have a natural immunity," she replied. "As for me...well, who knows? It's just bloody amazing, isn't it?"

As the men chowed down, Jock told Jillian the story of Russo, the snake, and Guess. "That poor lad," she said, gazing over at Guess, who was caring tenderly for Franz. "He must have been so terrified. I know exactly how he feels."

Jock's reply was a mix of surprise and skepticism: "You do?"

She was quiet for a few moments, staring vacantly into the distance. When she finally spoke, her voice had a fatalistic coldness, and she did not turn to face him. "Yes, I do. I killed someone today, too...Sato."

For a second, Jock thought she was kidding. "*Bob* Sato?" he asked. "The amorous Jap with the business card?"

Gravely, she nodded, and Jock realized this was no joke. His brain began to put the day's events together and he said, "So those soldiers at your house..."

"Yeah. They're looking for him...and I'm their number one suspect."

Now it was time for Jillian to tell her story. When she got to the end, she explained why the black men who brought the food had left so quickly. "They're getting the icehouse ready so we can get rid of the body quickly. Tonight, as soon as it's dark, we'll leave it on the Embley riverbank at a spot where a croc will be sure to find it. And if that croc leaves a little bit of him behind, all the better."

Jock wasn't convinced of her plan's wisdom. "Either way, aren't you still going to be a suspect?"

"Look, Jock…the *Kempeitai* aren't different from any other police. They're not interested in being Sherlock Holmes. They just want to frighten the bloody daylights out of people…and they're finally getting their chance. So it's time to get rid of the lot."

She fell silent again. As if she didn't have enough weighing down on her, there was still more. As her eyes began to fill with tears, she buried her face in her hands. Her voice trembling, she said, "One of my boats…it didn't come back. We don't know why…"

Then, just as quickly as she had broken down, Jillian composed herself. Jock envied the look of determination that came over her face. *The shit she's in is at least as deep as mine…and she seems to be handling it a whole lot better.*

Suddenly, she jumped up and started walking toward her horse. Over her shoulder, she said, "Damn, Jock…I almost forgot to give you something!" When she returned, she handed him a tubular map case. "Here are the charts I promised."

Jock unrolled the charts and placed them on his ground sheet. Using the data from his old map and notebook, he plotted the position of the Japanese airfield and headquarters on Jillian's chart, using the azimuth shots he got while up in the tree. Patchett double-checked and concurred with his work. When they compared the different results on her chart and his map, they said, in unison, "Holy shit!" The plotted positions were different by nearly a mile.

"I guess we're gonna trust this brand new chart over that old map, sir?" Patchett said, not really asking a question, just stating the obvious.

"So when are they going to bomb it?" Jillian asked.

"We'll call in the coordinates tonight...so I suppose the bombers will come tomorrow night," Jock replied. "Make sure that none of the blacks are anywhere near Airfield One then."

"I'll make sure of it," she replied. "Look, I've got to get going...I need to be back at the Mission before dark."

"Wait. There's something I need to ask you," Jock said.

He told her of his plan to assassinate the Japanese colonel at the Mission House. "The way I figure it," Jock said, "that's the only place we can count on finding him. They'll all come running out to get back to the airfield when they hear the bombs start falling. But there's just one problem...none of us know what this Colonel Najima looks like..."

"So you need someone to point him out to you," Jillian said.

"Yeah."

"Fine. I'll do it."

"No, wait," Jock said. "I didn't mean it had to be you. Anyone who knows what—"

"No, Jock. I said I'd do it."

She couldn't help but notice the scowl on Melvin Patchett's face. "I don't think your first sergeant wants my help," she said.

As Patchett bit his tongue, Jock said, "Let's just say the first sergeant thinks this part of the plan..." he paused and searched for the right word before adding, "...is unnecessary."

Patchett shook his head and said, "It's more than that, sir. There won't be no hiding this colonel's body. Ain't either of you worried that the Japs'll think a *civilian* knocked him off, too? If you think they're getting nasty with reprisals now, you ain't seen nothing yet."

Jock tried to reply diplomatically. "That's always a possibility, Top, but—"

Jillian interrupted once again. "There're no *buts* about it, Yanks," she said. "Sato was just a pencil-pusher. Kill their commander and it's a whole different story. I've been watching them for a while now...they're not exactly balls of fire when it comes to initiative, from the officers right down to the privates. They follow orders pretty well, but with nobody to tell them what to do every step, they stand around with their thumbs up their arses. I wouldn't hire a one of them. And if you're worried about reprisals against civilians, they'd have to find us to kill us, because once the fighting starts, we're all going bush. Nobody will be safer than us."

Neither Jock Miles nor Melvin Patchett had a rebuttal. She seemed so convinced in her logic they found themselves wanting to accept it, too.

"I've really got to go," Jillian said. "Shall we meet same time tomorrow?"

"Yeah," Jock replied, "but we're going to move camp at first light. We can't stay in one place too long. I was thinking of here..." He pointed to a spot on the chart closer to the Weipa Mission but still deep in the forest.

"That should be good," Jillian said after studying the chart. "Easy for me to find, too. Shall I bring dinner again?"

Their mouths may have been full, but every soldier in earshot responded, "YES!"

Taking the reins from Guess, Jillian climbed up on Franz and said, "Oh, by the way...the Jap wireless is setting up for the night in the Mission right now. I guess it's the radio operators' turn to visit the knocking shop."

As the horse stepped cautiously through the perimeter, Jock caught up and said, "Jillian, I hope everything turns out okay with your boat."

"Thanks, Jock," she replied, smiling in gratitude. Then she vanished into the forest.

A few minutes later, as Jock was preparing the target data for the night's radio transmission, Sergeant Botkin approached. "I heard what Miss Forbes said about the Jap transmitter, sir. Me and Mike...I mean Corporal McMillen...we started talking and came up with a little idea..."

Chapter Thirty-Seven

General Samuel Briley slumped behind his desk at the American headquarters in Brisbane. He hated after-hours meetings. *Never accomplished a damned thing at any one of them,* he thought as he rearranged the paraphernalia on the desk for a third time. *Men are at their best in the morning. After that, it's all downhill...and the only place to be at nineteen hundred hours is the club.* But the message that came down from MacArthur's headquarters two floors above had been specific: accommodate the governor immediately, in whatever manner you deem necessary and feasible.

That damned fool governor probably just wants to protest some more about our Negro troops slipping into downtown Brisbane...and slipping it to the local white girls. General Briley and Sir Malcolm Owens, Governor of Queensland, had discussed that topic several times already.

A knock on the office door. Briley's aide, John Joseph Pershing "Scooter" Brewster, stuck his head and shoulders just far enough into the office to display the shiny new captain's bars pinned to his collar. "The Governor is here, sir...and he's brought another gentleman with him. A police constable."

There was little need for formality or pleasantries between Briley and Owens. They were well acquainted with each other. The police constable, though, required an introduction.

"General Briley, this is Constable Mick Murray," Governor Owens said. "He's offered to join us and share his considerable expertise in the matter we are about to discuss."

Samuel Briley was finding it difficult to fathom what this coarse-looking, balding man—obviously ill at ease in their presence—had to share in any matter they might discuss. *Offered to join us, my ass,* the general thought. Anybody as uncomfortable as this constable appeared to be had obviously been ordered here against his will.

"I cannot emphasize enough just how concerned the prime minister is about this matter," Owens said. "It goes right to the very fabric of our Australian society."

The benign smile on Briley's face belied the thought in his head: *Oh shit...he's going to whine about my nigger troops polluting Aussie girls again, just like I thought.*

Governor Owens pressed on. "This morning, an Australian Navy patrol boat apprehended a fishing craft in the Gulf of Carpentaria. This boat, named *Andoom Clipper,* was crewed by four blacks from northern Cape York, who have been taken into custody. Once naval officers sorted out their childlike babblings, they told a story that strikes fear into the hearts of all good Australians."

The general stole a glance at his wristwatch and thought, *Oh, for fuck's sake, Governor...get on with it!*

"These black crewmen sail from Weipa Mission, high on Cape York—"

"I'm familiar with where it is," Briley interrupted.

"Very well, General," Owens continued. "Now, these blacks work for a *white woman*, who they say is doing business with the Japanese, wheeling and dealing...and turning a tidy profit in Japanese currency to boot. These fisherman had pockets full of Japanese money, as well. What's worse, this woman is organizing *all* the blacks on Cape York to support the Japanese. You can understand the prime minister's concern."

"Of course I can understand the concern," Briley said. "The loyalty of the blacks has always been a great question mark. Now, I must ask…are we sure the story these fishermen tell is true? And how did you even get word of it so fast?"

"Bad news like this always travels very quickly, General," Owens replied. "The Navy wisely alerted their headquarters immediately. The government wires have been abuzz ever since. As to the veracity of the blacks' story, Constable Murray can shed a great deal of light on that. He was the constable in Weipa for many years, and bravely maintained order there until the very last minute, when he was finally ordered to evacuate."

Sam Briley still wasn't sure why his time was being wasted by these two men. His mind wandered: he imagined long ranks of Aborigines in loincloths, armed only with spears, being mowed down like dominoes by his troopers' machine guns. But he knew he would have to do something to placate the prime minister's errand boy. MacArthur had dumped this issue into his lap, and his lap alone; he'd better not disappoint the boss. Maybe the Aborigines in his next daydream would be armed with Nambu machine guns and do a little mowing down of their own.

If only this constable inspired my confidence a little more, Briley thought. Mick Murray was sweating profusely. His well-worn suit seemed as dusty as the streets of Brisbane and was tailored for a larger man. His face was turning red—perhaps the buttoned-up collar was too tight? He certainly wasn't being choked by the necktie that hung loosely, its knot almost an inch below that top button. *Or maybe this man drinks a bit?* Murray had not once met eyes with Samuel Briley.

The general asked, "Do we even know this woman's name, Constable Murray?"

"Yes, General, we do. Her name is Jillian Forbes."

"And you know this Forbes woman personally?"

"Known her since she was born, General."

"Then tell me something about her," Briley said.

"She's just like her father was...thinks she's a law unto herself. When she was a kid at the Mission, she only played with the black kids, and she was wilder and more savage than any of them. When she got a little older, she took a strong liking to black boys...if you know what I mean. Her father sent her off to The Women's College here in Brisbane, but they threw her out."

"Why?" Briley asked.

"Moral turpitude, I'm told. Caught her sneaking away to have it off with boys...sometimes black boys. She didn't fit their image of a fine Queensland lady."

"How old is this woman now, Constable?"

"About twenty-four, I reckon," Murray said as he pulled a photo from his jacket pocket and handed it to the general. "That's from her days at the College. Her hair's longer and more wild now."

Briley asked, "Why wasn't she evacuated with the other whites?"

"She refused to go. I tried to talk reason with her, but she threatened me at gunpoint. She said she wouldn't abandon her fishing business."

"This twenty-four-year-old woman actually runs a

business?" Briley asked.

"Yes, she does."

"Successfully?"

"Yes, she's bloody good at it. She's bloody good at lots of things...and the *boongs* love her, just like they loved her father. She thinks like them...only she's much smarter. And much more dangerous."

"And you're sure all this makes her a collaborator?" Briley asked.

Before Murray could say a word, Governor Owens answered the question. "The prime minister is completely convinced. The opinion in Canberra is unified."

"This seems like quite the rush to judgment, Governor."

"Surely you can understand why, General. This represents Australia's worst nightmare becoming reality."

"Fine," the general said. "I suppose you'd like her taken into custody?"

Governor Owens shook his head gravely. "No, General," he said. "Canberra feels this situation calls for a far more expedient remedy. This treason must be nipped in the bud. Promptly."

Samuel Briley let those words swirl in his head for a moment, then leveled a stern look at the governor. "And the Australian military can't handle this task, either?"

Sir Malcolm Owens returned the general's stern gaze. "That would put our military...and our government...in a most awkward position, don't you think, General?"

Chapter Thirty-Eight

Stuart Botkin watched in the darkness as the phosphorescent second hand of his wristwatch swept around the dial. When it reached the 12, it would be exactly 2215 hours—time for the mobile Japanese transmitter to go on the air. Botkin was confident it would fail to do so on this night—or any night in the future.

He and Mike McMillen crouched among the trees that marked the eastern edge of the Weipa Mission. The radio truck sat unattended in the clearing, its engine idling, just 20 yards in front of them. The radio compartment on its bed resembled a large, windowless box big enough for several men to work in, covered in canvas, open only at the tailgate. With Captain Miles's permission, the two American soldiers had made their way back to the Mission at twilight to execute a plan Stu Botkin had been dreaming up ever since being assigned to Task Force Miles.

The captain had been hard to convince at first, probably because he was already down three men— Roper and Russo dead, Boudreau out of action—and couldn't afford to lose any more on some half-assed scheme. But Botkin needed somebody to guide him to the Mission, and Mike McMillen already knew the safest route. It would have to be just the two of them— or nothing. They'd be stuck out here all night, too—it wasn't safe to attempt a return to camp in darkness. But that would be the price of success. Maybe they'd even catch a little sleep while they waited for the dawn. As to Task Force Miles's nightly radio transmission, Botkin's men—PFC McGuire and PFC Savastano—were more than capable of handling that chore without their sergeant holding their hands.

In technical terms, the plan to sabotage the Japanese transmitter was very simple. *No step for a stepper,* First Sergeant Patchett had said as he nodded in approval of Botkin's plan. Captain Miles still had his doubts, though, asking, *Are you sure you'll know how to sabotage a Jap transmitter?* Botkin explained that there were only a limited number of workable radio circuits on God's green Earth, and he could recognize any one of them at a cursory glance. It didn't matter where they were made—each internal stage of the radio had to use one of those circuits. And if you knew how they worked, it was easy to figure out how to make them *not* work. A little bit of *shop trash*—bits and pieces of wire and metal—draped across critical connections inside the transmitter would turn it into a smoldering piece of junk in a split second. All Stu Botkin needed was a minute or two alone with that transmitter. If Miss Forbes was right about the Jap radio operators visiting the knocking shop, he'd get all the time he needed.

There had been only one tense moment in the whole affair. As Botkin worked alone on the transmitter, he suddenly heard voices speaking Japanese outside. It sounded like two or three men were arguing—everything in Japanese sounded so damned urgent! He had heard it spoken a few times before by Japanese students at the University of Illinois, where he was studying electrical engineering before his father died and the tuition money ran out. Unable to find a job in the Depression-torn American Midwest, Stu Botkin enlisted in the peacetime Army.

But what sounded like arguing turned to boisterous laughter. Botkin peeked over the truck's tailgate to watch three young Japanese soldiers swagger away, perhaps a little drunk. *Or maybe they just got laid.*

Stu Botkin carefully weaved his little pieces of sabotage into the transmitter's wiring, taking great care to not displace anything in the truck, including the stack of papers on the operator's desk. Even in Japanese, he could tell the papers were radio message forms, with printed blocks to separate the different parts of a transmission. No doubt, these were the messages to be transmitted tonight. When he was done, he took a moment to admire his handiwork:

That oughta do it. A grenade would do the job a whole lot easier...but then they'd have a pretty good idea what happened.

He was back in the tree line with McMillen a full 10 minutes before the radio truck's crew—there were four of them—returned at 2210, just enough time to warm up their set's vacuum tubes before tapping that first character on the telegraph key at precisely 2215.

The second hand on Botkin's watch swept through the 12. The truck's engine began to rev higher—*more power for the transmitter*—and Botkin was sure he could feel the air come alive with a surge of electricity—*or is it just my anxiety?* Within a heartbeat, a dull, white flash illuminated the opening at the truck's tailgate for an instant, followed by a persistent, orange glow that grew steadily brighter. One of the radio operators jumped from the tailgate to the ground, yelling words Botkin and McMillen couldn't hear over the truck's engine. The two men in the cab must have heard him, though; they spilled to the ground just in time to watch the side canvas begin to burn at its lower edge, spreading quickly in an ever-growing semicircle upward, promising to engulf the entire truck bed.

The second radio operator jumped to the ground, a sleeve of his tunic burning. He rolled on the ground trying to extinguish the flames. In the fire's glow, his face was a silent movie's vision of continuous screaming, with the sound of his agony blotted out by the rumble of engine noise. He kept screaming even after the flames burning his arm were out.

The truck's canvas sides had burned away, exposing the smoldering remains of the radio set. The flames now worked on the canvas roof over the bed and cab, dropping flaming patches down onto the truck body and tires.

McMillen started to inch backwards. "Maybe we should get a little more distance," he said, "in case the gas tank blows the whole thing sky high."

But Stu Botkin couldn't take his eyes off the spectacle he had just caused, one that far exceeded his expectations. He didn't move—couldn't move—until Mike McMillen grabbed him by the arm and pulled him away.

"That fire…," McMillen said, "if it gets much brighter out here, they'll be able to see us plain as day, Stu. Then we're really fucked."

They stopped their retreat about 100 yards deeper into the woods. The truck was still burning, even more ferociously than before. Every few seconds, a sharp *POOMF* was heard as one flaming tire after another exploded.

"I sure wasn't expecting anything like that," McMillen said, shaking his head in wonder. "You really know how to blow the shit out of something, don't you, Stu?"

No one was more surprised than Sergeant Stu Botkin. Over and over, he kept saying, "I had no idea...Incredible!"

Just when it seemed the inferno had finally burned itself out, the truck's gas tank exploded with a *BOOM* that shook the forest and a brilliant flash that ruined the Americans' night vision for a good 30 minutes. They clung to the base of a tree, fingers on their Thompsons' triggers, knowing full well that unless an enemy was accommodating enough to outline himself against the blaze, they'd never see him coming.

When the radio truck caught fire, Jillian and her men were still at the icehouse, pretending to be busy with something other than the disposal of a frozen corpse. They'd been waiting ever since nightfall for a chance to get Sato's body out of that icy tub, onto a cart, and over to the riverbank. On this particular night, though, the Japanese seemed to be everywhere in the Mission, and the opportunity to remove the body had yet to present itself. Once the truck began to burn, a state of panic gripped the Japanese troops. For the first time since they landed on Cape York, they thought they might actually be under attack. But from who?

"Oh, bloody hell!" Jillian mumbled from the icehouse's veranda, as she watched officers and sergeants, none too calm themselves, organize the frantic soldiers into defensive positions ringing the Mission. The few blacks wandering about the Mission wisely made themselves scarce, correct in their assumption the soldiers would be looking for scapegoats very soon.

A few minutes after the chaos began, Jillian saw Colonel Najima finally emerge from the Mission House, still fumbling with his sword belt, trying to get it buckled about his waist. A subordinate—from the tunic he wore, Jillian thought he was an officer, too—rushed up to report to the colonel. Just then, the truck's gas tank exploded, rocking both men and blowing their caps off. Even Jillian, much farther away, felt the shock wave like a brief blast of scorching tropic wind.

The subordinate scuttled off toward the flaming hulk of the truck. In short order, he returned to the colonel with four soldiers in tow. One seemed to have a sleeve burned off his tunic. The four braced in a line before the colonel. Najima walked down that line, saying something to each man, then slapping him soundly in the face. The subordinate then marched the four to a vehicle, which drove off down the road toward Airfield One. Even in the dim light, Jillian could see each of the four hanging his head like a man headed for the gallows—or the executioner's block. The fire was burning itself out and so was the anxiety of the remaining Japanese troops. A few even began to laugh and joke.

Jillian turned to the two black men beside her. "See?" she said. "The universe is in order again. Blame is assessed…authority has asserted its righteousness once more." She reached into the ice box and handed a beer to each of the blacks before taking one herself. "But, fellows, I'm afraid Mister Sato is going to be cooling off a little while longer."

Chapter Thirty-Nine

The duty officer at the Mossman radio station—a US Army Signal Corps second lieutenant fresh to Australia named Ernest Smith—was breathless as he spoke on the telephone to Headquarters, convinced he was conveying a crucial piece of intelligence. "That's right, sir," Lieutenant Smith said, "the Japanese transmitter did not go on the air tonight. We've been scanning all the possible frequencies. It's just not there."

Smith listened to what the voice on the other end of the line had to say and then turned to his radio operator, asking, "Did we get the position report from Task Force Miles, Corporal Welsh?"

With an air of irritation, Corporal Stanley Welsh slid the headphones off his ears and down to around his neck. He spun his swivel chair around to face the duty officer. "Yeah, we got it, Lieutenant. Already forwarded it to HQ. Don't they talk to each other down there?" As an afterthought, he added, "Different fist sent it tonight, though."

"Fist? What do you mean?" Lieutenant Smith asked.

Boy, this shavetail sure is green, Corporal Welsh thought. "Different fist, sir? It means a different operator sent it. You can tell…there's a different touch to the Morse. You never heard that expression before?"

Shrugging off his embarrassment, Smith once again listened to the voice on the other end of the line and then asked Welsh, "Did Task Force Miles mention anything about the Jap transmitter?"

Now the corporal was really annoyed. "How the

hell should I know, Lieutenant? Those transmissions are just a bunch of letters and numbers to me. The brass at HQ are supposed to figure out what it all means."

The waiter brought General Samuel Briley his fourth glass of whiskey. It was almost midnight, and the lounge of Lennon's Hotel in downtown Brisbane, crowded with American officers and Australian women just a short while ago, was emptying fast. The only officers from MacArthur's staff that remained were the diehard drinkers or those making a last, desperate attempt to procure female companionship for the night. The rest had retired to their rooms long ago.

Sam Briley knew sleep would elude him this night unless he sorted out the predicament dropped in his lap by Governor Owens. The Australian government wanted one of its citizens summarily executed for treason. A young woman, at that. No questions asked, no arrest, no trial. They couldn't risk even the possibility that a white person was encouraging the Aborigines to support the Japanese. He took the photograph of Jillian Forbes from his pocket and traced the outline of her face with his finger.

But the politicians need to protect themselves, just in case this all blows up in their faces...so let us Yanks do the dirty work.

He stuffed the photo back into his pocket.

He had spent the last two hours hashing the plan over in his mind. Actually, accomplishing the objective probably wouldn't be difficult at all: there was already an American patrol conveniently in the area—*Task*

Force Miles—who should be able to do the job. Miles and company were, like any other soldiers, considered expendable, their mission more a flawed gesture of moral support among impotent allies than a military necessity. If they lost their lives or just took the fall for a political decision gone terribly wrong, it didn't matter. There was just one problem: it wouldn't be very wise to transmit the order to assassinate a civilian by radio, even coded. Anyone with a receiver and the current code book could read it. Worse, there would be message forms filed, entries in transmission logs, and the long-term memories of clerks and radio operators. All quite capable of pointing accusing fingers for years to come. Such an order would have to be a written and sealed, eyes-only, burn-after-reading document, hand delivered to the man expected to carry them out.

So I'll need a courier I can trust implicitly...

Briley gazed across the lounge to the bar. His aide, Captain Scooter Brewster, looked forlorn as he leaned against the counter, nursing his beer. The woman he had been trying to chat up for the better part of the evening had just walked out the door, ditching the mere captain for a lieutenant colonel.

Rank does have its privileges...

The general summoned his aide to his table. "Have a seat, Scooter," he said.

Once Brewster was settled in, Samuel Briley asked, "Captain, how would you like to make an indelible contribution to the war effort? Maybe even pick yourself up a medal you can brag to the ladies about?"

Chapter Forty

Penicillin and real food had started to work their magic on Bogater Boudreau. The radio men, McGuire and Savastano, had made provisions to transport Boudreau on one of the *Radio Flyers* as Task Force Miles moved to the new position, but he wouldn't hear of it. He walked proudly, fully alert to any threat, carrying his weapon and pack without a hint of the weakness that plagued him yesterday. Even Doc Green was amazed how fast the Cajun trooper was bouncing back. "Your recuperative powers are amazing, young man," Doc told him.

"Couldn'ta done it without you and them needles, Doc," Boudreau replied.

Every man walking in that column wondered if they would ever see Botkin and McMillen again. Even those who had been off watch and catching some coveted sleep were jarred awake by last night's explosion from the direction of Weipa. They joined their on-watch comrades already gawking at the fire's glow lighting the sky. No one had any idea what had blown up or that Botkin had caused it. They could only hope whatever just happened in Weipa hadn't claimed him and McMillen.

As they reached the new position and began to dig fighting holes, their fears were put to rest. Stu Botkin and Mike McMillen ambled out of the forest, moving like very tired men but radiating a cocky, triumphant attitude that said *we just won the war all by ourselves.*

McMillen was gushing as he asked First Sergeant Patchett, "Did you see that fucking radio truck go up, Top?"

"Y'all did that?" Patchett replied, genuinely surprised. "You think they know it was the US Army that blew them up?"

"I don't think we'd be alive to talk about it if they knew that, Top," Botkin said.

Patchett took a good look at McMillen and Botkin's drawn faces and bloodshot eyes. "You two take the morning off and catch some shuteye." Almost as an afterthought, he added, "Y'all did real good, you know."

Jock Miles patted Botkin on the shoulder and asked, "Did you know that sabotaging the radio would be so..."—he fumbled for the right word—"...*spectacular*, Sergeant?"

"Hell no, sir," Botkin replied. "I figured it would just fry the transmitter. But I've been thinking...don't you suppose they'll just use the radio on one of those ships offshore now? At least until they can get a replacement unit?"

"Maybe," Jock said. "But with any luck at all, that'll be the least of their problems pretty soon."

PFC Savastano approached with a radio message form in his hand. "This just came in, Captain," Savastano said.

A smile spread across Jock's face as he read the message, but when he got to the last line, the smile faded.

"Bad news, sir?" Patchett asked.

"Yes and no, Top. The bombing raid's going to happen after midnight tonight, around oh two hundred hours. That's the good news."

Patchett girded himself for the rest of the message.

"They want us to supply a damage assessment,"

Jock added, "and await further orders."

Patchett frowned. "So it says nothing about pulling back and coming home?"

Jock shook his head and said, "Not yet." He heard Patchett mutter something. It wasn't very distinct, but it definitely included the words *sons of bitches.*

Melvin Patchett went back to supervising the defensive preparations. "Dig them holes good and deep, boys," he said. "The Air Corps is gonna be laying some eggs tonight."

Chapter Forty-One

At the moment, no soldier in the US Army was more upset and disoriented than Tech Corporal Grover Wheatley. He couldn't understand why he had been the only man awoken in his Brisbane bivouac tent in the middle of the night, told to grab the horseshoe field pack he never had the occasion to use, and draw the M1 rifle he had never fired. He was then hustled into a jeep and driven to Archerfield airstrip. There, he was issued a hand-held radio receiver/transmitter—an SCR-536 "walkie-talkie," just developed for the Army. Its transmitter's range was only about one mile, but it could receive any signal strong enough to reach it and was small and light enough to be carried by a foot soldier. The radio came complete with an accessory loop antenna for radio direction finding, a set of replaceable tuning coils which enabled the operator to change frequencies, and a box-full of spare batteries. He was then thrown onto a C-47 transport plane with some stick-up-the-ass captain from headquarters he didn't know named Brewster. The captain announced only this: Grover Wheatley had been detailed to be Brewster's radio operator for a very special courier mission.

They were airborne before the dawn, heading northwest to someplace he had never heard of, whose name he couldn't even pronounce. The only thing he fully understood was the workings of the walkie-talkie. He had been trained at the factory producing them and was an expert on that brand new marvel of American engineering.

Once the C-47 landed, they were driven to a tiny

anchorage on the lower end of the Gulf of Carpentaria—*wherever the hell that is*—and put onboard a Royal Australian Navy patrol boat. *Patrol boat* seemed a bit grand as a description of this vessel, Wheatley thought. It was nothing more than a pleasure boat—a big cabin cruiser captained by an aging petty officer—with a Bren Gun bolted to a stanchion on the foredeck. Her crew consisted of three of the most slovenly sailors Grover Wheatley had ever seen. The patrol boat didn't cast off from the dock until darkness began to fall. It then motored north making surprisingly good speed, hugging the eastern coast of the Gulf, bound for a place called Archer Bay. Only then did Captain Brewster reveal to Wheatley the barest outline of their mission. Grover Wheatley was no longer disoriented. Instead, he was incredulous.

He voiced his displeasure over the loud rumble of the boat's engine, the necessary volume of his words masking their insubordinate tone. "Let me get this straight, Captain," Wheatley said. "I've got to find some guy with this crummy hand-held direction finder…in the middle of nowhere…so you can deliver him that sealed envelope? And with Japs supposed to be crawling around, too? This has got to be a joke, right?"

Scooter Brewster decided the best way to handle this cranky corporal was to ignore his complaints entirely. He knew well the old Army game Wheatley was playing: *the squeaky wheel always gets the grease. If you bitch all the time, they'll back off giving you shit to do just so they won't have to listen to you. That's probably how I ended up with him…his CO wanted to get rid of him.*

"It's no joke, Corporal," Brewster said, without a hint of annoyance. "You're eminently trained for the job at hand. You come highly recommended."

"I'll bet...by someone who wants to see me dead, probably."

"Just try to catch some sleep, Corporal. We'll be back on shore before dawn. Then we've got a bit of walking to do."

"Sleep? On this noisy old tub? I wouldn't count on it, Captain."

Scooter Brewster said nothing in reply. He handed Wheatley a booklet with the transmission schedules and frequency assignments used by Task Force Miles.

"Let me ask you something, Captain," Wheatley said, dismissively thumbing through the booklet. "What happens if we can't find him?"

"In that case, I'm authorized to abort the mission and destroy the envelope and its contents."

Wheatley latched on to the ray of hope that statement seemed to contain. "Who decides when it's time to do that?"

"I do, Corporal."

Jillian arrived at the task force's new position a few minutes after 1700 hours. Once again, two black men accompanied her with the donkey cart loaded with seafood for dinner and fresh water. This time, Jillian was on foot, with her rifle slung from her shoulder.

"No Franz tonight?" Jock asked.

Jillian shook her head. "He'll be better off in his stall," she replied.

First Sergeant Patchett took a look at the food on the cart and said, "If we keep eating like this, pretty soon we'll be spending most of our time just burying our own shit."

Doc Green added another concern. He asked Jillian, "Any chance of bringing some toilet paper next time? We're going to run out at this rate. We don't want these lads to be wiping themselves with leaves. That leads to all sorts of irritation."

"Amen, Doc...Amen," Patchett added.

Jillian looked surprised. "Wait a moment," she said, "there's going to be a *next time?* I thought you blokes would be gone once the bombers came."

"The bombing raid is scheduled for oh two hundred," Jock replied. "About nine hours from now. But we're not done, it seems. We've been ordered to stick around and assess the damage...and await further orders. So we're not out of your hair yet."

A smile spread across Jillian's face. "Maybe that's not such a bad thing, Jock," she said. Her hand touched his arm and lingered there for a moment.

It was Patchett's turn to smile, for he was now certain: *the captain'll be puttin' it to her before too long.* The first sergeant noticed Doc was smiling, too. They exchanged knowing nods.

As the two black men prepared to depart, Jillian told them, "It's tonight." The men nodded and led the donkey cart away, vanishing quickly into the forest.

"They'll make sure all the blacks are nowhere near the airfield," she told Jock. "When do we go after Colonel Najima?"

"Let's get into position around dusk," Jock replied. "Maybe we can get a glimpse of the guy when there's still some light. It'll be you, me, Corporal McMillen, and Guess."

"I suppose Guess will be the sniper?" she asked, cradling her rifle in her arms like she couldn't wait to use it.

"Yeah...let's let him take the shot, okay?"

She seemed truly disappointed as she replied, "Fine."

It had been dark for several hours when the staff car rolled to a stop in front of the Weipa Mission House. The driver shut off its engine and extinguished its lights, then jumped out to hold open one of the back doors.

"That should be Colonel Najima's car," Jillian whispered to Jock and Guess as they crouched in the tree line 150 yards away. McMillen, a few yards away covering the rear, strained to hear her words. As she raised Jock's binoculars to her eyes, she added, "Let's see who gets out."

In the dim light of the lanterns flanking the Mission House's front door, she saw a Japanese officer exit the car and stand, cap in hand, facing the building. The lantern light framing the doorway was sufficient to illuminate his face. "That's Najima...no doubt about it," Jillian said.

Colonel Najima took giant strides across the short distance to the Mission House steps, as if he were marching in some parade. Guess followed his movement, the crosshairs of the sniper rifle's telescopic sight centered on the colonel's head. "Sure seems to be making a ceremony outta getting himself laid," Guess said. "He'll be moving a whole lot faster, though, when them bombs start falling. I'll probably have to shoot him once he's back in the car." His finger began to gently caress the trigger. "It'd be easier if I could take him down now, Captain…"

"And tell the whole Japanese Army we're here?" Jock replied. "Keep your drawers on, Guess. We wait until the fireworks start."

Chapter Forty-Two

Climbing out of Cairns in darkness, the crew of the B-17 bomber *Peggy V* was growing more apprehensive by the minute. They were the lead ship in the 12-plane *conga line* that would make its way to Weipa—each plane separated by about five miles—and attempt to drop their bombs on the coordinates identified by Task Force Miles. Unfortunately, *Peggy V's* crew found the prospect of this mission terrifying. This crew—like everyone else in the US Army Air Force—had little proficiency in night flying and even less in night bombing. Droning into harm's way through the darkness of night was the most frightening thing they could think of doing right now. Even worse, they had been ordered to do it at a much lower than normal altitude—only 7,000 feet.

They were told there was little to fear from Japanese night fighters, whose pilots were supposedly less skilled in the dark than the Americans. Aside from straying into mountains, the sea, or the vast emptiness of Australia, anti-aircraft fire would be their greatest nemesis. Flying at only 7,000 feet made it easier for the gunners on the ground to hit them. The B-17 squadron at Cairns had been chosen for this mission for a single reason: they were the only one that had enough fuel on hand to mount a 12-plane raid. The other squadrons were still waiting for that sparse flow of seaborne tankers from the States to refill their tanks.

They flew northwest, homing on a signal from the US Army radio station at Mossman some 50 miles from Cairns. Once over Mossman, they turned a few degrees north, keeping the radio compass needle pointed straight at the tail of their aircraft while they flew a course of 320 degrees away from Mossman. They would fly that course until the Iron Range station signal, on a different frequency, showed a magnetic bearing of 90 degrees, an event that wouldn't happen for about 95 minutes after passing over Mossman Station. There, they would drop their bombs. The plan was simple in theory, crude in practice, and guaranteed to be of questionable accuracy—winds aloft and anxiety-driven human errors would see to that. But bombing by radio beams was the best system available for locating a target in the dark. Headquarters at Brisbane had dictated the reduced altitude to shorten the bombs' freefall and negate some of the inherent inaccuracies. There was a risk that steady signals from the two radio stations would allow Japanese bombers to home in on them, but an impatient Washington demanded a demonstration—*any* demonstration—of its Air Force's prowess. There were high hopes: at least *some* of the squadron's 48,000 pounds of bombs were bound to land on or near the target Task Force Miles had identified. *Any* success could be trumpeted as a major victory.

One hour past Mossman, the *Peggy V's* navigator called to the pilot over the interphone. "We've got a problem, skipper," the navigator said. "The Mossman signal is getting weak fast. The DF needle is spinning all over the dial."

"Do you think it's the mountains causing it?" the pilot asked.

"I don't know, skipper. We aren't that far from the station...only about one hundred eighty miles. I can't update our drift correction without it."

"Can you go celestial? Get us some star shots to keep us on course?"

The navigator laughed, but the irritation in his voice was obvious. "Sure I can...but down here at seven thousand...with all the clouds above us...I may not get enough good shots in time for a decent drift correction. We're only about thirty-five minutes from target."

The pilot asked, "How's the Iron Range signal?"

"It's pretty strong," the navigator replied, "but one good signal's not enough. How come the Brits and Krauts have better radio systems for night bombing than this Mickey Mouse setup we've got?"

"You're preaching to the choir, my friend," the pilot said. "I'm going to hold this heading until you tell me differently. Try to get some star shots."

Peggy V's radio operator chimed in, asking, "Skipper, do you want me to contact Mossman and see if they're having problems?"

"Negative," the pilot replied. "Maintain radio silence."

Jillian couldn't believe she'd dozed off. She awoke with a start, finding her head pressed against Jock's shoulder. She looked around; they were still in the woods at the edge of the Mission. Guess was a few yards to their right, his Springfield trained on the front door of the Mission House. McMillen was still a few yards behind, covering for any surprises from the rear. Jock was quietly humming a tune. She recognized it instantly.

"Ahh, you're back," Jock whispered.

"How long have I been asleep?"

"About an hour. I was about to wake you. It's nearly oh two hundred."

Oh two hundred. The time the bombers were due.

"That tune you were humming," Jillian said. "It's Wagner...*Ride of the Valkyries.* That's really what's crossing your mind right now? Songs about dead warriors being carried to Valhalla? A bit fatalistic, isn't it?"

"Maybe the dead warriors will be Japanese this time," Jock replied. "It seems like a fitting musical score for all this. Do you hear something different?"

She thought about it for a moment and said, "I don't know...but if you're in the mood for Wagner, I was thinking *Tristan and Isolde.*"

"But that's a love story, Jillian."

"They're all love stories, silly boy," she whispered.

She wasn't sure if he saw her knowing smile in the darkness. And he certainly wouldn't know the thought behind that smile: *it doesn't matter what part of the world they're from...all men are thick as bricks.*

McMillen heard it first—the distant throbbing of engines from the sky. It took a few seconds to convince himself he wasn't imagining it. He turned to alert the others, but there was no need. The sound had grown stronger, and now they heard it, too.

Jillian looked upward, seeing nothing but the silhouettes of treetops in the moonlight. "That noise," she said. "Is it...?"

"Yeah," Jock said. "It's an airplane...with more than one engine. A bomber, I'll bet."

"It sounds so close," she said, "like it's coming

right over us. Do you think—"

A brilliant, vertical column of light suddenly appeared from the direction of Airfield One—an anti-aircraft searchlight. Then there was another, and in a few seconds, half a dozen more searchlights were scanning the night sky.

"The Japs sure don't think it's one of theirs," Jock said.

Chapter Forty-Three

To the crew onboard *Peggy V,* the searchlight beams sweeping the sky before her looked like fingers of death. The beams hadn't found her yet, but once they did, she'd be a sitting duck, clearly illuminated for the anti-aircraft gunners.

"We need to get this the hell over with," her pilot announced over the interphone, his words tumbling rapidly from his mouth. Panic had raised the pitch of his voice nearly an octave, making him sound like a terrified child. The sudden revving of her four engines was an unmistakable signal to the rest of the crew: the pilot had rammed her throttles forward to the stops.

"Hold on, skipper," the navigator said as he scrambled to complete his last calculation before the drop. "If you change speed, it's gonna screw the numbers up! We'll never get on target!"

The navigator drew the last line of position onto the chart, completing the intersection of his celestial plot with the Iron Range signal. He was happily surprised to find they were much closer to the target than he thought they'd be—but they were off course by a few degrees. If they held this course any longer, they would miss the target by several miles. If *Peggy V* sped up, he'd have to calculate the release point all over again—and there wasn't enough time for that.

"Navigator to pilot…come left, heading two niner five…and for God's sake, skipper, keep the speed at one eight zero!"

The searchlight beams kept dancing across the sky in broad arcs, but they still hadn't found *Peggy V.* Ahead of her, pinpoint flashes of orange light began to dot the darkness. It was hard for the crew to judge exactly how far ahead the flashes were. For a brief moment, they seemed captivating and harmless—almost beautiful. But that moment passed quickly, for they remembered even beautiful things can kill.

"Shit...*flak,*" the pilot said, fixated on the light show playing before him. He shoved his hand against the throttles again, hoping—praying—for more power, but they were already as far forward as they would go. He knew each of those orange flashes was the explosion of an anti-aircraft shell, 75 or 105 millimeters in caliber. In daylight, you'd be able to see the hideous puff of black smoke that lingered, suspended in the air long after the flash. If a shell detonated close enough, it would send red-hot metal fragments tearing through the ship—and through him. *Peggy V* continued to accelerate slowly but steadily toward the deadly mayhem.

"Skipper, are you gonna turn or what?" the navigator said, his voice now climbing in pitch to match the pilot's. He had already accepted the pilot had no intention of reducing speed.

Turn...maybe that's not such a bad idea, the pilot thought as he jerked the control wheel counterclockwise. *Throw those Nip gunners off a little.* The big bomber responded reluctantly—almost grudgingly—as she banked left.

At a speed of more than three miles a minute, they were less than one minute from the target. The navigator's final calculation would be simple arithmetic—still an approximation, but one that should be close enough. *Close enough for government work,* as the instructors in flight school used to say. The bomb bay doors were opened; the navigator picked his second on the stopwatch's face for release, calling them out to the bombardier as they ticked down.

Five...four...three...two...one.

Bombs away.

Peggy V's crew held their collective breath as she plowed west-northwest, lighter now without her bomb load, able to climb higher or fly faster at the pilot's option. Once again, he chose speed. The searchlights had never found them; the anti-aircraft fire had remained just a benign fireworks display, never scarring them or their plane. They'd been told that Japanese anti-aircraft techniques were primitive and almost useless in the darkness. That knowledge came as little comfort, however, when you were the target.

Just when they thought they were clear, one more moment of panic was forced upon them. A lone searchlight beam appeared and a few orange flashes dotted the sky, this time much too high above them to be of concern. The threat evaporated quickly in their wake, and over the emptiness of the Gulf of Carpentaria, they began to breathe again.

"That last bit of flak...we probably passed over some Jap warship sitting off Weipa," the pilot said, his voice returning to its normal register as he guided his aircraft to the safety of a higher altitude.

It was time to set a course for home. The navigator was already deep into the task. It was a simple exercise: fly south to clear the stream of bombers following you to the target before turning southeast, back to Cairns. As soon as he picked up his plotter, his error struck him like a punch to the gut:

That computation for that last leg before the

release point...the speed...I did it in knots instead of miles per hour. A schoolboy's mistake. We didn't drop those bombs where we thought we did. We were short. A couple of miles short.

So short, in fact, the 500-pound bombs from *Peggy V*—all eight of them—cut their deadly swath through the position occupied by Melvin Patchett and all but three of the men of Task Force Miles.

Jock's head jerked southward, toward the sound of the impacting bombs. "That doesn't seem right," he said. "They're dropping too far inland, I think."

Jillian grabbed his chin and pulled his face back in the direction of the Mission House. "Never mind," she said. "Pay attention to what we came here for."

What we came here for—the killing of Colonel Najima. The ultimate decapitation of the Japanese command. J.T. Guess was curled tight into his firing position, waiting for the colonel to appear. Even in the darkness, Jock could tell his sniper was calm and focused, ready to put that final, gentle squeeze on the trigger the moment his target entered the crosshairs.

"You got enough light?" Jock asked Guess.

"Plenty."

Jock was relieved to see just how right he had been: the Japanese in the Mission had become completely disoriented by the bombs, even though they fell a few miles away. Sergeants and lieutenants barked orders that did little more than add to the confusion. It seemed every Japanese soldier was running in crazy circles, trying to process answers to the three questions that suddenly held sway over his continued existence:

What just happened?

What am I supposed to be doing about it?

How do I keep myself from getting killed?

Japanese soldiers and *comfort women*—a dozen or more of each—began to spill from the Mission House, adding to the bewildered throng. "Right on cue," Jock said, not bothering to keep his voice down. "Surely, that house is gonna empty in another second or two."

"Be patient," Jillian said, "those men who just ran out are ordinary soldiers, not officers."

The colonel's driver, who had been sleeping soundly in the front seat, was now doing a fidgety dance alongside the staff car. He alternated between holding the rear door open in anticipation of the colonel's hasty arrival and crouching low against the car's fender, seeking cover.

"So where the hell is this colonel?" Guess asked, his voice placid, his eye still glued to the rifle's scope.

"Good question," Jillian replied.

Miss Directed, the second B-17 in the *conga line* of bombers, was less than five minutes behind *Peggy V* and having just as difficult a time finding the target. Her navigator had never fully given up on the wavering Mossman signal. He kept trying to interpolate that oscillating needle in his radio compass into a usable bearing. It worked, after a fashion; when she dropped her bombs, they were only slightly more inaccurate than *Peggy V's.* This load sketched its line of destruction across the southern edge of Weipa Mission settlement. It bisected the northern end of Yellow Vermin Road, killing several truckloads of Japanese soldiers being rushed back to defend Airfield One. It also wiped out the docks, sinking Jillian's remaining four boats and a number of Japanese barges tied up there. The final bomb in the train landed squarely on Jillian's icehouse, blowing the building and its contents to smithereens.

Jillian's vantage point was some 500 yards away from where the icehouse had stood only moments ago, too far to see clearly in the dim light but close enough to sense the devastation that had just befallen her. But she found one serendipitous glimmer in the terrible scene: Sato's body was hidden in the icehouse.

"Well, at least we don't have to worry about getting rid of Sato anymore," she said, her voice deadpan. "Your Air Force blokes just took care of that for me. But overall, I'd say your flyers aren't very good at their jobs."

Colonel Najima's car still stood before the Mission House. It was unattended, its driver having joined the mob of Japanese now scurrying north, away from the bombs that had just fallen.

"What the fuck happened to the colonel?" Jock asked.

Jillian's reply was adamant. "He's still inside."

"You're sure?"

"I'm positive, Jock. He never came out."

Mike McMillen hadn't said much of anything since the four of them arrived at this sniper's nest. He could sense the plan unraveling, though, and the irritation in his hoarse whisper was obvious. "He's still inside...that's just swell," McMillen said. "What the hell do we do now, Captain?"

There was no hesitation at all in Jock's reply. "We go in after him."

Second Lieutenant Ernest Smith had never been a night person. A Midwestern farm boy, he believed in rising before dawn and hitting the sack early. He had dreaded his first night shift as officer-in-charge at the Mossman radio station, and the experience was proving to be 10 times worse than the anticipation. He could hardly keep his eyes open. Parked in the rolling chair behind the OIC's desk, his body felt detached from its surroundings, like it was packed in thick cotton. It hurt to hold his eyes open.

An officer can never fall asleep on duty, he chastised himself. *What kind of example would that set for the men...especially a goldbrick like Corporal Stanley Welsh?*

Ernest Smith cursed the bad luck that had given him the cantankerous Corporal Welsh as senior radio operator this night. Since coming on duty at 2200, Welsh had ignored him, for the most part, only acknowledging his presence when he needed a message approved or log entry signed. When Smith asked Welsh if the station was ready to comply with Special Operations Order 6-107, Welsh had merely grunted and nodded once. Lieutenant Smith took that as an *affirmative.*

The requirements of Special Operations Order 6-107 were concise: Mossman was to broadcast a continuous wave carrier on a specified frequency—at full power of 450 watts—commencing at 2300 hours. This signal was to remain on the air until 0600 hours of the following day. Radio traffic on other frequencies was to be handled as normal. No other explanation for the continuous signal was given in the order, but it didn't take a genius to figure out what was going on. The Air Force would be flying around in the dark, something they didn't do very often. They needed radio beams to help navigate in the dark. At precisely 2300, Smith watched as Welsh closed the key on the designated transmitter while grumbling something that sounded like, *Fucking HQ and their stupid orders...they want the Japs to home right in on us.* The corporal then flopped into his chair, put his feet up on his console, and became deeply engrossed in an old copy of *Life* magazine.

It was now 0215, and Lieutenant Smith decided the only way he'd ever manage to stay awake through this 12-hour night shift was to stay on his feet. He decided he'd check on the transmitters that lined one wall of the station. There were four of them, each a rack of electronic components two feet wide and twice as tall. Three transmitters were in standby mode, their vacuum tubes warmed up but sending nothing over the air. The fourth was broadcasting the continuous signal per Special Operations Order 6-107. Smith scanned the row of meters on the transmitter's front panel several times before the alarm went off in his sleepy head:

This thing isn't putting out full power! Nowhere near it! It's not tuned properly!

"CORPORAL WELSH," Smith said, rousing himself from his sleepwalk by the sheer volume of his command voice. "WHY IS THIS TRANSMITTER

NOT TUNED FOR FULL OUTPUT? IT'S PUTTING OUT LESS THAN FIFTY WATTS."

Stanley Welsh was actually startled by the lieutenant's harsh tone. He had never heard Smith raise his voice before. But Welsh knew he'd been caught in the act: *I'd better snow-job this dumb shavetail before he tries to stick it up my ass.*

"What do you mean, Lieutenant? Something gone wrong with the transmitter?"

"Nothing's wrong with the damned transmitter," Smith said as he spun the knobs and watched the meters climb to full scale. "You didn't tune it properly."

Welsh made a show of tapping the meters and tweaking the knobs himself, trying to find something— anything—to discredit the lieutenant's correct assumption.

Smith pulled the copy of Special Operations Order 6-107 from the clipboard on the wall. He waved the sheet of paper in Welsh's face. "You're aware this order specified *full power,* Corporal?"

"That just don't make no sense, Lieutenant," Welsh said, still grasping for the upper hand. "It's against SOP to broadcast a continuous signal at full power. It's an invitation for the Japs to bomb us. You know that."

"Direct orders supersede SOP. *You* know that, Corporal. Are you telling me you ignored orders and detuned this transmitter on purpose?"

"I don't know why you're getting on my ass, Lieutenant. Can't a guy make a little mistake every now and then?"

"This was no mistake, Welsh. God only knows what problems you've caused. You're relieved from duty and restricted to quarters, pending court martial."

Welsh played his last card. "If this station didn't follow orders, I ain't the only one who's gonna get court martialed. You're the officer-in-charge, ain't you?"

"Your concern is touching, Welsh...but I'll take my chances. Now get out of my sight."

Chapter Forty-Four

Before Lieutenant Smith retuned the Mossman transmitter to full power, two more B-17s had stumbled toward the target and dropped their bombs. The next plane behind *Peggy V* and *Miss Directed* was *The Wanderer.* Her name proved to be appropriate as she scattered her bombs wildly into the forest some five miles south of the target, nowhere near any human beings. All the searchlight activity miles to the north—and the probability these searchlights further identified the target area—did not vex *The Wanderer's* crew greatly as her bombardier toggled the drop switch.

Five minutes behind *The Wanderer* came *Beauteous Belinda.* More by stroke of luck than any airman's skill, she was fairly close to being on course. Her bombs would have landed within a few hundred yards of the designated coordinates—if they had actually fallen when her bombardier hit the drop switch. Something in the electrical circuitry that released the bombs in sequence malfunctioned. As *Belinda* flew on past the drop point, her crew struggled to fix the problem with the bomb release. They debated turning around and trying again, this time using the manual bomb release lever. That maneuver was unanimously rejected; it was simply too dangerous. There were eight more aircraft strung out behind *Belinda* in that long, invisible line. The odds of colliding with one of them was just too great.

Almost 90 seconds past the drop point, they gave up their tinkering with the faulty circuit. As they prepared to close the bomb bay doors, the electrical bomb release circuitry suddenly came alive, as if some magic hand had fixed the problem. All eight bombs released and plunged into the dark void below.

Beauteous Belinda's crew gave a collective shrug: *a war machine can be as cantankerous as a woman.* Her pilot began the turn south, the first leg of her homeward journey.

Halfway through the turn, *Beauteous Belinda* was jostled by a shock wave. Her tail gunner reported there had been the flash of an enormous explosion in their wake a few seconds before the wave hit. The explosion had probably been at ground level, but in the darkness, with no visual reference, he couldn't tell for sure. The gunner didn't notice that last searchlight tracking his plane had extinguished simultaneously with the explosion.

Beauteous Belinda's crew would never know just how lucky they were that night. Instead, they were sick with worry. The explosion might be one of the other bombers crashing. Worse, it could be one of the others colliding with their accidental stick of bombs and exploding in flight. They never imagined the true source of the explosion: they had just sunk the only Japanese warship—a destroyer—lying at anchor off Weipa.

As she went to the bottom, so went the regiment's only remaining radio link to the Japanese headquarters at Rabaul.

For the navigators onboard the eight remaining aircraft in the *conga line,* finding the target suddenly got much easier. The Mossman signal had stopped its wild dance around their radio compass dials and settled down to a rock-steady bearing, a bearing solid enough for precise course adjustments. They had no idea how the four planes before them had fared; strict radio silence had been maintained. But the eight navigators knew they now had a far better chance of getting a bomb close to target than their predecessors in the *conga line.*

The navigators of the first four ships, bombs gone and on courses for home, shared the same thought when they noticed the return of the Mossman signal: *Son of a bitch! NOW it decides to get strong! Oh well...at least it'll make finding our way home a whole lot easier.*

They knelt in a circle as Jock laid down his plan to storm the Mission House, sketching its details in the dirt beneath the dim red glow of his flashlight. Jillian listened intently, fascinated by his focus and the infectious enthusiasm he radiated. Guess and McMillen obviously were, too. She wasn't sure whether to chalk it up to pure leadership on Jock's part or simple charisma. Either way, it was working its magic. By the time Jock said, "Let's show these bastards what the American soldier can do," his two men had been whipped into such a blood lust they looked ready to take on the entire Japanese Army.

Even Jillian startled herself by offering up a silent cheer. She took a deep breath and got a hold of herself. *Look at us,* she thought. *We're ready to do his bidding full stop...no matter how bloody crazy his plan is.*

"Okay, that's how it'll work," Jock said in

conclusion. "Any questions?"

"Just one," Jillian said. "What am I supposed to be doing in this plan of yours?"

"You're supposed to stay right here and wait for us," Jock replied.

"And how the bloody hell will you recognize Najima without me?"

"There can't be too many people still in there. Shouldn't be too hard to figure out. He'll be the only full colonel in there."

Guess added, "If we've gotta shoot a couple extra to be sure, it don't make no nevermind."

"I really think I should go with you," Jillian said, begging more than contradicting.

Gently, Jock took her face in his hands. He stared into her eyes—softly, deeply—telling her heart things no words could express.

"No," he whispered. "Stay here. Please."

As he stood, she held his hands, brushing his fingertips with a tender kiss as they left her face. She was sure Guess and McMillen knew exactly what was brewing between her and their commander, even though they were facing away, watching for the enemy. They probably had some crude Yank slang for it, no doubt, to match the leer she had caught earlier on the first sergeant's face. She didn't care who knew. Not anymore.

Before she released him, she said, "Good hunting, Jock...and hurry back."

The interior of the Mission House was darker than

Jock imagined. As he led Guess and McMillen down its long hallway, each step they took made the wooden floorboards creak, announcing their approach no matter how carefully they put their feet down. The house seemed deserted at first, but halfway down the hall they began to hear two muffled voices. One was a man's, making what sounded like furious demands in Japanese. The other was a woman's, sobbing words in what might have been fear or simply frustration. As they reached the end of the hallway, they knew the voices could only be coming from behind the last door on the right. It was closed tight.

Wordlessly, Jock positioned his two men on either side of the doorway. His Thompson poised to fire from the hip, he kicked the door open—and froze. He was totally unprepared for the scene that greeted him.

Jock had no doubt he had come face-to-face with Colonel Najima. There was no mistaking the likeness he had seen from afar a few hours ago. Jock lowered the muzzle of his Thompson, thinking:

I can't shoot a man this way...not in the predicament he's in. But I can't let him slip through my fingers, either.

Najima was bound hand and foot to a simple wooden armchair. He was naked as a jaybird, glowering at the Americans with an air of superiority that seemed ridiculously inappropriate for the circumstances. There were welts across his legs and torso, fresh and bright red, probably inflicted by the stout bamboo stick now lying on the floor. A comfort woman, very young, clad in a kimono—perhaps the person who had put the colonel in this compromising position and administered the corporal punishment—was kneeling behind the chair, the colonel's sword in hand, trying and failing to cut the thick, coarse ropes that bound him. She dropped the sword and slumped into the corner, trembling with fear, pleading with her hands. She babbled indecipherable words that could only come from one begging for her life.

Jock pulled her to her feet. "GO," he commanded, pointing to the door.

McMillen swung into the doorway. He had expected to hear the deafening chatter of a Thompson, not words. He was no more prepared than his captain for what he saw.

"Son of a bitch!" McMillen said. "I've seen some fucked-up shit in my life, but this takes the goddamn cake." He wasted little time scooping up the colonel's sword and hanging it from his pack. Quite satisfied, he said, "Man, this is a better souvenir than those uniforms we swiped."

"I'm letting the woman go," Jock said, propelling her toward the door. She bounced off McMillen and into the hallway, where she found herself staring down the barrel of Guess's rifle.

"Captain says let her go, Killer," McMillen said to Guess. "You ain't gonna believe the queer-ass bullshit that's been going on in here."

Guess lowered his rifle and waved the comfort woman away. She backed a few steps down the hall, still cringing in terror. Then she turned and ran as fast as her bare feet would carry her toward the entranceway. Just before she reached it, there was the sound of bombs exploding again, not in Weipa this time but farther to the south, where they were supposed to be. The woman shrieked, dropped to the floor, curled her knees to her chest and covered her head with her arms.

"GO ON...GET OUTTA HERE," Guess said, pointing his rifle at her. "YOU AIN'T GONNA GET ANOTHER CHANCE LIKE THIS, LADY."

The comfort woman looked frantically out the doorway, then back at Guess's rifle before coming to a decision. The rifle was deadly close; the bombs were not so close. At least not this time. She bolted out the door.

No sooner had she vanished from sight, the *thud-thud-thud* of the bombs' impact melded into a tremendous explosion that shook the Mission House. Its bright, orange flash lit the night sky like apricot daylight and cast its eerie brilliance into the house for a brief moment.

"What the fuck was that?" McMillen asked.

"Ammo dump...or fuel depot," Jock replied. "Nothing else goes up like that. Maybe those flyboys finally dropped something in the right place."

Guess took a glance inside the room. Seeing the bound, naked colonel, the expression on his face registered more than shock. He was *offended*. "Whoring's bad enough," he said as he trained his rifle on Najima, "but whatever sex stuff's been going on in here gotta be an abomination in the eyes of the Lord."

"Put the rifle down, Guess," Jock said, "and save that shit for the padre."

"But it just ain't *normal,* Captain,*"* Guess continued. "Look at him! He ain't even embarrassed. This man needs to die for a whole lotta reasons."

"I said put the rifle down, Guess. We're not going to kill him."

McMillen suddenly seemed as offended as Guess as he asked, "What do you mean, Captain? What the hell did we come here for?"

"He's our prisoner," Jock said. "First Jap POW of this damn war, I'm guessing...and we've got him. Grab the chair and carry him out of here just the way he is."

Neither McMillen nor Guess could believe what they had just heard. They stood in place, shaking their heads, mouths agape.

"Don't I speak English? Pick up the chair and let's get out of here," Jock said as he gathered the colonel's clothing from pegs on the wall. "Move it!"

Still silent, McMillen and Guess slung their weapons on their shoulders and, one on each side, picked up the chair with the colonel still bound to it. They maneuvered their human cargo into the hallway, and with Jock leading the way, headed toward the door that led outside.

Najima had yet to utter a sound since the Americans found him. The colonel's silence so far came as small comfort to Mike McMillen, though. He asked Jock, "What if he starts to make noise, sir?"

"Butt-stroke him in the head. That'll shut him up for a while."

Guess asked, "Do you think he knows what we're saying, Captain?"

"Right now, I couldn't care less."

Guess started to chuckle. "Miss Forbes is gonna get a real kick outta this."

"I'll bet it ain't nothing she ain't seen before," McMillen replied, "just a whole lot smaller."

They all looked to see if that comment got a rise out of the Jap colonel, but his facial expression never changed. That same glower was still there. No look of indignation, annoyance, or shame came over him.

"Nah, he doesn't understand us," Jock said.

They were outside now, in the faint glow of the fire raging to the south. It lit the settlement with that same apricot light from the initial explosion, only continuous and muted now, casting long, dancing shadows against the tree line in the distance where Jillian was waiting. Jock still led the way. McMillen and Guess, encumbered with the chair-bound colonel, moved more slowly and lagged behind. As Jock neared the colonel's abandoned car, a new shadow fell on the ground before him, its source still obscured by the car's mass. This new shadow advanced across Jock's path with a halting yet rhythmic motion, like the second hand of a wind-up clock. Or the gait of a limping man.

The *Kempeitai* sergeant—that same, game-legged bastard Jock had seen beating Jillian yesterday— stepped into his path from behind the hood of the car. Jock could just make out the thin moustache—and the dull, metallic glimmer of something in his raised hand:

A pistol...

He was only 20 feet away. The *kempei* took one last, tottering step as he steadied his aim.

To Jock, it felt like a year of his life passed in the split second it took to train his Thompson on the *kempei.* Trapped in this bizarre, slow-motion world of impending death, Jock couldn't believe his weapon had not yet fired. He could swear he was squeezing the trigger hard enough to break it off, yet it seemed to be moving slower than a glacier.

But there was no burst of automatic gunfire, just a dull *thump,* like a coconut being cleaved with a machete—and then a hot, wet spray hit Jock's face, stinging and blinding him. Only then did Jock hear the *crack* of a distant gunshot.

Maybe another year went by until Jock drew his next breath—and then time snapped back to its normal cadence. He wiped the spray's sticky residue from his eyes and realized, *Oh shit! It's the Jap's brains!*

Jock could see again. The limping *kempei* was no longer standing before him. His body was face-down in the dirt. Even in the dim, flickering light, Jock could tell his head was gravely misshapen, the skull shattered and emptied. The dark pool growing around it could only be blood. Someone had done the *kempei* in with a killer head shot. Jock was fairly sure it hadn't been him.

It hadn't been McMillen or Guess, either. At the sound of the gunshot, they had dropped the chair holding Najima, unslung their weapons and flung themselves to prone firing positions. But they had no idea who or what to shoot. They never saw the *Kempeitai* sergeant until he was dead on the ground.

With one glance backwards, Jock could see McMillen and Guess shared with him the same thought: *We need to get the fuck out of here.*

The three Americans covered the remaining distance to the tree line—complete with their seated captive—on the dead run. "I think we just broke the record for the hundred yard dash," Mike McMillen said as they collapsed among the trees to catch their breath. Najima's chair was tipped on its back, its immobile occupant staring at the sky.

McMillen asked Jock, "Who the hell shot that guy back there?"

It was Jillian who replied, "I did," as she

approached out of the dancing shadows. She skidded to a halt at the sight of Najima, who shot a hateful glance at her and finally uttered some guttural words no one understood—but they all easily grasped it wasn't a friendly, *Hello...nice to see you again, Miss Forbes.*

After a moment of staring incredulously at the naked colonel, she said, "What in bloody hell have you done, Jock?" She sounded like a frustrated parent scolding a delinquent child.

"We didn't do anything," Jock replied. "We found him like this, and we took him prisoner."

Jillian threw up her hands. "I thought you wanted him dead!"

"Change of plans. Captured is even better than dead. I'll explain later."

McMillen was still trying to come to grips with what they had just done. "First time I ever heard of a recon unit taking prisoners, sir," he said.

"There's a first time for everything," Jock replied. "Now we've got to figure out where to stash the good colonel."

"I know just the place," Jillian said. "Follow me. We shouldn't have any trouble navigating, with that fire as bright as it is now. We need to get farther upwind anyway. This is *the dry...*and any fire is going to spread fast."

As they made their way deeper into the woods, Jillian cast another, bewildered glance at the bound colonel, asking no one in particular, "What is it with these Japanese and their bloody ropes?"

Melvin Patchett awoke from unconsciousness to a strange glow in the sky. His eyes hadn't focused yet—they wouldn't for a few minutes—and he could hear nothing but a high-pitched siren screaming in his ears. He was lying on his back in a hole several feet deep, unable to move very much. His entire body ached, as if every square inch had been battered by powerful blows—but all the parts still seemed to be there. Slowly, a thought came together in the murky labyrinth of his mind:

Them Gerries sure shelled us good this time. Knocked me right on my ass.

A dark shape materialized and hovered over him. *A fucking Hun,* Patchett thought, his hands scrambling frantically around him for his rifle, a bayonet, an entrenching tool—anything to thwart this soldier of the Kaiser moving in to finish him off.

"Whoa, Top! Take it easy!" It was Doc Green's voice, but Melvin Patchett couldn't recognize it. Not through the distortion of his fiercely ringing ears.

"Sprechen sie Englisch?" Patchett asked, his voice weak and raspy.

Doc's ears were ringing like sirens, too, but he was pretty sure he understood, even if the words were in German. "OF COURSE I SPEAK ENGLISH," he said, pumping up the volume to be heard more clearly. "WHERE ARE YOU HURT, TOP?"

Top? That made no sense to Melvin Patchett. He was a private, not a first sergeant. Other details filtered back into his head: he was 18 years old. This was France. The Great War. *Over There* and all that crap.

"Did we hold?" Patchett asked.

"HOLD *WHAT*, TOP?"

"The Marne. We're supposed to hold at the Marne River."

Doc Green eased himself to a sitting position on the ground next to the first sergeant. All the squatting and kneeling to check on casualties was causing the wound on his leg—a jagged gash through the calf—to throb painfully. He needed to rest it for a moment. He'd use that time to bring Melvin Patchett back to reality.

"Top, listen to me carefully," Doc said, his mouth right next to Patchett's ear. "You're not in France anymore. This is Australia. And it's not 1918...it's 1942. We're in a new war. We've just been on the receiving end of a bombing raid, probably by our own blokes."

Melvin Patchett propped himself up on his elbows. His head was clearing and his eyes were beginning to focus. He recognized the man sitting next to him—*it's that Aussie doc.* He knew now he was no longer 18, no longer a private. There were men he was responsible for.

"How many dead and wounded, Doc?" Patchett asked.

"Everyone's wounded, one way or the other. Nobody's dead, but it looks like a giant bloody buzzsaw went through this place. I reckon your making us dig in deep saved us all. How do you feel? I can't see any wound on you...except your ears are bleeding."

Patchett shrugged off Doc's concern. He checked his wristwatch but couldn't read it. His eyes weren't working well enough for that yet. "What time is it, Doc?" he asked.

"About oh two twenty-five."

"Hmm. Looks like the middle of the day with all this damned light. What's burning over there?"

Doc shrugged. "Not sure...but whatever those bombs hit started one hell of a fire. Bloody good thing we're not downwind. It's going to spread and burn everything in the forest from the airfield to Weipa."

First Sergeant Patchett struggled to his feet, picking up his helmet and Thompson in the process. "Hey, you're wounded, too," he said, pointing to the bloody bandage on Doc Green's leg.

"No problem. I'll stitch it up later, when I get a chance."

"Outstanding," the first sergeant replied. "Now let's get off our asses and check on the others."

It was the middle of the night—a little after 0200—and Corporal Grover Wheatley still hadn't gotten a minute's sleep since leaving Brisbane almost 48 hours ago. He and this lunatic—this Captain Brewster—had trudged 25 miles up the coast since that tub of a patrol boat dropped them off at Archer Bay. At least that was Brewster's estimation. To Grover Wheatley, it seemed like they walked 500 miles. He was exhausted. His feet were killing him. Even though he showed little exposed skin—just his forearms, face, and neck—he'd been bitten by about a million mosquitoes. The K rations they carried were like eating nothing at all. And without sleep, he wouldn't last much longer.

Wheatley's frazzled mind began a silent rant against his captain. *Look at him, all snug in his bedroll like his mommy tucked him in. How on earth can this idiot sleep? It sounds like every animal in this fucking jungle is circling, waiting to make a meal out of us! And I don't even need to be here! I got to track exactly one transmission from this Task Force Miles so far...and guess what? It says they're north of here somewhere. Whoop-dee-fucking-doo! I could have told you that just looking at a map in Brisbane. I should stick this rifle up the captain's ass right now and pull the trigger...*

His rant was cut short when he felt the first tremor right through the soles of his boots. A few seconds later, he heard a dull rumble, like thunder. It seemed to be coming from the north. Wheatley turned and looked in that direction. A brilliant orange cap sat on the horizon like a vivid brushstroke on a black canvas. Something was burning. How far away, he couldn't tell. But he was sure there was one hell of a fire going on someplace.

Chapter Forty-Five

Making their way slowly through the forest, it took them almost an hour to reach the place Jillian had in mind. Guess and McMillen carried Colonel Najima—still naked and bound to the chair—the entire way, declining offers by Jock to alternate with them. When even Jillian offered to take a turn carrying the chair, Guess said, "No, thank you, ma'am. This little booger ain't heavy at all."

"Yeah, he's no problem," McMillen added. "Me and Killer could carry this guy all the way to Brisbane if we had to."

Every five minutes—just like clockwork—there was another series of dull *thuds* from the direction of Airfield One. "The flyboys must still be at it," Jock said. "I sure hope they're giving the Japs a good pasting."

They had traveled farther from the fire, and its glow had grown faint when shadowy outlines of huts, some emitting their own dim lantern light, appeared through the trees. "We're here," Jillian said. She pointed to a spot inside the settlement. "Go to that bigger shack standing off by itself. I'll join you in a minute." She raced ahead and vanished among the huts.

The shack to which Jillian had sent them was deserted. Its walls and roof were corrugated metal. There was a weathered sign over the door: *Queensland Police.* Jock pushed open the unlocked door and entered, shining his flashlight around the shack's interior. The dust was thick and cobwebs reflected his light, looking like the lacy doilies that decorated his grandmother's house back in Massachusetts. Manacles and leg shackles hung by their chains from pegs on a wall. There was a tall, iron-barred cage, big enough for several men, nestled in a corner. Its door was swung open.

"Bring him inside, men," Jock called to Guess and McMillen, who soon trudged through the doorway carrying the colonel.

"Put him in the cell," Jock said.

As they placed Najima, still bound to the chair, inside the cell, McMillen asked, "You want to untie him now, sir?"

"No. Not until we figure out who's got the key," Jock replied, tossing the colonel's clothes onto the naked man's lap.

"Wait a minute, Captain…let's keep his uniform, too. More souvenirs," McMillen said.

"No, we'll let the man keep his clothes," Jock replied. "Tell you what, though…you've already got his sword, so take his rank insignia, too."

McMillen eagerly ripped the insignia of rank— three silvery-white stars on a background of yellow and red stripes—from the collars of Najima's tunic. He tossed one to Guess and stashed the other in his breast pocket. "I'll betcha we can get half a month's pay from some rear-area rube for one of them beauties," McMillen said.

Jillian reappeared with Old Robert in tow. He twirled a heavy key on a chain around his finger. His face broke into a triumphant grin when he saw Najima. "Constable Mick's nick finally has another guest," Old Robert said, "and this time it's not a black man." He made a scolding, *cluck-cluck* sound with his tongue and then asked the colonel, "How could a man of your high standing get yourself in such a predicament?"

"He doesn't understand English," Jillian said.

Old Robert replied, "He doesn't have to speak English to know what I'm saying."

"Cut him loose," Jock said.

With his bayonet, Guess sliced through the ropes. Free of his bonds, the colonel wasted no time pulling on his trousers. There was a loud *clunk*—like the sound of a vault closing—as Old Robert swung the cell's door shut and a softer *clink-clink* as he turned the key in the lock. "We'll do our best to care for him in your absence," he said to Jock.

Jock checked his watch. It read 0310. "It's still over three hours to sunrise," he said. "I was thinking of heading back now, using the light from the fire—"

"No, don't," Jillian said. "If that fire dies out, you'll be in trouble out there until sunrise. Stay here and get some rest."

"I guess you're right," Jock replied, then turned to McMillen and Guess. "I'll take first watch. You two get some shut-eye."

Jock, Jillian, and Old Robert stepped outside to the police station's veranda and sat down on its wooden deck, their backs against the metal wall. Jock had a question for them: "What if the Japanese come and find you holding their colonel captive? It may be a few days before my men can take him back east."

"If the Japanese come, they will not find us here, Captain," Old Robert replied. "Everyone has gone bush except the ones who work Miss Jilly's boats...and now she says the boats are gone."

"I'm very sorry about that," Jock said. "The bombers...they...I mean...destroying the boats and the icehouse was just an accident, I'm sure."

Old Robert cast a skeptical glance Jock's way as he said, "Accident, you say? It's very hard to tell the difference from where I stand." He paused, staring solemnly into the night before adding, "Did this *accident* at least end the problem of Mister Sato's corpse, Miss Jilly?"

"Yes," Jillian replied, "in a most dramatic fashion."

"But the war has still put us out of business," Old Robert said, his *I told you so* glance not lost on Jillian.

Eager to change the subject, she asked Jock, "So *now* will you tell me why you changed your mind and took Najima prisoner?"

"It's simple," Jock replied. "I got worried that the bombing might be a complete failure. Then, there'd still be plenty of Najima's staff alive to run the regiment...and with him shot dead, they'd unleash retribution against everyone who lives here. But if he just turned up missing, there'd be a period of confusion while they tried to figure out what happened to him."

"A wise decision, Captain," Old Robert said. "Thank you."

They let a few minutes of silence pass. Jock finally broke it by saying, "It's been over fifteen minutes since we heard the last bombs fall. I guess the bombers are done."

Not sounding terribly enthusiastic, Jillian said, "I can't wait to see if they did any good...aside from burning down half the forest and nearly everything I own."

"Those explosions from down south," Jock said, "those weren't trees blowing up."

Still unconvinced, Jillian replied, "We'll see."

Another moment of silence passed before Jock said, "That man you shot...do you know who he was?"

"Yeah...I saw the limp, Jock."

"That was some great shooting. You saved my life."

"Let's not get carried away, Jock. It was an easy shot...and I never gave you a chance to get off one of your own."

"Still, how will I ever repay you?"

An impish smile spread slowly across her face as she draped an arm around his shoulders. "Oh, I'll think of something," she replied.

It was nearly 0800 when Jock, McMillen, and Guess returned to First Sergeant Patchett's position. They wouldn't have recognized it if not for the mangled remains of the radio set and two of the *Radio Flyers*. They walked the compact perimeter and found its fighting holes all but empty. A few of the holes showed dark, blackened splotches where soil and blood must have mixed. The perimeter, some 40 yards in diameter, was at the center of a line of destruction 100 yards wide that stretched east and west for hundreds of yards in either direction. At regular intervals along the line were eight saucer-shaped depressions in the ground, wide and deep enough to swallow a deuce and a half truck, the depressions stripped clean of all vegetation as if the earth had been tilled by some giant plow. Trees outside the depressions had been raggedly pruned, their broken limbs and shattered trunks littering the area. Some debris of an Army unit was scattered about—K ration boxes and wrappers, a well-dented helmet, a metal canteen crushed flat—but Patchett and his men were nowhere to be seen. What was once part of a eucalyptus forest now resembled a moonscape.

J.T. Guess tried to make sense of what he was seeing. "What caused this, sir?" he asked Jock. "Artillery?"

"Nah," Jock replied. "This is bomb damage." He held his arms parallel to the line of destruction. "See the nice straight line of craters? That's just how a stick of bombs would impact. None of them landed inside Top's perimeter…but two of them straddled it pretty damned close."

Jock's explanation was a bit too cold and clinical for McMillen. Looking around in confusion, he asked, "So what the hell happened to our guys? They didn't get…"

Jock finished McMillen's sentence. "Vaporized? No, I doubt that."

But that still didn't explain where Patchett and the rest were. Mike McMillen's bewilderment was turning to anger. He asked, "*Our* bombers did this, Captain?"

"Looks that way."

"Son of a fucking bitch!" McMillen said, kicking what was left of a *Radio Flyer*. "Ever since we got here, the Japs have been the least of our fucking problems." He wandered away from Jock and Guess, swearing a blue streak all the way to the edge of the perimeter.

His profane tirade ended abruptly, as if shut off by a switch. Someone—he couldn't tell who—was approaching out of the woods. McMillen leveled his Thompson and tried to shout out the challenge word— but he couldn't remember what it was. He stood there, silent yet open-mouthed, a panicky mute with a deadly weapon in his hands.

"*Laverne*, McMillen…the password's *Laverne*," First Sergeant Patchett said in his unmistakable voice, much too loudly considering there could be Japs within earshot. "Now stop pointing that fucking Thompson at me."

Jock made an urgent hand gesture to Patchett that could only mean *keep it down!*

"Can't help it, sir," Patchett said. "My ears are ringing like church bells. Everyone's are. Can't even hear myself think, let alone talk quiet."

Everyone's are…that particular phrasing gave Jock a glimmer of hope no one had been killed. But surely his men had paid some price. He asked, "How bad are the casualties, Top?" He cringed as he waited for the first sergeant's answer.

"Pacheco's the worst," Patchett said. "His leg's broke bad. Tree fell on him. Everybody else is banged up, concussed, and half-deaf, but that'll pass. Damn lucky thing these trees ain't no stouter. We would've had tree bursts for sure then…and we'd all be fucking dead. No hole in the ground saves you when they're blowing up right over your head."

"Amen, Top," Jock said, feeling very mortal as he scanned the line of bomb craters one more time. "Looks like the radio's done for, though."

"Yep," Patchett replied, that single, clipped word sounding like a stoic, yet hopeless admission of defeat. "Leave it to the flyboys to fuck things up but good."

Patchett started walking, motioning for Jock and the others to follow. "We set up over here a ways until y'all got back," he said. "Looks more like an aid station than a combat perimeter right now. As I live and breathe, that Doc Green's doing one hell of a job...for a lady doc."

Jock smiled and asked Patchett, "See any Japs?"

"Nope. Don't see no airplanes this morning, neither. Maybe they all burned up in that fire." Patchett pointed in the direction of the airfield. "Still a lot of smoke from over yonder. Maybe they're still burning."

Patchett turned to Guess and asked, "Well, son...did you get your shot?"

"Negative, Top. The captain had another idea."

Patchett stopped dead in his tracks. He turned to face Jock and, as if bracing for a blow, asked, "Another idea, sir?"

"We took the colonel prisoner," Jock replied.

Now Patchett's face looked as if he really had just taken a blow. "You did *what*, sir?"

"Captured him, Top. Probably the first Jap POW of the war...and he's ours."

Jock watched and waited as Melvin Patchett's face wheeled through a variety of emotions. Disbelief, denial, and anger all took their brief moment, until his expression settled into one of resignation and acceptance. "So where the hell is he, sir?" the first sergeant asked.

"Jillian and the blacks are holding him for us."

Jock wasn't sure if Patchett's sigh was one of relief or muted exasperation. "Well, that's just fine and dandy," the first sergeant said, and started walking again.

In a few minutes they reached the new perimeter. Patchett was right: it did look more like an aid station than a combat position. Everyone—even Doc Green—

was wearing a field dressing somewhere. Teddy Mukasic and Frank Simms, both without helmets, were manning the machine gun, each with a bandage wrapped over his forehead.

McMillen walked over to them and said, "Hey, you guys look like the fucking Spirit of Seventy-Six."

Mukasic and Simms responded in unison with dismissive scowls and raised middle fingers. "Let's see what you look like when some fuck-up drops one on your head," Simms said.

Jock gauged the condition of his unit. It wasn't a pretty picture: *Shit...they're going to need a lot of rest just to walk out of this place, let alone do any combat patrolling.* His gaze fell on Corporal Pacheco, lying on a makeshift stretcher atop the *Radio Flyer* that had survived the bombing. Doc Green was putting the finishing touches on the splint supporting his shattered leg. *And Pacheco won't be doing any walking, period. Not for a long time.*

But somehow, I've still got to figure out if this bombing raid was a success...or just a colossal screw-up. And I've got to figure out how we're going to talk to Brisbane without a radio.

Jock noticed a new expression on Melvin Patchett's face, one he had never witnessed before. This time, his first sergeant seemed unnerved and searching, reaching out for some assurance that everything would somehow be all right. Even Patchett's voice lost its usual, blustery confidence when he asked, "So what the hell do we do now, Captain?"

Chapter Forty-Six

It was almost noon before Jock was ready to move out again. He'd take McMillen and Guess with him once more; they were the only ones fit to go on a recon patrol. They hadn't suffered the pummeling from American bombs the others had, and they had actually gotten some sleep last night.

After much deliberation, Jock selected one more man to join the patrol: Bogater Boudreau. He seemed amazingly fresh and fit, healed of the concussive battering still plaguing the others, although he confessed *my ears were bleeding a little from them bombs.* Even his shoulder wound—the only bandage he wore, obvious beneath his khaki tee shirt—was posing no problems. It seemed like ancient history now, having happened on the Catalina five days ago. Five days that seemed like a lifetime. When Jock asked Doc Green if he thought Bogater was medically fit to go on patrol, Doc said, "Look at him…the lad's made of steel. Take him, if you must."

But Jock's mind wasn't made up until Boudreau said, "C'mon, Captain…take me. It's high time I got off my dead ass." It was more than a request; it was a plea.

It didn't take the four of them very long to reach Yellow Vermin Road. Hunkered down among the trees near the road's eastern edge, they couldn't believe what they were seeing. It looked like the entire Japanese Army—a few in trucks, most on foot—was staggering up that road, heading north. They looked disorganized. There didn't seem to be any leaders, no senior officers at roadside viewing the ragged parade from staff cars or atop horses. This was just mobs of soldiers—lost, confused, and fearful—fleeing to safety.

Mike McMillen whispered to Jock, "What the fuck is going on, sir?"

Jock didn't answer. He was deep in thought, trying to remember something Jillian had said. He couldn't recall her words at first, but then those words came back to him loud and clear: *Kill their commander and they'll be running around like chickens without heads.*

"I think we're looking at a general retreat," Jock finally replied. "Since we can't cross the road yet…not without getting spotted…we'll shadow them and see where they're going."

Bogater Boudreau had walked point the whole way as they paralleled the Japanese troops moving north up Yellow Vermin Road. He showed no signs of tiring, staying crisply alert. He seemed truly in his element: *He's getting one hell of a kick out of this,* Jock thought. Their pace was steady, and they had no trouble remaining concealed among the trees and tall grass on the east side of the road.

Soon after Jock and his men started north, the forest on the opposite side of the road—the west side, the windward side—showed the hideous scars of the fire like a line drawn across Earth by some angry God. What was left of the trees looked like blackened, smoking toothpicks haphazardly stuck into the barren ground. The stink of combustion's aftermath filled their lungs and made it difficult to breathe. The devastation extended west and north as far as they could see: *Right to where Airfield One is,* Jock thought. He struggled to keep his optimistic thoughts of a total Japanese rout in check until they had more evidence.

They continued their pursuit for almost an hour, until Boudreau stopped abruptly and crouched down in the grass, raising his hand—the signal for the others to stop. The hand signal was passed down the line, from Jock, to Guess, to McMillen. Jock crawled forward, joining Boudreau on point.

No words were necessary; the view ahead provided the answer why they stopped. They were about to run out of concealment. The forest beyond this point had been flattened, the barren ground now decorated with a line of bomb craters instead. The ragged stumps of trees still smoldered, the tall grass that once blanketed the soil burned away. Surprisingly, the wooden bridge the Japanese had built across the narrows of the Embley River had been spared. Vehicles and soldiers on foot streamed across it into Weipa. Less than half a mile ahead, the Americans could see through binoculars the Mission settlement, teeming with aimless Japanese troops like the ones they had been following.

"How many of them you figure there are, sir?" Boudreau asked.

"Between the road and the Mission? Hundreds...maybe a thousand," Jock replied.

Bogater Boudreau said, "And it sure looks to me like they're running away." Then he asked, "So what do we do now, Captain?"

"We're going to double back and get on the other side of that road," Jock replied. "Then we're going to take a look at the airfield."

McMillen was a few yards behind and had overheard the conversation. "You think that's such a hot idea, Captain?" he asked. "Everything's burned away. We'll be out in the open."

With a steady and confident gaze, Jock looked McMillen dead in the eyes and said, "We'll never know what really happened over there unless we look, Mike."

Staying deep in the trees, Jillian skirted the Weipa Mission as she walked back to her house. The route took her well out of her way, but she wanted to see what was going on in the Mission. Maybe, she hoped, she would get a chance to see in daylight if there was anything worth salvaging on her boats or in the icehouse. It only took one look from afar to dash that hope.

The Mission was crawling with Japanese. They streamed in and out of every building like ants, many with arms full of plunder. Some appeared to be drunk. Despite their uniforms, these men weren't soldiers anymore; they were an undisciplined mob.

In front of the Mission House, the colonel's car was gone. The body of the *kempei* sergeant she had shot was still lying there. A group of soldiers walked by, regarded the corpse for a moment, then each kicked it in turn as they moved on.

I guess they don't think too highly of their policemen, either, Jillian thought. *They probably think one of their own killed him.*

Looting and drinking weren't the only things on their minds. Comfort women who thought it best to return to the Mission House had been proved wrong. They were dragged outside and gang-raped. Those who struggled were beaten and worse; one women was lying alone, naked, and motionless in a pool of blood, curled into the fetal position that hadn't saved her from the thrusts of bayonets.

Poor Alice Tookura, the young, black shop girl so dedicated to her job at the Mission general store, was the only non-Japanese person Jillian could see. Alice was kneeling against a post of the store's veranda, her arms bound behind her back around the post, her head slumped to her chest, her dress torn open. Jillian could just make out the traces of blood against the dark skin of her exposed thighs. Alice lifted her head and began a wailing protest to the sky until a soldier walked over, silenced her with a blow to the face, and casually walked away. The Japanese were finished with her; they were more interested in pillaging her store.

Far across the Mission, Jillian could see throngs of soldiers ringing the harbor, milling about, picking with curious wonder through debris around the bomb craters, looking seaward for the vessels that had disappeared overnight. The presence of the Imperial Japanese Navy had dissolved, with one notable exception. At the outer edge of the harbor, she could see the tip of the main mast of a Japanese destroyer rising above the surface. The rest of the warship was submerged beneath it. She could see nothing of her boats. *Probably no more than charred splinters, the lot of them,* she thought. Where the icehouse had once stood, a bomb crater had taken its place.

Some of the soldiers had given up on waiting at the harbor and were walking north, out of the Mission settlement, where they'd soon come to the mouth of the Mission River, too wide and deep to cross at that point.

They'd continue east nearly 10 miles along its southern bank until it could be forded—*an unlucky few becoming croc food along the way, no doubt,* Jillian was sure—then continue north into the 100 miles of wild territory between Weipa and the tip of Cape York, where Australia ended in the Torres Strait. Across the strait was Papua New Guinea, where the Japanese adventure to Cape York had begun. She reckoned several hundred soldiers had passed through the Mission as she watched, with more meandering that way.

And the sky...it's empty! No planes!

Jillian moved closer to the edge of the tree line, desperate to find a way to rescue Alice. Trying to free her now would be suicide: she was just one woman with a bolt-action rifle and a handful of bullets. There were hundreds of armed Japanese still wandering around the Mission and more seemed to be spilling in from Yellow Vermin Road. *I'd be just one more fanny to rape...if I didn't get shot dead first.* She'd bide her time—and wait for just the right moment.

Alice was standing now, bloodied and half-naked, struggling to free herself from the post. *Good,* Jillian thought. *As least she's still got some strength. I'm not so sure how well I'd do if I had to carry her.*

The number of Japanese soldiers around the general store began to dwindle. There wasn't much left to pilfer. In a few minutes, the last soldiers at the store moved on, joining the crowd heading north. Jillian weighed the chances of rescuing Alice:

It's still a long way across open ground...Someone will catch me for sure. But I've got to try...

She stayed concealed in the trees, waiting, praying for a miracle.

Colonel Najima only played with the food the old black man had slid under the cell door an hour ago before vanishing once again. Najima was hungry, but he found the offering repulsive. *It's some sort of charred snake...or a lizard,* he complained to himself. *And these berries...only a fool would eat them. Perhaps they're trying to poison me.*

But the colonel knew that was unlikely*: If those faint-hearted white men...those Aussies or Yanks, whoever they are...had wanted me dead, I would have been dead hours ago. That impertinent Forbes woman has more nerve than all of them put together. I should have had her done away with a long time ago.*

Whatever his captors' plans were, it made no difference: he wouldn't eat the food offered by the primitives. Najima kicked the wooden plate back under the cell door. *I don't need their food. Every minute that ticks by brings my rescue closer.*

His last thoughts suddenly seemed prophetic: there were footsteps on the veranda outside. The sound of a man barking orders in Japanese. The door of the shack swung open, and a long bayonet on the muzzle of a rifle poked at the empty air beyond the threshold. A second passed before the man wielding the rifle stepped through the door: a young, trembling Japanese Army private, his face and uniform filthy, as if he had been rolled in ashes. Another man, still unseen beyond the doorway, pushed the private inside before making his own, careful entrance. Once inside, that man stood with hands on hips, a cocky grin on his leathery face as he surveyed the dingy room and its inhabitant.

He was no cleaner than the private who had preceded him through the door. Despite his filthy uniform, Colonel Najima could see the man was a sergeant, old enough to be a veteran of every campaign waged by the Empire since the Siberian adventures of 1918. His tunic strained against the considerable paunch beneath it. There was no glimmer of recognition of either man by the other.

"Find the old Aborigine with the key to this cell," Najima commanded. "Free me at once."

The sergeant said nothing in reply. He merely wandered around the room, opening drawers and cupboards, looking for things to steal. Or eat. When he came to the plate on the floor, he stooped, and with grimy fingers lifted a handful of the meat to his lips. He began to chew the food with great relish.

Enraged, Najima said, "SERGEANT, I ORDER YOU TO FREE ME AT ONCE!"

The sergeant picked up another handful off the plate and stuffed it into his mouth. Chewing slowly and noisily, he stepped closer to the cell, taking the full measure of the man inside. He turned for a moment to the trembling private, motioning him to the nearly empty plate on the floor. "Go ahead," he said, the food still in his mouth muddling the words. "Finish what's left, Private."

The private fell upon the plate like a man who hadn't eaten in days, scraping the last morsels into his mouth.

Najima's next words had a decidedly threatening tone. "Do you not realize who I am, Sergeant?"

The sergeant shrugged. He didn't know and couldn't care less.

"I am Najima, your regimental commander."

The young private snapped to attention at the sound of the name, but the sergeant had no reaction. He wiped his mouth with a grimy sleeve of his tunic. When he was finished, he ran his fingers along the cell's bars, savoring their impenetrability, and said, "I doubt that very much. You wear no rank. You carry no sword. All the regimental officers are dead, burned to a crisp. You are someone's prisoner. You are nothing."

"You will die for your arrogance, Sergeant."

The sergeant thrummed his fingers along the bars once again and said, "Arrogance? You speak of arrogance? It was the arrogance of the regimental command that placed all that aviation fuel in one storage area…in the middle of that tinderbox forest. They paid for that arrogance with their lives…and the lives of countless men under their command. Those of us who survived the inferno will be lucky not to starve to death before we escape this godforsaken hell."

The sergeant turned and headed for the door, motioning for the private to follow. The confused young man held his ground, looking like some street urchin caught red-handed in some petty crime, food dribbling down his dirty chin. "Come on," the sergeant said, "he cannot hurt you."

Najima called to the two men, imploring them to wait. His voice had lost its imperiousness. Now he sounded like a man in dire trouble, begging for help from strangers. "Please," he said, "find the old black man with the key."

"There is no one to find. This village is deserted," the sergeant replied.

"Then do not leave me to this humiliation,

Sergeant. Lend me your bayonet...and I'll seek my freedom in eternity."

"You do not deserve such a favor," the sergeant said as he vanished into the bright sunlight outside, dragging the private with him.

Jillian's miracle was delivered by a most unexpected source. The mobs of Japanese soldiers moving through the Mission had thinned to a trickle, and there were none near Alice Tookura, still bound to the post at the general store.

I just might be able to make it to Alice, Jillian supposed, *if I can use the Mission House for cover. The Japs are spread so thin now...and they're all farther from me than Alice at the moment. This is my chance.*

Jillian moved forward to the edge of the tree line, readying herself for the sprint across the 150 yards of open ground to the Mission House. Just as she was about to leap from her concealment in the trees, a single Japanese soldier emerged from the Mission House and walked casually into the path she had planned to take. He didn't appear to notice Jillian and began to walk straight toward Alice Tookura. Jillian crouched down and, her heart racing, clung to a tree for cover.

It appeared at first the soldier would walk right past Alice and join the others drifting out of Weipa. He did pass her by a few steps. Then he stopped. As if by reflex, Jillian leaned against the tree for support and sighted her rifle in the center of the soldier's back.

If he so much as touches her...

The soldier turned, and Jillian could see he held his

bayonet, now detached from his rifle, in his hand. Just as she started her gentle squeeze on the rifle's trigger, he moved quickly, stepping behind Alice and spoiling her shot. Jillian released her finger from the trigger before the hammer could strike home.

Suddenly, Alice's hands were in front of her, free of the ropes.

Bloody hell! He cut her loose!

The soldier—that surprising Good Samaritan—was walking away to join his comrades.

Alice seemed unsure what to do with her freedom. She wandered in circles on the store's veranda, trying with difficulty to hold her torn dress closed and rub her sore wrists at the same time.

Jillian stepped from the tree line and waved an arm over her head to get Alice's attention. Once Alice saw her, Jillian gestured, *Come this way! Hurry!*

This was the second time that day Jillian had watched someone cover that distance on the dead run. If Jock and his men thought they set a new record for the 100-yard dash, Alice was in the process of shattering their record. Her bare feet flew across the ground in a blur; after 20 yards, she gave up trying to hold her dress closed and used her arm swing to full advantage. When she reached the tree line, she had every intention to keep right on running. Jillian's attempt to grab her turned into a tackle. They both tumbled to the ground.

"Steady on, Alice. You're safe now," Jillian said as she pulled the terrified woman to her feet. "Come on...let's get you some clothes up at my house."

Alice still seemed in a daze as Jillian pulled her along by the hand through the woods. The walk to Jillian's house should have only taken 10 minutes; the need to coax Alice along lengthened it to almost 20. The girl kept stopping and turning to look longingly back toward the Mission, as if she was searching for something lost.

The house finally came into view through the trees, still a fair distance away. Relief began to flow through Jillian's body. She was home again.

But that relief lasted only a moment. There were Japanese soldiers—a dozen, maybe more, she couldn't be sure—swarming all around it, and more inside. They were just like the ones she had seen in the Mission: leaderless, undisciplined, more like feral animals than humans.

They had looted everything they could get their hands on. Food, drink, blankets, and, of course, liquor were being removed from the house and loaded onto the horse cart they were about to steal as well.

"You have your rifle," Alice said. "Why don't you just shoot them all?"

"I don't have that many bullets, Alice."

"But your beautiful house, Miss Jilly…"

A raucous sound exploded from within the house, clearly audible even at their distance from it. Jillian knew exactly what it was: 88 musical notes played all at once. The piano had been overturned, its wooden frame smashed to pieces, no doubt. Then the sound of breaking glass: windows were being smashed by the blows of rifle butts. From a shattered window, there was a wisp of smoke and then the flicker of flames.

Casting her eyes away from the chaos, Jillian said, "Shit. They're torching it." The circle of destruction was being closed around Jillian Forbes's existence. What the Yanks hadn't managed to destroy by accident, the Japs were finishing off on purpose.

The only thing still outside that circle was Jillian's horse, Franz. He was led to the cart. A few soldiers inexpertly tried to secure him to the cart's harness.

"Oh, no," Jillian moaned. "He'll never submit to that." She closed her eyes, bracing for the inevitable gunshots that would signal Franz's death. The circle would be complete.

Franz reared and bucked like the wild horse he had once been. Two soldiers who had been trying to secure Franz to the harness were thrown to the ground, each with an arm snapped like a twig.

The interior of the house was ablaze. Flames licked from every window and doorway.

With one great swirl of his massive body, Franz overturned the cart, reducing it to splintered boards. The men who stood on the cart were launched on a quick and violent trajectory to the ground. Free of the harness, Franz bolted away, heading deep into the bush. Some gunfire chased him: two soldiers awkwardly fired and cocked their weapons repeatedly, each encumbered with a bottle of rum they preferred not to lose tucked beneath a forearm. They emptied their clips in poorly aimed shots at the fleeing animal. None of their bullets hit Franz, who had vanished into the woods long before the last errant shot rang out.

"There's a good boy," Jillian whispered through bittersweet tears. "Farewell, my friend...and keep running."

Flames were consuming more and more of the house. Soon, the entire structure would be ablaze—and so would the woods downwind as the embers took flight. The Japanese soldiers scooped up what they could of their plunder and hurried off to the northwest—exactly downwind—toward Weipa Mission.

Jillian and Alice didn't need to say a word. They had both gauged the wind and knew that the ground they occupied would soon be on fire. In a few minutes of running upwind, they were clear of the spreading inferno.

"That wildfire will burn all the way to the Mission firebreak, I'm sure," Jillian said. "With any luck, it'll kill those jackasses who started it, too."

Alice's composure was returning. She stopped to fashion a lace from vines and used it to stitch together her ripped-open dress. She made a bittersweet joke as she worked: "What would the missionaries say of me walking around like this? They'd think I was a loose woman."

Deadpan, Jillian replied, "Yeah, they'd probably think you were even worse than me."

Her mending done, Alice asked, "So where do we go now?"

Jillian picked up a stick to draw a crude map in the dirt. "Look, Alice," she said, pointing to a spot on the map, "we're here." Then she pointed to a different spot. "Your people have gone here, just across Peppan Creek. Go to them and stay there. Old Robert is worried about you."

"Aren't you coming with us, Miss Jilly?"

"Later. I've got to find the Yanks first and tell them what's happening."

After doubling back several miles to the south

along Yellow Vermin Road, past the boundary of the fire's destruction, Jock and his three men had no trouble finding an opportunity to cross it unseen. The Japanese presence on the road had thinned out until there were long stretches of time—sometimes as much as 10 minutes—when it seemed completely deserted. The Americans' crossing was almost leisurely. Reversing direction again, they walked north through the virgin forest. Their path was diverted only once, to skirt a linear clearing hundreds of yards long gouged from the woods by a stick of bombs. The devastation looked just like what the bombs had done to Patchett's position.

After a few more minutes, they reached a creek that marked the abrupt line between verdant nature and a barren hell. They stood at the southern edge of a slack-sided rectangle emblazoned into the earth some 20 miles square, bounded by the road on the east, the Gulf of Carpentaria on the west, and the Embley River at Weipa to the north. The occasional tree trunk which still stood, even in death, had been scorched and whittled down to nothing more than a jagged pike, pointing skyward. Gray ash several inches thick blanketed the ground. Jock called a halt to get the lay of the devastated land before them. His men hunkered down in the shade of the last stand of unburned trees, dreading the walk they feared was coming across the flat, open terrain ahead. In broad daylight, yet.

Perfect machine gun territory, Mike McMillen thought.

"I reckon this is about where Russo died," J.T. Guess said. The statement was made so off-handedly, so matter-of-factly, that it took several moments before the full, horrific recollection of what had happened on this ground just two days earlier reared its hideous head in Jock's consciousness.

As he struggled to shake off the memory, Jock thought, *Has it really been just two days?*

Oddly enough, Russo's murder had crossed Jock's mind right before Guess made his comment. It had nothing to do with the legal or moral implications of Guess's act or what his fate might be in a court martial once this mission was over. There was no time for that sort of deliberation. Jock's thoughts of Russo's death had been just a geographic place marker, a tactical waypoint. From the tone of Guess's comment, that's all it meant to him, too. What else could they use for landmarks in the middle of this wilderness?

If they were right about the location, that meant they were nearing the southern end of Airfield One. Jock scanned ahead with binoculars. From the looks of the destruction he saw before them, what *used to be* Airfield One would be a more accurate description.

"I don't see a living soul," Jock said as he squinted into the field glasses, "but I do think I see a whole lot of burned-up airplanes. Let's go check it out."

Mike McMillen was in no hurry to get up. "Hang on, Captain," he said, looking warily across the field of ash. "It could be a trap or something."

Bogater Boudreau let out a laugh and said, "A trap? By who, Mike? If they ain't dead, they're all running home to momma."

Bogater and Guess were already crossing the creek. Jock's helping hand brought McMillen to his feet. "C'mon, Corporal Mike," Jock said, "you're second in command here." Jock nodded breezily toward Boudreau and Guess. "If I buy it, somebody's got to save those two." He capped the sentence with a sly wink.

McMillen's feet shuffled in place for a moment, taking him nowhere, until the delicate balance between paralyzing fear and doing what you were told swung back toward obedience once again. *Son of a bitch! Maybe the captain don't think he's bulletproof after all*, Mike McMillen thought as his feet took their first, hesitant steps across the creek.

"Do me a favor, sir," McMillen said. "Try not to buy it, okay?"

"You do me the same," Jock replied.

As the Americans stepped across the ash, it floated into the air with each footfall and clung to them. It coated their clothing, boots, and skin just like it had on so many of the Japanese survivors they had seen on the road.

They spread farther apart—in deference to the open terrain, so *one mortar round don't get us all*—and walked deeper into the emptiness. It was all becoming clear now: this was, indeed, Airfield One. Burned-out skeletons of aircraft—scores of them, parked among the scorched remnants of trees at the runway's edge—were collapsed on the ground like ruined and discarded children's toys. Vehicles sat deathly still, axles terminally resting on the ground, their rubber tires burned away; paint stripped away from their metal chassis in jagged patterns by the white-hot flames of exploding gasoline tanks. Some still held the charred remains of their drivers and passengers, burned beyond all recognition, like so many badly overcooked lumps of meat.

There were more bodies to be found as they moved

ahead, roasted to death by the hundreds—so many that they quickly lost count in the horror and stench of all the seared flesh. The Americans had to put cloths over their noses and mouths to breathe. There was no sign of all the tentage they had seen on the last recon of the airfield. The fragile canvas offered no defense against the wildfire and was now reduced to nothing.

A battery of anti-aircraft guns, their barrels still plainly recognizable, were scattered in various, seemingly accidental places across the airfield, most on overturned and mangled carriages. What powerful, unseen hand had flung them about was difficult to say, but Jock had a theory: *probably their own ammunition cooking off.*

They came to an area that was still smoldering. The ash was darker here, almost black. A line of bomb craters had traversed this part of the field, forming circular mounds of bulldozed earth that would have made ideal defensive positions, had there been any Japanese left to do the defending. As Jock and his men approached with cautious steps, testing how close they could get, they could feel the heat still in the ground through the soles of their boots. The fire had been more concentrated here, more intense; metal had been turned molten and then cooled into bizarre, blackened sculptures. *Like ornaments in the devil's playground,* Jock thought. If there had been any humans here, they had been incinerated to dust, their remains indistinguishable from any other ash that littered the ground. They could approach no closer. It was simply too hot, like walking into an oven. Or hell.

Vivid *déjà vu* gripped Jock; he'd seen an inferno like this before: *Pearl. This is just like Pearl. This was their fuel depot. Looks like they were dumb enough to put it all in one place, too...all neat and compact. So efficient...a supply officer's dream...*

And a bombardier's dream, too. This is where the blaze that burned down the whole damned place started, I'll bet.

I'll bet something else, too...looking at these craters, one plane was all that hit this spot. Everyone else missed by a mile. What a stroke of luck.

They had pushed their own luck long enough. There was nothing left to see here. It was time to get back to Patchett and the others. Brisbane needed to know what they had seen today—and Jock had an idea how, even without a radio, they'd pass that intelligence along.

His men were all for going back—and as quickly as possible. "Hey, Captain," Bogater Boudreau said, "why don't we cut back straight to the road? Save us a lot of time."

"Yeah, it would," Jock replied, "but if there are Japs on the road when we get there, we've got no place to hide. Forget it."

Boudreau, Guess, and McMillen looked disappointed, but the captain was right. They set off south again, back to the closest concealment on the circuitous path home. They moved quickly now, almost jogging, kicking up clouds of the choking ash around them. The cloths were no longer covering their faces, and they ate a good deal of that ash. As soon as they hit the trees again, they needed a water break badly.

Boudreau, still the point man, crouched into the tall grass. He didn't even have time to open his canteen before something up ahead, some motion, some glint of sunlight on metal, caught his attention. The others saw his frantic hand signal—*Down! Down!*—and quickly dropped their canteens.

No more than 10 yards ahead was a Japanese officer kneeling in the grass. His tunic and shirt were opened to bare his midriff. The tip of his sword was pressed against his stomach. Both hands were held away from his body, clutching the sword's handle. A look of anguish was on his face; his entire body trembled. Every few seconds, he would utter a loud grunt, jerking his arms as if to thrust the sword into his gut. But with each attempt to run himself through, the tip of the sword hardly moved. The blade would pulse upward but never forward. The only damage he had managed to do so far was a small laceration above his navel. A flesh wound, hardly fatal.

Guess whispered a dry observation: "The fucker can't even kill himself."

Bogater Boudreau raised his Thompson to his shoulder and put the Japanese officer in its sights. "Are we still recon, Captain?" he asked in a hushed, urgent voice. "Do we just crawl away...or do I grease this bastard right now?"

McMillen pulled the sword he had taken from Colonel Najima from his pack, swishing the blade back and forth like some cinema buccaneer. "If he's set on doing it the old-fashioned way," he said, not bothering to whisper, "I'd be happy to oblige."

The Japanese officer jumped to his feet and turned to face the Americans. At first he looked merely startled, a split second later ashamed, and in another split second, full of murderous rage. He ran toward the startled Americans, the tip of his sword leading the way, his continuous scream piercing the stillness.

Maybe it was the sword in his hand or maybe the Japanese officer just saw him first. Whatever the reason, he was coming straight for McMillen, who took several panicky steps backward before falling flat on his buttocks. Perhaps sword play wouldn't be much fun, after all.

The shrieks of the Japanese man ended abruptly, punctuated by the *bup-bup-bup* of a three-shot burst from Jock's Thompson. The point-blank shots caught the Jap squarely in the chest, canceling his forward motion in a vicious back-flip that sent the sword flying into the bush and ended with his mortally wounded body lying supine at Jock's feet, his arms outstretched, his lower legs tucked beneath his thighs. He looked like a puppet that just had all its strings cut. They could see his insignia of rank clearly now: a lieutenant colonel.

Maybe he was second in command of the regiment, Jock thought.

"Oh, Jesus," McMillen said softly over and over, nervously scanning to see if the shots had drawn attention their way. But there was nothing around them but trees and ash, and they paid the Americans no mind. He quickly slid Najima's sword back into the straps of his horseshoe pack.

Guess retrieved the sword that had gone flying and brought it to Boudreau. "Here," he said as he offered the sword, "I ain't gonna be needing this." Then, Guess stood over the Japanese officer, regarding him closely as life flowed from him. He touched the man's chest, slowly circling the three bullet holes that formed a tight triangle there. Calmly wiping the man's blood from his fingertips, Guess nodded to Jock and said, "Nice shot group, sir."

Then J.T. Guess turned to McMillen, still flat on his backside, and hurled one harsh, judgmental word in his direction: "Asshole."

McMillen looked to Jock, then Boudreau, searching for any hint of sympathy, but he found none. Their faces issued the same rebuke as Guess without having to say a word.

Jock had heard many old soldiers' tales about the first time you killed a man, and they all ended the same way: you puked your guts out. Even Melvin Patchett affirmed that the first time he knowingly killed one of the Kaiser's soldiers—hand-to-hand with a bayonet, at that—he had painful, debilitating dry heaves for an hour after. But Jock felt none of the signs of impending nausea—no churning of the stomach, no mouth flooding with saliva. *It'll hit me later, probably, when I've got a little less on my mind. Or maybe I'm just as strange as Guess. Killing Russo didn't seem to bother him a bit, either.*

One thing seemed pretty obvious to Jock, and he said it out loud: "One way or another, this guy...this light colonel...committed suicide." Then he squatted next to McMillen's ear so the others wouldn't hear and hissed, "Don't ever pull anything like that again, Corporal. This ain't the fucking playground. Now get up off your ass and let's go."

Chapter Forty-Seven

Doc Green needed a rest. Now that all of Patchett's men had their injuries treated, checked, and rechecked, it was time for Doc to deal with his own wound. It would need a good cleaning, another dose of sulfa powder, and stitches. The wound was deep. There was a fair chance it would become infected out here in the bush, but he wouldn't use any of the remaining penicillin on himself. Not yet, anyway. There was less than a vial left; first Boudreau's burned shoulder and now Pacheco's shattered leg had used up the lion's share. Sewing up the gash on his own calf would be awkward, but he'd manage somehow. He'd have to. He just needed a bit of a break first. He sagged to the ground in the middle of the perimeter, rested his back against a tree that seemed relatively free of insects, and bit into a chunk of D bar. He knew Jock Miles would want to move the unit to a new location as soon as he returned from the bomb damage assessment. But at the moment, Doc couldn't imagine taking another step.

At least everything had been quiet and peaceful since the bombing raid that came within a hair's breadth of killing them all. It seemed almost criminal there was no one but afflicted soldiers to man the perimeter. If they wanted a decent chance of staying alive, though, they'd have to do it—patched up, brains rattled, ears ringing, and all. Only Corporal Pacheco was exempt from the ring of fighting holes surrounding their position. Groggy and uncomfortable, he laid on the makeshift stretcher a few yards from Doc. The last syrette of morphine he had been given was wearing off. He'd need another shot soon.

Doc Green pulled his slouch hat over his face. *Just give me ten bloody minutes to close my eyes...*

But there would be no rest. A burst from the .30 caliber machine gun jarred Doc awake. Something was happening on the south side of the perimeter. He grabbed his helmet, his Thompson, and his medical kit and started low-crawling that way, the rush of adrenaline blocking the pain in his leg. Halfway there, the machine gun stopped firing, and the voices of men, some yelling in English, some in Japanese, were engaged in a frantic, high-pitched dialog neither side understood.

Doc peeked over the cover of some fallen timber. There were the bodies of three Japanese soldiers stacked like cordwood about 10 yards in front of the machine gun. Beyond the bodies were a few more soldiers—*six,* Doc counted—in various poses of surrender. One, the closest, had dropped his weapon and fallen to his knees. The other five were still on their feet. Each held a rifle by its forestock in one of his raised hands, fingers nowhere near the trigger. Teddy Mukasic, his finger still wrapped around the machine gun's trigger, was yelling, "HANDS UP! DROP YOUR WEAPONS!" Frank Simms was trying to reinforce Mukasic's commands with gestures the Japanese couldn't see. Whether it was out of fear or wisdom, Simms kept his body down in the fighting hole, well out of sight, with only his hands visible over the edge.

Even Doc Green didn't understand what the Japanese were yelling. Their faces seemed genuinely panicked, their body language anything but aggressive. But he'd seen Japanese troops in action before.

"THIS IS A TRICK," Doc yelled. "EVERYONE

STAY DOWN."

Melvin Patchett scurried next to Doc in a rapid low-crawl that would exhaust a man half his age. He wasn't even breathing hard as he asked Doc, "Trick? You seen this in New Guinea?"

"Yeah, Top. They'll wait until we expose ourselves, then this lot drops to the ground and some gunners we can't see open up on us."

"I heard tell about that," Patchett said, his eyes searching the forest before them. "Kinda strange when you see it up close, though. Sure looks like they're wanting to surrender...especially with them three dead ones piled up over yonder."

Melvin Patchett paused, then sighed. A look of resignation came over him, a bit sad but unmistakably determined. "EVERYONE STAY PUT AND COVER YOUR SECTOR," he commanded. "MUKASIC, STOP YOUR YAMMERING AND CUT THOSE NIPS DOWN. NOW!"

"BUT TOP," Mukasic replied, "THEY'RE FUCKING SURRENDERING!" His voice cracked as he said it, a man shouting on the verge of tears.

"I'M GIVING YOU A *DIE-RECT* ORDER, PRIVATE," Patchett replied. "KNOCK THEM DOWN BEFORE I..."

His words were interrupted by the crack of a gunshot.

Doc saw it unfold: one of the Japanese soldiers had dropped his rifle. Maybe he released his grip on it; maybe it slipped from his sweaty hand; maybe it snagged on something on the way down; or maybe the soldier clumsily tried to catch it.

However it happened, the weapon fired. The bullet

struck the top of the berm behind which lay Mukasic and Simms with the machine gun. The bullet shattered on impact, spraying fragments of soil, rock, and hot metal into the hole. Mukasic shrieked, squeezed the machine gun's trigger closed and held it there. A strange tug of war for the weapon seemed to be going on between Mukasic and Simms, making the muzzle weave back and forth, fanning the gun's deadly spray.

Every Japanese soldier was struck down. So were a few of the smaller trees, their trunks sliced in half by the buzzsaw of bullets. A few of the Thompsons on the perimeter joined in, whether the men on their triggers could see the Japanese or not. The machine gun didn't stop firing until its belt of ammunition was used up, long after the last enemy soldier had been mortally wounded. Seconds after, the Thompson firing died out. The only sound left was Teddy Mukasic's wailing:

"I'M HIT OH GOD I'M BLIND I CAN'T SEE..."

The words repeated over and over, not always in the same order, but always with the same message.

"Keep everyone down," Doc said to Patchett. "If they're still out there, we'll probably get hit with knee mortars next."

Doc crawled to Mukasic and pried the young man's hands from his face. "Take it easy, Teddy," Doc said in the most soothing voice he could muster. "Let me have a look."

There wasn't a hint of blood. Just a dirty face.

"You've just got some dirt in your eyes, Teddy, that's all," Doc said. "Here...I'm going to flush them clean. Just relax."

Simms loaded another belt into the machine gun. "He kept yelling he couldn't see shit, Doc," Simms said, "but he wouldn't let go of the frigging gun."

"Ahh, I see," Doc said. "That's why it looked like you were wrestling him for it."

"Yeah...it needed a little *aiming.*"

Doc wiped the last of the dirt from Teddy Mukasic's face. "There you go, laddie...take a look around."

Mukasic could indeed see again. The first thing his eyes fell on as he peered over the fighting hole's edge was the slew of dead Japanese he and Simms had just killed. He sunk back down into the hole and began heaving up the little bit of food in his stomach. A few seconds later, Frank Simms was inspired to spew the contents of his stomach into the bottom of the hole, too.

"It's okay, boys," the first sergeant called from behind the fallen timber. "Happens to just about everyone the first time."

Mukasic managed to whimper a few words between the dry heaves. "But why'd they do that, Top?" he begged. "They were surrendering."

"Maybe they were, maybe they weren't, son. Either way, the captain already got us one too many prisoners."

Half a mile away, Jock and his men heard the shooting from the direction of Patchett's camp, the same direction in which they were walking. J.T. Guess, taking his turn at point, muttered just one word when the bullets started flying: "Shit." None of the four thought they could be much more alert than they already were, but the sound of an automatic weapon—

the unmistakable noise of the .30 caliber machine gun—fine-tuned their senses up another notch. They pressed on, their bodies instinctively hunched low to the ground, what some people back home called a *duck walk*. The smaller the target they could make of themselves, the better. They weren't sure if the silence they now heard—after that 15-second orgy of gunfire—was a harbinger of victory or catastrophe.

Guess thought he heard voices ahead. American voices. He pivoted toward Jock, a few yards behind. "I do believe we're there, sir," he whispered. "Should I give 'em the password?"

Jock nodded. Guess shouted, *"Laverne!"*

He was answered by the chatter of a Thompson's burst. Bullets splattered wildly around them for a few seconds, scarring only the trees. When the fusillade ceased, Jock's angry voice rang out:

"LAVERNE, GODDAMNIT! LAVERNE! NEXT MAN WHO PULLS A FUCKING TRIGGER ON ME IS ON MY PERMANENT SHIT LIST."

The next voice they heard was Sergeant Hadley's, berating someone: "That's the captain, you fucking idiot!"

Jock and his men drifted into the perimeter, looking mightily pissed off. There was little doubt who had shot at them: PFC Savastano, one of Botkin's radiomen, sat in his fighting hole looking white as a sheet, telltale wisps of smoke still floating lazily from his weapon's muzzle. Hadley crouched over him, face flushed with anger, looking ready to throttle the private if he as much as twitched.

"Sorry, sir," Hadley said to Jock. "Damn good thing Thompsons ain't worth a shit at that distance.

We're all a little jumpy. We just had a go with some Japs on the south side."

"Yeah, we know," Jock said. "I'll bet everyone within ten miles heard it. Where's Top?"

Hadley pointed him in the right direction, and in a few moments, Jock slid into the hole next to his first sergeant. "Glad you're back, Captain," Patchett said. "We've got to find a new place to lay low, on the double. I'm betting the whole Jap Army heard that little shoot out."

Chapter Forty-Eight

Jillian had heard the sound of the machine gun, too, but she was much farther from it than Jock and his men. The silence that followed left her with the same anxious confusion: did it signal good news or disaster? If nothing else, it sharpened the direction to search for them.

Her heart sank when she came to the place where she had shared dinner with them last night. As she stood at the edge of a gaping bomb crater, she couldn't conceive of anyone surviving such an attack. The old perimeter was a complete void. If Patchett and his men had met death there, surely there would be some grisly indication.

But no...they're just gone. The sound of that gunfire, though...Somebody's around here, somewhere.

She kept walking, more slowly and cautiously now, in the direction of the shots.

Sergeant Botkin was nothing if not observant. He saw her first, a long way off through the trees. From his spot on the perimeter, he could make out her distinctively female shape, her long hair flowing from under her decidedly unmilitary bush hat. Even though she had a rifle slung from her shoulder, he would never mistake her for a soldier. He even recognized the clothes and boots she was wearing. They were the same ones she had on last night.

After PFC Savastano—one of *his* men—had nearly assassinated Captain Miles not long ago, he wanted—

no, *desperately needed*—to make sure a mistake like that didn't happen again.

"Miss Forbes is coming...pass it down," Botkin called to the man manning the fighting hole to his left. He listened intently for the message to make the full circle of the perimeter back to him. By the time he counted to 15, it had. He breathed a sigh of relief.

Jillian found Jock and Patchett at the center of the perimeter. There was much information the three of them needed to share. Jock described the obliteration of Airfield One by the wildfire, the apparent exodus north of the Japanese forces, and the encounter with the suicidal Japanese lieutenant colonel. The first sergeant told of the errant bombing raid, the toll it had taken on the men, and the encounter with the Japanese soldiers.

Jillian asked, "You're sure you killed them all? None got away?"

"Don't think so," Patchett replied. "Not that I'm complaining, mind you, but I'm kinda surprised we haven't had more visitors...all that noise gotta attract some attention."

Jillian shook her head. "No," she said, "if anything, it's going to keep them away. They don't seem to be much interested in looking for trouble right now. They just want to get out of here."

She went on to describe what she had seen in the Mission—the disorganized troops fleeing north, probably the same ones Jock had seen farther down the road; the rape and murder of the comfort women; the lucky break that had saved Alice Tookura. Almost as an afterthought, she added, "And that *kempei* I shot this morning? He's still lying there. I saw some soldiers kick his corpse as they passed. How's that for a total breakdown of discipline?"

Melvin Patchett laid back and chuckled. "Just goes to show you," he said. "Don't matter what army it is, they all hate their military police." He looked to Jock and asked, "Remember the old saying, sir?"

"Sure do," Jock replied with a big grin. "I'd rather have a sister in the whorehouse than a brother in the MPs."

Jillian found herself laughing, too, although she pretended to scold them as she said, "You Yanks are bloody awful!"

There wasn't much time for laughter, though. She told them what happened at her house.
"Everything...all my music, my piano...it's gone," she said. "At least my horse escaped with his life."

There was little time to mourn what had passed. That battered group of men that was Task Force Miles needed to be moved to a safer place, and quickly. Someplace out of the way. Jillian knew just where to go.

"I'm going to take you blokes to the place across Peppan Creek, where the blacks have all gone," she said. "It's well east of the Mission, well away from this parade of Japs. You can rest, gather your strength...you'll even get fed well, if you don't mind eating snake and croc and the like."

Doc Green hobbled slowly over and joined them. "The bit about getting fed well...I'm glad to hear that," he said, the exhaustion evident in his voice, too. "The lads are already grumbling that you showed up without your food wagon."

Jillian rolled her eyes and threw her hands up. "Fucking men," she said, protesting to the heavens.

"You can never do enough for them, can you?"

Jock couldn't tell if she was kidding or not. "Jillian," he said quite seriously, "we're not complaining. Believe me we're not..."

She wasn't paying attention to Jock. She had become fixated on what Doc Green was trying to do. He had removed the sodden bandage from his lower leg and, wielding surgical scissors, proceeded to cut off the bloody trouser leg below the knee. The wound now exposed was jagged and deep. Doc was on his third try to thread suture into a surgical needle. For the third time, his tired and shaking hand missed.

"Here, let me do it," Jillian said, taking the needle and thread from his hands. "You'll never be able to stitch that yourself."

Grateful for the help, Doc offered no resistance. He rolled onto his stomach, giving her clear access to the wound.

Jock didn't mean for his next words to sound harried and sarcastic, but that's how they came out: "You sure you know how to sew someone up, Jillian? How long is this *little surgery* gonna take, anyway? We need to get moving." He wanted to put his foot in his mouth the minute he said it.

Jillian shot him an angry glance. "Yes, I'm sure...and it'll take as long as it needs to, Jock."

It was Patchett who defused the tension. He held up his open hands in a gesture to Jillian that meant, *Whoa...nobody's trying to rush you.*

The first sergeant's tone was mellow and soothing as he said, "Jillian, we just need to know when it's safe to collapse the perimeter and start walking, that's all. We're gonna be racing the sun."

Looking at Jock's contrite face, she wished she had stifled her words, too. Their eyes met, and they apologized to each other without saying a word.

"Ten minutes, I think," she said, gently cleaning the wound. "Does that sound about right to you, Doc?"

Chapter Forty-Nine

It had been a difficult walk for the men of Task Force Miles and their female guide, but they made the almost 13 miles to Peppan Creek in four hours' time, arriving as night began to fall. From time to time, a man would stop and sit down, mumbling words like, *I just need a minute.* A minute was all he would get, as a comrade, himself struggling to keep the steady pace, pulled him to his feet. Corporal Pacheco, drowsy from the morphine, rode on the *Radio Flyer* being pulled by McGuire from the radio section. Experiencing occasional moments of glee from the drug, Pacheco would pretend to flog McGuire as the words *"Giddyap, horsy!"* croaked from his dry throat.

Doc Green had a tougher time of it. Jillian had done a fine job stitching and bandaging the gash on his calf, but the leg stiffened painfully and he was soon exhausted. He had managed to eat half of a rock-hard D bar before they set out, but the reserve of energy from the bitter chocolate was spent within an hour. PFC Savastano became his human crutch for the rest of the walk, supporting Doc like a man doing fervent penance. After nearly shooting Captain Miles and his patrol, Savastano needed to atone for his panicky mistake and convince himself—as well as the others—he was someone you could depend on. When Sergeant Botkin asked if he needed to hand off Doc to someone else, Savastano replied, "I'm okay, Sarge. I want to do this."

Even the most fit of the group—Jillian, Jock, McMillen, and Guess—were exhausted by the time they reached Peppan Creek. They hadn't suffered the effects of the bombing like the others, but they had been walking since sunrise.

The sun was still low in the sky when they heard a series of strange, shrill sounds—like the steady shriek of some animal—very loud and close at first, then fading as it was relayed to the north. "Ahh, they know we're coming," Jillian said, smiling serenely.

Jock's head swiveled, trying to locate the source of the sound. He saw nothing. No one. Confused, he asked Jillian, "*Who* knows we're coming? Those are *humans* making that racket?"

"Indeed," she said. "That's the Aborigine telegraph...the *cooee.* Surely you've heard that sound before in the bush?"

"Yeah, I guess I did...but I never knew what it was."

The new camp at Peppan Creek was a collection of old, abandoned mining shacks and new, temporary shelters the blacks had constructed from whatever material they could find. In the twilight, the camp was a shadowy presence spread across several acres of thick woodland. Old Robert was waiting for them at the edge of the settlement. He had known of their approach a long way off. Deep within the camp, women tended small cookfires; children played happily.

"There is food and shelter for everyone," Old Robert said, nodding respectfully to Jock.

Melvin Patchett tried to come to grips with the physical dimensions of the settlement. "We've got a problem, sir," he said to Jock. "We can't defend all these people. The area's just too big."

Old Robert smiled and said, "There is no need to defend us. We are safe here. *You* are safe here."

"All the same," Jock said, "we need to set up some

kind of security. Perhaps a few listening posts..."

Old Robert simply shrugged. "This village is one big listening post," he said. "I doubt any Japanese that might blunder this way in the dark will be any less noisy than you were." Before Jock or Patchett could protest, he added, "I have much greater fear of your soldiers shooting my people in error than any Japanese doing so in earnest. Your men are exhausted, Captain. Put just one of them with my people while the others sleep. He will alert you if, by chance, the Japanese come near."

Thinking back over the day's events, Jock found it hard to disagree with Old Robert's logic. He was too tired to argue; so was his first sergeant. They both nodded in acquiescence.

Jillian guided Patchett as he went about the business of getting Task Force Miles fed and bedded down for the night. They had everyone squared away by the time the camp was enveloped in darkness. Jock and Doc Green were billeted in one of the old mining shacks, a small, corrugated metal structure Jillian dubbed *the officers' quarters*. As soon as Doc had finished his dinner—he hadn't even bothered to ask what was the strange, reptilian meat he wolfed down— he fell dead asleep. Jock wished he could just fall asleep, too, but there were plans to be made. He gathered Jillian and his NCOs—Patchett, Hadley, McMillen, and Botkin—around the fire pit outside his shack. A kettle hung from a metal rod above the pit's low flames. The men were about to enjoy their first taste of hot coffee in almost six days—since their early morning breakfast at Cairns, before the final flight leg of the journey on the Catalinas. They pooled the dried coffee powder from the K rations each of them had been saving for just such an opportunity. They would need the caffeine boost just to stay awake for the meeting.

"Looks like this settlement is as good a place as any to hole up," Jock began, "until we get new orders..."

"Or they get us the hell out of here," Patchett said, not sure if he was completing the sentence the way his captain had intended.

"Yeah, that's right, Top," Jock said. "How's our supply situation?"

"We're doing okay," Patchett replied. "We've got at least ten days' worth of K rations left, thanks to Miss Forbes here—"

"And the good people of Weipa," Jillian added.

"Right," Patchett agreed. "Plenty of water around, and we've still got plenty of Halazone tablets. Ammo for the Thompsons is okay, and Guess's Springfield hasn't fired a shot yet, but we're real light on machine gun rounds...a little over a hundred left...about one fifty if we belted Guess's ammo and shit-canned the sniper rifle. One more run-in with the Japs and that'll be gone. Still got all our grenades, though."

Jock asked, "Can you speak for Doc on the medical supplies, Top? How low are we?"

"Real low, sir. We've only got a handful of field dressings left, and most of the antibiotics are already used up. Getting bombed by our own guys really did us in there."

"How much penicillin?"

Patchett shook his head. "Hardly any, sir."

"Okay, could be worse," Jock said. He looked to

Jillian and asked, "How far are we from Najima's jail?"

"It's about two miles west of here...back across Peppan Creek."

"And Old Robert says the colonel's refusing to eat?"

"So far," she replied. "It looks like he's been drinking the water, though."

"Hopefully," Jock said, "we'll have him in Brisbane in a few days. He won't starve to death by then."

"It's better that he's in that cell," Patchett said. "We need him around here like a hole in the head right now."

"Amen to that, Top," Jock said as the others mumbled their agreement. "Now, we've got to tell Brisbane what's going on. Losing the radio was a tough break, but I think we've got other options. Jillian, are you sure there are no other transmitters around here that Sergeant Botkin might be able to get working?"

"Afraid not," she replied. "The only one was at the Mission, and the Japs smashed it to pieces first thing."

"And there's no telegraph link to the Mission...or anyplace around here?"

"No, Jock, we only had the radio. If it was on the blink, the constable...Mick Murray...would send one of the blacks as a runner to the relay station at Moreton on the *tele* track."

Patchett looked skeptical. "The telegraph line...that's forty miles from here."

"More or less," she replied.

The first sergeant's brow furrowed. "How long did that take?"

"The runner would leave at daybreak and be at the

telegraph station around midday. He'd rest overnight while waiting for the reply and be back at the Mission the next day."

Patchett threw up his hands in disbelief. "Over forty miles in six hours? On foot?"

"I did say he was a *runner,* First Sergeant."

Patchett snickered and said, "And he probably did it barefoot, too."

"Of course," Jillian replied.

"Don't any of these blacks ride horses?" Patchett asked. "If they had some horses, they could cover that distance a lot quicker." He paused, then added, "So could we."

Jillian shook her head. "The Weipa people aren't keen on breaking and keeping horses. They're not stockmen...fishing comes much easier to them than herding livestock. The missionaries had some horses, but they turned them loose before they evacuated. I had the only horse left, and now he's gone, too."

"Okay, okay," Jock said, taking back control of the discussion. "I'm glad you brought up the telegraph line, because it's been on my mind ever since our bombers were kind enough to destroy our radio. Now, we passed the Moreton relay station on our way here. That's where we got off the trucks and started walking. We know it's abandoned, but the relay stations south of there...are they abandoned, too, Jillian?"

"I don't think so. The next station is about fifty miles south at Mein, and there are a few more before the line hits the coast at Cairns. Last I heard, that part of the Cape wasn't being evacuated...at least not yet. But my knowledge of evacuations isn't exactly current...it's over a month old."

"That sounds promising," Jock said. "Sergeant Botkin, you're the communications expert. Would a relay station have to be manned in order to pass a message along?"

"That's a tough one, sir," Botkin replied. "Theoretically...provided the station's batteries were up to snuff... it could do the relay, but only in one direction. If you could send, you couldn't receive...and vice versa. We saw those wires...it's a very crude system. You'd need a relay operator to have two-way communications."

"There's another problem," Patchett said. "Suppose the Japs are listening in on the lines?"

"That could only be an issue way up at the tip of the Cape, a bloody long way north of Moreton," Jillian said. "South of Moreton, the line runs well to the east. The Japs never came near it. They didn't stray too far inland from the west coast."

Botkin's next words glowed with enthusiasm. "I could easily cut the circuit to the north and send a message south," he said. "As long as there's someone to relay it, there'll be no problem at all."

With that statement, the discussion arrived at an assumed conclusion. Nobody needed to say it; they were going to try to send their bomb damage assessment via telegraph from the Moreton station to Brisbane. It was just down to the details.

Patchett asked, "How many men you planning on sending, sir?"

"Let's make it four," Jock said, "Sergeant Hadley, are you up for another long walk?"

"Yessir," Hadley replied with exuberant pride.

"Good. Take Boudreau with you. I know he's up

for it. Sergeant Botkin, we need you on this one. Feel like taking another walk?"

"Absolutely, sir."

"Outstanding. Which one of your radiomen is fit enough to go with you?"

"McGuire, sir," Botkin replied. "I'd take him. Savastano's beat. He carried Doc all the way here."

"Okay," Jock said. "That settles that. Hadley, you're ranking man, so you're in charge. Be ready to leave at first light."

Patchett wrote the names down in his notebook. "Two infantry and two sparkies," he said. "That oughta get the job done."

Hadley had been doing some figuring in his head. "You know, sir," he said, "if we travel real light, we could make that walk in one day. We'd be there by nightfall. We know the terrain, so we could cover it quick."

"Just don't wipe yourself out," Jock said. "Save something for the trip back."

"No problem, sir," Hadley replied.

"Wait a minute," Jillian said. "What happens if the station's batteries are dead? Then you can't do anything, can you? And who knows…they might have taken the batteries, the generator to recharge them, even the petrol to fuel it when they left."

"No problem," Botkin replied. "We've still got two spare batteries for the radio. They were in the other *Radio Flyer,* the one that didn't get blown up. I can adapt them to run a telegraph if I have to. As long as there's still wire running there, I can make it work."

Patchett asked, "Those batteries are heavy. They won't slow you down, son?"

Botkin's reply was no-nonsense: "We'll manage, First Sergeant."

But then, Botkin's brow furrowed. "I've got one more problem, sir. Our code book…it got destroyed with the radio. Assuming we get through, they're probably going to ask for authentication. And I'll have to send the text in the clear, completely uncoded. Without the book, we're screwed."

"I'm not worried about it," Jock said. "You're one smart guy, Sergeant Botkin. You took the Japs off the air with just some scrap from your pockets. You'll figure it out."

Corporal Grover Wheatley swept the direction-finding antenna of the walkie-talkie through one final pass before giving up in disgust. He sank into a crouch and pulled the headphones off his ears. "They are just not on the air, Captain," he said to Scooter Brewster. "I can even hear Iron Range trying to raise them, but there's no response from Task Force Miles. Nothing at all. The poor bastards are probably all dead…"

He finished his own sentence in his head: *just like we're going to be real soon, if we don't quit this silly chase and get our asses out of here.*

The forest at night was too dark to read the expression on Wheatley's face; there was only the faintest red glow from his flashlight as he stowed the radio. It illuminated nothing but Wheatley's hands as he worked.

"I wouldn't worry about them too much," Brewster said. Secretly, though, he wished Grover Wheatley was right. It wouldn't be the end of the world if Jock Miles and his unfortunate task force had met their demise.

Miles was a weak officer, anyway.

Another thought shot into his head: *What's the difference if he's dead...or I just can't find him?*

Fumbling in the darkness, Brewster reached into his pack and pulled out the sealed envelope. When he switched on his flashlight's red beam, it gave Wheatley just enough light to see what his captain was doing. His hopes began to soar that the captain was finally giving up. He'd destroy that damned envelope, and they'd reverse course, go back to Archer Bay and wait for a boat ride home.

But Brewster didn't seem to be about to destroy anything.

"You're not going to open those orders, are you, Captain?"

"I certainly am. That is my prerogative, Corporal."

That was the last thing Grover Wheatley wanted to hear. "Haven't we done all we can do here, Captain? We gave it our best shot..."

To Scooter Brewster, Wheatley sounded like nothing more than a child whining. He said nothing to his corporal as he emptied the envelope's contents into his lap. There wasn't much there: a typewritten sheet on division letterhead, signed by General Briley himself, a printed map of Weipa and its environs, with a number of details penciled in, and a photograph of a young, dark-haired white woman. The legend on the map indicated it was a product of the Queensland Police.

As Brewster read the instructions on the typewritten sheet, he would be the first to admit he was initially stunned. He had not expected in his wildest dreams the orders would direct an officer of the United States Army to assassinate an Australian civilian. A female civilian, at that. But this was war, and strange things happened in war.

A poem by Tennyson popped into his head. It had inspired him through the trials of West Point, and he found it just as inspiring now. His favorite lines repeated over and over again:

Theirs not to reason why,
Theirs but to do and die...

He was a soldier. He would do whatever his country expected. He would not ask why.

Wheatley had crept closer as Brewster read, but he could still see nothing of the envelope's contents. Afraid of the answer, he asked anyway: "So what does it say, Captain?"

Brewster made the unnecessary gesture of shielding the page against his chest, as if the words typed on it were somehow legible in the dim red light to a man standing five feet away. "Sorry. Classified," Brewster replied, and went back to pretending Wheatley wasn't there.

Wheatley couldn't care less what the orders said. With a hint of optimism, he asked, "So we're going home, then?"

"Negative, Corporal. We've just gotten some new orders."

Just when the one reason for their being in this godforsaken wilderness had seemingly evaporated, this idiot captain had created a new one. Rather than give up on Task Force Miles, Brewster would assume the mission intended for it in that envelope. And Wheatley would still have to follow him around on this fool's quest.

Corporal Grover Wheatley stood there, mouth wide open, trying to speak, but no words came out. He expressed himself by the only means he had left. He started to weep.

Scooter Brewster looked up from the map he was studying just long enough to shoot a look of disgust Wheatley's way. "Stop that, Corporal," Brewster said. "You're disgracing yourself."

There was a final bit of administration: stamped across the bottom of the page—in large block letters— were the words *BURN AFTER READING*. Scooter Brewster decided that would have to wait until morning:

Any flame in this darkness will have the Japs on us like stink on shit.

Chapter Fifty

Am I really watching a movie? Or is it some newsreel footage, all black and white and scratchy? And it seems to be stuck, like it's in some kind of loop...the same stuff happens over and over again. A Jap rushes forward, points a pistol at me...I squeeze the trigger of my weapon but it doesn't fire. Why the hell is this Thompson jamming? Didn't I clean it well enough? Patchett will be riding my ass...I'll never hear the end of it.

Then the film stops, like it's waiting for me to catch up. In a second, the image flickers and vanishes as the heat of the projector lamp burns the film away...

But then it starts all over again. This time, a Jap is running at me with a sword. I squeeze the trigger...Nothing! The image freezes with the sword inches from my chest...and then the film burns again.

We're back to the beginning...the Jap with the pistol. He's closer this time. I can see the hairs of his thin moustache...the crazy gleam in his eye...and still my Thompson won't fire. I can see his finger tighten on his trigger...and the film stops and burns...

It's the sword again. I don't have a weapon in my hands anymore. Why would I? The damned thing didn't work, anyway. The sword's tip is closer to my chest than the last time. The distance closes in slow motion...it's almost touching me. I wait for the film to pause and burn, but it doesn't stop...it just keeps slowly advancing, frame by frame, until the tip is one with my chest. It's inside me...it's piercing my heart. I don't feel a thing for a second...and then...

Jillian thought Jock's heart would burst if it beat

any faster. His breathing was short, rapid, and shallow. Even in the darkness of the shack, he looked white as a sheet. She held him in her arms as they sat on the floor, his hands clutching the edges of his bedroll as if he was trying to pull it over his head. His eyes were as wide as saucers, terrified by something but seeing nothing.

"Jock...Jock," she said in a tone too frightened to be soothing, "wake up! You're having a bad dream."

His hands released the bedroll and tried to clutch his chest, to see if the dream sword had left a wound. Instead, they fell on Jillian's arms holding him tight. He was awakening, his eyes finally seeing what little they could in the slivers of moonlight filtering into the shack. It was nothing but silhouettes—his Thompson, unashamed of its failures in Jock's subconscious, propped silent, lethal, and ready at arm's length; Doc Green in the other corner, sleeping deeply, snoring with mechanical precision; Jillian nestled against him, the loose curls of her long hair brushing his face. His hands clutched her arms, the arms that were clutching him, pulling him back from an imagined death.

"Jill...what are you doing here?" he whispered. "What time is it?"

"It's oh two hundred. I came to check on my patient."

"Your patient? You mean Doc? Is he okay?"

"He's good," she replied. "No fever...and his sutures are holding up fine. Oh, I had to borrow your torch."

"My what?"

One arm released him and she held up his flashlight. "This is a torch, my good man."

He shook a few more cobwebs from his sleepy

head and said, "Oh, yeah...I forgot. So fucking British."

"No, not fucking British," she said, miming a playful clonk on his head with the flashlight. "Fucking Australian."

"I've been meaning to ask you...where did you learn to stitch someone up like that?"

"Jock...silly boy...I work on a small boat in a big ocean. We're always getting banged about. We would've all bled to death a long time ago if we couldn't mend each other." She put her other arm back around him, resting her head against his. "Besides, we're at the end of the earth," she whispered, her lips brushing his ear. "Medical help is not exactly abundant."

Neither of them started before the other. The kiss was a simultaneous act, a powerful convergence of wills that gripped them both with necessity and undeniable certainty. He fell back onto his bedroll, his head on the pillow he had made of his pack, and she lay on top of him. Their mouths had yet to part.

The kiss didn't stop until she asked, "But what about Doc? He's right over there."

Jock chuckled softly. "That old buzzsaw? It'd take gunfire to wake him now."

She didn't need much convincing. As he pulled her back down to him, he said, "It's a pity we don't have any music," before she surrendered to the next deep kiss.

His hands were free to explore her. She was wearing some sort of dress—loose, simple, a shift, perhaps—like he had seen the black women wearing. It was hiked up to her pelvis as she straddled his hips.

Beneath it, he found, she wore nothing at all. His fingertips sensed her arousal, without a doubt, and his gentle caresses made her longing all the more intense. Within moments, their lips parted and she slid back, struggling in the dark to undo his trousers.

"Bloody buttons," he heard her mumble, her voice growling in frustration.

But when that task was done, as she raised her hips to take him inside her, Jock could sense other emotions flashing through her as well—a rush of anxiety, a tremor of fear. Before he was fully nestled in the warmth of her flesh, she slumped forward, her palms on the floor, her rigid arms holding her off him. Their brief union was over. Her face hung before his, hidden in the curls of her hair that had closed over it. A low wail rose from her throat, like the agony of lost love—or of pain that should be pleasure.

She rolled off and lay next to him, sobbing softly, "Why? Why? Why? Why does it have to hurt so bloody awful?"

He couldn't think of anything to do but take her in his arms. He didn't know what had gone wrong, everything had seemed so ready, so perfect. Only one possibility crossed his mind. He stuttered, "You're not...you aren't a..."

"A virgin, Jock?" Irritation had displaced the desperation in her voice for just an instant. "No, I'm not a bloody virgin." They clung to each other in silence for a few more moments before she added, "There's something wrong with me down there. I don't know what it is."

Just lying quietly in each other's arms provided enough of the comfort they both needed, and they were soon drifting off to sleep. A few feet away, Doc Green was wide awake; he'd been that way since the first rustle of their attempted coupling, and he'd heard every word.

But I might know what it is, Jillian, Doc thought as he drifted back to sleep.

Chapter Fifty-One

Major General Samuel Briley had tried to sleep, but anxiety had kept him wide awake. Now it was nearly sunrise, and he was exhausted. He hated the feel of his body when it was deprived of sleep. It was like his insides were hollow and dirty, covered with a shell of sore, exhausted muscles that somehow managed to function but suggested with every movement they could fail with the very next attempt. Vision was painful; his dry, tired eyes felt as if pins were being driven into them. The urge to collapse to the floor, curl into a ball, and lose consciousness for as long as it took his body to recover was almost overpowering.

Samuel Briley hadn't felt like this since the trenches of France in 1918, when sleep was a luxury afforded only in the absence of German artillery. The demon that had kept him awake all night was none other than General MacArthur, who, while enjoying the benefits of a good night's sleep alongside his wife in their opulent Brisbane apartment, expected Briley to provide him with the bomb assessment damage from Task Force Miles the very moment the Supreme Commander awoke.

I will personally give Washington the good news you deliver to me, MacArthur had told him.

And Samuel Briley knew if *good news* was what the Supreme Commander wanted, *good news* is what you will deliver.

There was just one problem: the nightly transmission from Task Force Miles had not come through. All night, every frequency had been searched over and over again as Briley paced the floor of his

quarters, waiting for the phone call that would tell him
what he needed to hear. But none of the many calls he
received throughout the night—all from apprehensive
communications officers—provided that service. Not
one bit of a message, not one character of Morse code,
not even a hint of a carrier wave, was received at any
station around Queensland. It was as if Captain
Maynard Miles and his men suddenly did not exist. The
only good news Briley knew about the shaky venture
on Cape York was already old news: all the bombers
had returned from the raid with no serious damage to
the planes and no serious injuries to the crewmen. That
in itself was a cause for celebration in these dark days,
but that celebration was long over. Where their bombs
actually fell, Samuel Briley still had not a clue. Dawn
had broken, and there was still no news at all:

And no news is good news, right?

Scooter Brewster and Grover Wheatley hadn't
slept much, either, but for entirely different reasons.
Dawn had broken, and Captain Brewster was full of
adrenaline, eager to accomplish the mission he had
taken upon himself to assume. Wheatley, on the other
hand, was scared out of his mind, and the exhaustion
creeping through his body was only making the fear
worse. They were going further into harm's way, and
he had not been told why. He began to believe that if he
raised one more protest, this lunatic of a captain might
just kill him, for no other reason than not to have to
listen to him anymore.

A voice in Wheatley's head asked the simple

question: *Why don't you just murder the captain and be done with all this? There are no witnesses. Find your own way back. You can say the Japs killed him...or maybe the Aborigines.*

Tempting as the thought might be, Grover Wheatley was not an optimistic man. He had never escaped blame for anything he had done in his life, and he certainly would never escape the blame for homicide—of a superior officer, at that. Somehow, he'd be in front of a firing squad in no time flat. He was sure of it. He had become more afraid of the insane asylum known as the US Army—embodied at the moment in one Captain Brewster—than he was of the Japanese, a foe he had yet to meet.

When Brewster set the sheet of paper containing the orders alight, he recognized the faint glimmer of hope that came into Wheatley's bloodshot eyes, a look that meant *maybe he changed his mind after all...and we're going back!*

Scooter Brewster sneered and said, "Don't get your hopes up, Corporal. Now, let's move out. We're still headed north. You take point."

Brewster enjoyed watching the hope drain from Wheatley's eyes. The corporal shuffled off like a man condemned to the gallows.

They hadn't walked very far through the forest when they heard a loud voice. They couldn't make out the words being said. It certainly wasn't in English.

Brewster and Wheatley found themselves just a short distance—maybe 10 yards—from the edge of a wide, dirt road, running north and south. As they crouched in the undergrowth behind some sturdy trees, Brewster hastily checked his map. He was pretty sure where they were—about 15 miles due south of Weipa—and according to this map, there was no road anywhere near here. This wasn't some trail carved by natives. It had been laid out by engineers, straight and true as an arrow, intended for large vehicles.

The Japs must have built this recently, Brewster thought.

They looked to the south, and the origin of the voice became clear. What appeared to be a company of Japanese soldiers, perhaps 100 or more, were marching in a column of twos. A man marching alongside the column—probably a sergeant—was calling what sounded like cadence. Trailing the column in a small staff car was a young officer who seemed very apprehensive, constantly looking around like he expected calamity to befall them at any second. Brewster couldn't see the officer's rank clearly, but he was a lieutenant or captain, definitely not higher. Neither he nor the troops who marched before him looked much like soldiers of a victorious army. The men looked bedraggled and dragged their feet as they marched. Their packs seemed very full and heavy, as if they were carrying everything they owned on their backs. Their uniforms were sloppy and varied from man to man. Brewster got the impression they had set out on this march in great haste. He wouldn't have been surprised if he was witnessing a punishment detail. They passed to the north quickly, leaving only a cloud of choking dust in their wake.

The dust drifted away, and another group of men became visible down the road. They, too, were heading north, but they were definitely not Japanese soldiers. They were not soldiers at all. They were Aborigines.

Brewster counted 16 of them. They were dressed like construction workers in trousers and shirts of sturdy fabric and hats of all varieties. A few wore sturdy boots. The rest were barefoot. Each carried a rucksack slung over a shoulder. Unlike the Japanese that preceded them, they seemed quite happy, laughing and joking as they made their way up the road. Some of what Brewster overheard even sounded like English. Occasionally, one of the Aborigines would make a gesture in the direction of the Japanese column and yell something—loud enough to amuse his companions but not for the Japanese to hear—and the others would laugh uproariously. Even though Brewster couldn't make out the exact words, it didn't sound as if a compliment was being offered to the soldiers. They were being mocked, plain and simple.

"We're going to follow that group of Aborigines," Brewster said to Wheatley.

Wheatley's panic reached a new height. "You don't mean we're going to walk on the road, do you? Out in the open?"

"Don't be ridiculous, Corporal. Of course not. We'll stay hidden among the trees."

Jock had risen from slumber to find himself alone in the shack. It was well past sunrise, and he scolded himself for sleeping in. There was so much that needed to be done today.

He wasn't prepared for the sight that met his eyes as he stepped from the shack. In the middle of the camp, a number of his men were seated on the ground in a wide circle, being served breakfast, which they were consuming with great relish. It was like a big, friendly picnic—and it seemed totally out of place in the middle of a combat zone. They were being waited on by several Aborigine women. First Sergeant Patchett appeared to be in a place of honor, seated on a box that raised him higher than the others. One of the black women was apparently dedicated to serving only him. Jock was relieved to see they all had their weapons with them, at least.

Patchett saw Jock and gestured for him to join them. As he walked toward the circle, Jock noticed Jillian across the camp, talking with Old Robert and a few other black men. She was barefoot and still wearing the loose shift. She looked up and saw him, cast a shy smile his way, and went right on talking with the men.

"A little bit of paradise, Captain," Patchett said as Jock grew close. One of the black women approached with another box and placed it next to the first sergeant. "Your throne, sir," Patchett said. "Have a seat and dig into this chow. Not sure what it is, but it tastes just fine."

Jock counted the men in the circle. Five were missing. Hadley, Boudreau, Botkin and McGuire were already gone, he was told, on their way to the Moreton telegraph relay station. The fifth, Corporal Pacheco, was still riding the *Radio Flyer* and being pulled across the camp toward the breakfast circle by two young black boys.

"Hadley and his men were on their way the minute the sun broke the horizon," Patchett said. "They even got served a good breakfast before they hit the trail, too."

"While they're gone," Jock said, "we've got to figure out where all those Japs are off to."

Patchett pointed toward Jillian and the black men. "They're already on it. They've got a scout network set up from here all the way to the tip of the Cape. They've got the whole damn indigenous population to work with, and they'll cover a hell of a lot more ground than we ever could. From what they tell me, it looks like the Japs ain't gonna stop walking until they hit the Torres Strait. They even tried to cover ground last night, the damn fools."

Patchett shoveled another fistful of mashed fruit into his mouth before adding, "These blacks don't plan on staying in this camp forever. Once it's all clear, they'd like to get back to their homes in the Mission."

"Those who still have homes, anyway," Jock said, thinking of Jillian's incinerated house.

"You know, Captain…assuming we get that message through, do you really think they'll come pick us up at Weipa, right there at Albatross Bay?"

"I didn't think it would hurt to ask," Jock replied as he sampled from his plate, "especially after they know we've got a prisoner. I'd like to spare the men that long walk back, if I can."

"That'd be real nice," Patchett said, "but a couple days' rest and they'll be up to making long walks again." His taut stomach was now full and content, and he rubbed it happily.

Doc Green ambled slowly toward them from across the camp. He still limped on his wounded leg, but he looked clean and refreshed. He had even shaved, the only man to do so since they'd entered the bush six days ago.

"Where've you been?" Jock asked the doc.

"Down to the creek. Got myself freshened up. It might be a good idea to get the lads cleaned up, too. Hygiene and all that. The water's fine for washing...no crocs around...but no drinking without the Halazone first."

"No problem, Doc," Patchett said. "I've already got a bath schedule worked up. Maybe we get some of these filthy uniforms washed, too."

Doc Green asked, "A word, Jock?" Jock rose and followed Green away from the circle.

"I can probably help Jillian with her problem," Doc said.

"Problem? What do you mean?"

"The pain with sex...her *dyspareunia.*"

"*Dyspurrr-what?*"

"Never mind that," Doc said. "It just means pain with sex. Lady-parts are what I used to do for a living, remember?"

Now Jock was embarrassed. "You *heard* us?"

Doc grinned like a Cheshire cat. "It was hard to miss." He made the words sound like the understatement of the century. "Look, Jock...I'll need to examine her. You know...a vaginal exam. But I can't very well just walk up to her and say, *Good day, Jillian...how about giving me a peek at your fanny?*"

"So what do we do, Doc?"

"Make it *your* idea. Mention that I'm a gyno—"

"She already knows that."

"Right. Of course," Doc said. "So make the gentle suggestion that she pay me an *office visit.*"

"Can you really fix her, Doc?"

"Maybe not out here...but we'll never know if I

don't look, will we?"

Chapter Fifty-Two

It was nearly 1100 hours as Scooter Brewster peered through binoculars at the Weipa Mission, over a mile in the distance. Grover Wheatley nervously scanned the other three quadrants around their position without benefit of binoculars, wondering if he'd be able to pull the trigger of his M1—or even find a voice to sound the alarm—if any Japanese approached.

The only Japanese that could be seen, however, were that same column from earlier on the road. They had stopped once inside the Weipa Mission, milling around aimlessly while its members took turns relieving themselves. Now re-formed into a column of twos, they continued their march north through and out of the Mission.

The behavior of the Aborigine group they had shadowed up the road was far more interesting. Once they reached the deserted Mission, they split up, peered into a few of the buildings, and re-formed for a brief group discussion. It didn't take them long to arrive at a consensus. They walked straight into the woods, heading due east away from the Mission. They looked around as they walked, as if checking if anyone was following them. In a few moments, they had vanished into the forest. Scooter Brewster drew two arrows on his map: one for the direction of movement of the Japanese, the other for the Aborigines.

There was no point in Brewster seeking his quarry in the Mission. It was obviously deserted now. He put his finger on one of the details that had been sketched onto the map in the orders envelope. It was a crude drawing of a house. Next to it were the words *Forbes house.* Shooting an azimuth to the northeast with his compass, Brewster set out in that direction. "Get moving, Wheatley," he said to his corporal. "I'll be on point now, you cover my ass."

They arrived in less than half an hour, but his quarry wasn't there, either. The house wasn't there, for that matter. Obviously, a structure used to be there, but it and the woods around it had been burned to the ground. As they viewed it from 50 yards away, in the shelter of unburned trees, the only things recognizable in the charred rubble were a bathtub, a few sinks, and the tin roof panels. The wildfire that ravaged the forest swept west, carving a channel a hundred yards wide that looked like it might extend all the way to the Mission.

Brewster settled to a seated position on the ground, his M1 vertical between his knees, the muzzle pointed skyward. He needed a minute to think:

If this was her house...and it's burned to the ground...does that mean she died in this fire?

Or is she still someplace else...God knows where...in this big, empty wasteland?

That minute was all he needed. "Corporal," Brewster said, "search what's left of that house for human remains."

"What would I be looking for, Captain? I'm a radio tech, not some ghoul from Graves Registration."

"Oh, come on, man! Use your imagination! You're looking for a burned corpse...a skeleton...maybe just some bones. Now conduct the search. That's an order."

Wheatley resigned himself to his task. After all, he had been ordered. He was just as afraid of walking into the burned-out area—completely devoid of cover and concealment—as he was of actually finding a charred corpse. To make himself as small a target as possible, he employed the only tactical skill he retained from basic training—he low-crawled out of the tree line into the void the wildfire had left behind.

"For crying out loud," Brewster called after him, "is that really necessary, Corporal? We don't have all fucking day."

Wheatley pretended not to hear the captain and kept right on crawling. When he reached the pile of scorched debris that was once a house, he did a fairly thorough search, even peering under every fallen roof panel without ever rising higher than a crouch. It turned up nothing, though. There was no sign any living thing had died there.

Filthy with soot, he returned and reported his lack of findings to Scooter Brewster, who asked, "You're absolutely sure?"

"Yes sir. Absolutely."

"Well, that's just fucking great," Brewster said, as if this was somehow the corporal's fault.

"So can we go back now, Captain?"

Brewster sighed and shook his head. "Sit down, Corporal," he said. "It's time I explained to you what we're doing here."

Scooter Brewster proceeded to relate every detail of their mission to a stunned and silent Grover Wheatley. Brewster talked for a solid 10 minutes, relating the orders from the sheet of paper he had burned earlier that morning, augmenting those words with references to the map and the photo of the young woman. He concluded the briefing by saying, "If she's anywhere around here, we're going to find this traitorous woman…and we're going to carry out those orders, so help me God."

It had taken his five years of service to convince Grover Wheatley the US Army was insane. But at this moment, he felt his understanding of that institution's pathology had reached a new height. It was more than just insane; it was criminally insane.

Chapter Fifty-Three

Franklin Delano Roosevelt abruptly pushed his wheelchair back from the breakfast table and lit a cigarette with shaking hands. He had been in a good mood on this bright summer morning, enjoying the news his CNO, Admiral Ernest King, had just reported. The invasion of the Solomon Islands was definitely a "go" for late September, just three months from now. FDR's beloved Navy was finally getting back into this war. Then his Army Chief of Staff had to go and ruin it all.

"So you're telling me, General Marshall," the president said, "we have no earthly idea how well our bombers did on Cape York?"

Marshall swallowed hard and struggled to keep his normally calm and collected demeanor intact. Inside, though, his stomach churned. There was no denying what the president just said. He really had no earthly idea what, if any, good the bombers had done. The cables from MacArthur's headquarters in Brisbane had been silent on the matter.

"*Yet*, Mister President...We don't know *yet*," Marshall said, trying to stress the hope this lack of information was temporary in nature.

FDR pounded his fist on the wheelchair's armrest. "When? When will you know, General Marshall? I've given up trying to figure out what day this is in Australia, but by my count, it's been about thirty hours since those bombs were supposed to fall. How much time do you need?"

Marshall knew there was no answer to the president's question. His only hope of escaping this meeting without a major ass-chewing was to deflect the blame. He knew just how to do it.

"Mister President, I'm sure General MacArthur is carefully assessing—"

As Marshall expected, FDR flew into a rage at the mention of the name and cut Marshall off. "MacArthur!" the President said, spitting the syllables out like they were poison. "That self-serving, deceitful son of a bitch! And insubordinate, too! He's not assessing anything...he's playing politics again, like he always does. It's just like him to give us information when he, and only he, decides...and only after he's tampered with it, so it makes him sound as good as possible."

Roosevelt calmed himself and took a deep drag on his cigarette. His next words were a lament, a wish he had lost the power to make come true: "I should have left his pompous ass to rot in the Philippines." Wheeling himself from the dining room, he said, "Good day, gentlemen," abruptly dismissing his Army and Navy chiefs and leaving them in silence.

George Marshall tried not to smile; he had dodged the bullet. But across the table, Ernest King was smirking victoriously at him, for the Navy was on top once again in the president's eyes. Marshall had to fight the urge to scoop a knife from the table and stab King right in his smug face.

They were making great time across the flat plains of the eucalyptus forest, spread out in single file, keeping a brisk walking pace. Sometimes they even jogged. Sergeant Tom Hadley was on point. He and the three men following behind felt surprisingly good, despite the ordeal of the last five days in the bush. Hadley had a theory why that was so:

Because if we get this message through, it means we'll be back in Brisbane before you know it.

They had little fear of running into any Japanese this far inland. Hadley checked his compass; it was important to stay on course. "If we can keep up this pace," Hadley said over his shoulder, "and hit the telegraph road right near the station, I'm betting we'll be there by late afternoon. We've got plenty of K rations, so keep drinking and eating, especially the D bars. Don't let yourself get run down. We've still got a lot of walking to do."

Sergeant Stu Botkin wasn't as optimistic, though. "But Tom," he said, "suppose we hit the road and the station's nowhere in sight. Which way do we go?"

"That's easy," Hadley replied. "We'd have to be south of the station, so we'd go north. The only way we could hit the road north of the station is if we cross the Wenlock River, and I think we'd know if we did that."

Botkin wanted to kick himself for forgetting that basic bit of geography. "Oh, yeah," he said, "I forgot about the river."

"I forgot about something, too," Hadley said. "I know we're moving fast, but keep an eye out for snakes…and for God's sake, don't step on one."

Bogater Boudreau found that funny. "If ol' Russo remembered that," he said, "he still might be here."

"Shut up, Boudreau," Hadley said, his irritation flaring. "I was there and you weren't. You don't know what happened."

Botkin caught up to Hadley so the two sergeants could talk without the others hearing. "Tom," he said, "what do you think is going to happen to Guess once we get back?"

The tone of Hadley's answer was matter-of-fact, almost disappointed: "I think they're going to go through the motions of a court martial...and Guess will be acquitted."

"I take it you disagree with that," Botkin said.

"We all know they hated each other, Stu. Nobody knows if Russo would have died from that snakebite. Maybe we could have shut him up and saved him. As it stands, it looks like murder to me, plain and simple."

"That's a lot of *ifs,* Tom," Botkin said. "And in the heat of battle, at that."

Before Hadley could say anything, Bogater Boudreau—who had heard every word—said, with unswerving conviction, "Makes no nevermind. All I know, Sergeant Hadley, is that you and Guess and Billings and Captain Miles would be pushing up daisies right now if Guess hadn't done what he did. If them Japs didn't shoot you outright, they would've cut your fucking heads off. One man for four sounds like a pretty good trade-off to me...and it being that fucking Yankee Russo who did the dying is just icing on the cake."

"I'd go easy there, Bogater," Botkin said. "The rest of us here are all fucking Yankees, too. You're the only fucking redneck."

"It is what it is," Boudreau said with a shrug. "And I ain't no redneck, Sergeant...I'm a Cajun."

Hadley had nothing more to say. He had turned off the conversation and drifted into his memory of that fateful patrol, the one everyone survived but Nicky Russo. It had happened only three days ago, but it felt like an event from another lifetime. The words Captain Miles had said as they carried Russo's lifeless body repeated over and over in his head, like a scratched phonograph record whose needle was stuck replaying the same few grooves for eternity: *But I'm not sure I wouldn't have done the same thing myself if I'd gotten there first.*

Then Captain Miles had offered the question that really wasn't a question at all, just a statement of undeniable fact: *Wouldn't you?*

Tom Hadley finally had to admit it: *Yeah...I probably would have.*

Jock Miles and Melvin Patchett agreed this would be a day of cleanup and rest for the men but not one in which they'd let their guard down. As diligent about security as their black hosts were, they didn't possess firearms, and until it was known for certain where the Japanese had gone, they all would have to assume at least some of Colonel Najima's stragglers might still be wandering around the area. The arsenal of spears, arrows, and knives the blacks used for hunting and fishing wouldn't offer much of a defense against machine guns and aircraft. The Americans were grateful for the protection offered them last night, when any of their men put on guard duty would, no doubt, have fallen dead asleep. Now, though, it was time to become more of a proactive partner in this newfound alliance with the Weipa blacks.

Old Robert welcomed the support the American manpower could provide. He laid out the early-warning and surveillance network his people had established to Jock and Patchett, and the Americans were quite impressed with its thoroughness. They seemed to have every angle covered. When Jock suggested augmenting one of the black outposts with the .30 caliber machine gun, however, Old Robert frowned and shook his head.

"You must remember, Captain Miles," Robert said, "our plan is to locate and avoid the Japanese, not do battle with them. I thought that was your mission, as well."

"Well, then...how about this? Let's keep our firepower centrally located in the camp," Jock said, pivoting effortlessly to the role of conciliator. "That way, we can respond immediately in any direction."

Patchett and Old Robert nodded in agreement. The ground rules of cooperation established, Patchett stepped to the forefront to work out the manpower details. Unneeded now—only an observer in the first sergeant's realm—Jock set out to find Jillian.

He found her outside the shack she shared with Alice Tookura and several other black women. Jillian was actually standing guard, making sure no one entered. Doc Green was inside, she explained, treating Alice, the young woman who had been sexually abused by Japanese soldiers the day before.

"Jill, about last night," Jock said.

The look she gave him flashed from embarrassment to disappointed resignation. "What do you want me to say, Jock? I'm sorry. I can't help it..."

She convinced herself she wasn't going to cry.

"There's nothing to be sorry about," he said. "You

know…just maybe…maybe Doc can help you, too."

She looked at him quizzically, perhaps a bit suspiciously. "What does Doc have to…" She stiffened as if an electric shock had passed through her body. "Oh, bloody hell! Last night…did he hear us?"

His hesitation was all the confirmation she needed. "Bloody fucking hell, Jock," she said, crossing her arms defensively over her chest. "I don't want the whole damned world knowing my problems."

He tried to take her in his arms but she jumped away. "But if it's something medical," he said, "we've got a gynecologist right here. Maybe he can help, Jill."

"Why are you calling me *Jill* all of a sudden? It sounds ridiculous. Nobody calls me that."

"Nobody? Good. It'll be special if only I say it…because you're special to me."

He reached out for her again. This time she didn't back away.

Without a hint of animosity, she said, "You're so full of it, Yank." She was looking down, so he couldn't see her face. But he was sure she was smiling.

"Jock, why do you assume it's a medical problem? Did Doc tell you that?"

"Why can't it be medical?"

She sighed and rested her head on his shoulder. "Oh, it could be," she said.

"Then you'll go and see Doc?"

It felt to Jock like she took an eternity to answer, but he didn't mind. Not with her nestled against him like this.

"I suppose," she said.

There was a commotion from the western fringe of the camp. By instinct, Jock unslung his Thompson and brought it to the ready position. In a moment, it was back on his shoulder; the noises were happy ones. It was a celebration.

He quickly checked that none of his men were poised to fire, but they, too, understood it was no threat. All across the camp, Thompsons were being slung over shoulders once again.

Jillian got caught up in the excitement. "It's Nathan Gooreng," she said, "and the rest of the men from Airfield Two. They're safe!" She and Jock rushed to join Nathan and the 15 men with him—the same 16 Scooter Brewster had followed to Weipa Mission—as they were joyously reunited with their families.

Seeing Jock and his men, Nathan said, "So the Yanks have joined with us now. Good. They'll want to hear what we have to say."

With his three young children clinging happily to him, Nathan proceeded to tell his story. "The Japanese soldiers are terrified. They claim their enemies dropped fire from the sky. All their leaders are gone, they say...burned to death. There's no one left to give them orders at the airfield except one lieutenant. He told them to stay, but they didn't listen. They have no food...so they're leaving, hoping their Navy will take them back to Papua. But all the ships are gone, too."

"My God," Patchett muttered, "it's a rout."

Looking past the euphoria of the moment, Jillian said, "We'd better hope they get to Papua somehow, or they'll be wandering all around us, looking for something to eat."

Jock, Patchett, and Old Robert found themselves nodding thoughtfully in agreement with her.

"One more thing, Captain," Nathan said. "Your

men don't know how to hide very well."

"What makes you say that, Nathan?"

"Two of them followed us for a time on Yellow Vermin Road. They tried to hide from us, but we knew they were there."

"That can't be," Jock said, scratching his head. "All my men are either right here or on their way to Moreton."

"Then the ones going to Moreton must be very lost, Captain, because the men following us wore helmets just like you. They must be Yanks."

His story finished, Nathan and the men who traveled with him retired to be with their families. They were weary from their long walk. Once rested, they would be joining the others keeping track of the Japanese.

As delighted as Jock and Patchett were to get confirmation of the Japanese retreat, Nathan's last words still left them puzzled. "He's got to be mistaken, sir," the first sergeant said. "Even if Brisbane decided to send more troops here, it wouldn't be until they heard from us...or decided they'd never hear from us again. And it's way too soon for them desk jockeys to have decided something like that, slow as they are to come around."

"Yeah, I know," Jock replied. "It just doesn't make any sense there'd be another American unit in the area. But if there are more Yanks out there, I hope to hell they have a radio."

"You think we should go looking for 'em, sir?"

"No, Top. If anyone's out there, Old Robert's men will find them long before we will."

The young Japanese lieutenant was growing more fearful with each passing hour. Technically, he was leading the soldiers from Airfield Two as they fled north, but those men paid him no attention. Ever since they ignored his order to stay at the airfield and started their exodus, he knew he was no longer leading anyone. He had become just a follower, another traveler in the Cape York wilderness, alone, powerless, and feeling very vulnerable. He was on foot now, like the rest; his vehicle ran out of fuel a few miles past Weipa. Those outspoken ones who had provoked such disobedience would pay, he assured himself, once they got back to Papua—assuming, of course, *he* ever got back to Papua.

He needed a quiet place to relieve himself, away from the prying eyes of those jackals who used to be dutiful soldiers. He doubled back to a stream they had just passed, confident none of them would bother to follow him. His trousers were halfway to the ground when he saw the eyes of a crocodile rippling the surface of the water like tiny periscopes, staring right at him.

Perhaps this is not the best place, he thought, and turned to walk upstream.

He never got to take a step. Several soldiers rushed forward and pushed him into the stream. The croc—a very large one—wasted little time escorting the lieutenant to his underwater grave.

Chapter Fifty-Four

When they emerged from the woods at the dirt road that was Telegraph Track, they had only missed their destination by a few hundred yards. Up the road to the north, along the line of wooden poles carrying the telegraph wires high over their heads, stood the Moreton Relay Station, shimmering in the orange light of sunset. Nestled very close to the Wenlock River, the white structure very much resembled a typical Australian house, with a second-story veranda on all sides. Though it looked abandoned, just as they had expected, the house seemed to welcome these dog-tired travelers. They walked in the open on Telegraph Track, their journey moments from completion.

As they neared the station, something didn't look right to Sergeant Hadley. "Get off the road! Now!" he said as he dove into the tall grass that bordered the track. His three men wasted little time diving for concealment right behind him.

"This place isn't deserted," Hadley said, pointing to the station some 30 yards away, "We've got company...and I think they saw us."

What they couldn't see from down the road was obvious now. There were two scruffy white men with heavy beards, dressed in rough, working man's clothes and bush hats. Close by, two rifles were resting against the veranda railing. The two men were carrying a heavy object from the station.

"There's got to be more than two of them," Hadley said. "Look around back of the house. There's a cart with a mule...and there are two horses with saddles. So there're at least three of them. Maybe more."

The two men placed the object they carried onto the mule cart, which was already loaded with equipment.

"That's a storage battery they're carrying," Botkin said. "I need that stuff, dammit!" He stood and took one step in the direction of the station before Hadley pulled him back down.

"Stay the fuck down, Stu," Hadley said. "Let's figure out what's going on here."

"There's nothing to figure, Tom," Botkin replied. "If we're going to send that message, we need that equipment."

One of the bearded men called out to the Americans. "You diggers are on private property," he said. "Go play your bloody army games some place else."

"We're Americans," Botkin called back. "We need to send an urgent message to Brisbane."

The bearded men didn't seem impressed. "Yanks, eh?" the other said. "Makes no difference. This gear belongs to the telegraph company...and it's out of commission. You can't use it." The pair picked up the rifles from the railing.

"Bogater," Hadley said, "you and McGuire keep our ass covered. The others may try to slip behind us. And for God's sake, spread out."

"We got it, Sarge," Bogater Boudreau replied as he guided McGuire to a good firing position.

Hadley asked Botkin, "You really think they work for the telegraph, Stu? They look like plain ol' hillbillies to me."

"I'll give them a little test," Botkin replied. He called to the bearded men, "So you're telegraphers?"

"That's right, Yank. We work for the telegraph."

Botkin proceeded to shout a series of *dits* and *dahs*—a short message in Morse code, delivered verbally. It made McGuire laugh.

"What's so goddamn funny?" Boudreau asked.

"He just told them *fuck you* in Morse," McGuire replied.

There was not even the faintest glimmer of recognition on the bearded men's faces. They had no idea they had just been cryptically insulted. Botkin shook his head and said, "They ain't telegraphers, that's for—"

His words were cut off by a single rifle shot and then the chatter of Thompson submachine guns. Boudreau and McGuire had been fired on, and they were firing back in spades. McGuire was screaming his head off: "THERE'S ONE OVER THERE! THERE'S ONE OVER THERE!"

Each of the bearded men at the station got off one shot from his rifle before a long burst from Hadley's Thompson riddled both of them. They collapsed, lifeless, to the deck of the veranda. Hadley's burst also managed to shatter every window on that side of the station, generously perforate the wall, and scatter the frightened horses. Only the mule stood its ground.

In the seconds it took Stu Botkin to get his head up and try to fire, it was all over. He never got a shot off. It wasn't necessary anymore—and he was worried Hadley had already shot up the station beyond repair. There was no point adding to the damage.

"ANYONE HIT?" Hadley asked his men, his adrenaline-fueled voice raised nearly an octave.

Their voices breathless and reedy, Botkin and

McGuire managed to say they were okay. Boudreau was okay, too. His voice eerily calm, he added, "We got the other two. You had that situation pegged real good, Sarge." He scooped up the rifles from the bodies of the men he and McGuire had just killed. These dead men looked and dressed exactly like their now-deceased partners at the station. "Like Sarge said, they're just a bunch of thieving, hillbilly scumbags," Boudreau said as he nudged a dead body with his foot.

"You sure there were just those two, Bogater?" Hadley asked, struggling to get his voice under control.

"Sure as I can be," Boudreau replied. "Damn shame them two horses took off, though. We could have used them. That mule don't do us no good. Slow us down too much. Might as well cut him loose."

There was no time for regrets now. Pressing on, Hadley said, "We've got to clear the station...make sure there're no bad guys still inside. Stu, you and Bogater approach it from the north, I'll take McGuire and approach it from the south...stay in cover as long as you can...and for cryin' out loud, let's not turn this into a circular firing squad and shoot each other."

They found no one else inside. It took Stuart Botkin all of five minutes to determine Hadley's torrent of bullets had hit nothing of importance in the station and reassemble the components the bearded thieves had removed. In 10 more minutes, he had a confirmation from the Brisbane civil telegraph office his message was being forwarded to US Army Headquarters.

General Briley knew the message's content sooner

than anyone could have expected. The US Army liaison officer at the Brisbane telegraph office had the general on the phone within minutes. Briley was at a meeting of the American/Australian joint staff. The major acting as the general's aide in Scooter Brewster's absence interrupted that meeting, knowing Briley would want to know immediately of any communication with Task Force Miles. It was too late to worry about codes and message security now; everyone on the long telegraph line from Moreton to Brisbane knew what it said. Every operator at the telephone switchboard did, too.

Briley wasn't buying a word of it. Fuming, he said, "One little bombing raid and an airfield totally destroyed? A Jap *regiment* in hasty retreat? The regiment's *colonel* has been captured, to boot! All these improbable events described in a message sent in the clear, not by military radio but civil telegraph because they claim their code book was destroyed! Gentlemen, this is obvious Japanese trickery. A complete hoax."

Wing Commander Tim Wells, one of the Australians seated at the conference table, found Briley's dismissal hard to accept. "But if that message is true, General," Wells said, "are you willing to ignore the victory it would signify?"

Briley gave Wells an arrogant glance. "I believe your boys flew Task Force Miles in, didn't they, Wing Commander?"

"Yes, General, they did. I flew the lead plane."

"And would the Royal Australian Air Force be willing to fly in and pick them up at Albatross Bay, as this ridiculous message suggests?"

"If the message can be verified as authentic, then absolutely, General."

"And just how do you propose we verify it, Wells?"

"Quite simply, sir...by asking them the identifiers of the aircraft that flew them in. No Jap could ever know that."

Stu Botkin was startled when the receiver relay began clicking its reply. It had been less than an hour since he sent his message to Brisbane. His three comrades were lounging on the veranda, keeping a lookout while resting their weary legs. They weren't expecting an answer so soon. They came rushing in and crowded eagerly around the telegraph operator's table at the first click of the relay, straining to hear every *dit* and *dah* of Morse code—though only Botkin and McGuire understood it.

The reply was short; only a few sentences. By the time he finished copying it, Botkin seemed puzzled. He sighed and said, "Here we go...they want authentication. Get this...they're asking for the identifiers of the aircraft that flew us here." He buried his face in his hands and asked, "Who the hell would know that?"

Botkin could tell right away that Hadley and Boudreau didn't know; the blank looks on their faces were a dead giveaway.

McGuire, though, was busily flipping through a notebook he pulled from his shirt pocket. "I know that," he said. "It's all right here. The planes were called *L for Love* and *M for Mother.*"

Botkin was astonished. "You wrote all that shit

down, Pat?"

"Yeah," McGuire replied. "You see, I plan to write a book about all this...if we ever get out of here alive, that is."

The joint planning conference was still going on when General Briley's aide rushed back into the conference room. "The reply has come back, General," the aide said, pointing to the phone on the conference table. "I'll have them put the call through."

General Briley listened for a moment, and then cupped his hand over the phone's mouthpiece. Turning to Tim Wells, he asked, *"L for Love, M for Mother.* Is that it, Wells?"

Tim Wells smiled. "That's correct, sir," he replied.

Briley hung up the phone and began to pace the conference room as the eyes of 20 military officers nervously followed him. He had been so heavily invested in the idea the message was a Japanese hoax that now, with confirmation of the message's authenticity, he didn't know how to proceed. He didn't like being proved so totally wrong, either.

One thing still bothered Samuel Briley very much: what of Captain Brewster's courier mission? There was no mention of it at all in the telegraph message. Had that mission failed as spectacularly as Task Force Miles had succeeded? Perhaps there was another possibility, Briley thought:

The elimination of the Forbes woman has been accomplished, and my young captains are shrewd enough to make no mention of it in an unsecured message.

Whatever the outcome, it could not be discussed over civil telegraph lines.

After a few more moments of pacing, Samuel Briley had come to a decision. "All right," he said, "let's bring Task Force Miles in...but we're not going to pick them up at Albatross Bay."

Several voices rang out in dissent all at once, but Tim Wells's was the most prominent. "Why not, sir?" Wells said. "I'm willing to give it a go."

"Too risky...and I know my Air Force will back me up on this. We haven't had a successful air operation in daylight since we got here, and we're not going to try it now. Task Force Miles walked in...they can walk out the same way. Tell them to come home...and make damned sure they bring that Jap *colonel* with them."

Briley sensed the other officers in the room weren't thrilled with his decision. They wouldn't look him in the eye and shifted uncomfortably in their chairs. The general didn't care, though. They had no choice but to comply, and he wasn't there to make them happy.

"This meeting is dismissed," Briley said. "I've got to get upstairs and inform General MacArthur."

Chapter Fifty-Five

Samuel Briley walked purposefully into the reception suite of MacArthur's office. His step faltered only when the icy gaze of the receptionist fell on him. The woman, an Australian civilian in US Army employ, issued a cold greeting: "General Sutherland wants a word with you, sir."

Quite put out, Briley said, "I'm here to see the Supreme Commander, not the Chief of Staff."

"General MacArthur is unavailable," she said. "Please have a seat. General Sutherland will be with you shortly."

Briley knew what was going on: *I'm being snubbed. A two-star doesn't have to cool his heels just to see another two-star. Sutherland is just his gatekeeper...I know full well MacArthur's in there.*

It was one thing to know what was going on, but it was entirely another to know why. Right now, Samuel Briley didn't have a clue as to why MacArthur was snubbing him.

Generals do not wait well. In the five minutes it took Sutherland to appear, Sam Briley's face had reddened with annoyance. He was sure he could feel his blood pressure rising. He was well aware of his pulse pounding in his temples. His first words to Sutherland were anything but cordial: "What the hell's going on here, Richard? I need to see General MacArthur. I have some excellent news for him."

Sutherland's tone was like a schoolmaster scolding a pupil. "The general already knows your *news.* It's all over the radio...and he's very unhappy."

Briley realized this conversation was going to

happen right here, with the two of them standing in the reception area. He would not be ushered into Sutherland's office, let alone MacArthur's. He would not be offered a drink and a comfortable chair. He was not being afforded the courtesies owed to a two-star general. The snub was becoming more brutal by the second.

Although the men were roughly the same height, Sutherland seemed to be looking down at Briley. "That message from that task force of yours," Sutherland said, "the whole damned world knows about it now. It's all over the radio. Do you vouch for its authenticity?"

"Yes, Richard, I do."

"Then that was a damned foolish thing to do, General." Sutherland managed to make the word *general* sound like a slur.

Baffled, Briley asked, "Since when is victory foolish, Richard?"

"When MacArthur doesn't get the credit," Sutherland replied. "The only name being mentioned on the radio right now is yours…because your idiots on that task force put it in that telegram. Does anyone in your division have any concept of communications security?"

"This is ridiculous, Richard. I think—"

Sutherland silenced him with a wave of the hand. "Nobody cares what you think, General. You've forgotten two cardinal rules of this command. First, when there's a victory to be announced, MacArthur will announce it at a time and place that suits MacArthur. Second, only MacArthur will get the credit for said victory. Think about that in your new assignment."

Sutherland's last sentence knocked whatever wind

was left from Sam Briley's sails. He took a second to compose himself before asking, "What new assignment?"

"You're going home, General," Sutherland said. "A combat command no longer suits you. The orders are being typed as we speak."

The waiter at Lennon's Hotel bar left a freshly-opened bottle of whiskey on Sam Briley's table. The general had quickly emptied his glass several times already, and the waiter was tired of bringing refills. He had the usual nighttime crowd of American officers to tend to, and most were far better tippers than this two-star sitting alone in the corner.

"With the hotel's compliments, General," the waiter lied before scurrying away. The hotel had no intention of giving anything to the Yanks for free. They simply had too much money in their pockets to deserve such largesse. The bottle would be duly added to Briley's running tab, and the bleary-eyed general would never catch the charge even if he bothered to check.

Briley's mind was still clear enough to focus on two key facts. First, he had been sacked—relieved of his division command and sent packing to some nebulous desk job in the States, where he would probably spend the rest of this war rotting away in obscurity.

Second, if there was ever any fallout over the summary execution of an Australian civilian—an act he had ordered troops under his command to carry out—he was now out of favor and at the mercy of the political winds. Suddenly, the prospect of being found guilty of conspiracy to commit murder and spending the rest of his life in Leavenworth seemed very real. The politicians would skate free, like they always did, no matter what horrors they had perpetrated. And MacArthur, of course—despite his colossal blunders in the Philippines—was untouchable. If anyone in the high command was going to pay a price, it would be the newly-expendable Samuel Briley.

He removed a carefully folded piece of paper from his pocket and solemnly opened it. One last time, he read the order to kill Jillian Forbes that bore his signature. It had been locked in a file cabinet to which only he had the key, and it was the only copy of that document that should still be in existence. When he was done reading, he folded it once again, placed it in the ashtray sitting beside him, and reduced it to ashes with his cigarette lighter. In a room already thick with cigarette smoke and the effects of too much alcohol, nobody even noticed what he had done.

Refilling his whiskey glass, he thought, *Now, whether that woman is dead or not, it'll just be my word against the word of some little captain.*

Jillian and Jock sat on the steps of the *officers' quarters,* counting the stars in the quiet of night. He played gently with her hair, absently wrapping its curls around the fingers of one hand. One of her hands sketched lines on his back, as if keeping a running total of the star count on some imaginary blackboard. Neither could remember a time in recent days when things seemed so peaceful.

"Where's Doc?" she asked.

"He's bunking with the first sergeant tonight."

"How thoughtful," she said, pulling him closer.

"Jill...Doc said you went to see him today."

"Yeah, I did," she replied, taking back her arm to clasp her knees to her chest. She kept looking at the stars.

"So what did he say?"

"He said there's nothing wrong with me. Not physically, anyway. I'm a perfectly healthy young woman."

Jock was too puzzled by what she had just said to put a coherent question together. Disjointed words began tumbling from his mouth: "But...why...why can't..."

She assembled the sentence for him. "Why can't I have normal sexual relations? We talked about that. Quite a bit, actually."

Jock's puzzlement was giving way to frustration. "Come on, Jill...aren't you going to tell me?"

"Fucking hell, Jock...why do you keep calling me *Jill?* It sounds like we're in some bloody nursery rhyme...*Jock and Jill went up the hill...*"

He became more soothing than he ever imagined he could be. He pulled her close, with a firm but protective touch that chased every bit of tension from her body. She melted into him. He kissed her forehead.

"There...that's the problem," she said.

"I don't know what you mean."

"My head. Doc says it's all in my head."

"Why? How could that be?"

"It might have something to do with my mum. She

died giving birth to me. I never told you that, did I? He thinks maybe I'm just afraid that sex can lead to pregnancy...and death."

"But there are things we can do about that," he said.

She slipped her hand into the pocket of her shift and pulled out a fistful of condoms. She waved them in front of his face.

"Ahh, very good," Jock said, reaching for the condoms. "Seems the doc's got a cure for everything."

"Not so fast, Yank," she replied, putting the condoms back in her pocket. "I'm going to need a lot of help loosening up. He thinks it would be a good idea if I got a little pissed before trying it again."

"Pissed? You mean angry...or drunk?"

"Drunk, Jock. It means drunk."

"Hmm...that could be a problem around these parts. Is there any liquor around?"

"Not that I know of," she replied. "Not anymore, anyway. There's something else, too...I don't get drunk very easily."

"Oh, come on...everyone gets drunk."

"Is that so, Yank? I can drink every man I've ever known under the table."

"We'll just have to find ourselves a big enough supply of spirits to suit your requirements, then," he said, hoping the words didn't sound too lecherous.

"We'll need to get back to civilization for that, Jock. And speaking of civilization...when you and the lads do go back, can I come along with you?"

Jock could not have imagined a more pleasant suggestion. "Sure! Of course you can!"

"Good," she said, "because I really need to get to

Brisbane. I was afraid I'd have to walk all the way there. I need to see my aunt…and we'll need to talk to the bankers."

"Bankers? What for?"

"For the money to rebuild my business," she replied. "The Forbes family is, as you Yanks say, *loaded,* and Aunt Margaret controls the money."

"Holy cow," Jock said, truly surprised. "You're an heiress or something?"

"Yeah, something like that…but that's not my fault, Jock." She kissed him and added, "And of course, you and I might want to sample the abundant stocks of liquor available there…and hopefully reap the benefits. You can wait that long, can't you?"

"If that's what you want, Jillian."

Kissing him again, she said, "Thank you. Oh, and I didn't mean to snap at you before. You, and only you, Captain Maynard Miles, are hereby allowed to call me Jill. And never in public."

"Agreed," Jock replied. "So what do we do now?"

She started to giggle and replied, "How about we listen to some music? Maybe some Wagner? Let's just crank up the old Victrola…Oh, wait. I forgot. It got torched."

They laughed away the sad truth until it ended in a mutual sigh—there would be no music for them until they were back in Brisbane.

"How about we just go to sleep, Jock? It's very late."

Chapter Fifty-Six

The new day brought more good news. The Japanese seemed to be completely gone from Weipa. Not one had been sighted since that final, large group passed through the Mission yesterday. The atmosphere in the Peppan Creek camp had become more relaxed—even idyllic—until, at twilight, a shrill, distant *cooee* shattered the serenity. Every man of Task Force Miles grabbed his weapon and hurried to the rally point at the center of camp. Old Robert hurried there, too. He needed to coax the Americans' fingers off their triggers, for the *cooee* signaled good news. "It means your men are returning from Moreton," he told Jock. "Please, Captain...no shooting."

Thirty minutes later, Tom Hadley and his men walked proudly into the camp, to be greeted by the rest of Task Force Miles. They were exhausted but thrilled to be back. To silence the barrage of anxious questions, Hadley summed up the information they carried concisely: "We're going home, boys."

Sergeant Botkin handed the message from Brisbane to Jock, who began to study it intently. As he did, First Sergeant Patchett looked over Hadley's men and said, "Very good. Four men went out, four men came in. Run into any problems?"

The story of the shoot-out with the thieves came tumbling from Hadley's mouth. Jillian became apprehensive as she listened. "These men you call *hillbillies*," she said, "they were white?"

"Yes, ma'am," Hadley replied.

Jillian blew a sigh of relief. She couldn't imagine one black thief, let alone a mob, inclined to shoot it out with soldiers.

Everyone noticed Jock's face falling as he read further. Patchett asked, "Bad news, sir?"

"Yes and no," Jock replied. "Yeah, we're leaving, but we're going back the same way we came in. Walking. We're to hook up with the Nackeroos at Moreton again, and they'll take us to the planes at Temple Bay. Headquarters nixed the idea of an Albatross Bay pickup. *Too risky,* they say."

The news didn't seem to depress anyone in the assembled company. All they knew was they were going home, and they were thrilled about it. Their war would be over for a little while, at least. It would be worth the walk.

"When do you want to move out, sir?" Patchett asked.

"Will everyone be ready to go at first light tomorrow, Top?"

Patchett turned to Hadley and asked, "Are you and your boys up to it?"

Hadley gave a thumbs up and replied, "We're in great shape! We even slept with a roof over our heads last night. Just give us another night's sleep and some chow and we'll be ready."

"Then the unit will be ready to move out at first light, sir," the first sergeant said to Jock. He added, "I guess that was the *further orders* we've been waiting for?"

Deep in the woods east of Peppan Creek, Thaddeus, the young black man who spotted Hadley's men approaching and sounded the *cooee,* was preparing to return to the camp. His tour on watch was done for the day. It would be dark soon, and new sentinels were already setting up a line of outposts nearer the settlement. His eagerness to get home didn't dull his senses, though; there were more men approaching—not as many as before, maybe only two—but they were definitely heading toward the camp. And they were walking slower—more cautiously—than the men before, as if—despite the racket of their heavy boots on the undergrowth and the rattling of their gear—they were trying to sneak up on somebody.

The men couldn't see Thaddeus, but he could see them. They were Yanks—two of them—wearing the same silly helmets but with longer rifles than the men of the captain Miss Jilly fancied. And these rifles had bayonets affixed to their muzzles.

But they're just more Yanks...and they look lost. I'll help them get back to the camp.

Thaddeus didn't recognize the men even as they drew closer, but he wasn't worried:

Those helmets...they hide the face.

He stepped from behind a tree into the path of the two Americans. With a smile of greeting, he said, "Hello, Yanks...I can take you back—"

But the words caught in Thaddeus's throat. The Yank closest to him had those same bars on his collar, just like Captain Jock—*are there two captains?*—and he was lunging forward toward Thaddeus, the tip of his bayonet leading the way.

The smile was still on the black man's face as Scooter Brewster's bayonet sunk into his chest and pierced his heart. His knees buckled, and Brewster pushed him over, the bayonet still stuck in his ribs, the watery gurgle of his breath escaping his throat.

In a few moments, Thaddeus was dead. He did not carry his smile into the afterlife. In its place was a look of innocent confusion, much like a child being punished but not knowing why.

No matter how hard Scooter Brewster pulled, Thaddeus's chest would not release the bayonet. Just then, he remembered a bit of wisdom Melvin Patchett had once dispensed to the troops: *If it don't come out, you gotta put a foot on his chest and twist the son of a bitch while you're pulling it.*

Scooter Brewster did just that, and with the *crack* of ribs breaking, the bayonet pulled free. Rubbing the blade against Thaddeus's trousers, he wiped the blood clean.

"We're very close to *something,*" Brewster said to the ashen-faced Corporal Wheatley. "Let's try to find out what it is before dark."

Nobody knew J.T. Guess had been carrying a camera in his pack. He had yet to have a chance to use it, and this seemed as good an opportunity as any. He needed to hurry, though; soon the light would be completely gone and the Peppan Creek camp would be in darkness once more.

First Sergeant Patchett was not thrilled to see the camera. He leveled his stern gaze on Guess and said, "Have you been carrying that fucking thing the whole damn time?"

"Yes, First Sergeant."

"Did I not strictly forbid heavy objects in a man's pack before we left Brisbane? We're supposed to be traveling light, remember?"

"Come on, First Sergeant...let me take a couple of shots. It's my last chance."

It's my last chance—those words hit Patchett like a brick. It literally could be J.T. Guess's last chance. A few days from now, he just might be in the stockade, awaiting a court martial for murder.

Patchett felt his anger softening, being quickly replaced by sympathy. "Go ahead, son," he said, "take all the pictures you need to."

Guess began eagerly snapping the shutter; his first subjects were his comrades. The soldiers were posing—sometimes individually, sometimes in small groups—proudly brandishing their weapons. They were too preoccupied with their fun to notice the blacks had retreated in fright. When Melvin Patchett tried to include Old Robert in the photo with Jock Miles, he pulled away, terrified.

With panic in her eyes, Jillian came streaking up to J.T. Guess and tried to grab the camera from the startled soldier. Guess would not release his grip, and they were quickly in a tug-of-war.

"NO, J.T.," Jillian said, as they danced in a small circle. "DON'T EVER TRY TO PHOTOGRAPH THE BLACKS. THEY'RE SUPERSTITIOUS. THEY—"

For a second frozen in time, no one could believe a shot had rung out. It seemed incomprehensible that J.T. Guess had been thrown to the ground by some mighty, invisible force, his head split open, droplets of his blood and brains splotched all over Jillian's face, arms, and torso.

"SNIPER," Patchett screamed, and time unstuck just as instantaneously as it had stopped. It was now racing to the future in fast-forward, with every man in Task Force Miles—and Jillian, too—hitting the deck, heads swiveling in search of the shooter. The blacks, confused and in shock by what they were seeing, stayed on their feet, retreating even farther from Jillian and the Americans.

"HE'S GOT TO BE SOUTH," Jock said. It was a deduction based on simple ballistics even mortal terror could not distort: the spray of Guess's brain matter was fanned out to the north.

"I THINK I SEE HIM!" Jillian said, pointing south. "HE'S CLOSE…AND HE'S RUNNING AWAY."

Jock had his men organized in seconds. Half went with Patchett, flanking the shooter to the east. Jock took the rest to flank west. Doc and Jillian were to stay in the camp with the blacks.

Patchett's team wasn't 30 yards into the woods when a hysterical American soldier appeared from behind a tree, his hands in the air, screaming, "I'M AMERICAN…DON'T KILL ME…I SURRENDER."

They captured Corporal Grover Wheatley. Mike McMillen snatched Wheatley's M1 rifle from the ground where it had been thrown and sniffed the receiver. "Top, this weapon ain't even been fired," McMillen said.

Jock's team plunged deeper into the darkening woods. The sun settled on the western horizon. Soon it would slip from sight, and the chances of finding the man who killed J.T. Guess would slip away with it.

They could hear him running—but they couldn't

see him.

The last shadows of a thousand trees backlit by sunset merged like a spreading pool of blackness. The footsteps they were following slowed and stopped. Jock imagined the man reaching some obstruction—and trying to decide which way to turn.

He had to be close. Maybe just feet away. In a few more minutes, the sky above them would darken as the sun moved on to the other side of the world. He could be inches away then—and they would never see him.

It was Teddy Mukasic's voice that called out: "CAPTAIN! BEHIND YOU!"

Jock whirled around to see the silhouette of a man—so close, he could hear him breathing.

So close, he could smell the cordite from a recently-fired rifle.

The dream flashed before Jock's eyes again—the one in which he kept trying to fire and nothing happened. But unlike the dream, he knew he was firing this time.

The forest lit up in the strobe light flashes from his Thompson's muzzle. He heard nothing but the weapon's bark and could only see a brief glimpse in each flash of the silhouette crumpling to the ground, like watching a movie a frame at a time. He released the trigger.

Now, he could hear nothing but the ringing in his ears from his weapon's noisy burst. He could see nothing; for the moment, the flashes had ruined his night vision.

A new fear gripped Jock Miles: he had fired in the dark. He had no idea who he had hit. Was it an enemy? Or had he just shot one or more of his own men with that reflexive squeeze of his trigger?

None of them had a flashlight. Working by feel alone, Jock was, at first, relieved as he took the rifle from the dead man's hands. It was obviously an M1, with a bayonet at its muzzle. None of his men carried an M1 on this mission.

But just about every other dogface in the US Army did.

He commanded his men to count off—and they were all alive and well. At least he hadn't killed any of them—just this mysterious GI who seemed to be playing for the wrong team.

They stumbled back through the woods toward the camp with only the phosphorescent needle on Jock's compass to guide them. They prayed they hadn't gotten so turned around—even in the short distance this pursuit covered—that they would miss the camp completely. It was slow going—they were dragging the body of the slain American soldier, and it had grown so dark they couldn't see their hands in front of their faces.

They prayed for something else, too: that they wouldn't get into a confused shootout in the dark with the first sergeant's team.

Chapter Fifty-Seven

In the oil lantern's glow, not one man believed what they were seeing. Lying next to the dead body of J.T. Guess was the body of his killer—their old XO, John Joseph Pershing "Scooter" Brewster.

As he stared down at Brewster's body, Melvin Patchett asked Jock, "Just what the fuck is going on here, sir?"

"Wish the hell I knew, Top," Jock replied. He could not come to grips with any possible scenario, short of mental illness, that could have led to what had just happened.

"That corporal you caught," Jock said, "is he talking yet?"

"Are you kidding? He won't shut up," Patchett replied. "Trouble is, he's talking nonsense. Doc's trying to calm him down."

What Grover Wheatley told Jock Miles and Melvin Patchett—even after Doc Green had calmed him—was so bizarre they couldn't believe it, either. But Wheatley was insistent. "I'm telling you, Captain Miles," he said, "when we couldn't track you down, that lunatic took it on himself to kill that woman. What could I do to stop him? I'm just a little ol' tech corporal...I do what I'm told."

At this moment, Jock was very glad Jillian wasn't present to hear this. He asked, "So he was aiming for her...and he missed?"

"That's about it, Captain."

"But you never fired your weapon, Corporal," Jock said. "Why's that?"

Wheatley seemed offended at the question. "Hey, I

may be stuck in *this man's Army* for the duration, but I'm not stupid. I'm a radio tech, not a sniper. And I'm definitely no murderer." He paused, collecting his thoughts. "It all seemed like some stupid Army game, but I never figured in a million years he'd actually find her. It was just luck we saw those guys of yours and followed them here."

Patchett squatted before Wheatley, looked him dead in the eyes, and asked, "You got any proof to back up your story, Corporal?"

"Like I said, First Sergeant, he burned the orders. I never got to read them."

Patchett asked, "Do you know who signed them?"

"Nope," Wheatley replied. "But if you want some kind of proof, check his body…there's still a picture of her and a map somewhere." Glancing toward Old Robert, Wheatley added, "You might want to check the woods, too. Captain Brewster bayoneted some Aborigine kid out there."

That last, sad truth was the only thing Wheatley said that made any sense to Old Robert. He had feared such a truth, for one of his men was missing. "Thaddeus," Old Robert whispered, solving the mystery.

Jillian's profane rant had been going on for a good five minutes. Jock, Patchett, and Doc Green looked on helplessly, surrendering any hope of calming her. Their only function now—until she grew exhausted—was to keep her from hurting herself. She had already launched Jock's pack across the room with one powerful kick of her bare foot. Several times, she had to be restrained from kicking the metal walls in the shack. They already had enough people who couldn't walk very well.

After traversing the interior of the shack for what seemed like the hundredth time, she stopped in the middle of the floor, shot the three a withering gaze, and said, "Isn't this fucking wonderful? That gentle lad takes a bullet because your bloody Army wants me dead. I suppose if I went back to Brisbane now, I'd be arrested and hung as a traitor?"

"As far as a treason charge goes," Jock said, "we only have some corporal's word on that."

That came as small comfort to Jillian. "Why else would they want to assassinate a civilian in wartime?" she asked. "Or is helping your sorry arses suddenly an offense punishable by death?"

Doc said, "It is a bit confusing, though. How the hell would anyone in Brisbane know anything about what's going on up here, outside of the few wireless messages we sent?"

"Yeah," Patchett said, "and those messages never said a damn thing about Miss Forbes, one way or the other."

"Right, Top," Jock said. "So who the hell would want Jillian killed...and why?"

None of them had the answer to that question until revelation struck Jillian a leveling blow. Head in hands, she sank to a seat on the floor.

"Oh, God," she said, "my boat! *Andoom Clipper!* The one that never came back. My crew...the Navy seized them, I'll bet. Somehow, they found them and seized them."

Jock and Patchett weren't following. Jock asked,

"So what?"

Jillian's words had struck a revelation in Doc Green, too. He sat down beside her on the floor, a show, perhaps, of Australian solidarity. "You Yanks don't understand Australia quite like we do," Doc said. "Can you imagine what their story will sound like to those who consider the blacks little more than feral animals...and are terrified they'll join forces with the Japs?" He turned to Patchett and added, "Hell, Top...you were ready to call her a collaborator at first, too."

Jock wasn't buying it. "You're making her sound like she's *the Queen of Cape York,*" he said.

Doc replied, "To the blacks, she is. That's why the Army...and the government...would consider her so dangerous."

Jillian was lost in her disturbing thoughts. She shook her head as she mumbled, "The flag...that bloody white flag on the boat. And the money...I'll bet they had Jap money on them."

"This is starting to make some sense," Jock said. "I really can't see the US Army targeting a civilian unless the Australian government wanted it."

Patchett nodded in agreement. "I'll go along with that, sir...I know a little something about MacArthur and his people. They like playing God."

The three men might have come to a consensus, but Jillian still seemed in another world. "I need my life back," she said, talking to no one but the ceiling. "I need my business. It means something to these people...and it means everything to me."

Jock took a seat on the floor with Jillian and Doc, the three forming a tight circle. He put his hands on her shoulders and said, "And we're going to help you do just that. We're going to get you to Brisbane and fix all this."

She looked deep into his eyes and asked, "How?"

"We're going to tell the world just how heroic you are...how you saved our mission."

Again, she asked, "How?"

He said nothing and kept holding on to her. He hadn't thought his plan through that far yet. Jock's proclamation had sent Doc Green's mind racing, though. He was already filling in the blanks Jock couldn't.

"The newspapers," Doc said. "That's our answer. An old school chum of mine is editor at the Brisbane Telegraph, and this country is dying for heroes right now. I'll get him to publish Jillian's *real* story...and nobody will dare lay a finger on her after that."

Melvin Patchett was already finding the devil in the details. "How are you so sure he'll publish it, Doc?" he asked.

A coy smile came over Doc's face. "Let's just say *he owes me,* in a very big way."

Patchett smiled right back and asked, "Does it involve money? Or a woman?"

"Both."

The answer impressed Patchett, and he nodded respectfully. But he had another question. "Once we get back," he asked, "this'll take a little time, won't it? And while we're traveling back to Brisbane, how do we explain why she's with us?"

"We don't explain anything," Jock said. "If anyone asks, she's our prisoner."

"Prisoner?" Jillian said, snapping back to reality

and not liking what she had just heard at all. "You're going to sort this out while I'm in *prison*? I say bollocks on that, Jock Miles."

"Wait...hear me out," Jock said. "The military mind will believe the prisoner story quicker than just about anything. This mission to kill you was *Top Secret* stuff, so nobody is going to know about it, anyway, except for us and the high-level assholes who thought it up. The cops won't have a dragnet out for you."

Doc added, "And yes...Top's right. This will take a little time, but I'm betting there's someplace you can hide out until they're ready to pin the Victoria Cross on you."

"Perhaps your aunt can stash you away for a bit?" Jock asked.

With a mixture of reluctance and blind hope, Jillian replied, "I suppose so."

"Good," Jock said, "then it's settled. You're coming with us."

"Just one thing, though," Doc added. "This article can't mention a bloody thing about any plot to kill Jillian."

"Of course it can't," Jock said. "Then we'd all become targets, right? We'd know too much."

"Exactly," Doc replied, as Patchett and Jillian nodded in agreement.

The unsettling sound of shovels piercing earth drifted into the shack, numbing everyone's mood. They filed outside to find a burial site being dug by lantern light.

"I made them dig two graves," Patchett said to Jock. "I don't think Guess deserves to be in a common grave with that man."

"I agree," Jock replied.

"But I've gotta say, Captain...first Roper, now Guess...the men in this company do seem to find the damnedest ways to get out of court martials."

His voice just above a whisper so only his first sergeant would hear, Jock said, "I wasn't going to court martial Private Guess, Top."

The slightest of smiles creased Melvin Patchett's stolid face.

Chapter Fifty-Eight

A traveling circus…

Those were the only words Jock Miles could find to describe what his charges looked like as they walked east across the bush to Moreton Telegraph Station. Having buried Roper, Russo, and Guess, they were down to 12 American members of Task Force Miles, one of whom—Corporal Jorge Pacheco—couldn't walk. He rode the *Radio Flyer,* pulled by a rotating pool of men, two at a time. In addition, the *circus* now featured a small cart donated by the Weipa blacks, pulled by another rotating pool. On that cart rode Colonel Najima, secured in irons taken from the jail, and Doc Green, whose leg wound prevented him from walking at any decent speed. Jillian Forbes walked easily among the soldiers, her rifle cradled and ready in her arms. She had given up the casual dress and bare feet of the Peppan Creek camp for her trousers and sturdy riding boots.

Finally, there was Corporal Grover Wheatley, walking sullenly in front of Jillian, without a weapon, carrying only the walkie-talkie he had left Brisbane with four days ago. He had been stripped of his M1 rifle since he surrendered and he wasn't getting it back until Brisbane. He had complained constantly from the moment they set out from the camp, and First Sergeant Patchett had given him a simple ultimatum: "If you don't shut that whining pie-hole of yours, son, I'm gonna plant you like your Captain Brewster."

"But what if the Japs hit us, First Sergeant? I ain't got no gun!"

Patchett scowled and replied, "You ain't got no

rifle, sparky. It's a goddamned *rifle,* not a *gun.* But I'll tell you what…if we come across any Japs, just throw that useless, piece of shit radio at them, with its one fucking mile range."

Jock Miles and Melvin Patchett weren't worried in the least about Corporal Wheatley, though. Jillian had assured them if Wheatley made as much as one wrong move, she'd shoot him herself. They believed she'd do it, too. To her mind, he was guilty by association with Scooter Brewster.

Patchett asked, "How far do you reckon we've gone, Captain?" It was more an expression of pessimism than a question.

"Not far enough," Jock replied. "Pulling those wagons…Hadley and his boys doing this trip for the third time…we'll be lucky to make 15 miles today."

"That's about what I figured," Patchett said. "That makes it a three-day trip—"

"Even longer if those Nackeroos aren't there to pick us up," Jock added.

Even thought the pace of the march wouldn't break any records, everyone with Task Force Miles took solace in one article of faith: they were fairly confident they'd seen the last of the Japanese. But this wasn't a carefree stroll across the bush. They remained vigilant and kept a well-dispersed tactical column, for they were far more concerned with encountering hostile wildlife than enemy soldiers. As Melvin Patchett summed it up, "We lost two to Mother Nature, two to our fellow soldiers…and zero to the Japs."

Jock asked, "You're counting Russo to Mother Nature, Top?"

"Yes sir, I am."

"Yeah, me too."

The sun was setting at their backs. It was time to stop and set up camp. As Melvin Patchett directed the perimeter setup, he was met with a barrage of protests.

"Come on, Top…there ain't no Japs around here," Mike McMillen said. "You're not really going to make us dig in, are you?"

"You bet your sweet ass I am, Corporal," Patchett replied. "What gave you the idea this was some admin bivouac?"

The grumbling continued from all quarters—but so did the digging.

Jillian said to Jock, "Lend me one of the lads and I'll fetch us some supper." Bogater Boudreau volunteered to join her on the hunt before she had even finished speaking.

"Okay," Jock said, "but you two be real careful out there. We can eat K rations if we have to."

"Lovely as that sounds, we can do much better," Jillian said. "Now, promise no one will panic when my rifle fires."

Boudreau added, "But if you hear my Thompson let loose, y'all better come bail us out, because it won't be shooting at no game, that's for damn sure."

They were gone half an hour, and in that time, there were three shots from Jillian's rifle. Boudreau's Thompson remained silent. They returned to the perimeter just as the sun had dropped behind the trees. Jillian carried two bush turkeys—large flightless birds with black bodies and red heads—by their feet, their heads dragging lifelessly along the ground. Bogater Boudreau had several long, fat snakes—quite dead— draped over his shoulders.

"Dinner is served, chaps," Jillian called as they dropped their quarry at Patchett's feet.

"Outstanding," the first sergeant replied, and then added, "and since our Corporal McMillen didn't appreciate the need to dig in, one of his men gets the honor of digging the fire pit to cook these vittles."

Later, after the sun had set and the meal was consumed, Jock and Jillian relaxed by the dwindling flames of the cookfire with Melvin Patchett. There hadn't been much said; they were all spent from the walk. Their feet ached and the muscles in their legs felt like taut elastic bands, stretched to the breaking point. But they all knew that after some rest, they would loosen those limbs and be ready to do it all over again, tomorrow and the day after that. There was no landmark to prove it, but they were quite sure they weren't even halfway to Moreton yet. All considered, though, Jock found the stamina of his soldiers simply amazing. He told the first sergeant, "You did one hell of a job whipping these men into shape, Top."

"It was my pleasure, Captain," Patchett replied. "I'll tell you what, though…this lady here is the one who really impresses me."

Jock could find no argument with that statement.

The second day of the walk passed much like the first. They pushed a little farther into the sunset before making camp on the off chance they were nearer to

Moreton than dead reckoning led them to believe. There would be no light to hunt for supper. K rations would have to suffice. Moreton Station, the Telegraph Track, and the Wenlock River were still nowhere in sight.

Colonel Najima had grown noticeably drawn and weak, his refusal to eat for the past four days finally taking its physical toll. Doc Green offered Najima each item in a K ration package one at a time as Patchett watched, and with each offering the colonel turned his head away.

"That son of a bitch better not die before we get his ass to Brisbane," Patchett said. "Can't you force feed him an IV or something, Doc?"

"Even if I could, it would just be wasted, Top. He'd find a way to tear it out."

Mid-afternoon of the third day, the poles along the Telegraph Track came into view. The euphoria of finally getting there swept over everyone except Jillian. She caught up with Jock and said, "Wait a minute…If the diggers are there, I'm supposed to be your *prisoner,* am I not?"

"Damn it! You're right," Jock replied, feeling sheepish for overlooking that part of the plan. "Better give me your rifle."

She handed it over. "Better tie my hands, too," she said.

"No. There's no need for that," he said, as he slung her rifle over his shoulder.

She pointed to Najima on the wagon. "Look…he's a prisoner, and you've got him shackled hand and foot." She handed him a length of rope from her pack. "Let's make this look right, at least."

"I said no, Jillian. We have no idea what's going to happen. You might need those hands...and this rifle, too."

A half hour later, they were at the Moreton Station. There was nobody there to greet them.

"Shit," Jock said as he took a look around the big, empty house. "Sergeant Botkin, can you send another telegraph message?"

Botkin had already checked the equipment. It was exactly as he left it three days ago. "Sure, Captain," he replied. "No problem."

"Excellent. Tell Brisbane we're here, awaiting rendezvous."

Patchett had just finished his own recon of the area. "How about we set up in the woods by the river, sir?" the first sergeant asked. "This building is a little too out in the open for my taste."

"Agreed," Jock replied.

Chapter Fifty-Nine

It was well after dark when the telegraph receiver relay began to chatter with Brisbane's answer. The message was terse: HOLD POSITION. NACKEROOS ADVISED.

Patchett chuckled as PFC Savastano read the telegram aloud. "A little light on specifics," the first sergeant said. "It'd be real nice to know when they planned to get here."

"It won't be tonight, that's for sure," Jock said. "Not in the dark."

A few miles to the east, Corporal Harry Cockburn and his three Nackeroo privates had settled in for the night. The negotiation to procure the trucks had taken far longer than they planned—a day and a half longer. The miners were far more reluctant this time than last to hand them over. Petrol was harder than ever to obtain, and the miners ultimately demanded the Army repay *in petrol* at a rate five times over what they'd use for the journey. Knowing he could never get his hands on such a quantity, Cockburn quoted with great assertiveness a nonexistent wartime regulation he made up on the spot. The imaginary regulation threatened the Army would confiscate the mine if the miners didn't cooperate. That seemed to do the trick. He had pulled off the bluff—it just took too long. Finally in the vehicles, the Nackeroos raced the setting sun to Moreton Station—and lost.

Harry Cockburn took the order from his pocket and

read it one more time. He found the instructions within more and more unsettling. He had expected to be told to retrieve Captain Miles's patrol—or at least what was left of it—in a straightforward manner, the reverse of how he had inserted them into the bush. The order he held in his hand made the task sound much more risky.

Cockburn had no way of knowing the order had been the product of a chain of military services and organizations, each reviewing and reproducing the message, passing it down the chain to arrive at the next link with a slightly different meaning. It was no different than the parlor game of *telephone,* where a message is whispered from one person to the next in a circle. By the time it arrives back to the first player, its original meaning has been totally corrupted.

The order was first drafted by General Briley's operations officer—his G3—and was what Cockburn might have expected: instructions to retrieve Task Force Miles at Moreton Telegraph Relay Station. Anticipated arrival time of the task force at Moreton was one to three days from date of the order, an accurate estimation. Somewhere along the chain, though, the concept of *imminent Japanese threat* was introduced. Whether this came from Briley's original suspicions of a Jap trick—before those suspicions were set aside by Tim Wells's clever verification technique—or simply the figment of some overcautious officer's imagination was difficult to say. All Harry Cockburn could see—plastered below the header of the orders—were the words *IMMINENT JAPANESE THREAT.*

He asked himself, *So what? Isn't that why we're here in the first place? Because of an imminent*

Japanese threat?

Harry Cockburn let those words spin around in his head, their implications amplifying and turning more sinister with each revolution until he envisioned a Japanese invasion force sweeping across the Cape from the west.

Sure...Task Force Miles needs to be retrieved, but I'm betting they're being chased by a bloody mob of Japanese. And if I'm not careful, I'm going to drive us right into those Japs. We may already be too late to save the Yanks, thanks to those bloody miners!

Cockburn made up his mind then and there: in the morning, they would leave the trucks parked right where they were and advance toward Moreton on foot. *Trucks make noise and attract airplanes. On foot, we can be stealthy...and if we do come across the Japs, we've got a chance to sneak away without them ever seeing us.*

The new sunrise marked the start of the eleventh day Task Force Miles had been on the ground at Cape York. It would be the first day in four they had no plans to walk anywhere. That sounded good in theory, but it didn't get them any closer to the comfort and safety of Brisbane.

First Sergeant Patchett was releasing men from the perimeter in pairs, sending them to the river to wash themselves. When it was Mike McMillen's turn, Patchett told him, "You and Simms go get cleaned up, and take the Jap with you. Let him do his business, if he's got any...and don't you dare come back without him."

McMillen and Simms led the weakened, stumbling Najima down to the river. The leg shackles gave the colonel just enough freedom to maintain an awkward, throttled stride; the arm shackles allowed him to undo his own trousers. McMillen mimed the act of urination for Najima's benefit as Simms kept a firm grip on the chain functioning as a leash. The colonel responded with a trickle of urine against a tree by the riverside and then dropped to his knees to wash his hands and face in the river's anemic flow.

"I don't know about you," Simms said, "but I could sure use a bath."

"Good idea," McMillen replied, "but we've got to make it quick. Let's chain the Jap to a tree and get to it. Stand him up over here..."

With Najima secured, the two Americans stripped to their skivvies and waded into the knee-deep water at the middle of the river. "It ain't much, but it'll have to do," McMillen said, throwing himself flat and rolling around in the cool water. "I figure we've got about three minutes."

It took a lot less than that for Simms to get nervous, though. "Maybe we'd better get back, Mike. Top will shit all over us if he thinks we're fucking the dog."

"Relax, Frankie...we've got plenty of time. Just keep an eye on the Jap so he—"

They felt the bullet slice the air above their heads a split-second before they saw Najima's chest blossom in a crimson spray. His body recoiled off the tree trunk and sagged to its knees, its torso still upright, held by the restraining chain. His head hung lifelessly against his chest.

McMillen and Simms shared one thought: how silly it would be to be killed taking a bath in your skivvies—with your weapon well out of reach.

Their weapons weren't out of reach for long. The Thompsons were pointed across the river now, their bearers out of the water and crouched in firing positions behind trees. McMillen and Simms could make out something nearing the opposite bank, a low silhouette moving slowly. It was too far way for an easy kill with the Thompson.

"Let them get closer," Mike McMillen whispered.

"I don't see a *them,*" Frank Simms replied. "I just see one."

"Let *him* get closer, then."

The figure kept coming until there was no mistaking what it was: an Australian soldier—a Nackeroo, standing on the far bank. The shorts, slouch hat, and Lee-Enfield rifle were a dead giveaway. His anxious, wide-eyed gaze was fixated on Najima, hanging dead against the tree.

Still concealed behind the tree, McMillen called out, "NICE SHOT, NUMBNUTS...BUT WHY THE FUCK DID YOU KILL OUR PRISONER?"

When the two Americans—wearing only undershorts, holding submachine guns—popped out on the other bank, the Nackeroo was so startled he lost his footing on the slippery rocks and fell face-first into the river.

Doc Green shook his head. There was nothing he

could do. Colonel Najima was dead, shot through the heart.

Jock Miles was trying as hard as he could to be civil, but he was losing the battle. "Corporal Cockburn," he said, "your people have a real knack for accidental killings."

"With all due respect, sir," Cockburn said, "our orders warned of an imminent Jap threat."

"And your men took that to mean one guy chained to a tree is a *threat?*" Jock asked. "Is that your battle doctrine, Corporal? Shoot the first man you see? Isn't that like poking a hornet's nest? What if he was the point man for a company...or a *division?*"

"My man panicked, sir. He saw a Jap, he fired. Simple as that. And he didn't see your men."

Jock let out a sigh of frustration. "The Japs are gone, dammit," he said. "The ones that aren't dead are running back to New Guinea. We've already told Headquarters that. Don't they pay any attention down there?"

"No, sir, I guess not," Cockburn replied. Eager to change the subject, he added, "Now, as far as getting out of here, the trucks are about two miles—"

Jock cut him off. "Go get them, Corporal. My people have walked enough. And try not to kill any more of us today."

As Cockburn rounded up his three men, Jock turned to Sergeant Botkin. "Better get a message off to Brisbane, Sergeant," Jock said. "Advise them our Jap regimental commander has met a most untimely end."

As they waited for the trucks to arrive, Jillian tried to understand why Jock was in such a funk. "You did a brilliant job out there," she said. "Losing Najima doesn't change that, does it?"

Jock mumbled his answer: "The brass like trophies, Jill...and we just got ours taken away."

Chapter Sixty

It was four more days before Task Force Miles was back in Brisbane. After cooling their heels at Temple Bay for two nights, the Catalinas finally arrived just after dawn. They stayed onboard the Cats for nearly 24 hours—including a fuel stop at Cooktown, featuring a fistfight that erupted when the flight engineers demanded more aviation gasoline than the fuelers felt they were authorized—before touching down with the new sunrise on the Brisbane River. They were delighted when they found their company vehicles—a jeep and a deuce and a half—still secure in the seaplane base motor pool. It would not have been uncommon for the vehicles to be gone, *appropriated* by some other outfit, who would paint bogus unit markings over the authentic ones.

As he made his way through the base's hangar, Jock picked up a week-old newspaper. Its headline—in bold, two-inch-high letters—announced:

YANK AIRMEN DRIVE JAPS FROM CAPE YORK!

He scanned the article, searching for any mention of the ground recon patrol—*his* patrol—that had made it all possible. He tried to tell himself he wasn't surprised when he found none, but something in him refused to believe it. The ache of disappointment—tinged with a feeling of betrayal—would not go away.

Across the hangar, Jillian hung up the telephone and found Jock standing next to her. "Aunt Margaret is expecting us," she said with apprehension written all over her face. "She doesn't like to be kept waiting."

The deuce and a half rolled to a stop at the Division Signal Company bivouac. Melvin Patchett stepped down from the cab and met Corporal Grover Wheatley as he climbed down the truck's tailgate. The men of Task Force Miles, still lounging on the truck's bed, didn't bother to say goodbye to him.

Patchett said, "I reckon it's best you keep quiet about that business with Captain Brewster and Miss Forbes, son."

Back on familiar, safer soil, a bit of cockiness crept back into Wheatley's demeanor. "And what if I don't?" he asked.

"Then we just might start recollecting it was *you* that took the shot that killed our boy Guess," Patchett replied. "Last time I checked, you still get the firing squad for murder."

Patchett could tell he had made his point; the cockiness had drained from Wheatley's face. Sounding sheepish once again, he asked, "Am I dismissed, First Sergeant?"

"You bet your sweet ass you are, son."

The corporal grabbed his gear and vanished into a tent without saying another word.

Back in his quarters, Dunbar Green—the *doc*—couldn't believe the radio announcer was still carrying on about how the Yank airmen had evicted the Japs from Cape York. *Like nobody on the ground helped them,* he thought, mixing amusement and annoyance.

He allowed himself the luxury of an extra-long shower and 15-minute nap before donning clean khakis and driving to the offices of the Brisbane Telegraph newspaper. Harry Giggs, editor for the Telegraph and old school chum, met him in the lobby. They embraced like long-lost brothers.

"Dunnie, you're limping," Harry said. "Are you all right?"

"Nothing serious," Doc replied. "I'll be fine."

"So what's this hero story you've got for me? I can't wait to hear it."

"You're going to love this, Harry. That bombing raid that drove the Japs off the Cape? I'm giving you the exclusive story of the Aussie *woman* who made it all possible."

"Really? This sounds brilliant," Harry said, leading Doc down the hall to his office. "They'll love it all the way to Canberra!"

First Sergeant Melvin Patchett had cleaned up, too. He was in downtown Brisbane, waiting to see his old buddy, Master Sergeant Johnny Jarvis. He and Jarvis went back a long way—all the way to the trenches of France in The Great War. Their bond of trust was forged in blood all those years ago. He would be the one man—the top sergeant for the whole division, unofficially its *sergeant major*—who knew everything that was going on within it, secret or not. Of all the men on God's green Earth, Melvin Patchett knew Johnny Jarvis was the one who would never try to bullshit him.

Patchett sat on a bench in the hallway and watched

as a workman scraped the gold leaf lettering off the door of the big office down the hall. Half the letters were already gone, but he could tell it used to read MAJOR GENERAL SAMUEL BRILEY.

Johnny Jarvis, a fireplug of a man who seemed to always be moving at the speed of an Olympic runner, smiled with delight as he raced down the hall. "PATCH," he said at thunderous volume, "glad you're back! How the hell are you, you old son of a bitch?"

They settled into Jarvis's office. "Pretty fancy digs you got here, Johnny," Patchett said, eyeing the spacious, well-appointed room.

"Got me two secretaries and everything, Patch. Sweetest little Aussie girls you ever did lay eyes on." Jarvis came around and propped himself against the front of his desk, within arm's length of Patchett. He lowered his voice as he said, "So tell me, Patch...what's it like fighting them Japs?"

"Hard to say, Johnny. The only ones I saw were either running away or surrendering."

The roar of Jarvis's laughter rattled the office windows.

"That's my old Patch...ain't a man alive not scared of you...except me, of course."

Jarvis snuck a hurried glance at the clock on his desk. "But I know this isn't a social call," he said. "What do you need, Patch?"

"A couple of questions. First...are we getting a new division commander? Or did Briley just change his name?"

"Well, Patch, it's like this...let's just say General Briley has fallen from favor with the man upstairs."

Patchett knew *the man upstairs* meant MacArthur.

"Who's replacing him?" he asked.

"Some brigadier named Horace Cash."

"Never heard of him," Patchett said.

"I haven't heard much, except he's a pencil-pusher...but somebody's pushing him for another star and he needs a command for that, so here he comes. We expect him to arrive tomorrow."

"*Somebody,* you say, Johnny. You mean MacArthur, don't you?"

Jarvis smiled and said, "Who else?" His eyes narrowed as he continued, "But you didn't come all the way here to ask me that. Hell, you could read the change of command order on your dayroom wall. What's really on your mind, Patch?"

"I'll get right to the point, Johnny. We ran into Captain Brewster out there—"

"Briley's aide?"

"Right...and my company XO before that. Seems he might have been carrying some secret orders about assassinating an Aussie civilian."

Jarvis looked truly shocked. "Are you sure, Patch?" he asked.

"Let's just say a couple of the details are real fuzzy...but yeah, I'm sure."

Jarvis slid off the desk and slumped into his chair. He looked truly upset.

Patchett asked, "You didn't know anything about that, did you, Johnny?"

Jarvis shook his head. "No, Patch...I surely did not. I don't want to believe we'd do shit like that." After a pensive pause, he added, "It might explain where that little son of a bitch Brewster vanished to, though."

"He ain't coming back, either, Johnny. We buried him out there."

Johnny Jarvis didn't look in the least bit upset to hear that news.

The only word Jock could think of to describe the home of Margaret Forbes-Masters was *palatial.* Sitting on top of a hill that overlooked Brisbane and the Pacific Ocean beyond, it obviously belonged to someone extremely well-heeled. Jock began to feel very out of place in his filthy fatigues—like some grubby street urchin—as he drove the jeep up the long, winding driveway. Seated beside him, Jillian seemed to be steeling herself for the reunion with her aunt. She tied her wild hair back and tried to primp her hopelessly grimy shirt and trousers into something presentable for what seemed like the hundredth time since they left the seaplane base.

"Quite a little house," Jock said.

"Yeah, and it's just one of them," Jillian replied.

A maid escorted them into the drawing room. Seated in a plush chair by the window was a tall, stern-looking woman, wearing an exquisite silk dress that probably cost as much as Jock's pay for a year. Her graying hair was tightly pulled back and twisted into a bun, framing her face like an ancient warrior's helmet. Jock found the mere sight of her intimidating.

Aunt Margaret hadn't so much as glanced at Jock yet. Her disapproving glare was fixated on her niece. "I can smell you from here, my dear," she said, her voice cold, her words brutally frank. "I don't suppose that piscine odor has come from working on your little boats."

Unflustered, Jillian replied, "Sorry. It can't be helped." She took Jock's hand and pulled him closer to the seated woman. "Aunt Margaret, I'd like to introduce Captain Jock Miles, United States Army."

At last, she turned her withering gaze to Jock. She looked him up and down twice, and then, to Jock and Jillian's great surprise, smiled at him. "I trust you two have a good reason for visiting me in such a"—she paused, searching for just the right word—"*defiled* condition."

They told her their story. As they related the plot to kill Jillian, Aunt Margaret's eyes flared with incendiary fury. Jock was sure anyone targeted by that gaze might as well be standing in front of a flamethrower.

When their story was done, Aunt Margaret said, "Jillian, go stay at the Hope Island cottage. You'll be well hidden there"—she smiled at Jock again before continuing—"and your young man won't have far to travel when he visits."

How about that? She's scary and clairvoyant, too, Jock thought.

He rose to take his leave. "Very nice meeting you, ma'am," he said, "but I've got to report back to my commander. And I've still got a company to run."

"Don't be silly," Jillian said. "The first sergeant can run the company all by himself. He doesn't need you." She winked so he would be certain she was just pulling his leg.

Aunt Margaret had one more thing to say: "Soldiers don't hatch plots like the one you just described. Politicians do…and no wanker from the

King's bloody government will ever threaten a Forbes and not pay a dear price. I'm going to make a few discreet inquiries of my friends at Government House. I wouldn't be surprised if someone there is involved in this up to his bloody eyeballs...and when I find out who he is, I'll rip those eyeballs out with my bare hands."

Jock had no doubt she could, too.

As they watched him drive off, Aunt Margaret said to Jillian, "Now, my dear, let's get you into a nice hot tub and find you a decent frock to wear. You've *gone troppo* long enough."

Chapter Sixty-One

First Sergeant Patchett let out with a wolf whistle as Jock Miles, cleaned up and outfitted in crisp khakis, complete with tie, entered the dayroom. "You cleaned up real good, sir," Patchett said.

"You don't look so bad yourself, Top. Let's you and I have a little chat in private."

They retired to Jock's office and shut the door.

Jock asked, "What did you find out up at Division?"

"Johnny Jarvis don't know a damn thing about it, sir...and you can bet your life on Johnny's word."

Jock thought that over for a minute. "So the order was some big, goddamned secret, and it either came from Briley...or MacArthur himself."

"I'm betting MacArthur, sir. That would make Briley just the middleman...and Briley owned Brewster lock, stock, and barrel. That'd make him the perfect errand boy."

Jock told Patchett about Jillian's Aunt Margaret and her theory some politician was ultimately behind the whole thing. Patchett thought it over for a moment, but he obviously had serious reservations.

"Politician, you say? MacArthur ain't nothing if he ain't a politician, sir. What general ain't?"

Jock had to admit his first sergeant had a point. Suddenly, he was a lot less confident in their little plan to protect Jillian Forbes. MacArthur was untouchable, a goddamned *national treasure.* He could crush them all like bugs if he so chose and nobody would raise a voice against him—not in Australia, not back in the States. Reality was what he said it was—and if he wanted

Jillian dead, she'd be dead.

The voice in Jock's head said, *This newspaper friend of Doc's better come through in a big way...and quick.*

The formal after-action report for Task Force Miles would take Jock a few days to write, but the new division commander, Brigadier General Cash, wanted a verbal debrief that afternoon, before happy hour began at Lennon's Hotel bar. The first thing that struck Jock about General Cash was he looked more like a bank clerk than a general. His eyes always seemed to be staring intently at the papers on his desk, papers he shuffled constantly, as if the neatness of their stacks was more important than the information printed on them. The one star on each collar seemed to be a weighty burden, bending his slight frame constantly forward, forcing the general to frequently correct the resulting unmilitary posture. His staff officers seated around the conference table seemed to be feeding him basic information about his division far too often. Jock figured that was information any general should already know.

I guess Top had him pegged, Jock thought. *A pencil-pusher, over his head in a combat command.*

When the floor was given to Jock, he moved to the large map of Queensland on the wall and, pointer in hand, proceeded to relate the tale of Task Force Miles. He left out no details except one: he credited the *residents of Weipa*—without mentioning any names— for their unfailing support of his mission against the

Japanese.

The division intelligence officer asked, "So, Captain, you're telling us the abos are *definitely not* supporting the Japanese?"

"That's correct, sir," Jock replied.

"You're sure about that?" the intelligence officer asked.

"Yes, sir. Absolutely sure. My men and I are living proof of that."

When Jock finished his presentation, the room went deathly quiet. The next words were supposed to come from the division commander, but General Cash just kept shuffling those papers before him. Finally, after the pause had gone past awkward into discomforting, Cash began to speak.

"I'm concerned about a few points, Captain Miles," the general said. "First, your use of civil telegraph lines to relay battlefield intelligence was a serious breach of communications security."

Jock couldn't believe what he was hearing. "Sir," he said, "we had no choice. Our radio—"

Cash cut him off. "You've already told us about your radio, Captain," the general said, "but a wise commander takes better care of his assets."

Jock began to protest. "Sir," he said, "our own planes bombed us."

"Yes, Captain, you mentioned that, too. At least that's what you think happened. You did say you observed Japanese artillery in your area of operation, did you not?"

"Yes, sir, but—"

"Then I'd say it was far more likely that Jap artillery is what *bombed* your position. Wouldn't you agree, Captain?"

"No, sir, that's not—"

Cash cut him off again. "Enough excuses, Captain Miles. I have another problem. That Japanese colonel you say you captured, then lost in a tragic accident. Do you realize what an asset to this command you allowed to slip away?"

There was no point trying to explain it anymore; the verdict was already in. Jock's reply was only, "Yes, sir, I realize that."

"I'm glad to hear it," Cash said. "Now, my final problem. This Captain John Brewster, who you say killed one of your men before meeting his own tragic end by friendly fire. Can you tell me what in the world this man was doing in your area of operation?"

"Actually, sir, I was hoping you could tell me."

Jock looked around the room and got nothing but blank stares in response. He couldn't help but smile, for now he was sure: *This guy and his whole damned staff don't have a clue about the order to kill Jillian.*

"Perhaps we can ask General Briley," Jock said, "but I'm betting he's halfway to California by now."

Nobody seated around the table seemed interested in asking General Briley anything.

"Permission to speak freely, sir?" Jock asked.

General Cash impatiently checked his wristwatch before nodding his assent.

"I'd just like to add, sir, that my men did a heroic job against incredible odds. Their physical stamina alone allowed—"

General Cash was having none of it. His voice was strident as he interrupted. "It seems to me, Captain, that your men just barely did what they were supposed to do, and sloppily at that. I'll be expecting your written report within two days. You are dismissed."

The debriefing over, General Cash was in a hurry to seek some relaxation at Lennon's. As he shuffled the papers on his desk one last time, his new aide—Scooter Brewster's successor—appeared in the office's open doorway. He held a file in his hand.

With great impatience, Cash asked, "What is it, Captain?"

"Sir, I was clearing out my predecessor's effects from my desk, and I came across this. I thought you might want to look at it."

Cash motioned him closer and snatched the file away. His blank expression became a scowl as he scanned the documents within, documents proposing to decorate Jock Miles for his actions at Pearl Harbor.

"Very good, Captain," Cash said. "I'll take care of this. Shut the door on your way out."

Once his aide left the office, Cash hesitated for just a moment before ripping the documents to pieces.

Chapter Sixty-Two

Jock's jeep crunched to a stop in front of the Hope Island cottage. It was partially hidden among palm trees, set well back from the narrow road and overgrown with tropical flowers, their vibrant colors muted in the early evening darkness. Jillian was waiting for him on the veranda, scrubbed clean, hair washed and silken, barefoot, and in a simple cotton dress that flowed softly in the breeze as if she was standing at the rail of a ship underway. She already had a drink in her hand.

He had no trouble driving right up to the cottage. "Is this place really a safe hideout?" he asked as he stepped onto the veranda.

"Sure," Jillian replied. "This is private property, and there are guards. You wouldn't have gotten in quite so easily if I hadn't arranged it."

"Are they *armed* guards?"

"Are there any other kind, silly boy?"

"But I didn't see any guards, Jill."

"You would have if you weren't welcome. Now, would you stop bloody worrying and kiss me?"

The kiss was long, slow, deep, and magnificent. When it was done, she led him into the cottage, using his khaki necktie to pull him along. Strains of Liszt rippled from a phonograph in a corner of the tiny sitting room. As they settled onto the couch, she said, "I've always liked it here. It reminds me of my place in Weipa, just with different trees."

"I see this place comes complete with music by Liszt," he said.

"Don't worry, there's some Wagner for you, too.

Courtesy of Aunt Margaret."

"That's very nice, but your Aunt Margaret still scares the crap out of me, Jill."

Jillian laughed as she replied, "She scares the crap out of everyone. But you have nothing to worry about. She *likes* you...and that's an honor not handed out lightly. Or frequently."

She poured him a drink from a bottle of dark rum. Taking the glass, he asked, "How much of a head start do you have on me?"

"I've been drinking rum ever since I got here this afternoon."

He was amazed to hear that. "But you seem perfectly sober," he said.

She slid closer and buried her tongue in his ear. "Looks can be very deceiving, Captain," she whispered. She gave her half-filled glass a long, hard look, and then added, "Maybe I should stop, though. I do want to *remember* this..."

They fell asleep as soon as the lovemaking was finished. It had been fast—they were so eager, so hungry, and so tired—but the act had at last been consummated. When Jock stirred just before midnight, he found Jillian wide awake next to him, propped up on an elbow, smiling down at his drowsy face.

"I just realized...I never gave you a chance to tell how the debriefing went," she said.

"Forget that," he replied. "Tell me how it was for you...the pain, I mean."

She threw her head back against the pillow, splaying the dark curls of her hair across it and stretched her entire body like some contented cat. "Let's just say it was a very, very good start," she replied. Her hand slid beneath the sheet covering his lower body. "I was wondering if perhaps you'd like to test the waters again, Captain? We've got lots and lots of condoms..."

The second coupling put them to sleep until dawn. When the first rays of sunrise fell across their bed, Jock was already slipping into his uniform. Jillian wiped the sleep from her eyes and said, "I just remembered...I don't have any coffee for you. You Yanks and your coffee..."

"That's okay, honey. I'll manage."

She liked the sound of *honey*. She liked it very much.

She pulled a man's tee shirt over her head, turning it into a short dress, and shuffled to the kitchen. "How about some juice instead?" she called back to him.

"I'd love some, thanks."

She carried him a full glass. "Before you go, Jock," she said, "you've still got to tell me about the debriefing."

Shrugging, he replied, "Not much to tell. It was pretty much a waste of time...just like I figured. They've already anointed their heroes. All the credit is going to the flyboys. I guess since it was Jap airpower that took us out of this war, they need to show it's *our* airpower putting us right back in it."

"You don't seem very upset, Jock. Weren't you the man all worried about *redemption*?"

Jock smiled and took her in his arms. "There isn't any *redemption*, Jillian. Not in this business."

She looked up at him, wanting to believe, desperate to gauge the sincerity of his words and the change in him they signaled. "You really don't care what those stupid old wankers think anymore?"

His reply convinced her beyond all doubt. Looking her straight in the eyes, he said, "Nope. To hell with them."

She responded with a deep and powerful kiss, expressing her relief, approval, and joy in a way words never could. Jock took the silent discourse a step further—he swept her off her feet and carried her back to the bedroom.

Chapter Sixty-Three

First Sergeant Patchett appeared in the doorway to Jock's office and said, "Doc Green's on the horn for you, sir."

The telephone line's distortion could not dilute the breathless excitement in Doc's voice. "The newspaper story comes out later today, the evening edition," he said. "It's got the front page headline!"

Jock was beaming as he hung up the phone. "Good news, sir?" Patchett asked.

"Yep. The article comes out this evening."

"Perfect timing," Patchett said, "with the after-action report due today and all."

Jock picked up the manila envelope holding the report. "It's time we hit them with both barrels, Top."

"Amen to that, sir."

Master Sergeant Johnny Jarvis eyed the manila envelope his secretary had placed in General Cash's "in" box. He knew what the envelope contained—the after-action report from Task Force Miles.

They beat the deadline with minutes to spare, Jarvis thought as he slid the report from the envelope. *Let's have ourselves a little look-see at what this thing has to say.* His eyes widened with surprise as he flipped through its pages; his mouth twisted into a grimace. He was sure of one thing:

This report ain't gonna go over real big upstairs, that's for damn sure. It could sure use a healthy dose of sugarcoating, especially the parts about the inaccurate bombing, the Nackeroo screw-ups...and fuck me up the ass and call me Sally, but this part with the gun-toting woman and her abos saving their asses? Didn't old Patch teach that young captain of his how to play the game with the brass hats?

General MacArthur sat down to supper in his private dining room. His orderly had placed the evening edition of the Brisbane Telegraph beside his napkin, folded neatly, as always. Ordinarily, the general would begin eating before even glancing at the paper, but tonight something in the visible fragment of the bold, oversized headline caught his eye. He began to unfold the paper. If the headline said what he thought it might, he would surely lose his appetite.

When it was unfolded, he was correct—*was MacArthur ever wrong?* The headline screamed:

AUSSIE WOMAN BAILS OUT YANKS

The subheadline, right below the picture of a smiling young woman, was no less unsettling:

SHE MADE CAPE YORK CAMPAIGN A SUCCESS

When he had read the whole article, he called for his orderly. "Generals Sutherland and Cash are to report to me immediately," MacArthur commanded.

The orderly scurried from the room. MacArthur ran his finger down the article, pausing over the Aussie woman's name as he asked himself,
Forbes...Forbes...Where have I heard that name before?

His chief of staff, General Sutherland, arrived first.

"Richard," MacArthur said as he held up the headline for Sutherland to see, "how did we lose control of this story so thoroughly? And why does this Forbes woman's name ring a bell?"

Sutherland had a quick reply; he had just finished reading the article when he was summoned. "I believe, sir, this Jillian Forbes was the woman Governor Owens wished to neutralize. He claimed she was organizing the blacks to side with the Japanese, or something like that. Briley was instructed to deal with the matter."

MacArthur furrowed his brow. "I don't recall any such conversation, Richard. Neither do you."

"Yes, sir. I understand completely."

General Cash knocked on the open door, hoping no one would notice his knees trembling. "Reporting as ordered, sir," Cash said.

Sutherland stepped aside and let the full weight of MacArthur's wrath fall on Horace Cash.

Again putting the newspaper headline on display, MacArthur said, "General Cash, have you read this article?"

"Yes, sir...a few minutes ago."

MacArthur asked, "Does it reflect what is written in the after-action report of Task Force Miles?"

"Almost word for word, General."

"And who is this Australian Army doctor...this Major Dunbar Green...the man listed as the source for this article?"

"He was the medic with Task Force Miles, sir," Cash replied.

MacArthur's face was reddening as he said, "That's just dandy. How in God's name did an *Australian* doctor become the medic for an *American* patrol?"

Cash replied, "I have no idea, sir. That all happened on General Briley's watch."

Sutherland had an idea. "Perhaps, sir, we can tout Green's presence as an outstanding example of cooperation between allies?"

A withering glance from MacArthur convinced Sutherland to say no more.

MacArthur had one last question. "This aide of Briley's...this Captain Brewster...do you have any idea what he was doing in the Weipa area when he was killed?"

Cash shrugged and said, "Again, sir...I have no idea. That was on General Briley's watch, not mine."

Those were the words MacArthur wanted to hear. He relaxed into his chair.

"Cash," MacArthur said, "I'll expect you to correct the many *inaccuracies* in that after-action report. Remember, this was *my* victory...an *American* victory...not the work of some Aussie woman and her band of pickaninnies playing soldier. Have the revised report on my desk by fifteen hundred tomorrow. That is all."

Cash snapped to attention, about-faced, and headed for the door as fast as he could without breaking into a trot. Sutherland remained, standing at ease, knowing not to speak until spoken to.

The orderly appeared once again. "There's a secretary in your office, General. She says there's an urgent telephone call for you."

With a wave of his hand, MacArthur dispatched his chief of staff to deal with the caller. *Finally,* the Supreme Commander thought, *I can enjoy my supper.*

Sutherland returned in a few moments, though.

"It's Governor Owens on the line, sir," Sutherland said. "He sounds very upset."

"He should be," MacArthur replied.

"He demands to speak to you, sir," Sutherland said.

MacArthur flung his fork down on the table.

"*Demands? Demands*, does he? Tell the Governor if he needs to speak with me so desperately, he can get his royally appointed ass over here. Now leave me in peace to finish my supper, Richard."

Chapter Sixty-Four

Governor Sir Malcolm Owens was wearing a track in General MacArthur's office carpet. He couldn't stop himself from nervously pacing the floor. The general, on the other hand, puffed contentedly on his pipe while seated behind the desk and couldn't have seemed calmer.

"She's still alive," Owens said, "and she's here, in Brisbane. I'm sure of it."

MacArthur shook his head and asked, "How could that be, Governor?"

"My wife saw her yesterday, General, while attending a tea at the home of Margaret Forbes-Masters, Jillian Forbes's aunt. Miss Forbes wasn't introduced…in fact, she stayed out of sight. But my wife caught a fleeting glimpse as she passed through a hallway. She's seen the girl many times before…it was unmistakably her. She's still alive!"

MacArthur glanced at the evening paper headline. "I'd say that's a very fortunate turn of events, Governor."

"No, General, it's not. By morning, Canberra will know all about the article…and how we've failed to thwart a very dangerous threat to this nation. A *white* woman, leading the blacks in consort with the Japanese—"

"We now know that to be nonsense, Governor," MacArthur said, "at least as far as northern Queensland goes. My own troops serve as witness."

"I notified the police commissioner," Owens said, sounding more desperate by the moment, "but he just laughed. He refuses to take any action against the

Forbes-Masters family. Not without formal arrest papers, signed by a magistrate."

"And I suppose, Governor, you can't find a magistrate willing to do that, either?"

Owens shook his head. MacArthur supposed he had never seen a man looking so forlorn.

"Good for them," MacArthur said. "At least there are still some officials in this country who know how to act judiciously."

The Governor was begging now. "General, we must find and eliminate her before it's too late."

MacArthur's roar of laughter made Owens tremble. "On the contrary, Governor. I'm going to find her...and *decorate* her. I need this to blow over quickly, and that's the best way to end this unfortunate sideshow."

Owens was terrified. Almost in tears, he said, "But General...Canberra—"

"Canberra can kiss MacArthur's ass," the general interrupted. "In fact, when I do honor this Forbes woman, not only will *you* be there, but I think I'll invite Prime Minister Curtin as well."

Once MacArthur dismissed the governor, he called General Sutherland into the office. There were a few more details of the Jillian Forbes affair to work out.

"Richard," MacArthur said, "find this Forbes woman. I plan to make a big show of acknowledging her *accomplishments.* I've met her aunt, this Margaret Forbes-Masters...some function at Government House last month, I believe. She's a formidable woman, but get her cooperation somehow to produce her niece."

"Yes, General," Sutherland replied.

MacArthur moved on to his next order of business. "Now, what do we know about this Captain Maynard Miles, Richard?"

Sutherland had the information on the tip of his tongue. "I had Cash's people pull his records. He's a West Point man, class of thirty-five. He was a real comer once...an aide to Short at Pearl...but he fell from grace like a stone. Short crucified him, probably one of the last things he did before getting the ax himself."

MacArthur thought that over for a minute before saying, "Find a slot for him on our staff somewhere...make up a job if you have to, like *Special Liaison for Northern Queensland,* or some bullshit like that. We need to keep a close eye on our young captain for a while..."

But then MacArthur changed his mind. "No, never mind, Richard," he said. "His company will be on its way to the Solomons very soon. Let him rot in hell."

Chapter Sixty-Five

The note from Aunt Margaret had sent Jillian into a panic. Never one to beat around the bush, her aunt's words were simple and direct:

Dearest Jillian,

Two of MacArthur's officers visited me today. They said the general wishes to honor you in a public ceremony. They suspect you are in Brisbane. I did not confirm their suspicion.

I believe they are sincere. The choice is yours.

Love always,

Aunt Margaret

When Jock arrived to spend the night at Hope Island, Jillian was still in turmoil.

"They want to *honor* me?" she asked. "How? With a firing squad?"

Jock reached out for her, but she spun away from his grasp. "Jill, calm down," he said. "This is exactly what we hoped for. Better, even."

Not convinced at all, she asked, "It is?"

"Sure," he replied. "Top's got a *little birdie* at Headquarters that tells him everything. MacArthur just wants this whole affair to go away—"

"You're sure he doesn't just want *me* to go away quickly, Jock? To my grave, perhaps?"

"No, honey...nothing like that. He'll give you a brief moment in the spotlight, then he can have the spotlight back, all to himself, just how he likes it. That's all there is to it."

He could tell she was coming around to his way of thinking, but very slowly.

"Besides," Jock said, "Aunt Margaret thinks it's on

the level. You told me she can figure out a person in a glance…and we know how good she is at that. After all, she likes me, doesn't she?"

Jillian couldn't help but smile. "Yes…you, of all people, she likes. The scoundrel who's defiling her beloved niece."

Now Jock was smiling, too, as he took her in his arms. This time, she didn't resist. "Speaking of *defiling*," he said, "would you care to step into the bedchamber?"

"*Scoundrel,*" she said over her shoulder as she led the way.

Jock awoke to find himself alone in the bed. Moonlight washed the room in its dim glow, outlining Jillian's silhouette as she stood by the window, gazing into the night sky.

"Jill, come back to bed," he said, his voice rough with sleep.

"I can't. Too much on my mind."

He moved to the window, enveloping her in his arms, his chest against her back. "Like what?" he asked.

"I have to go back, you know," she said, wrapping her arms tight around his. "I don't belong here, Jock. I'm not *needed* here."

He knew her words were true—but he hadn't wanted to hear them.

"You don't think *I* need you?"

"That's different," she said, "and you're not going to be here very long, either."

He knew those words were true, too.

"You know, Jill...Weipa's going to be a very different place if you go back. One of the other regiments is shipping out tomorrow to secure those abandoned Jap airfields. Our planes will be flying out of them before you know it. There'll be Yanks all over the place."

"Good," she said, gazing dreamily at the heavens. "Then the trading boats can start back up...and I'll be back in business. I sold tons of fish to the Japanese...I can sell them to you Yanks, too."

She rested the back of her head against his shoulder and said, "And maybe, when this is all over..."

She stopped in mid-sentence to kiss him. When the kiss ended, he asked, "Okay, so when this is all over...*what?*"

"Nevermind," she replied. "Let's go back to bed."

They were awake before the dawn. This time, there was coffee percolating on the stove. As Jock pulled on his khakis, he said, "You know, Jill, we need pictures of each other."

"I was afraid you'd say that," she replied, her voice tinted with dread.

"Afraid? Why?"

She poured him a cup and placed it on the nightstand and then slumped into an armchair. Reluctantly, she began her explanation.

"Do you remember when I tried to stop poor J.T. Guess from photographing the blacks?"

"Yeah...right before Brewster—"

"Correct," she interrupted, not wanting to plunge

any deeper into the memory of the shooting. "The blacks are superstitious about photographs. They believe that once people are dead, there mustn't be any images of them. You can't even speak their names."

"But what does that have to do with us, Jill?"

Her response was nothing but a look that sent a chill down his spine. It was sadness. It was an apology. It was resignation to the inevitable. But beneath it all was a yearning—a fervent hope—that the sorrow and pain would never come to pass.

He was about to tell her, *But I'm not going to die, Jill*—but he knew he couldn't promise that. He was stuck in the business of war—the business of dying—and he would be for the duration. But surely she didn't think they could hide from cameras forever?

"There'll be photographers when MacArthur honors you, Jill."

She walked to the window as the first rays of sunrise began to brighten their little world, illuminating her face as she said, "You can keep one of those photos, I suppose."

Chapter Sixty-Six

Master Sergeant Johnny Jarvis strolled into Melvin Patchett's dayroom carrying a cardboard box under his arm. He dropped the box on the first sergeant's desk.

"What's this, Johnny?" Patchett asked. "You giving out presents?"

"Yes, indeed, Patch. Yes, indeed," Jarvis replied, a big grin on his face. He stuck his hand into the box and produced a manila envelope.

"First," Jarvis said, "here's the revised after-action report for your Task Force Miles."

"Revised in what way, Johnny?"

"Let me start by telling you what General Cash's staff didn't revise. All that stuff about *unconditional support from the indigenous population* stands. MacArthur was real insistent about that. But he did make them tone it down a teeny little bit."

"All right," Patchett said. "What else did they change?"

"A few key points have been corrected or clarified, Patch. For example, it now says *all bombs struck the designated target within probable error criteria.*"

"That's complete bullshit," Patchett said. "They bombed *us*, for cryin' out loud."

"I know, Patch...I know. But it's gospel now."

Patchett scowled and leaned back in his chair, laced his hands nonchalantly behind his head, and said, "Go ahead...you might as well kick me in the ass with the rest of it."

Jarvis dumped the remaining contents of the cardboard box on Patchett's desk. Eleven small, identical rectangular boxes spilled out—the type of boxes that might contain jewelry. Or military decorations.

"No, Patch," Jarvis said, "you've got this all wrong. Getting back to that part about the bombing...since we now know it all hit its designated target, that bombardment you and your men suffered is no longer classified as an unfortunate accident but the result of enemy action—"

Patchett interrupted, asking, "Like a Jap artillery barrage?"

"Exactly, Patch."

"Bullshit, Johnny. I know a fucking artillery barrage when I see one. So do you. We've damn sure been in enough of them in the last war."

"Bear with me here, Patch," Jarvis said, not missing a beat. "As a result of these new findings, General Cash is proud to award the eleven men who were wounded in that bombardment the Purple Heart, including that Aussie doc. In fact, the Purple Heart for your"—he fumbled to find the name on the pages of the after-action report—"for your Private First Class Marcel Boudreau comes complete with oak leaf cluster, since he was wounded twice on that mission."

Patchett shook his head in disgust. "General Cash may be proud," he said, "but I don't see him *awarding* shit. We don't ask for much...hell, we didn't even ask for these damn medals...but it'd be real decent of him if he, or at least Colonel Snow, showed up to pin these medals on my men."

Jarvis shrugged as he backed toward the door. "Sorry, Patch. I really am...but the general and the colonel are both very busy men."

Melvin Patchett's burst of laughter shook the walls.

"I'll bet they are, Johnny," he said. "So that's it? That's all the ceremony my men get? Some old warhorse drops a box on my desk like he's delivering parcel post? Why don't you just line them up and shit on their heads while you're at it?"

"Seems like someone's already done that, Patch," Jarvis said before slipping out the door.

At MacArthur's headquarters, in a conference room crowded with US Army officers, civilian newsmen, and photographers, a very different sort of awards ceremony was taking place. In front of the podium, before a fusillade of popping flashbulbs, the 12 bomber pilots stood proudly in a row, snapping to attention, to be decorated by the Supreme Commander himself. The squadron leader and aircraft commander of the *Peggy V*—the plane that unwittingly bombed nothing but the men of Task Force Miles—was the first to receive his medal: the Distinguished Flying Cross. He puffed his chest proudly as MacArthur pinned on the decoration, the highest the nation bestowed for heroic exploits in the air. The general moved down the line, dispensing an Air Medal, the newly-established award for aerial achievement, to each of the other 11 pilots.

Despite the honors being bestowed on them, the pilots weren't kidding themselves. They had seen the original bomb damage assessment from Task Force Miles. They knew their bombing accuracy had not been nearly as good as MacArthur was telling the world. Only one plane had dropped its load close to the designated target, but thanks to luck and Mother Nature, that one had been enough. As each pilot felt the dignifying presence of the medal just pinned to his chest, he was buoyed by the hope he might be the lucky man who sent the Japs running. Each would cling forever to the solace offered by that one in twelve chance.

After the last pilot received his medal, MacArthur took a few moments to further cement the message he wished to convey. As reporters recorded his every word, he said:

"Thanks to the unselfish heroism of these twelve brave men I see before me, the world has now seen the awesome, unleashed might of American airpower. We offer our continued and steadfast support to our allies, and we caution our enemies to think twice about any further acts of aggression, lest they wish to experience the swift and merciless vengeance dealt by thousands upon thousands of courageous airmen just like these fine men."

Waiting at the back of the room, Jillian thought, *That's right, you wankers, the flyboys did it all by themselves. Didn't need a bit of help from Jock and his boys on the ground.*

As the pilots filed out, MacArthur cornered General Sutherland, his chief of staff, and whispered, "Why is Governor Owens not here yet?"

"Bad news, sir," Sutherland said. "The governor's office just called. He expresses his regrets, but a pressing matter keeps him from attending. He's sent Premier Granville in his place as representative of the Queensland government." Sutherland nodded toward a man standing alone at the back of the room, looking disinterested and restless. "He's the fidgety gentleman in the red tie."

MacArthur muttered, "Why, that treacherous little worm. Owens has made a serious mistake to trifle with me."

The American generals couldn't help but notice that Prime Minister Curtin had ignored his invitation, as well. Then again, they hadn't really expected him to make the trip from Canberra for a 15-minute ceremony. But a snub was a snub; he hadn't even bothered to cable his regrets.

"Well, Richard," MacArthur said, "let's get the rest of this circus over with."

Jillian Forbes, wearing an expensive dress, hat, and pumps Aunt Margaret had managed to procure on very short notice, was escorted to the podium on the arm of a young staff officer like a debutant strolling into a cotillion. Approaching General MacArthur as the cameras flashed, she realized she had no idea of proper etiquette:

Am I supposed to curtsey to this wanker? No, of course not...he's not the bloody king. Maybe a handshake?

She decided a smile and a simple *Nice to meet you, General* would suffice.

MacArthur got right down to business, rolling into his second and final speech of the ceremony. It concluded with these words:

"For the substantial assistance selflessly provided by you to American forces in northern Queensland, on behalf of the President of the United States, I present you, Jillian Forbes, with this plaque for meritorious service."

On cue, the same staff officer who escorted Jillian into the room appeared with the plaque, a mahogany oval with the brass eagle-and-shield crest of the US Army at its center. Below the crest was an engraved brass plate. She didn't bother to glance at the plaque but displayed it as she posed politely for pictures with the general.

But Jillian's polite expression faded. As she took a good look at the plaque, her lips pursed and she began to gently shake her head.

"You know, General," Jillian said as a stunned hush fell over the onlookers, "this is all very nice…but I, and the people of Weipa, could surely use a little more than kind words."

Startled this young woman had the audacity to speak without invitation, MacArthur played the benevolent straight man and asked, "And what would that be, my dear?"

"I believe you are holding two of my fishing boats and four of my crewmen," she replied. "I'd appreciate it if you'd return them to me so my community can rebuild and return to normal life."

Photographers who tripped their shutters at that moment recorded for posterity the dumbfounded look on MacArthur's face; the general had no idea what Jillian was talking about. All of Queensland, though, would know about her request as soon as the evening papers hit the newsstands. Shaken and struggling to keep his irritation in check, MacArthur turned to his equally clueless chief of staff and said, "I'll trust Miss Forbes's concerns to you, General Sutherland."

His magisterial air returning quickly, MacArthur faced the audience and said, "Thank you all for coming.

These proceedings are closed."

Sir Malcolm Owens figured he was safe. As long as he avoided the downtown office building that served as MacArthur's headquarters—as well as Lennon's Hotel—for a few days, his odds of running into MacArthur or any members of his staff would be close to zero. In those same few days, this Jillian Forbes affair would be forgotten, dissolved in the constantly changing panorama swirling around a nation at war.

And the blacks will be considered a subversive threat once again, as they bloody well should be, he thought.

Owens wasn't worried about MacArthur visiting him at Government House. The general had grudgingly paid the customary courtesy call when first arriving in Brisbane. He wouldn't bother calling again.

The governor couldn't avoid being in public, though. Like now, for instance: he was lunching with two comely young secretaries from Parliament House, young enough to be his daughters, in the dining room of the Gresham Hotel. Owens was following the rule *Dine with a woman not your wife and it's called adultery. Dine with two, though, and it's called business.*

One of the young women had caught his eye a few weeks ago; his confidence was high he would bed her very soon. The other was a more recent find and had been invited along for the appearance of propriety. She also served as insurance: if the first decided some archaic tenets of morality were more important than keeping her job, perhaps the second could be convinced to see reason. If things went really well, one of these lucky ladies might join the governor upstairs this afternoon in his private suite—*The Guv's Knocking Shop,* the hotel staff called it—while his driver spirited the other back to Parliament House, perhaps to complete her last day in the government's employ.

As Sir Malcolm saw it, things were indeed going really well, but then he saw something else: Margaret Forbes-Masters striding across the dining room, coming straight for him. The two plainclothes policemen who were his bodyguards, each at a separate table, rose from their chairs to intercept the determined-looking woman.

"That's all right, lads," Owens said to the policemen as he rose to greet her. "That lady is a dear friend."

"Dear friend, my arse, Malcolm," Aunt Margaret replied, spitting fire with her words.

Owens suddenly seemed very small and timid. His luncheon guests hastily excused themselves and fled to the powder room. Aunt Margaret stood very close to Sir Malcolm; what she was about to say was meant for his ears only.

"Malcolm, you little shit," she hissed, "if you ever so much as threaten a Forbes again, I'll see—"

"Now see here, Margaret," Owens said, trying to puff himself up, "I represent the king. You cannot speak to me like that…and it's *Sir* Malcolm."

"I'll speak to you any way I bloody want, Malcolm. As I was saying, if you're ever stupid enough to threaten a Forbes again, I'll make sure you become a member of the *penniless aristocracy* overnight. I'll also make sure there's no place in Australia you'll be able to show your face, you lecherous old bastard."

Owens tried to act offended, but he could fool no one. He couldn't hide the fact he was terrified. In a quavering voice, he said, "But I represent the king…"

"That's very impressive, Malcolm. But it doesn't make you immortal." As she made her exit, Aunt Margaret added, loud enough for everyone in the dining room to hear, "Good day, Sir Malcolm. I do hope I didn't spoil your little ménage a trois."

The photo hit the front page of every Brisbane newspaper that evening. There was MacArthur, a shocked look on his face, with mouth wide open, as the determined young woman beside him spoke her mind.

Actually, Jock thought, it was a lovely picture of Jillian in her stylish outfit: *Trim MacArthur out with a pair of scissors and the picture was a definite keeper.* He was hoping when he arrived at the Hope Island cottage she might still be wearing it. He knew full well, though, she'd probably peel it off at the first opportunity, to be replaced with something far more casual and comfortable.

He was right. When he drove up, Jillian was waiting on the cottage's veranda, barefoot and wearing a flowing, full skirt and cardigan to ward off the cool evening breeze.

She still looks lovely.

Jillian smiled when she saw the newspaper tucked under his arm. They kissed and settled into the veranda's wicker loveseat. "So what did you think?" she asked, pointing to the newspaper.

With a straight face, Jock replied, "The men in my company decided you have the biggest pair of balls in Australia."

She threw her head back and roared with laughter. His poker face broke, and he laughed, too.

When the last giggle died out, she said, "Actually, I was quite furious after I saw all those pilot wankers get their bloody medals...and nothing for you and your lads."

"I really wasn't expecting to be decorated, Jill."

"Still, Jock, they made it sound like I was the only one on the ground who made it possible. That's not bloody fair."

Jock shrugged and said, "I wasn't expecting it to be fair, either. I don't expect much of anything anymore. All I wanted was to get that bull's-eye off your back, and we did that. So how about that drink?"

She dashed inside and emerged a few moments later. The two glasses of rum she had poured were balanced on what looked like a wooden tray. As she held it in front of him, he took his glass and realized what the tray was—the plaque.

Jock started to laugh again and asked, "You're going to use it as a serving tray?"

"Sure," she replied, "or a doorstop, paperweight...you know, something actually useful."

She took her glass and dropped the plaque to the veranda's deck. It landed with a resounding *thunk*. Jillian gave the plaque an admiring glance and said, "Good wood, eh?"

They clinked glasses in triumph and downed the rum. As the rich liquid traced a warm path to their souls, Jock asked, "Do they really have your boats...and your crewmen?"

"Looks like it," she replied. "General Sutherland said he'll have confirmation in a day or two."

"And after that?"

"I'll be getting them back, I believe."

"And after that, Jill?"

She gazed into the distance and replied, "Who knows what that day will bring?"

Chapter Sixty-Seven

It was Christmas in July as far as Franklin Delano Roosevelt was concerned. There seemed to be nothing but good news from his military chiefs. The report of Admiral Ernest King, the CNO, was especially gratifying.

"Yes, Mister President," King said, "we have met our fuel resupply target figures for the Pacific fleet on schedule...a little ahead of schedule, in fact. Hawaii remains safe, and our offensive operations against the Japanese in the Solomons will begin on schedule. Twenty-one September has been selected as D-Day."

"Excellent," the president said. "What about the Japanese on Midway and in the Aleutians?"

King snickered as he replied, "What about them, Mister President? They're not doing much of anything. It looks like a clear case of biting off more than they could chew. They're holding on to rocks in the water with miniscule forces that pose no real offensive threat. They're just soaking up resources for their defense, resources that could be put to better use elsewhere. Once the entire Pacific fleet is back at fighting strength, I say we bottle them up and let them rot there."

Roosevelt said, "We'll see about that, Admiral. Now, General Marshall, I see the great MacArthur has finally seen fit to advise us on the situation in Australia, and I must say, I like what I'm hearing. I like it very much."

"Yes, Mister President," George Marshall said, "the Air Force did a magnificent job evicting the Japanese exploratory force on Cape York. Commendations are being prepared for General Arnold and his theater commanders as we speak."

A look of concern crossed the president's face. He asked, "What of our boys on the ground...the young lads who did the reconnaissance for the bombers? How did they fare?"

"They paid a steep price, Mister President," Marshall replied. "Of the sixteen that began the mission, three were killed, and almost all were wounded. The survivors are recuperating at Brisbane."

The president was disturbed to hear those numbers. He asked Marshall, "So, you're saying they took nearly one hundred percent casualties?"

"Unfortunately, yes, Mister President."

FDR sadly shook his head as he said, "Let it be our fervent hope, gentlemen, that in future ground engagements with the Japanese we incur a significantly lower rate. It was bad enough to be bled dry of fuel, but we'll recover. We simply cannot afford to be bled dry of manpower. We could never recover from that."

Stoically, Admiral Isoroku Yamamoto watched as barges deposited the last of Colonel Najima's devastated regiment on the shore at Port Moresby, Papua New Guinea. The men he saw were frightened, exhausted, and, for at least the foreseeable future, worthless as soldiers. What had been promised as easy occupation duty on Cape York for them had turned, instead, into a costly nightmare.

General Hitoshi Imamura, the commander of the Japanese Army on New Guinea, stood beside Yamamoto and tallied the crippling toll.

"Approximately one thousand men...a third of the regiment's strength...is lost," the general said.

For the last week, Yamamoto had been watching the numbers, too. One particular detail, though, struck him as very odd. "The officers," Yamamoto said. "Is it true not one officer of this regiment survived?"

General Imamura replied, "Unless there are some on these last barges...and considering the disgraceful rabble we're seeing, it certainly doesn't look like there are...then, yes, Admiral, none of the regiment's officers survived."

Yamamoto looked grim as he said, "Let us pray this is a most unique aberration. We cannot hope to prevail against the Americans with such a casualty rate."

Imamura felt no need to reply. He knew that fact all too well.

"I should never have allowed this," Yamamoto said. "We should have used this regiment to bolster our sparse forces in the Solomons...on Guadalcanal, especially. Any fool can see that is where the Americans will try to strike back, at the farthest, most vulnerable tip of our conquests."

Admiral Yamamoto had seen enough. Beginning the short walk back to his staff car, he added, "It was all so easy when they couldn't fight back."

Chapter Sixty-Eight

They hadn't expected the attack—at least not from that direction. It was a shame; their defensive positions were meticulously crafted and impenetrable—as long as the attack came from the front. The defenders had simply gotten used to the routine. The enemy would arrive in dependable waves—just like clockwork—to be mowed down by their machine guns, with their inexhaustible supply of ammunition.

The defenders thought it was all getting a bit boring until the corporal-in-charge found Tom Hadley's submachine gun pressed against the small of his back. The corporal looked to his left and then to his right. All along his defensive wall, his squad had dropped their weapons and had their hands in the air, taken prisoner by the attackers.

"Bang," Tom Hadley said. "You're dead."

"Wait a minute," the corporal-in-charge said, waving his arms in protest. "Where the fuck did you guys come from?"

"From behind you," Hadley replied.

"But that's cheating! You're supposed to come from the front!"

The men of Hadley's platoon got a huge kick out of the corporal's complaint. They taunted their opponents in this war game with those words over and over again: *But that's cheating!* Bogater Boudreau tucked the butt of his Thompson under his chin and pretended to play it like a violin. "That's some sob story," Bogater said, "but you're all still dead, you clowns."

A cocky young second lieutenant with a white

band around his helmet—the mark of a war game umpire—walked purposefully toward Tom Hadley and spewed the words, "What do you think you're doing, Sergeant? Your mission was to stage a frontal assault on this position, testing your ability to use fire and maneuver to achieve your objective."

Hadley laughed and said, "Begging your pardon, Lieutenant, but even with everyone shooting blanks, a frontal assault sounded like a real dumb idea. Our way worked a whole lot better."

The lieutenant scribbled on his clipboard as he said, "Unacceptable. What's your name, Sergeant?"

"Hadley, sir. Thomas P.," he replied in a polite yet confident tone.

"Well, Sergeant Hadley, Thomas P., you just delayed the whole afternoon's training schedule with your little stunt. Not to mention you exhausted your men by walking miles out of your way to get behind this position."

Hadley took a look at his men. They were hardly exhausted—and they were quite delighted with what they had just done.

The arrogant lieutenant had more preaching to do. "I'm here to tell you, Sergeant, when you're up against the Japs—"

That wiped the smiles from the faces of Tom Hadley and his men.

"With all due respect, sir," Hadley said, "what would you know about being up against the Japs?"

The lieutenant took Hadley's question like the insult it was meant to be. "That's it! I'm putting you on report, Sergeant. What's your unit?"

With great pride, Hadley replied, "C Company,

First of the Eighty-First, sir."

The lieutenant became so ham-fisted, the point snapped off his pencil before he could write the second letter. He realized who the men of this unit were. There were hints of awe and reverence in his voice as he stammered the words, "You men...you men are..."

"That's right, sir," Hadley said. "We're Task Force Miles. We know a little something about being up against the Japs. And we don't give a damn about how far we have to walk...hell, we could walk a hundred miles. Or more. In spades."

The lieutenant's attitude changed drastically. Now, he wanted to be their buddy. "Is Captain Miles here?" he asked. "I'd like to meet him."

"Sorry, Lieutenant," Hadley replied, "but the captain got called up to battalion. We'll be sure to give him your regards, though."

At the battalion headquarters tent, Jock received two pieces of bad news. One was expected. The other was not, and it shook him so badly he needed to sit down.

The expected news: within a week, his unit would relocate from the tactical training camp near Toowoomba, where the division had been bivouacked for the past three days, to Hervey Bay—a five-hour drive north of Brisbane—for amphibious assault training. The amphibious training would take three weeks. After that, they would be off to staging areas— well to the north, probably near Townsville—for the invasion of the Solomon Islands.

The news he hadn't expected came at mail call in a letter from Jillian. He'd read the letter a dozen times since opening the envelope a few minutes ago. But he'd read it again, hoping against hope it would say something different this time:

My darling Jock,

I beg you not to think me cruel or heartless, but by the time you read this, I'll be gone. My boats are waiting for me at Karumba. My crewmen are being held close by at the prison camp in Normanton. I've been given the paperwork to secure their release.

It's my fault they've been rotting in that prison camp. They did nothing wrong. They're not at war with anyone. It's not fair that they stay there another day. Please understand.

You know where to find me.

I love you, Jock Miles,

Jill

It had only been four nights since they lay in each other's arms. He thought they would have so much more time.

The deepest cut of all: he never told her he loved her. *Maybe if I had, she'd still be waiting in Brisbane...*

But he knew her better than that.

Chapter Sixty-Nine

They were finally cut a break. Once the division finished tactical training at Toowoomba, it was allowed to return to its Brisbane bivouac for five days before shipping off to Hervey Bay. They'd need two of those days to refit. The other three, they were granted leave.

First Sergeant Patchett asked Jock, "What are you gonna do with your three days' leave, sir?"

"I'm going back to Weipa, Top."

Patchett didn't need to ask why Jock was going. He had a more practical concern, though: "How on God's green Earth do you plan to do that, Captain? It's a thousand miles from here."

"I'm going to fly," Jock replied.

The RAAF Catalina amphibian—named *G for George*—lifted off from the runway at Archerfield and turned north. Once settled in at cruising altitude, Wing Commander Tim Wells turned the controls over to his co-pilot and joined Jock in the cabin.

"Thanks for letting me come along, sir," Jock said, "and bending your schedule a little to accommodate mine."

"Call me Tim, Jock...and you're very welcome. It's the least I can do, and you bloody well deserve it. Everyone knows what a farce that was, pinning medals all over those Yank pilots...and you lads not even getting a mention. That Jillian is some feisty sheila, though, to stand up to MacArthur like that."

"That she is, sir...uhh, Tim."

"No wonder you want to see her again," Wells said. "Anyway, when they told me to scout the Weipa area for a possible seaplane base, I thought to myself, *It couldn't hurt to take along someone who knows the place really well...someone who's actually been there.*"

With a wry smile, Jock said, "My colonel thought I was out of my ever-loving mind, volunteering to give up my three-day leave to do this."

"Ahh, the things we do for love, eh, Jock?"

Gazing over the Pacific from the Cat's gun blister, Jock couldn't believe how different the maritime traffic looked from the last time he had flown this route. Then, there was just a pitiful trickle of vessels plying their way to Brisbane. Now, it looked like an armada of freighters, troop ships, and tankers—carrying that all-important fuel—was on its way to save the world. The columns of ships stretched across the ocean like a band of steel in the spotlight of the low, early morning sun.

"Looks like we're finally getting the stuff to do this job right," Jock said, smiling at the spectacle on the sea below.

"Yes, indeed," Tim Wells said. "Things are definitely getting better. This was the first week I haven't had to fight to get enough fuel for my planes."

"That's good to hear," Jock said. "You know, when we came in to refit, we got everything we needed without any bullshit. Every last damned thing."

"It's about bloody time, too," Tim Wells added before heading back to the cockpit.

The sun was making its orange dome on the western horizon as the Cat splashed down on Albatross Bay. Two American fighter planes streaked low overhead as she taxied to the harbor, waggling their wings in greeting. Lighters from cargo ships anchored out in the bay crowded the shore, transferring their loads to US Army trucks. Where Japanese soldiers once prowled the Weipa Mission, now there were only Yanks. As the Cat plowed past the mast of the sunken Japanese destroyer, still protruding high above the surface, one of the Aussie gunners bowed in mock-Japanese style, and then flicked the V sign in its direction.

Tim Wells cut the engines and *G for George* coasted to a stop. As the crewman in the nose turret dropped the anchor, a boat slowly approached and turned a lazy circle. Jock recognized the name on her bow—*Andoom Clipper.* One of Jillian's boats.

As the boat pulled alongside, one of her black crewmen recognized Jock immediately. He smiled broadly as he said, "Captain Jock...you come back! Remember me? I am Nigel. I brought food to your camp."

Jock climbed into the boat, exchanging hearty pats on the back with her crew. In complete innocence, Nigel asked, "You want Miss Jilly?"

"Yes, I do," Jock replied, imagining the snickers that question would cause in the barracks. "Where is she?"

"On shore. The supplies just came."

He found her where the icehouse used to stand,

tallying stacks of crates and barrels, her back to him. Black men and women were busy loading the goods onto wagons.

"Need a hand with anything?" Jock asked.

She was turning at the first sound of his voice. Like a perfectly choreographed dance, they were locked in each other's arms at the precise moment her pivot was complete.

They kissed and kissed again. She asked, "How long do you have?"

"Two nights."

"And then?"

He didn't need to answer. The faraway look in his eyes told her everything she needed to know. She hugged him tighter and asked, "Why'd you come all this way, my silly boy?"

His faraway look vanished. Looking deep into her eyes now, he said, "I forgot to tell you something..."

***

About the Author:

William Peter Grasso writes on historical and aviation topics. He is retired from the aircraft maintenance industry and served in the US Army. He also participated in Desert Storm as a flight crew member in the Civil Reserve Air Fleet (CRAF). He resides with his wife in Tulsa, Oklahoma.

Contact the Author Online:

wpgrasso@cox.net

Also by William Peter Grasso:

June 1944: A recon flight is shot down over the
Japanese-held island of Biak, soon to be the next jump
in MacArthur's leapfrogging across New Guinea.
Major Jock Miles, US Army—the crashed plane's
intelligence officer—must lead the handful of survivors
to safety. It's a tall order for a man barely recovered
from a near-crippling leg wound. Gaining the grudging
help of a Dutch planter who has evaded the Japanese
since the war began, Jock discovers just how little
MacArthur's staff knows about the terrain and defenses
of the island they're about to invade.

After surviving a deadly plane crash, Jock Miles is handed a new mission: neutralize a mountaintop observation post on Japanese-held Manus Island so MacArthur's invasion fleet en route to Hollandia, New Guinea, can arrive undetected. Jock's team seizes and holds the observation post with the help of a clever deception. But when they learn of a POW camp deep in the island's treacherous jungle, it opens old wounds for Jock and his men: the disappearance—and presumed death—of Jillian Forbes at Buna a year before. There's only one risky way to find out if she's a prisoner there…and doing so puts their entire mission in serious jeopardy.

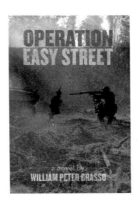

Port Moresby was bad. Buna was worse.

The WW2 alternative history adventure of Jock Miles continues as MacArthur orders American and Australian forces to seize Buna in Papua New Guinea. Once again, the Allied high command underestimates the Japanese defenders, plunging Jock and his men into a battle they're not equipped to win. Worse, jungle diseases, treacherous terrain, and the tactical fantasies of deluded generals become adversaries every bit as deadly as the Japanese. Sick, exhausted, and outgunned, Jock's battalion is ordered to spearhead an amphibious assault against the well-entrenched enemy. It's a suicide mission—but with ingenious help from an unexpected source, there might be a way to avoid the certain slaughter and take Buna. For Jock, though, victory comes at a dreadful price.

Alternative history takes center stage as *Operation Long Jump,* the second book in the Jock Miles World War 2 adventure series, plunges us into the horrors of combat in the rainforests of Papua New Guinea. As a prelude to the Allied invasion, Jock Miles and his men seize the Japanese observation post on the mountain overlooking Port Moresby. The main invasion that follows quickly degenerates to a bloody stalemate, as the inexperienced, demoralized, and poorly led GIs struggle against the stubborn enemy. Seeking a way to crack the impenetrable Japanese defenses, infantry officer Jock finds himself in a new role—aerial observer. He's teamed with rookie pilot John Worth, in a prequel to his role as hero of Grasso's *East Wind Returns.* Together, they struggle to expose the Japanese defenses—while highly exposed themselves—in their slow and vulnerable spotter plane. The enemy is not the only thing troubling Jock: his Australian lover, Jillian Forbes, has found a new and dangerous way to contribute to the war effort.

In this alternate history adventure set in WW2's early days, a crippled US military struggles to defend vulnerable Australia against the unstoppable Japanese forces. When a Japanese regiment lands on Australia's desolate and undefended Cape York Peninsula, Jock Miles, a US Army captain disgraced despite heroic actions at Pearl Harbor, is ordered to locate the enemy's elusive command post.

Conceived in politics rather than sound tactics, the futile mission is a "show of faith" by the American war leaders meant to do little more than bolster their flagging Australian ally. For Jock Miles and the men of his patrol, it's a death sentence: their enemy is superior in men, material, firepower, and combat experience. Even if the Japanese don't kill them, the vast distances they must cover on foot in the treacherous natural realm of Cape York just might. When Jock joins forces with Jillian Forbes, an indomitable woman with her own checkered past who refused to evacuate in the face of the Japanese threat, the dim prospects of the Allied war effort begin to brighten in surprising ways.

Congressman. Presidential candidate. Murderer.
Leonard Pilcher is all of these things.

As an American pilot interned in Sweden during WWII,
he kills one of his own crewmen and gets away with it.
Two people have witnessed the murder—American
airman Joe Gelardi and his secret Swedish lover, Pola
Nilsson-MacLeish—but they cannot speak out without
paying a devastating price. Tormented by their guilt and
separated by a vast ocean after the war, Joe and Pola
maintain the silence that haunts them both...until 1960,
when Congressman Pilcher's campaign for his party's
nomination for president gains momentum. Just as the
nomination seems within Pilcher's grasp, Pola
reappears to enlist Joe's help in finally exposing Pilcher
for the criminal he really is. As the passion of their
wartime romance rekindles, they must struggle to bring
Pilcher down before becoming his next victims.

EAST WIND RETURNS

William Peter Grasso

A young but veteran photo recon pilot in WWII finds the fate of the greatest invasion in history--and the life of the nurse he loves--resting perilously on his shoulders.

"East Wind Returns" is a story of World War II set in July-November 1945 which explores a very different road to that conflict's historic conclusion. The American war leaders grapple with a crippling setback: Their secret atomic bomb does not work. The invasion of Japan seems the only option to bring the war to a close. When those leaders suppress intelligence of a Japanese atomic weapon poised against the invasion forces, it falls to photo reconnaissance pilot John Worth to find the Japanese device. Political intrigue is mixed with passionate romance and exciting aerial action--the terror of enemy fighters, anti-aircraft fire, mechanical malfunctions, deadly weather, and the Kamikaze. When shot down by friendly fire over southern Japan during the American invasion, Worth leads the desperate mission that seeks to deactivate the device.

Made in the USA
Columbia, SC
06 March 2019